MEDICAL

Life and love in the world of modern medicine.

Melting Dr Grumpy's Frozen Heart

Scarlet Wilson

Neurosurgeon's IVF Mix-Up Miracle

Annie Claydon

MILLS & BOON

Scarlet Wilson is acknowledged as the author of this work
MELTING DR GRUMPY'S FROZEN HEART
© 2024 by Harlequin Enterprises ULC
Philippine Copyright 2024
Australian Copyright 2024
New Zealand Copyright 2024
First Published 2024
First Australian Paperback Edition 2024
ISBN 978 1 038 93545 8

Annie Claydon is acknowledged as the author of this work
NEUROSURGEON'S IVF MIX-UP MIRACLE
© 2024 by Harlequin Enterprises ULC
Philippine Copyright 2024
Australian Copyright 2024
New Zealand Copyright 2024
First Published 2024
First Australian Paperback Edition 2024
ISBN 978 1 038 93545 8

Published by
Harlequin Mills & Boon
An imprint of Harlequin Enterprises (Australia) Pty Limited
(ABN 47 001 180 918), a subsidiary of HarperCollins
Publishers Australia Pty Limited
(ABN 36 009 913 517)
Level 19, 201 Elizabeth Street
SYDNEY NSW 2000 AUSTRALIA

Printed and bound in Australia by McPherson's Printing Group

Melting Dr Grumpy's Frozen Heart

Scarlet Wilson

MILLS & BOON

Also by Scarlet Wilson

Cinderella's Kiss with the ER Doc
Her Summer with the Brooding Vet

Night Shift in Barcelona miniseries

The Night They Never Forgot

California Nurses miniseries

Nurse with a Billion-Dollar Secret

Scarlet Wilson wrote her first story aged eight and has never stopped. She's worked in the health service for more than thirty years, having trained as a nurse and a health visitor. Scarlet now works in public health and lives on the West Coast of Scotland with her fiancé and their two sons. Writing medical romances and contemporary romances is a dream come true for her.

To my darling sister, Jennifer Mary Dickson.

Thank you for being my biggest writing cheerleader.

Will love you and miss you for ever. x

CHAPTER ONE

SKYE CAMPBELL WAS BUZZING—literally. She could feel the hum in the air around her. As she walked along the frosty Edinburgh pavement, she smiled in pleasure at the crunch of her steps. She loved this time of year. And Edinburgh did it so well.

Even though it was mid-November, the large Christmas tree that sat near the Scott Monument was already up and decorated in shades of purple, pink and silver. The Edinburgh Christmas market started this weekend, and her Christmas shopping was part way done. Skye only shopped online for things she couldn't find in the shops. Whilst others hated the busyness of the shops at Christmas, she absolutely loved it. There was nothing nicer than watching people buying gifts for their loved ones, puzzling between colours or styles, sniffing samples of perfume in the department stores, or staring at the dazzling array of trainers in a sports shop. She was here for all that.

The Great Northern Hospital was lit up before her with a warm glow. Seven floors of glass, which had been specially constructed to allow patients to see out, but no one could see in. The effect from outside gave a tinged yellow and orange colour like a warm hug. She loved it. If she could meet the architect, she would shake their hand. She gave a sideways glance to Edinburgh Castle in the distance, proudly sitting on its ancient volcano site. She did this every morning, and today there was a hint of white around it. The temperature had dropped suddenly overnight and it seemed like Scotland had remembered it was the most wonderful time of the year.

As the main doors of the hospital slid open before her, her stomach gave a little flip. The whole main entrance was now decorated for Christmas. She'd been campaigning for it since the first of November, so she was glad they'd finally caved. Truth was, it was likely they'd caved to coincide with the city's decorations outside.

White fairy lights were everywhere. A giant tree was cordoned off and could be seen from the few floors above that overlooked the main reception.

'Morning.' Skye waved to Ellis, who sat behind the reception desk, as she headed over to the lifts. She joined the lift with Max Robertson, the very serious paediatric surgeon. She shot him a smile, which he almost returned.

A few minutes later she was striding down the corridor towards her office. She was a tiny bit nervous this morning. She was continually driven in her job as an oncology doctor and researcher. Losing her father to the disease during her medical training had made her realise which direction she wanted to take.

Her friends joked about her being a double doctor. Being a doctor of medicine as well as a doctor of research had meant hard work. Long days and long nights. But she'd been used to that when she'd helped nurse her father towards the end. Other students had been partying. Enjoying the student and hospital social life. Skye had been exactly where she should have been—with her family. And part of the reason she was so determined to make this new project work was due to the subject matter. Time.

Her new ground-breaking study aimed to predict the growth of cancer. It didn't sound pleasant. But anyone who'd worked as an oncologist knew that the first question a patient asked was how long they had. And it was a question a doctor could rarely answer with any confidence. It was always a best guess.

With a new wave of technology, and several early studies, Skye's premise was that AI—artificial intelligence—could help answer that question. It held promise. The battle against cancer was fought on many levels, and hers—the art of learning about the disease and its progression—was only one.

The only downside was she'd just learned that world-renowned oncologist Jay Bannerman was temporarily transferring up from Great Southern Hospital in London. He was going supervise her research for the next six weeks. She needed someone with his credentials to sign off on the next stage of the project. He had huge credibility, and his patients loved him. He'd led lots of cancer studies in the past. But there was a downside—from reputation alone, and whispers from their sister hospital, he was not-so-secretly known as Dr Grumpy.

Skye was more than a little worried. He didn't really fit with her personality type. She always tried to be positive, and tried to bring out the best in people around her.

Her colleagues had nicknamed her Miss Sunshine and she didn't mind it one bit.

But a research supervisor for this project was essential. Her original supervisor had gone into hospital for a knee replacement and was expected to be off for six weeks. As the surgery had been planned, so had the coverage. So, whoever Dr Bannerman really was, she'd just need to hope for the best. All she really needed him to do was give her a green tick.

As she did every morning, she bypassed her office—stopping only to throw in her laptop and bag—and headed to the nurses' station in the oncology ward. It was the heart of their department—and where she could find out everything she needed to know. Indira, the ward sister, was doing a handover to all staff—allocating patients, making sure all tests would be followed up. She ran a tight ship. Skye loved working with her, and the rest of the staff in this ward. There was a real team spirit.

Connie, the ward receptionist, appeared with a large tray of biscuits, a wide smile on her face. The rest of the staff gave a little cheer and helped themselves. Skye listened to the rest of the handover, making a few mental notes of things to follow up.

One of the nurses handed over a firm envelope addressed to her. The writing on the envelope was beautiful, and as Skye opened and pulled out the cream card, her face broke into a wide smile, a warm feeling spreading inside her.

'It's an invite,' she said, 'to Fiona and Armando's wedding.' Fiona was a patient they'd treated over the last eighteen months, who'd finally managed to ring the bell that signalled the end of her treatment.

'That's fantastic,' said Lleyton, the ward physio. 'Didn't they have to postpone initially because she was so sick?'

Skye nodded. 'They did. But Fiona finally gets to have her special day.' She hugged the card close to her chest. She'd sat next to Fiona whilst she'd sobbed during her treatments, and when she'd felt so sick. Seeing her out the other side was a delight. And it reinforced the hope she had for all her patients—that good things can happen, and life can get better.

A moment later she was distracted by the sight of a dark-suited man striding down the corridor towards them. She didn't recognise him, but they often had visiting staff in the Great Northern.

Connie turned and held out the biscuit tray towards him. He didn't even acknowledge her. Just kept walking, coming to a sharp halt and glaring at the white fairy lights strung from underneath the nurse's station to the tops of the walls.

His gaze stopped dead on Skye. She had no idea who he was, but he better change his attitude fast. No one got to ignore Connie. Not on her watch.

She met his glare as she pointedly leaned forward to lift one of the delicious smelling biscuits.

'Thank you, Connie,' she said, smiling at Connie, but still side-eyeing the gentleman in the hope he would get the not-so-secret message.

He did get the message, looking her clearly in the eye. 'I'm here to meet Dr Campbell, not eat sweets.'

There was an instant chill across her skin. That Irish accent. It sent shockwaves through her system, making her catch her breath. There was only one person who would be looking for her that she didn't know. But she hadn't expected him here for another few days. Wasn't he moving up from London? How could he have got here so quickly?

And why did he have to look like that? Tall, with dark wavy hair, penetrating brown eyes and a lean body. He should be a leading man in some Hollywood rom-com.

In a wave of panic, she hoped her gaze hadn't been obvious. Because she knew exactly how she wanted to come across to this man. It was clear he had no idea who she was, because he started to glance around, as if he expected Dr Campbell to appear out of thin air.

Skye took a quick glance down at her outfit. She wasn't wearing her white coat, but was dressed in a long-sleeved, mid-length pink patterned dress, with buttons down the front and tied at the waist. It was a favourite.

'I'm Dr Campbell,' she said, knowing that all eyes were on them. 'Follow me to my office.'

She didn't wait. She walked back down the corridor, opening her office door and waiting as he came inside. Her nerves were jangling. She needed this guy to be on board with her research project, she really didn't want to get off on the wrong foot—but it seemed that Dr Grumpy might not extend her the same courtesy.

She closed the door firmly and walked around her desk, sitting down and placing her arms on the desk. She leaned a little towards him.

'Can I assume that you are Jay Bannerman?'

He gave the briefest nod, so she started talking. Better just to take the bull by the horns.

'Dr Bannerman, we are a team around here. A team that works well together. I don't want anything to disrupt my team. And a few moments ago? That was downright rude.'

His body gave a little jerk and he straightened up. 'Excuse me?'

'I'll just put my cards on the table.' She was careful with her tone, mindful that she knew nothing about this man, or his background. She tried to give him a smile. 'No one is rude to Connie, not on my watch.'

'Excuse me?' he repeated. He kind of looked like a deer caught in headlights. His reputation as Dr Grumpy had travelled from one hospital to another. Had no one ever spoken to this guy about his manner?

She took a breath. 'Connie is our receptionist. She's been here since the hospital was built.' Skye paused for a second. What she was going to reveal was generally known by everyone who worked here, but it felt like breaking a confidence.

'Connie has had a really hard life. She was a victim of domestic abuse for years. It took her a while before she could tell someone and make plans to leave. Her grown-up daughter has alcohol issues. Connie deals with all this on her own. When Connie gets stressed,' Skye gave a wave of her hand, 'she bakes.'

His shoulders relaxed just a touch, as if he was beginning to understand where she was going with this.

'So,' Skye continued, 'when Connie appears with tins of biscuits, or traybakes or loafs, we know. We know something is going on with her, and that she needs some support.' Skye licked her lips and met those brown eyes. 'That's why I'll never let anyone be rude to Connie on my watch, and…' she paused '…I hope you won't either.'

'I'm not a social worker.'

Skye bristled, but her words stayed calm. 'I'm not asking you to be a social worker, Dr Bannerman. I'm asking you to be kind and considerate to your colleagues.' Then she just couldn't help herself. 'But with your length of time in the job, I really shouldn't have to.'

There was a long silence. She hoped she'd handled this the way she should have. Tone was everything—Skye knew that. She hadn't spoken angrily, or accusingly. She hoped everything she'd said had come across as kindly as possible.

This guy didn't know her background. He didn't know why she was here. For Skye, cancer research was personal. And she didn't know his background, what had made him do years of training and decide that oncology was the place he wanted to work. She wasn't here to make an enemy. But from the expression on his face, she was doubting she was making a friend.

She decided to push in another direction. 'You know,' she said breezily, 'I am a huge Christmas fan. You'll learn that over the next few weeks. My favourite movie is *The Grinch.* I'd hate for people to start calling you that.'

The edges of his mouth hinted upwards and he gave a sigh, as his eyebrows raised. The expression had the hint of a cheeky teenager about it. 'My nickname is Dr Grumpy, and yes, I know that,' he replied in that delicious, thick Irish accent.

'And mine is Miss Sunshine,' she replied, holding her hand out to his.

Jay Bannerman didn't even hide his groan as he shook her hand. 'This is going to be a disaster, isn't it?'

For a second—at least in Skye's head—things froze. She was captured by the man sitting in front of her. Now she'd stopped focusing on everything else, she realised just how handsome he was. Discounting the fact that every time he spoke with his lilting accent, which sent a whole host of vibrations down her spine, even if he hadn't opened his mouth, and she'd seen him in a bar, this guy was hot.

Skye didn't mix business with pleasure. She'd never been interested in dating her colleagues.

But at least he was semi-smiling now, and she would take that. He stood up and straightened his suit jacket. 'Let me go back and make a better impression on our staff, then you can show me where my office is, and hopefully point me in the direction of where to pick up my laptop. We need to talk about your research project.'

She felt a tiny chill on her skin. 'Of course.' She didn't like the way her voice sounded.

He gave her the briefest of glances and then walked to the door. Jay didn't waste any time—he walked back down the corridor to where Connie was sitting behind the nurses' station. The tray of biscuits was sitting above her.

Jay walked around beside her and held out his hand. 'Hi, Connie? I'm Jay Bannerman. I'm an oncologist from the Great Southern and I'm up here with special privileges to see patients, and to oversee Dr Campbell's research project. We'll be working together.'

Since Skye had been on his heels she'd heard every word. It appeared that Jay could turn on the charm when he chose to, and his Irish accent was almost therapeutic. If Connie was surprised, she hid it well, and shook his outstretched hand.

She didn't get a chance to respond, as Jay lifted his other hand to grab a biscuit. 'And I have it on good authority that you're a wonderful baker, so thanks for the biscuit.'

It wasn't an apology as such. But at least he was making an effort.

Connie gave a cautious nod. 'If you need any assistance with anything just let me know, Dr Bannerman. I'm happy to help.'

He gave a nod. 'Dr Campbell's just about to get me set up with a laptop. I'll let you know if I need anything.'

Connie gave a nervous glance and handed Skye a slip of paper. 'You've just had a call about an emergency admission. GP is sending them straight up as he doesn't want the patient going through A&E.' Connie was very switched on and knew exactly what that meant. 'Why don't you go and call him and I'll get Dr Bannerman his ID, show him his office and get his laptop set up?'

Skye took the piece of paper and read it quickly. 'Sorry, Jay,' she said automatically, 'I'll have to prioritise this patient.'

His brown eyes met hers for a moment. She couldn't quite make out that expression. Calculating? He gave a small nod. 'Since I have privileges, I'd like to see how things work. Why don't you give me a shout when the patient arrives so I can familiarise myself with all the processes? I'm sure I'll be in good hands with Connie up until then.'

She wanted to say no. She wanted to refuse to let him oversee her. She didn't need him for that. The only thing he was supposed to do was oversee her research project. But that was making her oddly nervous too. She glanced down at the name on the paper. Leah McLeod—a teenage girl. That's where her focus had to be.

Not on this doctor. Or what he thought of her. Or her project.

She fixed a smile to her face. 'No problem at all. Thanks Connie, I'll give you a shout when our patient arrives.'

And she walked quickly back to her office, phoned the GP and organised some tests for Leah's arrival.

Jay Bannerman wasn't quite sure if this was a good day or a bad day.

He hadn't exactly made the impression he'd wanted to. But then again, he didn't spend much of his life worrying about what people thought of him.

But the truth was—he wasn't happy to be here, and he was having trouble putting a 'face' on. Yet another trick he'd never really mastered.

He'd worked at the Great Southern in London for ten years. Five of those years he'd been engaged to Jessica Morris, a fellow doctor. They'd agreed on a long engagement, not wanting to rush into marriage. But a year ago she'd broken things off, saying she wasn't ready.

Now, she apparently was ready. But not for marriage to him. She'd just announced her surprise engagement to one of their colleagues—Peter Benson. And Jay really didn't want to stay around and witness the fun.

He knew he had a bit of reputation for being serious and introverted. But since his break-up with Jess, he'd definitely got worse. As far as he was concerned, his patient care was still excellent, but he was reluctant to form any new friendships here in Scotland. He didn't want any romantic entanglements with colleagues. He didn't really want people knowing his business. The truth was, when it came to personal relationships now, he wasn't sure he could trust his own judgement.

So, the fact that the person he was directly supervising looked as gorgeous as a movie star, and could clearly hold her own, was making every part of his body groan. Skye Campbell had dark curly hair that had been pulled back from her face, with surprisingly dark green eyes. Her pink dress suited her, it covered up every part of her, but still managed to show off her curves. Something he absolutely shouldn't have noticed, or be focusing on.

His nickname of Dr Grumpy had clearly been no surprise to her. But, somehow, he knew it wasn't his rudeness that had rattled her. He sensed something more. It was almost as if she were wary of him.

And she should be. He was there to assess her work, and to investigate any potential controversies over the use of artificial intelligence in the prediction of cancer growth rates. As with all research projects, it had gone through countless committees before approval and funding. But he still had a number of valid questions he needed to raise with her.

'Dr Bannerman?'

He looked up from the desk. Connie had escorted him to HR, security and then IT. He now had an ID badge and security pass, white coat, his emails transferred and his laptop set up. Connie was just linking him to a few hospital systems specific to their ward now.

She took a few moments to show him where to access test results and how to order bloods, X-rays, ECGs and a whole range of other tests—all things that happened on a daily basis in the oncology unit.

She showed him where the research study data was stored, and how to access patient records. Connie was exceedingly good at her job.

'I don't think I've missed anything, but if you think of something, just let me know.'

She pulled up the ward details and nodded at the admission list. 'Looks like Leah McLeod has arrived.' She turned the laptop around to Jay and pointed at the young woman's name. 'If you click here, you'll be able to pull up her records.'

Jay sat back and nodded. 'Thanks very much, Connie, you've been a big help.' He shot her the best smile he could. 'It's much appreciated.'

He could see the expression on Connie's face, and the slight relaxation of her shoulders. He got it. He got why Skye was protective over her colleague. There were good intentions here, and he would be more mindful in future.

He scanned Leah's records and the brief notes from the GP that had referred her. Leah had presented at the surgery with some classic signs, and the GP had taken some bloods before he'd sent her to hospital. Jay could see the blood results now.

He gave a nod and stood up, asking Connie which bed, and heading to the side room where he knew Skye would already be. He wondered if she would have told him Leah was here or just ploughed on without him. But as he reached the door, she gave him a smile and waved him in.

'Leah, this is Dr Bannerman, the other doctor I said would see you too.'

Leah was as pale as the hospital bedsheets. Her father—an extremely anxious looking man—was standing against a wall. He looked like he might be sick.

Jay walked over and put a hand on his arm. 'Mr McLeod? I'm Jay Bannerman. Let me assure you that we're going to look after your daughter.'

Skye positioned herself next to the bed, glancing at Jay. 'I've got the notes from your GP, and I spoke to him earlier when you were on the way up. He told me you had a UTI last week, and it looks like you've a chest infection this week. You've noticed some bruising. You had a couple of knocks recently and it's been difficult to control the bleeding.'

Leah gave an anxious nod. 'I play hockey. At least I did until last week. But this week I just couldn't breathe.'

She pulled back the covers to show Skye the top of her leg. 'I clashed with someone else. I've never bruised like this before.'

The angry bruise was still red and purple. A week-old bruise would normally have faded slightly, and the edge turned yellow. There were also plasters on her knees.

Jay moved to the other side of the bed. 'Did you skin your knees at the same time?'

Leah nodded and frowned. 'But they just keep bleeding. They haven't even scabbed yet.' She looked down at the inside of her elbow, where a cotton wool ball was held in place with some tape. 'Even where Dr Gillespie took blood—it's still bleeding.'

Skye lifted her stethoscope from around her neck. 'If it's okay, I'd like to listen to your chest. If we think you have a chest infection, we'll start you on antibiotics right away.'

Leah leaned forward and Skye gave her instructions to breathe in and out slowly, before moving her stethoscope around to the front and nodding as she listened.

She looked over to Jay and Leah's father. 'I'm going to pull the curtains for a second, just to check Leah's lymph nodes.'

Jay helped tug the curtain around. Leah's dad looked a bit confused. 'There's lymph nodes at your neck, under your arms and in your groin area,' he explained. 'Because your daughter's a teenage girl, we try to give some privacy.'

He nodded, still looking overwhelmed by everything. 'My wife's away on a business trip in Germany. She says she'll get the first flight back she can.' He shook his head and blinked back tears. 'As soon as the doctor said he was sending us up to the oncology ward…' His words tailed off.

Skye pulled the curtains back. 'So, Leah's lymph nodes are swollen.'

'What does that mean?' asked Leah. 'Why is everyone so worried? And why do I feel so rubbish?'

Skye gave him the briefest look. She was doing a great

job. He was impressed. And he wanted to be clear they were a team.

He sat down next to Leah. 'We'll need to run a few more tests. But from your symptoms, and your initial blood tests, we think you could have a condition called acute lymphoblastic leukaemia. The only way we can get a definite diagnosis is if we do something called a bone marrow biopsy. And we'd like to do that tonight if we can.' He watched Leah carefully. 'Your dad says your mum is coming back. If your mum can get a flight today, we can wait until she's here to do the next test. Dr Campbell and I are happy to wait.'

Skye reached over and squeezed Leah's hand. 'I'll explain everything about the test to you. Don't worry.'

'Leukaemia is cancer.' Leah blinked.

Skye nodded and kept her hand over Leah's. 'It is. It's a cancer of the blood. And we have lots of ways to treat it. We can talk all that over too.' She looked over at Mr McLeod. 'Would you be able to find out if your wife has managed to get a flight tonight? And is there anyone else you would like to call?'

Mr McLeod looked like a deer caught in headlights.

Jay put an arm behind him, guiding him to the door. 'Leah, why don't you write a list of everything you want your dad to bring from home? It's likely you'll need to stay with us for a few days. So, comfy clothes, a tablet if you have one, any toiletries you want, books?'

Skye pulled a tiny notepad from the pocket of her satin dress and handed it over. 'Favourite sweets,' she said with a smile. 'That's what I always tell people to put first on their list.'

'Am I going to lose my little girl?' asked Mr McLeod as soon as they stepped outside.

The door was still open and Jay could see Skye talking to Leah and keeping her occupied. He was always honest with his patients and their relatives and he hated this part. But this was him, this was his job. 'I certainly hope not. The odds are in her favour. She's fifteen—the younger the diagnosis, the better the chances. Overall, we look at the five-year survival rate and for this disease it's around sixty-five percent. Lots of things affect this, and I'll talk to you about it all. But first, let's get her chest infection sorted and her bone marrow biopsy done. We have lots of treatments, and it all depends on how Leah reacts to them. If one kind of treatment doesn't work as well as we hoped, we have other options. We also have some clinical trials. Honestly?' He looked Mr McLeod in the eye. 'Your daughter is in one of the best hospitals. And we'll be with you every step of the way.'

For a moment Jay honestly thought the man in front of him was going to collapse. There was no one else around them. He could hear quiet voices in the unit. After a few seconds he saw a wave of a hand at the bottom of the corridor. It was one of the healthcare support workers dressed in a grey tunic. The staff member pointed to a chair in a kind of query, and Jay gave a small nod, as the guy quickly retrieved one and brought it along the corridor to them.

The healthcare support worker was an older man, built as if he did weights. He slid the chair next to Mr McLeod and put a hand on his shoulder. 'What can I get you? Tea? Coffee, or something sweet to drink?'

'Coffee,' said Mr McLeod automatically, his legs folding beneath him as he collapsed onto the seat. 'Thank you,' it came out absentmindedly as his phone beeped.

He looked up at Jay. 'I almost didn't take her to the GP. My wife usually takes care of that kind of stuff. But her colour—she was just so pale. And she'd felt off for the last few days. We just couldn't really put our finger on anything but…' His voice tailed again and Jay lowered himself so he would be at eye level with Mr McLeod.

'Onset can be really rapid. You did the right thing.' He took a breath as he let the man collect himself a bit. 'Your phone—was that your wife?'

He looked surprised for a moment, then pulled the phone from his pocket. Jay could see how relief swamped his body. 'She got on standby at Berlin airport and someone gave up their seat for her.' His voice broke a little. 'How nice is that?'

Jay gave a smile. 'People can surprise you sometimes.'

He was conscious of Skye and Leah still in the side room. He could tell that Skye was having a serious conversation with Leah, and was holding her hand as she spoke to her. He could only hear a few words, but Skye was encouraging Leah to ask questions.

Mr McLeod took a deep breath. 'Her flight takes off in forty-five minutes. She lands at five o'clock and will come straight here.'

Jay gave him a smile. 'That's great news.' He looked up as the healthcare support worker approached, carrying a tray with two steaming cups and a plate of chocolate biscuits—and some of Connie's cookies.

'Why don't I take this into Leah's room? Hot chocolate for her, and coffee for you.'

The healthcare worker headed in and put the tray down on the table next to Leah, who immediately looked up in surprise. Skye took her cue to leave, to let dad and daughter talk to each other, and walked out to join Jay again.

He was impressed by how seamlessly the team did things around here. The ward had a calm atmosphere, and the staff seemed to anticipate the needs of the patients well.

'Who is the healthcare assistant?'

'That's Ronnie, he's our gentle giant, but also our security guard when required.'

'You have trouble on the ward?' Jay was surprised by this.

'Emotions are always heightened on an oncology ward.' She gave a sad smile. 'Either it's warring sons and daughters over their mum or dad, or divorced parents over a child.' She gestured her hand down to the fairy lights on the desk. 'And whilst I love Christmas, for some families it's a hard time of year.'

She licked her lips for a second and gave him a careful stare. It was hard not to be captivated by those dark green eyes. But his heart had already sunk a little. He generally knew what a look like that meant.

'Dr Bannerman,' she said quietly.

'Yes?' He kept his face straight. He wasn't going to show any sign of weakness.

'I appreciate you have a great deal of knowledge in treating cancers. But…' she glanced over her shoulder, back to the room where Leah and her dad were '...I'm not sure Mr McLeod was ready for news like that.'

'I'm not sure he was either. But he asked me a direct question. I don't lie to my patients or their relatives, Dr Campbell.' If she wanted to be formal, so could he.

He'd already seen her in action with Leah. She was one of these people who had a natural rapport with others, who could engage at their level and be their friend.

'I'm their doctor,' he reiterated. 'Not their friend.'

Skye pulled something slightly bent from the pocket of her dress. 'But sometimes we can be both,' she said easily.

He could see from first glance it was a wedding invitation.

She held it up. 'This is from a patient we all treated for the last eighteen months. I find it impossible not to form therapeutic relationships with my patients.'

And he could already see that. He'd love to be that kind of doctor, but that had always been a struggle for him.

She bowed her head a little, though it wasn't in any way deferential. She was obviously finding a way to say something. She lifted her head again and met his gaze. 'We'll find a way to work together well. I would have waited until Mrs McLeod was here to do the biopsy and give the news to the family together, but that's too late now. Perhaps,' she licked those lips again, and Jay tried to focus on something else, 'in future, we could have a chat about breaking bad news and maybe I could do that part?' She gave a wary smile. 'You could do the part about what type of treatment you recommend, since that's your area of expertise?'

She framed it as a question, but he wasn't naïve enough

to know that this woman had just told him how this should go.

'I'll consider it.' He tried not to outwardly bristle.

Her face broke into a wide smile. 'Good,' she said, then gave him a cheeky wink as she started down the corridor. 'And here was you thinking this was going to be a disaster.'

CHAPTER TWO

THE NEXT WEEK was slightly odd. Skye concentrated on her patients, trying to find a way to work well with Jay Bannerman. He hadn't really revealed much of his character, and seemed so guarded at times. Skye had never been one for gossip, but had made a few casual enquiries with colleagues at the Great Southern. She'd learned that his previous fiancée had just announced her engagement to another doctor. Was that why he had come up here?

She would have loved it if she'd thought that Jay Bannerman had wanted to come up here to supervise her meticulous research project. But, so far, he'd barely mentioned it to her, with the exception of requesting a few files.

Leah McLeod's mother had arrived on the day she'd been admitted to the ward. She was with her daughter whilst she had her bone marrow biopsy, which had confirmed the diagnosis she and Jay had suspected. Her chest infection had taken hold, and she'd had a few days of intravenous antibiotics, before they'd even had the conversation around treatment and the fact it could cause immunosuppression. She'd then been allowed a day at home, before coming back in to start her treatment regime.

Leah's mother had been a steadying force on both her husband and daughter. She was a business woman—she was used to being in control. But both Skye and Jay had caught her crying at moments, and taken her out of the ward to talk to her and let her gather herself. Skye knew just how overwhelming the first few weeks could be, and wanted to ensure she supported the whole family the best way she could. She didn't need to worry about the rest of the staff. They knew exactly what was needed for newly diagnosed patients and their families, and she trusted them. This was the good thing about working in a ward with people she knew well.

The hospital had started to play Christmas music, and people were starting to complain that it was only the third week in November. But Skye would happily play Christmas music all year round. She reached the nurses' station that morning and plunked down a Christmas container. One of the staff picked it up and looked through the plastic edges suspiciously. 'What is this?'

'Christmas chocolate tiffin. Made by my own fair hands.' She was laughing already as they all knew she wasn't entirely skilled in the baking department. 'It's a tray bake,' she added. 'Nearly impossible to burn.'

Her colleague lifted up the edge of the container and sniffed. 'Smells okay. It might be edible.'

'I'll have you know that I nearly offered Max Robertson a bit in the lift this morning, in order to try and coax a smile out of him.'

Lleyton, the physio, laughed. 'If it's anything like your sultana muffins, it wouldn't have got you a smile.'

'You're being mean now,' she shot back.

'Only to you. But honestly, what's it going to take to

get that guy to crack a smile. They're actually taking bets on it now.'

Skye frowned. 'Who?'

'All the other wards.'

She waved her hand. 'No, that's definitely mean. He's good with his patients, the kids love him and, apparently, he helps out at a local children's home. Maybe he just uses up all his smiles there?'

The rest of them groaned and Lleyton leaned forward. 'Maybe we should take bets on our own guy. He's a bit serious too, isn't he?'

And this is why she tried not to get involved in hospital gossip. Because it really wouldn't do if her research supervisor came out here and caught her talking about him.

'Leave me out of it,' she said breezily as she headed down to her office.

She had work to do, patients to see. The unit had been even busier than usual. As well as her research work, she'd been covering extra duties since one of her colleagues was on maternity leave. But Skye didn't mind. Returning to an empty home at night wasn't always the best thing in the world. She knew she was lucky to be able to afford her own place to live, but since she didn't have a partner or a flatmate, the place sometimes seemed a little hollow. And Skye still didn't like too much time on her hands. It gave her too much time to think.

To think about her father, and how treatments had potentially changed, and how he might have had a better outcome if he were diagnosed now instead of then.

She'd contemplated getting a cat. She thought she was likely more of a dog person, but the hours she worked weren't conducive to owning a dog, so a cat was a definite possibility.

'Dr Campbell?' The unexpected Irish voice caught her by surprise. She thought he'd gone home already.

'Jay? What are you still doing here? And call me Skye. Dr Campbell makes me feel old.'

He glanced over his shoulder. 'I don't like to be overly familiar in front of patients.'

She held up her arms in her empty office. 'See any patients?'

He gave a sigh and came in and sat down. 'We haven't really had a chance to talk about your research project. I've read the documents you sent, and wondered if you had some time to discuss it?'

Her stomach gave a nervous flip. She'd actually prepared for this conversation virtually every day since last week, but as he hadn't approached her she'd sort of relaxed about it. Now it felt like he'd caught her on the hop.

But...he was still the person to oversee her research, so she painted an appropriate smile on her face and gestured to the chair on the other side of her desk. 'Of course.'

How weird. To get any research proposal off the ground, the proposer had to sit through countless research committees, both in hospitals and at universities, often being grilled within an inch of their life. Skye had done this on more than one occasion. She'd always been passionate about her work, and had researched things fastidiously. So, she should be confident about this. But Jay Bannerman was having an unnerving effect on her—and she wasn't quite sure why.

'Where would you like to start?' He leaned back in the chair. He'd taken off his white coat and was wearing a mid-blue short-sleeved shirt and navy trousers. He had a bit of a rumpled look about him. A bit like that TV doc in the show set in Seattle.

The question he'd just asked rattled around her brain. She knew exactly where she would start in front of an ethics committee. But she'd done all that. She didn't want to do those practised spiels again.

Maybe it was the long day she'd just had. Maybe it was the fact she hadn't quite got the measure of Jay Bannerman yet. Maybe she was just a little tired. So, she did what she did when talking to friend. She spoke from the heart.

'The unofficial name of the project—and the name I always use when talking about it, is the Hope Project.'

She blew a few strands of hair out of her eyes. 'My dad died of cancer when I was doing my medical training. It immediately changed my course as a doctor. It was clear I didn't understand cancer, but I did have experience of what a cancer diagnosis did to a family. I understood the ripple effect better than anyone, and I realised that the tiny spider web wasn't just the picture of what a cancer cell could do in a body, it was also the impact of cancer on everything surrounding the person. Their family, their relationships, their job or their ability to work, their insurance, or lack of chance of getting any. The impact of the treatment, the changes to their everyday living. Sometimes changes in their appearance. The hopes and dreams that they lost, along with their family members or friends who were on that journey with them.'

She sighed and sat back, fixing her eyes on the wall instead of Jay. She knew his gaze was fixed on her, but she didn't want to lose focus now she was in full flow.

'What's the one question every patient diagnosed with cancer asks? What's the question every parent asks? Once they think there can't be a complete cure, they ask about time. All of them. Everyone. I can't remember a patient in that position who hasn't asked me. And what do we tell them? Our best guess. Sometimes we are right, and sometimes we are wrong. And when we're wrong, we hate ourselves. Even though we try to reason with ourselves about it.' She took a deep breath. 'So, time. That's essentially what's at the heart of this project.'

He leaned forward on the desk, pulling her attention. A frown creased his brow. 'Do you honestly think that telling someone how much time they have left is really a good thing?'

She held out both hands. 'For some patients? Yes. But not for all. That's where we come in. That's where we will know our patients well enough to understand whether they can deal with news like that. Artificial intelligence can help us predict how cancers will evolve and spread. It can pick out patterns in DNA mutations and use that information to forecast future genetic changes. We will know if a tumour is likely to become drug resistant and change treatments accordingly. We'll be able to predict cancer's next move, and eventually its lifecycle. There's been some earlier work of this nature done in breast cancer, and now it's time to look at cancers of the lung, bowel, liver and kidney.'

'And artificial intelligence is really the way forward to do this?' He ran his fingers through his hair.

She tilted her head to one side. 'You have something against artificial intelligence?'

He gave a small shrug. 'My sister is a writer as well

as being a university lecturer. She has lots to say about artificial intelligence—particularly around the amount of fake essays it generates, and the amount of fake books that haven't been written by real people.'

Skye raised her eyebrows. 'And your sister would be right. But this is different. This is just the latest version of our technology. Don't you remember the pictures of the NASA mathematicians standing next to their huge stacks of paper—Katherine Johnson—when they made the calculations to get to the moon? Don't you remember that computers used to fill a whole room?' She held up her phone. 'Or the fact that our modern smart phones have more technology than the guidance system Apollo Eleven used?'

He gave a small smile. 'You like your space trivia.'

'I'm just fascinated that I live in a world where technology seems to be progressing at a tremendous rate. And whilst some students want to use it to cheat on their essays, I want to use it help our patients, and help find some of the answers that cancer has hidden from us for years.'

He tapped his fingers on the table for a moment. 'I read a book recently, where people could find out how long they would live.' He shook his head. 'It really didn't work out well for most of them.'

She met his gaze. Those brown eyes were really something, but they wouldn't dissuade her. 'My dad's cancer progressed extremely quickly. We thought we'd have more time. If I'd known,' she put her hand on her heart, 'I would have taken a year off university and spent it all with him.'

Jay didn't speak, just watched her carefully.

'I absolutely expect your area of interest to be around

the tracking of the mutations,' she continued, 'identifying repeating patterns and predicting the future trajectory of tumour development, and how different treatments can impact on that. I fully expect we could work on this for the next twenty years. Maybe it will revolutionise how we treat certain cancers.'

She paused again. 'But time—the bit that no one really wants to talk about, and pays the least attention to? That's the bit of information I wanted when I was eighteen years old. And I'll never forget that.'

Jay was trying to take everything in. This was the heart of the project for her. And she was right. It fundamentally was the least important part, because the prediction for how a certain tumour might grow, and to know how to treat that most effectively, was the part that the majority of the world would consider the key aspects. They certainly were for him.

But all of a sudden he was glad he'd had this conversation. He'd read her proposals. And this part had been hidden in amongst everything else. He would never have found out her family history, or the impact it'd had on her world.

He was struck how much she'd gone through at such a crucial point in her life.

Her hair had released itself from the clasp at the back of her head as she'd spoken, and now her dark curls were sitting on her shoulders. The green dress she wore reflected her dark green eyes, enhancing their colour. It was almost like Skye Campbell had just unwrapped herself in front of him, and he couldn't imagine how vulnerable that might make her feel.

If this was his history, would he have been able to tell her the same?

Every cell in his body cringed at the mere thought. Since his love life had previously been the business of everyone in the Southern, he'd spent the last year wanting to live his life in a private bubble. Revealing any part of himself might make him open to being hurt again. It was a road he just didn't want to take.

'So, you qualified as a doctor, then did a research doctorate?'

Skye smiled and shook her head, sliding open a drawer in her desk and bringing out a large box of chocolates. 'I'm essentially a glutton for punishment.'

He bit his lip. 'What kind of doctor might you have been?'

He asked the question just as she bit into a chocolate and pushed the box towards him.

'What?' As she asked the question some gooey caramel dripped down her chin. She made an elaborate mission of trying to catch it, and failed miserably.

He laughed, then repeated, 'If that hadn't happened to your dad, what kind of direction do you think you might have taken?'

She grabbed a tissue and wiped her chin, biting the inside of her cheek as she contemplated the question. 'No one has actually asked me that before,' she admitted.

'Really?'

'Really.' She sat back and licked her lips of caramel. She sighed. 'If you want absolute honesty, I was thinking medicine wasn't for me. I fancied myself as a Lara Croft type and wanted to switch to archaeology.'

'No way.' The words were out before he had time to think.

'Maybe I just wanted to wear an Indiana Jones type fedora?'

'You would have changed your course?'

She nodded. 'I was young and naïve. The first year of medical school is dull. You know that.' He raised his eyebrows and she laughed. 'Go on admit it. The only thing good about first year is telling people you're going to be a doctor. The actual study part is hideous.'

He'd never thought about it that way, and now he actually laughed. 'You could be right. I never loved the biochemistry.'

Her face lit up and she leaned towards him. 'I *hated* it. But when dad got sick my whole world just turned. I became extra focused. I wanted to learn about cancer. I was interested in the cellular level, the pathology, the journey. Every aspect of it drove me on. I never even considered any other speciality. It was always oncology. There was no other option for me.'

'That's interesting,' he said. She had leaned towards him, and now he could see her face in much more detail. She had tiny lines around her eyes, smiling lines or laughter lines from what little he knew of her. Those dark green eyes were something, and her dark curls framing her face. She had tiny freckles over her nose, but her skin was pale. He found himself wondering if she got a tan in the summer.

The aroma of her perfume was drifting towards him. Hints of amber and spice. It suited her. And it made him want to lean closer.

'Why is that interesting?' she asked, and her voice brought him back to the topic sharply.

He gave a wry kind of laugh and sat backwards, leaning into his chair. It seemed the right thing to do, even though he was reluctant to move away from her.

He didn't tell people much about himself. But she'd revealed a piece of herself that was almost at an intimate level. And it was he who had directed this conversation. It was only fair.

He slipped up his sleeve, revealing a white disc on his outer arm.

'You're diabetic?' She recognised the device immediately. It was fairly common place now.

He nodded. 'Since I was eight. I had measles, and went on to develop Type One. I was pretty good as a teenager, didn't stop taking insulin, no crazy diets, no drinking binges. I had a great diabetic nurse who also wrote a reference for my university application. But from the second I started medical school I knew what area I *wasn't* going to study.'

Her eyes widened, and she seemed fascinated. 'Really? But why? Don't you want to know everything?'

He gave a slow nod. 'I do. But I live with diabetes every day. I realised quickly I didn't want to work with it every day too.'

He could see the recognition of those words hitting home with her. She was clearly thinking back to her own training.

He held out his hands. 'I know I'm at higher risk for basically everything. I have this sensor,' he patted his arm, 'I get an annual review, my bloods are checked, my eyes and feet are checked. I'm lucky. I haven't had any major problems.'

'But as long as you look after yourself, you shouldn't have.'

He pulled a face. 'That's kind of an idealistic view.'

'You think?'

'Well, what do you think your risk of cancer is? Some studies say that one in every two people will develop some form of cancer.'

She nodded. 'We know that some cancers have genetic components, we know that some have contributory lifestyle factors, others environmental, and some are just bad luck. So, I guess I have the same chance as everyone else.'

He liked how she was willing to have these kinds of conversations. It gave him a good sense of her. This had started off being about her research project, and had taken them both down another path.

'Okay,' he said, 'so, from my perspective, if I'd specialised in diabetes, I would have seen all the problem patients. The ones with end-stage issues. The patients with renal failure that require dialysis. The teenagers who don't accept their condition and come in and out in ketoacidosis, who play with their life, not realising how close to death they come, or the long-term damage they do to every part of their body.'

She took a deep breath. 'Okay,' she said. 'But devil's advocate?'

Jeez, he actually liked this woman more and more every minute. She was intelligent, insightful and also really, really easy to talk to. Jay couldn't remember the last time he'd had a conversation like this.

He gave a soft shoulder shrug. 'Go on.'

She actually laughed. 'Please say that again.'

'What?'

'Those words, the go on. With your accent it's just…' She didn't finish the sentence.

He gave a smile. 'Go on then.'

She gave a shiver and a broad smile that made tiny hairs on his body stand on end.

'Okay,' she shook her head, 'I'll get back to where we should be.' She swallowed and continued, her fingers going to her throat, toying with the gold pendant around her neck. 'Think of studies you could have got involved in—all around those sensors,' she pointed to his arm, 'or new insulins, the pumps or even the beta cell implant work.'

He sighed. 'I read the studies. I keep up to date. But I don't want diabetes to consume every minute of every day for me.' He licked his lips and leaned forward, keeping his voice low. 'Because the reality is, it already does.'

His gaze connected with hers, and again he saw some recognition. She stopped leaning on the desk and sat back herself.

'Wow,' she said.

He took a deep breath. 'Maybe this just proves what we already know?'

She frowned. 'And what's that?'

'You said you're Miss Sunshine here, and I'm,' he pulled a face and raised his eyebrows, 'Dr Grumpy, or Grinch, since it's coming up to Christmas.'

Her smile broadened. 'But what does that mean?'

'We're opposites,' he said decisively. 'You saw cancer

in your family and jumped in, immersed yourself in everything about it, to take part in both caring for patients and studies. You've actively pursued everything around it.' He gave another shrug. 'I was diagnosed diabetic as a child, and whilst I look after myself, I've purposely chosen to walk in a different direction. I don't want to immerse myself in it. I want my work to be about something else.'

She leaned an elbow on the desk and put her face in her hand. 'I'm not sure we're opposites,' she said in a complacent tone. '*I* wasn't affected by cancer. If it was me, I might have felt entirely differently.'

'You might,' he agreed, 'and I might have felt differently if my sister had been the one diagnosed with diabetes, and had issues that I would've wanted to assist with.'

'Jelly babies?' she asked out the blue.

'What?' He shook his head in confusion.

'Other diabetics I know keep jelly babies around them in case they go low. Is that what you eat?' She gave him a cheeky wink. 'I need to know if I should buy a bag to keep in my drawer.'

He shuddered. 'I absolutely hate jelly babies.' He paused and looked at her. 'Digestive biscuits. That's what I like. Chocolate digestives even more.'

'Don't they take too long to be absorbed and work?'

'We're all individuals. They seem to work for me.' He tapped his arm. 'My alarm usually gives me plenty warning. It's not as if I'm a surgeon and on my feet for twelve hours at a time, or have people's lives in my hands. If I alarm, I have a seat for five minutes, eat a biscuit and give it time to kick in. I never get so low that I'm irritated or incoherent.'

She tilted her head to the side. 'You must have as a child. Alarms didn't exist then.'

He smiled and nodded. 'My mother spent her life at the side of football or rugby pitches with an array of things in her pockets. But I did have hypo warning signs, so I always knew if I needed to come off.' He raised his eyebrows. 'I didn't always want to come off. At times I ran past with my hand held out for her to stuff something into it.'

'I bet she loved that.'

He kept grinning. 'I had to be quick in case she made a grab for me. But I was speedy back then.'

Her eyes ran over his frame—it gave him a tingle that she was obviously sizing him up.

'You still look speedy,' she said simply.

'I run,' he said, wondering if this was verging on flirtation. Tiny red flags started waving in his brain, but he ignored them.

'I don't,' she replied so swiftly he laughed out loud.

He let his eyes take in her curves underneath her dress. 'You look just as speedy yourself,' he said, following her backward compliment.

'I would like to say that I walk my dog, but I don't have one.'

He looked at her curiously. 'You want one.'

'I've contemplated one for the last three years. But I think it's going to be a cat for me. Hours here are too long.' Then she breathed in and added, 'So, until I get a dog, I swim.'

'You swim?' And he tried his absolute best not to think about what she looked like in a swimsuit.

'There's a swimming pool near where I live, so I try and do half a mile every morning. It only takes thirty minutes.' She lifted her arm to her nose and sniffed. 'So, if you ever think I smell of chlorine, that's why. But I do shower,' she joked.

'I'm sure you do.' He didn't let himself think on that subject any further. 'How many lengths is half a mile?'

'It depends entirely on the length of the pool. But for the one I go to, it's thirty-two lengths. There are quite a few people in at that time in the morning. There's no chat. Just in, swim and back out. There're a few kids too, mainly teenagers who are swimming competitively, so there's no one deliberately annoying me by swimming the wrong way.'

Now he couldn't help but laugh. 'You mean the people that swim widths, instead of lengths?'

She gave him a stern look. 'You know the way you hate jelly babies?' He nodded. 'That's the way I hate people swimming the wrong way.'

He laughed. 'Watch out, I might pay someone to come in and do that, just to annoy you.'

Her eyebrows went straight up. 'And I will fill your room with strings of jelly babies and tack them up on your wall like Christmas decorations.'

'This could be war,' he teased.

'It could.' She glanced at the clock on the wall. 'But it's too late. I need to get home. I have an imaginary cat to feed.'

Honestly? He didn't quite know what to make of Skye Campbell. But was he intrigued? You bet.

He watched as she picked up her bag and lifted her coat from the hook behind the door.

'Are you going to steal my sweeties if I leave you unsupervised in here?' she joked.

He stood up quickly, almost sad that she wanted to leave. But as he glanced towards the office window, he could see it was black outside. Just how late was it?

She was just like him. A fellow workaholic. Whilst they might be at opposite sides of the spectrum for other things, at least at some points they overlapped.

'See you Monday,' he said as he headed out, back to his own office.

He could rush along to grab his stuff and walk out with her. But that seemed too forced. He'd found out so much more about his colleague tonight—there had even been some mild flirtation—and he wasn't entirely sure how he felt about that. Best just to leave things.

'Goodnight, Skye,' he said.

'Night, Jay,' she replied.

And for some weird reason that he couldn't explain, he watched her walk down the corridor until she reached the double doors to the lifts.

He was sorry to see her leave.

And for a man who'd vowed never to have a relationship at work again, that might be a troublesome thing.

CHAPTER THREE

'WHAT ON EARTH are you doing?'

It was just after seven in the morning and Skye had an array of bags at her feet. She stood behind the nurses' station in the ward, staring at the back wall. Her curls were pulled back in a ponytail, and he noticed the ends were slightly damp. She must have been up extra early for swimming.

She flung up her hands. 'I'm sorting out the advent calendar.'

Jay decided to stop peering over the station and walked around until he was beside her. 'Doesn't an advent calendar just have a bit of chocolate behind it every day?' He was bewildered at the paraphernalia at her feet.

'Amateur,' she scoffed. 'And those chocolate ones aren't real. I prefer the cardboard ones, you know, where they have a picture behind every window, like a robin, or a present, or a Christmas tree.'

'Anyway, it's not December yet.'

Skye dropped to her knees, picked up one of the bags and dumped the contents out on the floor. There was a whole array of small bags with numbers on them in a variety of Christmas colours.

'That's why I have to get things prepared. We're only two days away.'

He bent down and picked up a red bag with the number thirteen hand-stitched in green. 'What are these for?'

She waved her hand at the untouched wall. 'I hang them all up here in order, put things in them, and every day a staff member gets to open the bag for the day and the contents are their present.'

Jay stared at the small bag, opening it, and looked at her again. 'What on earth can you fit in here?'

This is where her face lit up. 'Oh, lots of things, they're all in here.' She gestured to another bag and he peered inside. Tiny perfume and aftershave, candles, a few decorations, some sweets from an exclusive chocolatier in Edinburgh, a bag with crystals, a knitted hat, some gloves and a tiny book.

He shook his head. 'Where did you get all this?'

'I buy them all year around. I know what people on the ward like. I've got something for everyone.'

'You've done all this yourself?'

Her smile just widened. 'Christmas is my thing. It's my absolute favourite time of year. I do one for the staff, and one for the patients.'

'Doesn't this cost you a fortune?' He was slightly stunned.

She waved a hand. 'As I said, I buy things all year round, so don't really notice. Here, help me pin up the bags in order, then I'll fill them.'

If anyone had told Jay Bannerman that he'd be pinning up bags on a wall at seven in the morning, he'd have thought they'd had some kind of weird dream. But instead, he bent down to sort out the bags in order and started pinning them to the wall.

'Won't we get in trouble for this?' he asked.

She gave a half-hearted shrug. 'Indira the ward sister doesn't mind. The maintenance guy sometimes has something to say about it, but I always have a secret gift stashed for him somewhere. So, he forgives me.'

'And you do this every year?' he asked incredulously.

She nodded. 'Of course. It's Christmas.' She shot him a wicked smile. 'I also have a number of Christmas dresses, earrings, a speaker to play Christmas music and a real love of the Christmas movie channels.'

He kept pinning bags to the wall and she started to fill them. 'When you've finished these ones,' she said, 'the patient ones are in the other bag.'

Her arm brushed against his and he automatically caught his breath.

'Are you always this bossy?' he teased.

She gave him a shocked look. 'I'm not bossy. I'm just a good organiser.' She took a breath. 'Anyhow, the guys here would wonder what was wrong if I didn't put up the calendar.'

He narrowed his gaze. 'Do you think you might be getting taken advantage of?'

'Grumpy Grinch,' she muttered under her breath, still smiling.

'I'm being serious,' he said, turning towards her, realising how close they actually were.

Since that late-night chat in her office, he'd sensed they were holding each other at arm's length slightly. Even now, when the ward was quiet, with some patients still sleeping, and the rest of the staff quietly going about their business, it seemed as if they were the only two around.

He caught a waft of her perfume. It was different from before. Lighter, but with a definite hint of Christmas. Was it trees?

He let out a laugh. 'Why do you smell of Christmas trees?'

She touched her hair, her eyes bright. 'Do I? Great, it's working. I thought it was just some kind of gimmick. I changed my shampoo. It's supposed to be Christmas Evergreen Woods.'

He put his hand over his mouth as he sneezed. 'Sorry.' But he couldn't help but laugh again. 'It's certainly working.'

He ducked into the nearby treatment room to wash his hands, before coming back out to pin up the patients' bags.

He picked up a few vouchers that Skye had left on the station. 'What are these for?'

'One is for Lleyton, the physio—that's his favourite coffee place—and other will be for Ronnie. He's an avid reader. It's for his favourite bookshop.'

'Ronnie? The man mountain?'

She wagged her finger. 'You mean Ronnie, the gentle giant.'

'I didn't take him for a reader.'

'I dare you to find a subject or author he hasn't read. The guy should be on mastermind with books as his specialist subject.'

She really had thought about everything. 'How do people know what number to pick?'

'Oh, I check the off duty and make sure everyone is scheduled to get their present on a day they're working. I leave little tags on the bags.'

Jay folded his arms. 'You really think about this.' It was a statement, rather than a question.

She folded her arms too, mimicking his stance. 'I was actually joking about you being a Grinch and a grump. But any second now I'll think that you'll refuse to dress up as Santa for the ward Christmas party.'

He froze, taking a few seconds to work out whether she was joking or not. But she couldn't hold it together and laughed out loud.

'Your face, it's a picture.' She playfully hit his arm. 'There's no way you'd get that job. It's Ronnie's. Every year.' She winked. 'I think he might even fight you for it.'

As they'd been talking, the ward was starting to get busier. More patients had woken up. Drug rounds had started. And one of the nursing staff appeared next to them with an observation chart in her hand. Almost everything was done electronically now, but clipboards with observation charts were still at the bottom of every bed.

The nurse, Ruby, handed it over. 'Leah's starting to run a temp and has tachycardia. Can someone listen to her chest again, and I'll get a urine sample and check that?'

Skye let out a low groan and looked over Jay's shoulder as he read the chart. 'Did she get a central line inserted yet for her chemo?'

Ruby nodded. 'I've checked that. Nothing obvious.'

Skye pulled her lilac stethoscope from around her neck. 'I'll listen to her chest. I'm pretty sure her chest infection has completely cleared, but I'll listen again.'

Jay nodded to Ruby. 'You'll let me know if anything shows in her urine. And can you observe her wound site every couple of hours, please? Last thing we want to do is stop the chemo, but if she's not fit we'll have to.'

Ruby nodded and disappeared.

There was another nurse on the computer at the station, so Jay headed into the nearest office to use another. It just so happened to be Skye's.

The phlebotomist was due in the ward soon, and he wanted to add another few things onto Leah's blood tests. The most dangerous thing for any patient was to develop sepsis. At this point he would put her on the potential pathway, which meant she would have regular obs, and be watched very carefully.

As he sat down at Skye's computer he noticed two paper Christmas calendars on her desk, alongside two chocolate ones.

She walked in as he was inputting Leah's requirements. 'Chest is clear,' she said, and as Ruby walked in at her back she turned. 'Anything?'

Ruby shook her head. 'Nothing obvious when I dipsticked her urine, but I'll send a sample down to the lab.'

He looked at them both. 'Potential sepsis pathway?' they said in unison.

It was oddly comforting. The staff in this ward knew exactly how dangerous things were for these highly vulnerable patients. He nodded. 'I've just ordered a few extra tests.'

Ruby nodded. 'I'm looking after Leah today, but I'll let Indira know too.'

The staff here worked twelve-hours shifts, and all

staff needed breaks, so it was essential that someone co-ordinated the next few hours for Leah's care.

'Thanks,' he murmured as she left. He sat back, sighing. 'This is the last thing she needs.'

Skye agreed. 'We're both here all day. We can keep a close eye on her. I can cancel our meeting if you want?'

Jay looked at her. Today was his first online meeting with their counterparts in London, South Africa and Chicago, where a parallel study was running.

'I hope we can avoid that,' he said. 'Instead of going to the IT suite, would you be happy if we just sat together in one of our offices here? That way, if there's any change in Leah's condition, we're right at hand.'

'Fine with me,' she said easily. 'I don't want anything happening to our girl.'

Our girl.

It was the way she said those words so easily. Jay wasn't always good with people—probably because he didn't like wasting time, and he didn't always do the niceties that could be expected.

But something about this place was affecting his manner. He found himself stopping to think before issuing sharp instructions. And all the staff here had gone out of their way to be friendly.

Before, at the Great Southern, whenever anyone had asked any kind of personal question it had always felt like prying. But back there he'd been dating a fellow doctor. He'd hated being part of the hospital gossip mill, and that's how it had always felt.

But just yesterday, someone had asked him a general question about running, then had given Jay some routes through the city to try that he hadn't known about. Someone else had told him which petrol stations to avoid because they always overcharged, and another member of staff had casually told him in the canteen queue where to get the best coffee in the city.

Scottish people had a vibe very similar to the Irish. His accent gelled well here. People were interested to know what part of Ireland he was from, and everyone seemed to know a person who lived in a city or village near his own.

It was almost as if he was finally working in a place he could…breathe. Relax a little. Without looking over his shoulder to see who might be talking about him.

Maybe he was just a bit paranoid, but he'd walked in on a number of conversations about himself back at the Great Southern. First, when he was dating Jessica—then, when they'd split up—and then, when the whole hospital had suspicions about who she was dating now. He'd lost all of that when he'd come here, and it wasn't until now he realised what a relief that was.

Now, he was beginning to feel like part of a team. And those two simple words, *Our girl*, let a gentle heat spread through him.

Skye sat down opposite him. 'Pick your calendars.'

'What?'

She turned them around. 'I bought you one of each for your office. But—' she pointed to the chocolate one '—only to be used in an emergency.' Then she winked. 'And open my drawer.'

He looked at her suspiciously before pulling open her drawer to see a packet of chocolate digestives.

'Have to look after my colleague.' She beamed.

Something in him prickled. It would be easy. Easy to let himself flirt with this woman, and easy to be attracted to her. But that would take him back to the situation he was relieved to be away from.

'I don't really do Christmas calendars,' he said.

Skye paused, thinking for a few moments, then stood up. 'Oh no, you don't get to do that around here.'

'I don't get to not like Christmas calendars?'

She put her hands on her hips. 'You don't get to refuse a gift.'

Oh, no. And now he felt crummy.

He wasn't quite sure what to make of all this.

His brain was clear that he didn't ever want to have a relationship with a colleague again. He wanted his private life to be exactly that—private.

But from the moment he'd set foot on this ward he couldn't ignore what was straight in front of him. An attractive, intelligent, committed woman with fire in her belly. He could keep telling himself that he didn't like her, and wasn't attracted to her—but that wouldn't be true.

They'd fallen into flirtation the other night, and it had come too easily to them both.

Maybe this was all in his head. Maybe there had been no flirtation. But the cheeky smiles, winks and way that they gelled together was playing havoc with his senses.

And even when he tried to draw a little line in the sand, like now, she wasn't having it.

'You pick the one you like best. Advent calendars are clearly your thing. I will be happy to take what's left.'

'What's left?'

He nodded, knowing he hadn't made the situation any better. It might be better not to say anything at all. But he couldn't stay silent for long.

'We have to prepare for our meeting with your research colleagues,' he said. 'Somehow, I think our time would be better served preparing for that and keeping an eye on Leah, rather than worrying about Christmas decorations.'

It came out more cutting that he intended, but he was exasperated. He was here to do a job. He needed to focus on that. The meeting today was important, and he would have thought Skye would be taking things more seriously. Even though her research project had gone through all the relevant ethics committee, at any point a research supervisor, such as himself, could ask for things to be called to a halt. Truth be told, he was yet to be convinced by the use of AI in tracking cancer growth reliably.

Skye's eyes widened for the merest second, then narrowed again. He'd annoyed her. And maybe things were better that way.

'That's the thing about women and their ability to multitask,' she said, her tone full of disdain. 'We can do all things well, at the *same* time.'

She picked up two of the advent calendars from his desk and left.

That was the moment he realised the chocolate calendar she'd left behind had a picture of the Grinch on it.

Skye was fuming. She'd thought that she and Jay were getting somewhere. She'd finally stopped inwardly swooning over his accent every time he spoke. His serious manner was starting to filter away, and then, in the blink of an eye, it was back.

She was beginning to think he was a Christmas hater.

Part of her brain was shouting at her, telling her to keep her research supervisor on side. But she didn't feel the need. The heart to heart they'd had the other night had surely shown him how passionate she was about this project. She knew she hadn't overlooked anything in her countless challenges through the ethics committees. There were no issues with her project—whether Jay Bannerman liked the concept or not.

She hung her own advent calendars on the wall. In two days, she could start opening the doors. It made her smile, no matter how annoyed she was. There was something magical about the countdown to Christmas.

She gave a little sigh and looked out her office window. Even though it was daytime, she knew that by nightfall the famous Christmas market would have started, the Christmas tree on the Mound would be lit up and the streets would be decorated.

She loved this time of year. But she'd been so busy that she hadn't had a chance to really enjoy the city's festive spirit yet. Walking the streets at night, with the lights around her, hearing her feet crunching on the ice forming beneath her, with a woolly hat pulled around her ears—it was one of her favourite things on earth.

In the next few days, she was definitely going to visit the market at night again. It just had to be done.

Her phone signalled, letting her know her meeting would be starting soon. She bit her lip. She had enough time to check on Leah first, but as she walked along the corridor, she could see that Jay had already beat her to the room. He was wearing a mask, apron and gloves, and was peeling back the dressing at her central line. It wasn't unusual for staff to wear protective equipment around patients who were immunosuppressed, so Skye grabbed an apron and mask for herself and hurried in.

Jay was talking in a low voice to Leah, who was lying back against her pillows. Her pallor was still obvious. The nurse was around the other side of the bed, checking Leah's temperature and blood pressure.

As Skye stepped up behind him, Leah had her eyes closed. She was listening to the melodic tones of his voice as he told her exactly what he was doing, and reassuring her along the way. He did have patient skills when he concentrated on it.

But Skye's attention was on the wound site. As he pulled back the dressing, she could see the tiniest hint of red around the edges. She had to press her face closer, making Jay jerk a little as he clearly hadn't realised she was behind him.

'So, this is our site of infection?' she queried.

She heard him take a deep breath behind the mask. 'It could be, or it could just be a little irritation from the compounds in the central line. It's really too early to say, but I'm starting her on some broad-spectrum IV antibiotics.'

'That'll be her second set,' she murmured, knowing exactly what the ongoing problems were for patients who were immunosuppressed.

He nodded. 'We have to treat her symptoms. We both

know I can't wait for all the lab results to come back. She has clear signs of infection somewhere.'

He nodded to the nurse to cover the wound site again, before removing his gloves and giving Leah's hand a squeeze. 'Leah, we're going to start some antibiotics again. We'll give them through your vein so there is chance of them working quicker, and hopefully you'll start feeling a bit better soon.'

'I'll give your mum and dad a quick call. Explain what's happened and that we'll talk to them later today.' Her eyes went to the clock as Jay electronically prescribed the medicine on a nearby tablet.

Since they hadn't agreed what office to work in, Skye wasn't surprised when, as soon as she replaced the phone on her desk, Jay walked in with his laptop in his hands. 'We've already connected,' he said, pulling a seat up next to her, as he sat the laptop down.

She could see the faces of her colleagues in London, South Africa and Chicago. A few looked slightly tired, but it was hard to coordinate appropriate time zones across the world.

Skye was caught a bit off guard, but settled in her chair and took a breath. 'Shall we do introductions?'

The camera on the laptop required her and Jay to sit close together, their shoulders almost brushing. She fixed a smile on her face. 'So, you've already met Dr Bannerman, who will be my research supervisor for this project, and is also our new temporary Director of Oncology at the Great Northern Hospital. He previously had the same role at our Southern counterpart.'

All colleagues took a few moments to introduce themselves, and she could see Jay start to pick up. He recognised research studies that they had been involved in, and they in turn recognised some of his published studies.

The conversation quickly turned to the actual samples collected. There were over eight hundred, all from a variety of different forms of cancer. A pathologist joined at this point to explain that each sample was examined by three different pathologists, to ensure agreement on the cancer type, stage and any anomalies. Cancer journeys were then plotted in real life, and once new sample cancer cells had been confirmed by type and stage, AI plotted their likely path. This was the part where Jay became most vocal. He questioned the best pathways of care for each journey, and if patients were being given their optimum path. He talked about the new data learned every day from cancer, and if changing treatment types would affect the results of their study.

Skye understood that. He didn't want any patients to be compromised because they were part of the study. She didn't either. And although most cancers had guidelines for stages and treatments, every person had to be treated as an individual. Their counterparts in Chicago and South Africa talked about their own guidelines and when they would make a different decision based on a patient's presentation. A few specific patients were brought to the table for discussion. There were no concerns about the pathway decisions, but there were questions about whether it was feasible for them to remain part of the study. These things always happened in research studies, and were necessary to ensure the studies remained reliable and robust.

Skye herself became more animated as the discussion continued. The AI mapping so far was exceeding expectations for breast and renal cancer, and they spent a long time debating why these types of cancer appeared easier to predict. By the time the meeting came to an end, she honestly felt exhausted.

She didn't even try to hide it as she slumped back in her chair, lifting the paperwork from one of the cases that AI had plotted and predicted. She looked at Jay. 'Do we really think that breast and renal cancer are easier to predict, or are they just easier to predict for AI because it has so much data behind it?'

Jay looked at her in interest. 'What do you mean?' His words sounded a little sharp, and she wondered what he had actually thought of the meeting.

She ran her fingers across the page. 'Look at how many vectors it has taken into consideration. My brain couldn't even begin to compute that many things.'

He made a noise. She wasn't quite sure if it was in agreement or dispute.

She should be happy. Jay had taken part in his first meeting of the research project. And although he'd asked questions, most of which she felt were valid, she was hoping he would be more reassured by now, and certainly a bit more enthusiastic.

She gestured to some patient files. 'Think of the difference we can make to these patients whose cells have been categorised now.'

'I'm not ready to think like that yet,' he said. 'I still want to look at margins of error.'

'It's all covered in the research proposal and the plans.

The data is there.' She was becoming a bit hostile, and she didn't really like that, but the bottom line was that Jay Bannerman was annoying her.

Then he ran his fingers through that slightly too-long hair and glanced over at her with those brown eyes. Did he know how good looking he was? Was he trying to irritate her?

'Take your time,' she said smoothly as she stood up. 'I'll go and check on Leah.'

His mouth opened, but she watched as he visibly stopped himself from answering. It was likely he wanted to check on Leah himself. But she was a doctor on this ward, and she didn't need his permission to check on her own patient.

She strode along the corridor, irritated. Her mind was spinning in circles. Was he going to throw a spanner in the works for her research? Did he even really understand it? Why couldn't he be as enthusiastic about it as she was? Her stomach clenched as she turned into Leah's room, meeting the nurse at the door.

'No change,' the nurse said. 'I've been monitoring her wound site. It's not showing obvious signs of infection. The first lot of IV antibiotics went in with no issues, and she's due the second set in an hour.'

Skye kept her voice low. 'Any sign of improvement?'

The nurse shook her head. 'Not yet. But there's not really been enough time.' She looked at Skye. 'Could you phone the lab and see if there's any news on the potential urine infection?'

Skye nodded, glad to have something to do, but knowing that her colleague was trying to placate her.

It was worth it. The call to the lab meant a diagnosis of a more unusual urinary tract infection, which needed specific antibiotics. Skye listened carefully, then telephoned a colleague who was a urologist to ask for some advice on the treatment. Some antibiotics could affect patients with a weakened immune system more severely, and she wanted to tread carefully with Leah. The last thing she wanted was to make her sicker than she already was.

She prescribed the new antibiotics, along with some anti-sickness meds, and phoned the pharmacy to make sure the ward would have them on site in the next hour.

When she went back to check on Leah, she found Jay in the room talking to her. Leah was slightly more awake than before, although she still looked exhausted.

She gave Skye a weak smile. 'Dr Jay was just telling me about what he used to get up to back in Ireland with his sister.'

Skye's eyes widened. 'Well, that's a story I haven't heard. Should I pull up a chair?'

Colour heated his cheeks—she couldn't really imagine him telling personal stories to a patient.

But for the first time in a few days, Leah was smiling. 'I told him that I loved horses, and he told me about him and his sister stealing one from the farm next door.'

He sat up straighter in his chair, and she could almost see all his defences clicking into place.

Skye's smile was completely genuine. 'Oh, do tell.' She sat down and crossed one leg over the other.

For a second, his eyes went to her legs.

No, she hadn't imagined that.

'We...were adventurous kids,' he said easily. 'My sister was annoyed she hadn't got a toy horse for Christmas. So, we decided to steal a real one.'

'That's a bit of jump,' said Skye.

Jay shook his head. His accent even thicker. 'Na, the actual bit of a jump was the hedge between our farms. Our mams and dads didn't like each other. We had to climb the hedge to get over to their place. And our Marian, she didn't just want the pony—because they had a number of horses over there. No, she wanted the palomino—the golden and white beauty that was their pride and joy.'

'And did you actually steal it?' Skye leaned forward. She was fascinated with this insight into Jay's childhood.

He pulled a face and waggled his hand. 'Eh…we borrowed it. Just for half an hour or so.' He shrugged. 'Then we got caught.'

Leah put her hand up to her mouth. 'What happened when you got caught?'

'No, wait.' Skye held up her hand. 'How did you actually steal it?'

She nodded as the nurse walked in with the new IV infusion bag.

'They had a big old house. We had to duck under their windows to get to the stables. The stables were kind of at an angle. So, no windows from the house directly looked on to them. It was easy enough to get into the stables, we just had to take Whitmore Shores out of his stall. The bridle was right there. And we could both put a bridle on in our sleep.'

'The horse was called Whitmore Shores?' asked Leah, her brow furrowed.

He exchanged a glance with Skye as she realised what that meant. 'You stole a race horse?' she asked.

He gave a small grimace. 'We called him Goldie.' He sighed. 'So, we put the bridle on, and Marian got on his back and just took off across the fields.'

'Did she have a saddle?' asked Leah, her eyes wide. It was the most awake and focused she'd been all day.

He shook his head. 'She didn't need one. Marian was always a natural on horseback.'

'Didn't she fall off?'

'I can honestly say I've never seen my sister fall off a horse.'

'Wait a minute,' said Skye, 'how did you get caught?'

He waved a hand. 'Oh, that's easy. Marian decided the fields weren't enough and she wanted to take the horse over to our house. So, instead of picking a way across the fields again, she marched the horse right past their front window and down their driveway. It took Mr Rogers about ten seconds to be out of his front door, roaring his lungs out at us.'

Skye and Leah started to laugh at once. Jay laughed too, wagging his finger at them both. 'And the lesson learned that day was, don't take Marian Bannerman with you if you want to pull off a heist.'

He looked a bit wistful for a moment. 'I miss that house.'

'They don't live there anymore?'

He shook his head. 'They live in Brighton now, and they absolutely love it. I keep expecting them to tell me they're moving back home, but my sister is over here too now.' He tapped his eye. 'I think they stay in this country because they think they can keep an eye on us.'

Leah was laughing now, clearly distracted and liking the chat.

Skye's eyes went back to the IV. The nurse had connected it whilst they were talking and the medicine was running in. She'd left a medicine cup next to Skye.

She picked it up and held it out to Leah. 'Take this for me. It's a medicine to stop you being sick.'

Leah frowned. 'I've not been sick.'

Jay replied before Skye could. 'Your new medicine is quite powerful and can make some people sick, we're just trying to stop you feeling like that.'

Leah looked at the fluid-filled bag. 'So, do you know what it is yet?'

Jay nodded. 'You've got a urine infection, and it's one that responds best to the medicine that's in the drip.' It was clear he'd read the lab report, and the notes that Skye had put in Leah's file. He really didn't miss much. And Skye wasn't sure if that made her happy or sad.

She'd always thought of herself as meticulous and thorough. Why on earth would she not admire those traits in someone else?

Jay leaned forward and started telling Leah another story. He was watching her, monitoring her whilst this new drug infused. And it seemed that, whilst he did that, he didn't seem to mind sharing a little part of himself.

It was a new side to Dr Bannerman. He'd mentioned he wasn't too good with patients. And their first encounter had seemed a little clunky. But maybe he wasn't as bad as he thought.

Or maybe he'd been affected by new surroundings, or a new job.

Whatever it was, the man she was watching now—relaxed in his chair, small laughter lines around his eyes and completely engaged with their patient—was extraordinary to watch.

She was quite sure that Leah wouldn't know the real reason they were both there. And that was just as important.

Skye settled back, smiling. She was quite happy to watch the Jay Bannerman show, and learn as much as she could.

CHAPTER FOUR

IT WAS FINALLY the first of December and, as Jay approached the ward, he didn't know what to expect.

He was slightly later this morning, having had to attend a consultant meeting with the medical director, and as he walked onto the ward it was slightly quieter than he'd expected. Yes, he could hear Christmas music playing, but it was low and subdued. He could see that the first little advent bag had been taken down, and couldn't remember which staff member's name had been attached. He was gradually getting to know people a little better, becoming familiar with all their names and quirks.

Connie was behind the desk as he walked up.

'What's wrong?' he asked, scanning the ward for more people. He could see that some patients were up at the side of their beds, and nursing and physio staff were in the six-bedded rooms.

Connie gave him a sad smile. 'Mr Kerr was admitted this morning. He's a long-time patient. On his third type of cancer. He lost his wife last year and is now on his own. He's not looking good at all.'

She tapped a tablet, bringing up the man's records, and handed it to Jay. 'We all love him. He's such a nice man.' She gave a long sigh and looked out one of the windows.

'We hate it when it gets to this stage with someone we've looked after for years. It's just so hard.'

Jay scanned the notes. Frank Kerr was in his late seventies. He'd had bowel, lung and now bladder cancer. Each one treated in succession, and to all intents and purposes cured. But that was the thing about cancer. Cells could be like spiderwebs instead of round capsules, and could reach unpredictable places.

Unpredictable. He wondered if Frank Kerr was part of the study. He'd have to ask Skye later.

'Where is Skye?' he asked.

Connie pressed her lips together for a moment.

'What is it?' he asked.

'She's with Mr Kerr. He was one of her father's friends. He was a good bit older, but I think they'd worked together.'

'Oh.' It was all he could say. He could only imagine how this was hitting her. Should he ask to take over Mr Kerr's care? He didn't want to offend her, but this might all be a bit too close to home. 'I'll go and join her.'

He turned to go and Connie pushed something towards him. It was a plate with some slightly lop-sided scones. 'Take these for Frank. Cheese scones are his favourites.'

Jay gave a nod and lifted the plate, watching the scones precariously skid around as if they were on a skating rink. He concentrated, tucking the tablet under one arm, eyes focused on the plate as he made his way to the patient's room.

The first thing that struck him was how thin Mr Kerr was. Was this normal for him? The second thing he noticed was that Mr Kerr and Skye's hands were intertwined.

He moved forward and put the scones on Mr Kerr's bed table.

'Hi there,' he said in a soft voice. 'I'm Jay Bannerman, one of the new doctors. Connie sent me to give you some scones.'

Frank had the palest blue eyes, which opened as he smiled. 'She's an angel.'

Skye looked up. Her hand hadn't moved. She clearly wasn't embarrassed about how close she was to this patient. Jay nodded to the scones. 'Can I get one of our support workers to bring you some tea to go with the scones? Then maybe we can have a chat about your care.'

He could see Skye visibly bristle. 'I'm looking after Frank,' she said.

He put a hand on her shoulder. It was a friendly gesture, but also one to remind her where she was. 'Of course you are, Dr Campbell, but we're a team here, and I gather Frank's a special guest. I want to make sure I'm up to date on all his needs, so we can make him comfortable.'

He wasn't trying to tell her off, and was careful with his words, but her shoulders slumped a little. She squeezed Frank's hand. 'I'll get us tea, then I'll be back.'

She gave a tiny nod of her head to Jay and he followed her to the ward kitchen. As the boss, there was a whole host of things he should say. All about trying to keep a line between themselves and the patient, and about looking after friends who end up in the ward. But he went with the most important.

'Skye, are you all right?'

She shook her head as she opened the cupboard to pull out cups. 'No,' she said, her voice shaky.

'What can I do to help?' He put his hand on her arm. It wasn't just her voice that was shaky, her hand was trembling too. 'Let me make the tea.'

He gently moved her sideways, finding the rest of the equipment and getting water from the HydroBoil.

She dipped her head as he worked, her voice broken. 'I can't believe how he's deteriorated. There was a package of care in place for him. He looks like he hasn't eaten in weeks. No wonder the cancer has taken hold. He's got nothing left to fight with.'

She started to sob and shake. Jay put his arms around her, pulling her close.

He didn't say anything. He just held her in place, rubbing her back gently as she sobbed.

He'd never seen her upset like this. One of the support workers came to walk in, saw Jay's gentle shake of the head and discreetly walked away.

Little flags shot up in his brain. Would people talk? Would rumours start? But he took a breath. Petty rumours be damned. Whilst it might not be for everyone, if a colleague needed a hug, he would do it.

Her sobbing quietened, and she pulled back a bit, her face streaked with mascara, part of her make-up on the shoulder of his white coat.

'Sorry,' she breathed.

'Don't be,' he replied, then took another breath. 'What do you want me to do? As your boss I should ask you if you want me to take over Frank's care? I don't want you to feel compromised in any way.'

She bit her lip. She still hadn't moved fully away from him—his arm was still at her waist. 'My first reaction is to be angry and say no.' She waited a moment then shook her head. 'But I do feel too attached. I want him to be comfortable and have a good end. I want to make sure his wishes are in place. But...' She paused a moment, then nodded. 'But I know Frank is terminal. I know this will be his last visit. I don't want anyone to have a chance to insinuate anything about this unit.'

The thoughts were clearly forming in her head as she spoke. 'I'd prefer it if you could prescribe his meds, and review his pain relief. I'm not a family member, but last time around Frank's son was in Japan. I'm happy to talk to him, to let him know it's time to come over.'

She sighed, and held up her hands. 'You know the first time he came in I didn't really remember him. He recognised me straight away and asked me if I was Evan Campbell's daughter. He could tell me about parties he'd come to at the family home, and once he did that, I remembered playing in my back garden with his son. And he told me a million stories of my dad from when they were young—things my dad never got a chance to tell me. He and his wife were so close. They did everything together.' She put her hand on her chest. 'I just think he doesn't want to be here without her.'

Jay nodded. 'I noticed in his notes that he told his GP he'd had symptoms for months before he attended. He knew what he had, Skye. Let me talk to him. Let me be the independent person that you can't possibly be. Let me talk to him about treatment—which I think he'll refuse—and his end-of-life care.'

'I want to help,' she said quickly.

'And you will,' he reassured her. 'But let's have a

clean line about who his doctor is, and who makes medical decisions.'

She pressed her lips together. 'I hate this.'

'Then let me help you.'

They'd had this whole conversation face to face, only inches apart. It was intensely personal. But so was the subject matter.

'Thank you,' she said breathily, their eyes connecting.

They stood there for probably a moment more than they should. He didn't want to lift his hand away from her waist, or the other from her elbow. He hated that her face was tear-streaked. He hated that she felt in this position. But it was natural. He'd had patients that he'd treated for more than ten years himself, and they almost became friends.

He was the boss. He had to let her be a friend without compromising her role as doctor. And he could do that.

She wiped her face. 'I better clean up before we go back in.'

'I'll make this tea,' he said with a smile.

'Frank likes builder's tea,' she said, her eyes bright with tears, 'so to be sure to let it stew. Oh, and butter for the scones.'

She disappeared to the toilets and Jay organised the tea, putting everything on a tray.

'I could have done that.' One of the healthcare support workers was bringing back some dishes to the kitchen.

'It's fine,' he said over his shoulder, as he headed back into the ward area and Frank's room.

Skye joined them a few moments later, and once Frank

had started to eat his scone and drink his tea, they had a long chat about his life and wishes.

Every doctor wanted to wave a magic wand and cure every patient. And whilst treatments mainly got better year on year, and research studies helped find out more and more about the disease, sometimes there reached an end point for patients.

Jay was always respectful of patients' wishes. But his heart strings tugged when Frank said he'd wished he'd just slipped away at home with no fuss. He was emaciated, and frail. He didn't always take his medicines, as his water tablets had him up too many times at night. His package of care had dwindled—the council didn't have enough staff to maintain everyone at home.

Skye kept her cool, although he saw her wiping away a few angry tears.

'You should have told me, Frank,' she said. 'I could have come and helped you.'

Frank gave her a sad smile. 'But I didn't want you to, Skye. I wanted you to stay here, and do the job you do, helping those that want help.'

She reached out and took his hand again. She might not be family, but she was the closest that Frank Kerr had to family until his son got here.

In his head, Jay got a vision of a younger version of Skye—how she'd coped with her own father's death. It gripped him like a vice. He was sure this would bring back memories, and trauma, and he wanted to make sure he looked out for her.

He might only have been here a few weeks, but he already could sense the dynamic around the whole unit, and Skye was a huge part of that. Her normally sunny demeanour seemed to rub off on everyone. He'd yet to hear anyone say a bad word about her—even in jest—and from what he'd witnessed her colleagues seemed to admire her.

Today was the first time he'd seen her without her normal festive spirit. She hadn't even mentioned Christmas.

He made a mental note to try and brighten her mood later. These would be a hard few days. And, whilst he could take care of Mr Kerr, he wasn't quite sure how much he could take care of Skye Campbell.

'You finished?'

Jay appeared in her doorway with his jacket already on and zipped up. It wasn't too late, only eight o'clock, but she couldn't believe how tired she was.

'I'm just finishing a few things,' she said with a weak smile.

He walked over and looked down at her notes. 'Anything that can't wait until tomorrow?'

Now she was a bit confused. She looked up. 'Why?'

'Because it's been a tough day, and I wanted to make it a bit better for you.' He gave a wink. 'I'm not always the Grinch, you know.'

She pushed her chair back and stretched out her tired legs. She was intrigued. 'What did you have in mind?'

'Do you have warm clothes?'

She let out a laugh and pulled out a drawer stuffed with hats, scarves and gloves in an array of colours, then pointed to her bright pink wool coat hanging behind the door.

'I think I might be able to manage that.' She grabbed some items from the drawer, slid on her coat and put her bag across her body. 'This better be good,' she teased.

'It will be. Have you said goodnight to Frank?'

She nodded. 'He's already sleeping.'

'Then let's go.'

He led her out the hospital and along the main road towards the centre of town. 'First time in Edinburgh at Christmas,' he said. 'So, I thought I would ask the expert to show me the Christmas lights.'

Her face lit up and her body seemed to straighten. She glanced at him, a renewed sparkle in those green eyes. 'Oh, I think I can manage that. Just how far do you think you can walk?'

'Is that a challenge?' he asked, his smile widening. It was clear this had been the right thing to do. Her mood had lifted instantly once they got outside the hospital.

'It could be,' she teased. 'We'll just need to see if you're up to it.'

'Well,' he said, 'in that case, let's start this night the right way. What's your festive drink? Hot chocolate or mulled wine?'

The streets around them had a number of other people out admiring the festive lights, and there were a few street carts along the way, with a few more regular wooden stands offering a range of food and drinks.

'Mulled wine is for nearer Christmas,' she mused, breathing out a long visible breath in the cold air. 'Hot chocolate would certainly be welcome.'

They joined a short queue for hot chocolate with

marshmallows, flakes and cream, and she was soon sipping as they walked.

Skye had put on a grey woollen hat that had a dog emblem on the front. He nodded at her. 'So, is that the kind of dog you would like—a Scottie?'

She sighed. 'Dog talk. My favourite kind of dog.' She put her hand to her hat. 'I would like a Scottie. But I would also consider a Labrador, because of their good nature, a spaniel for their cute faces, or a cockapoo because I think I might have a similar nature.'

He laughed as he looked at her. 'I'm not entirely sure how to react that one, so I'll just let it go.'

She kept smiling as she sipped. 'You know my favourite actor, Patrick Stewart, fosters pit bulls in America, to show how loving and good-natured they actually are—I'd think about one of them too. Apparently, they are the dogs always left at the shelters.' She turned to him as they walked. 'Have you ever had a dog?'

'We looked after our next-door neighbour's dog when they emigrated to Australia. It was about six months before the dog could join them. It was a mongrel, some kind of collie mix, and Dora had wandered in and out of our house since they'd got her. I think she got fed there, then came to ours to get fed too.'

Skye nodded, her dark green eyes barely visible beneath the edge of her hat. 'Dogs are far more intelligent than we give them credit for.'

They continued down the streets, heading for St Andrew Square, where most of the buildings had their own light displays.

As they rounded the corner, Skye let out a sigh. 'One

of my favourite places at Christmas. I could stay here all night and look at the lights.'

He smiled. The stress and anxiety that had been written all over her face had vanished. She was back to her normal smiley self, and whilst at first he'd thought her naturally bright demeanour would annoy him, it had only taken a few hours of its absence to make him realise what an essential part of her it was.

'Glad you're feeling a bit better,' he said lowly.

She slid her arm into his as if it were the most natural thing in the world. St Andrew Square was busier, and it kept them together, but Jay couldn't ignore the little buzz going up his arm. They stopped into a bar and had a beer, then headed up towards the castle.

There was a special light show on at Edinburgh Castle for the Christmas period and hospital staff had free tickets. They showed their passes and went on in.

It wasn't just lights, it was sounds and history. They followed the light trail to the castle courtyard. Depending on where you stood, you could watch a number of different stories take place. They watched a tale about the castle's history and battles fought, another about Scottish mythical beasts like the kelpies and Nessie, another was more like a party, sharing snapshots of artists who had performed at Edinburgh Castle, and the last story was around Scotland's most famous queen—Mary Queen of Scots.

They then followed a light tunnel, with white and red lights arched above them, and a dramatic spinning earth at the bottom, giving the illusion that they were actually in space, looking down from above.

'Wow,' Skye gave her head a little shake, 'I think I'm seeing stars after that one.'

She had left her hand where it was, slid through his arm, and Jay had seen several people looking at them. He knew they looked like a couple, and it was doing curious things to his brain. One part was thinking how nice it was, and how normal this all felt. The other part was shouting, warning him about his history of dating a colleague and how that all felt for him. Having his humiliation played out in front of everyone he worked with, and the whole hospital thinking they were entitled to know his and Jessica's business. That experience was hard to push aside.

He'd vowed not to walk that path again, and yet here he was, a few weeks after starting his new job, arm in arm with a new colleague in Edinburgh.

It went against everything he'd told himself. But being around Skye was…special.

He already knew parts of her history that he wasn't sure she shared with everyone. He'd watched her passion for her patients, and he'd seen her fall apart knowing she was going to watch someone she cared about die imminently.

'Hey,' someone said and they both jumped.

A small woman in a bright red coat was next to them, clutching the hand of a primary-school-age child.

'Hey, Roseann,' said Skye brightly.

Jay watched as Roseann's eyes went from one to the other, obviously taking in how close they looked.

Skye bent down to talk to the kid. 'Hi, Fletcher, are you enjoying the show?'

The boy nodded enthusiastically.

'Did you use the hospital tickets?' Skye asked as she stood back up.

'Aren't they great? It's about time there was some kind of bonus for working in the health service,' said Roseann, before leaning towards Skye. 'Heard the latest gossip?'

Skye gave an anxious glance at Jay before she shook her head. Jay knew exactly what was wrong. Skye didn't seem like the gossip type.

Roseann beamed and spoke in a not-so-low voice, even though she glanced around to see if anyone was listening. 'You know that Poppy Evans is pregnant?'

Skye gave a careful nod. 'Yes.' Jay had no idea who they were talking about.

'Word on the street is that the father of the baby is Dylan Harper, her fellow neurosurgeon.'

Skye's mouth dropped open, but she tried to cover it up. 'Well, I guess the only person who really knows that is Poppy. It's not really for us to say.'

'Of course not,' said Roseann conspiratorially. 'But wouldn't they make a nice couple?'

'I suppose,' said Skye with caution. Thankfully, Fletcher tugged his mother's hand and pulled her in another direction.

'Best be going,' said Roseann. 'See you at work.' She waved as she walked away.

Jay waited a few moments before he looked at Skye. 'What was all that about?'

'Hospital gossip,' she said uncomfortably. 'I hate it.'

It was like something washed over him. Relief. 'I have no idea who the people are she was talking about.'

'Good,' Skye replied, 'then you won't pass gossip on.' She stopped for a second and looked thoughtful. 'They would be a good-looking couple though.' Then she shook her head and smiled. 'None of my business.'

They started to walk again, finishing the light show in the castle and leaving by the main exit.

'Want another drink?' he asked, feeling hopeful.

There was a second of hesitation from her. 'Coffee. I'd like coffee. I'm getting cold again.'

They found a nearby street vendor and ordered two coffees, taking them over to a small bench under a tree.

'I've had a wonderful night,' she breathed, the steam from her coffee mixing with her breath in the air.

'I'm glad,' he said simply, trying not to stare at her too hard. She was beautiful in the warm lights from the nearby shop fronts. It pulled out the green in her eyes, and the darkness from the strands of hair that had escaped from her hat.

She lowered her head. 'Today was harder than normal. I care about all our patients. But seeing how much Frank had deteriorated shocked me. The same happened with my dad, but it seemed much more gradual.'

Jay nodded and, after a moment, slipped a hand around her back. 'I could see how it affected you. Here's hoping his son arrives soon.'

She leaned into him. 'I think he's honestly just waiting for his son to get here.'

'But until then, he has you. He obviously values the relationship you've had.'

Her head rested against his shoulder, and he got a small

waft of her amber perfume. It suited her. Warm, rich-smelling, like a big hug.

This was the first time Jay had felt a connection to someone in so long. Even with Jessica, their last year together had almost seemed automatic. The romance and fun had fallen by the wayside. Work had overtaken everything.

But he hadn't had a chance for that to happen here. And all he could really think about was this beautiful woman at his side. The heat seeping through his coat from her to him. The fact he really just wanted to take her in his arms and…

Jay moved, just slightly, and her face tilted upward towards his.

Their lips met naturally, gently at first, and then as if they were feeling their way—with more passion.

Her hand came up to his cheek, and he slid his hand around her back, up and into her hair.

Their bodies shifted towards each other as their kiss deepened. He could taste the coffee on her lips. Feel the warmth of their bodies next to each other. For a second, he wished they were a million miles away from a public place. His lips moved from hers, first to her ear, and then to her neck. She was still holding on tightly, not letting go.

Then their lips naturally came together again, and heat started to spread across his chest and down his body. He would happily sit here all night kissing this woman.

Then Skye drew in a sharp breath and pulled back. Her pupils were dilated, her cheeks flushed.

'What?' he asked. 'What's wrong?' The pullback had

been sudden, as if there had been a shout, or she'd been hit by something.

She blinked and bit her lip, her eyes darting all over the place—anywhere but meeting his.

'This was a bad idea,' she said suddenly.

His stomach plummeted.

She stood up quickly, but placed a hand on his shoulder when he went to stand up too. 'No, don't.' Her voice was firm. 'I need to go home. Get some beauty sleep. I want to be up early in the morning and get back to see Frank.'

Jay went to stand again but her hand was firm.

'I'll walk you,' he offered, but she shook her head.

'No. I don't live too far, and I've walked these streets alone for years. I'll be fine.' Then she took a breath. 'Please, just let me go alone. I'll text you when I'm home.'

She started walking briskly away, dodging the other people on the streets until her pink coat and grey hat were lost in the crowd.

Jay felt frozen. What had he done? What had gone wrong? He stared down at their empty coffee cups before standing and putting them in a nearby rubbish bin.

It had been Skye who'd been the one to take his arm and to lean against him. She'd seemed so comfortable in his company all night. And she'd responded to his kiss in a way that made him know he hadn't been the only one thinking about it.

Jay stood and stretched his back. Stared in the direction she'd gone. He wanted to go after her, to talk to her again. But she'd asked him not to, so he would respect her wishes. Would he worry if she didn't text to say she was home safe? Of course he would. But he didn't know her address, and it would only be his place to raise an issue if she didn't appear at work tomorrow.

He sighed, shaking his head as he walked back towards his own place, his feet crunching on the pavements. All he could see right now were visions of her face throughout the night. When she'd smiled, the sparkle in her eyes. And when she'd been sad, the way his only thought had been to comfort her.

As he kept walking, the thoughts kept circling. It had been a long time since he'd thought about any woman this way, and that confused him. They'd only known each other a short time, and they'd kissed once. This wasn't like him. Not at all.

As he approached his front door, his phone sounded. He pulled it out. One word.

Home x

He gave a smile as he opened the door. Who knew if that kiss even meant something—or if it meant nothing at all.

What he did know for sure was what he'd dream about tonight. And that was a woman called Skye.

CHAPTER FIVE

EVEN THOUGH IT was early when he reached the ward next day, Skye had still beat him to it.

'She been here long?' he asked the ward sister.

Indira gave a sad nod. 'She's been here since about six. But Mr Kerr's son's plane is due to land about eleven this morning. So he should be here shortly after that.'

Jay gave a nod, not wanting to intrude on her time with Mr Kerr. He sat down next to Indira and took Mr Kerr's chart. 'Any concerns about his chest, pressure areas, urine output?'

Indira shook her head. 'All fine. His IV line tissued last night and had to be re-sited, but that was it.' She gave a smile. 'He did say that "everything hurt". But it's likely that his cancer might have moved to his bones.'

'Have we started an infusion yet for his pain?' Jay knew that bladder cancer could affect surrounding organs, even the bones in his pelvis.

'I was waiting for you to come in to talk about it.'

Jay nodded, drawing up the prescribing regime that they normally used for terminal patients. It gave them a low and steady amount of painkiller, with a chance for the patient to supplement themselves with the push of a button.

'Do you want me to go in and talk to him about this?'

Indira shook her head. 'I'll set it up and get it started. I think Skye will be fine to explain this to him.'

Jay paused for a moment. 'Once you've got that set up, let's go over the rest of the patients she normally would deal with—and I'm happy to speak to Mr Kerr's son if she's not comfortable doing it. They knew each other as kids, it might be difficult for her.'

Indira's head tilted to the side, and she gave him a cross between a curious glance and a warm smile. 'She seems to have opened up to you.'

He felt a small wave of panic. Had that person they'd met last night—Roseann—told people she'd seen them together? To be honest, he wouldn't be surprised in the slightest, but he hadn't been entirely sure she would have recognised him as a doctor from here.

The stare from Indira was making him feel as if he were under the spotlight, but maybe he was imagining it.

'She told me a little of how she knew Mr Kerr,' was all he replied in explanation.

'Okay,' was Indira's response as she left to go and set up the infusion pump.

Jay spent the next few hours examining the ward patients who needed reviews, checking over test results when required, and answering a few queries from GPs. He walked around to the day unit, to see those who came in for daily chemotherapy, and made sure everything was problem-free before he headed back to the ward.

As he arrived, he saw Skye hugging a tall, thin man as she left Mr Kerr's room. She walked down to the nurse's station, clearly blinking back tears.

'Mr Kerr's son?' he asked.

'Jason,' she said in croaky voice.

'Need me to talk to him, to do anything?'

She shook her head firmly. 'I've done it. He knows everything he needs to know, and now they just need some time together.'

Jay licked his lips, wondering if she wanted some space or not.

'I've seen all the ward patients, and those in day care. How do you feel about an early lunch?'

For a moment his heart was frozen, wondering if he might see a flash of panic in her eyes.

But instead, she just gave him a grateful nod. 'Yes, please.'

They headed down to the canteen, grabbed some hot drinks and bacon rolls, and found a table in the corner of the room.

Once they were seated, Jay didn't wait. 'I wanted to apologise,' he said quickly.

'Apologise?'

He nodded. 'For last night. I didn't mean to upset you, or step over a line. It was never my intention to offend you.'

Skye blinked and sat for a few seconds, trying to decide what to say. She wasn't quite sure where to go with this.

Sure, she had made excuses and left hastily last night, and it was likely odd, given they'd had such a nice evening together. But she'd just been shellshocked by what that kiss had actually done to her. What it had actually *awoken* in her. She hadn't actually expected him to apologise for the best kiss she'd had in her life.

'I think I should tell you something,' he continued.

Uh oh. Her stomach gave an uneven flip. That didn't sound good. She licked her lips. 'What?'

'I don't know how much you might have heard about me on the grapevine.' Jay looked extremely uncomfortable.

'Nothing,' she replied. There had been a few rumours, and she knew he'd been known as Dr Grumpy down south, but she had no idea why.

He took a deep breath, and she sensed he was a little relieved. Something flicked in her brain from last night. She'd spent her whole time thinking about the kiss since then, but something had just jarred her. When they'd met Roseann, and she'd clearly been gossiping. Jay had looked a little wary. It was clear he was just as uncomfortable with that sort of thing as she was.

'When I worked at the Southern,' he started, 'I was engaged to another doctor for five years.'

Skye shifted a little uncomfortably in her chair, not entirely sure she wanted to hear about another woman.

'We'd agreed to a long engagement—neither of us wanted to rush into marriage. But, last year, she broke it off suddenly. Then, a few weeks ago, she announced her new engagement to a guy we both worked with. I'd been uncomfortable already in the hospital.'

He paused and looked at her. 'When you have a relationship with anyone inside the hospital, the whole place thinks it's their business to have an opinion on it. I never liked it. I like my private life to be just that—private.

And then, when it was clear that our relationship was over, and it became pretty obvious that she was likely dating him whilst still engaged to me, I just felt that everyone had their eyes on me, and that most people had likely been talking about me behind my back. Probably saying what a fool I was.'

'Oh, Jay, I'm sorry. That's horrible.'

He stared at his coffee cup for a moment. 'It is,' he agreed, then pressed his lips together. He leaned his head on one hand. 'Trouble is,' he said in that lilting accent, 'when you've likely been the talking point in your place of work, it makes your defences go up.' He raised his eyebrows. 'I might have got a bit of a reputation for being grumpy at work, and standoffish. But I just didn't want my business to become the hospital's grapevine. I stopped going to nights out, or anything like that, because I just hated the thought of being made a fool of again.'

Skye gulped and reached over, giving his hand the briefest touch. Now she knew why he came across as prickly at times, and why he didn't seem particularly friendly.

'You're at a new place,' she said quietly. 'A new hospital, with a whole group of people that don't know you, or anything about you. Surely you should just take some time to take a breath, and get to know everyone?' She paused, then added, 'And let them get to know you.'

Something was nagging at her. The way he'd spoken about his ex. He hadn't even said a name. Was he still thinking about her? Was he really up here because he didn't want to see her with her new fiancé? Was Jay Bannerman actually just on the rebound?

Anger flickered deep inside. She'd really enjoyed last night's kiss. Yes, she might have panicked for a second. But she'd sent him a text to let him know she was home and ended that with a kiss.

Skye had always struggled with relationships herself—mainly because she hadn't ever been inclined to give them the time and attention they probably deserved. She'd dated a lot. Meeting men was never a problem. But sooner or later, no matter how great the guy, they always got fed up with her devotion to work, and most relationships just petered out.

She blinked as she sat in front of Jay now. Did she even want a relationship with him?

He gave her a sad look. 'So, you're telling me to give Northern a chance?'

'I don't think people are talking about you, Jay. They have no reason to.'

He gave a slow nod. 'I guess.' Then his gaze met hers. 'Unless someone saw us last night?'

She froze. She literally froze. That hadn't even occurred to her. Of course, other hospital staff might have taken the same opportunity that they had, using the tickets to the show. It was always popular.

'It's just as likely no one saw us,' she countered, 'and if they did, you've only been here a few weeks, most people wouldn't recognise you.' She shook her head. 'There's no rumour to start.'

He gave a slow gulp. His head tilted slightly to the side. 'So, what about our kiss last night? What did that mean?'

Now she was on the spot. She would like it to mean

something. But, on the other hand, what had really changed for her?

She was still entirely focused on her work. Was that likely to change any time in the future? No.

The kiss had made her feel special. It had made her feel connected. And whilst she hadn't felt that way in a long time, it didn't have to mean anything.

She met his gaze. 'I think we can put that down to a wonderful night out between friends. It ended the evening in a nice way.'

His eyebrows went up again. 'Nice?'

She gave a small smile, knowing he was pushing. 'Well, it wasn't exactly unpleasant,' she said, stringing the words out. 'But…' She straightened, trying to look a bit more serious. 'It's probably not a good idea for us. We work together. You're the supervisor of my research project. Things like that could become complicated. I don't want to be in a situation where either of us is uncomfortable working together.'

Now it was Jay's time to shift in his chair. 'Of course not,' he said quickly. 'Maybe we can just put it down to getting carried away with the Christmas spirit?'

Now she did laugh out loud. 'You?'

He pretended to look wounded, putting his hand to his chest. 'Yes, me. You think I can't be festive?'

She leaned across the table. 'Name Santa's reindeers.'

For a second he looked panicked. 'Rudolph,' he said triumphantly.

'There's eight more,' she replied, deadpan.

He shook his head. 'Give me something else.'

'Name five Christmas films.'

His brow furrowed and he concentrated. *'The Grinch,'* he said, almost wickedly—she'd called him that too.

'One.'

'White Christmas.' It was like he'd pulled that from the dregs of his mind.

'Two.' She drummed her fingers on the table, doing her best impression of being unimpressed.

'Eh…'

'Nope, I don't know a Christmas film called that.'

'Give me a moment.' He actually did look a bit worried, and that made her want to laugh out loud. After what seemed like the longest time, he let out a breath and frowned. 'I give up.'

She counted on her fingers. *'Santa Claus: The Movie, Miracle on Thirty-Fourth Street, Elf, The Polar Express, Last Christmas, The Christmas Chronicles, The Holiday, It's a Wonderful Life, Die Hard—'*

He cut her off. 'That is *not* a Christmas movie.'

She folded her arms. 'It is. And I'll fight to the death over that one.'

The tension between them appeared to have eased, because they both took long breaths.

He gave a resolute smile. 'So, Christmas spirit. Is that what we're going with?'

She wondered how he felt deep down. Because she wanted to say no. She wanted to tell him she was more than a little annoyed at getting kissed on the rebound by a handsome doctor with distracting brown eyes and a lilting accent. If she was in some kind of Jane Austen adaptation, she would declare it terribly unfair.

But she wasn't, so she kept her expression impartial.

'I guess if we want to keep working together—well, it should be.'

He slid his hand across the table, and, for a brief second, she wondered if he was going to squeeze her hand, give her some kind of secret sign that this was just all nonsense.

But…his hand was in the position for shaking. So, she gripped his hand, probably just a little too tightly, and shook it. 'Agreed.'

He glanced over at the clock. 'Time to get back, you probably want to see Frank again.'

Frank. For about ten minutes she actually hadn't thought about him. That made her feel instantly guilty. Her chair scraped as she stood up quickly.

'Yes,' was her reply before she turned and left him to pick up their cups, and head back to the ward.

The next few days were hard on Skye. This was her time of year. And although her walk with Jay had been good, the kiss—and their conversation after—had left her feeling low.

She'd sat with Frank and his son Joe on and off for a few days until Frank had finally passed. He'd been comfortable and had slipped away whilst both Joe and Skye had been in his room.

Skye had promised to help Joe with the funeral, and had given him a list of their fathers' mutual friends so he could start arrangements. It was only proper to help him. But it sparked a lot of old memories for her, and made her sad.

Her mum lived in Spain now, and had met someone last year. Skye was happy for her, because her mother had been sad and lonely when her father had died, and then for years afterwards. She'd lost her oomph for life, and this new man was only a couple of years older and was also a widower. He was good company for her mum, and Skye did approve. But it also meant it didn't feel appropriate to phone and be upset about all the memories of her father.

She was trying her best to keep things bright on the ward. But the last two nights she'd gone home and just hugged herself with a blanket on the sofa. Had that kiss unsettled her too? Her work ethic meant that she hadn't really dated any colleagues. She'd never really wanted to. But being alone wasn't always good. Being alone was just sometimes lonely. No wonder she wanted a dog or a cat.

The next morning, even though it wasn't even light yet, she found her most festive dress, bright red and decorated with tiny Santas, and a pair of knee-high black boots.

There were a few research meetings over the next week, and she needed to be prepared. More data was ready on the tumour samples, and she wanted to see how the AI had plotted them.

When she got to the ward it was barely seven o'clock. Indira was on the phone at the desk and she gestured Skye over.

'Why has the patient been down there so long? They could have come up to us at any point in the middle of the night?' Indira paused, then sighed and nodded. 'Send them straight up, our own doctor will deal with them.'

'What is it?' asked Skye as soon as Indira put down the phone.

'Renal cancer. Transfer in from a hospital in Ayrshire.

We didn't receive the notification, and A&E have been slammed. The patient's been in there all night.'

'Oh no, poor soul,' said Skye. 'Are they sending them right up?'

Indira nodded. 'I'll get Ronnie to get the bed ready and find some breakfast for them.'

'I'll clerk them in.' Then she turned. 'Or, will we wait and see how they are? They might be knackered and need a sleep.'

Indira nodded. 'Thanks Skye.'

Skye hated when things like this happened. They shouldn't. But occasionally a referral would get lost—between ambulance transfers, messages not being passed on, consultants or GPs being on annual leave. It was rare, but it always made her feel terrible.

She liked to think the NHS offered a wonderful service. The thought of some poor patient—who was likely getting admitted because of worsening symptoms, or pain not being controlled—lying on an uncomfortable A&E trolley all night made her insides curl.

'What's wrong?' The deep voice was right at her shoulder.

She jumped. 'Where did you come from?' Then she frowned. 'And how do you know something is wrong?'

'I'm not blind. I can see the expression on your and Indira's faces. Is it something I should know about?'

She quickly explained. He looked around. 'It'll be breakfast time soon. Most of the porters will be delivering food trolleys.' He caught sight of Ronnie. 'How about Ronnie and I go down and pick the patient up?'

'You'd do that?' She was shocked. Most department

heads wouldn't consider it their role to do something like that.

'Of course I will,' he replied and went to get Ronnie.

Fifteen minutes later the guys wheeled the trolley onto the ward and gently moved the patient over to their waiting bed.

Indira took a few moments to speak to the forty-year-old woman, who looked exhausted, and then came back with some tea and toast.

Jay met Skye at the nurse's station. 'Metastatic disease, she's tired, hungry and needs some pain relief. She also let me know she prefers female staff. Are you happy to take the lead?'

Skye took a few seconds to answer—she knew it had been two male staff who'd collected the woman from A&E.

'She was okay on the way up?'

He nodded. 'One of the female healthcare assistants came up with us.'

Skye nodded. 'Absolutely, I'll let her finish breakfast, sort out some pain relief and take it from there.'

She handed Jay another chart. 'I'll do you a trade. Leah's on her second day of chemo today and needs to be checked over later to see how she's tolerating it. Do you mind doing that?'

He gave a slow nod. There had been nearly a full two-week delay in her treatment because of her underlying infections. Those were now resolved, but they were both worried about her.

She ought to feel awkward around Jay because of their previous kiss. But with their conversation in the canteen—where she had been the one to insist that their kiss didn't have to mean anything deeper—a line had been firmly drawn in the sand. And since then, it hadn't been as awkward as she might have expected.

He was treating her just the same. But instead of feeling relief at having no tension at work, it was actually annoying her!

Had their kiss really meant nothing to him? She hated that she found herself occasionally staring at him, wondering what might have happened if they'd been in a different location, somewhere more private.

Maybe he spent his life just kissing girls? Because he was good at it. She had *never* been kissed like that, and that's what annoyed her the most.

It's what had been causing her dreams to sizzle over the last few days—it was proving very distracting. No matter how much she tried to push 'that' kiss into a box and lock it away, somehow it was sneakily managing to get itself back out.

She kept wondering what he made of all this. Maybe she had misjudged the fact he was on the rebound. It certainly sounded like that, but annoyingly enough she couldn't see into his head, to see if that was how *he* actually felt.

The last thing she wanted to do was compromise their working relationship, but as much as she could tell, there was still a vibe in the air. She could feel it.

The ward was busy at this time of year. It was strange, but there always seemed to be a spate of people who received a cancer diagnosis just before Christmas. For the majority of people, even though the diagnosis was scary, they had a good chance of a cure. Jay was always honest with patients. Screening tests were invaluable, and often picked up a diagnosis before a person had a single symptom. Most people were grateful to be able to start treatment as soon as possible.

But Jay had just spent the last few days giving people diagnosis after diagnosis. It seemed like a revolving door. As a consultant oncologist he should be used to it, but even he was getting down.

As he stood as the nurses' station, he picked up a flyer about a drive-in Christmas movie experience, in Portobello, a coastal suburb of Edinburgh. That wasn't too far from him.

'Know what film they're showing?' he asked Indira.

She lifted her head and looked at the leaflet. 'They never tell you until you're actually there and parked up. Some people go, and hate what's been selected, others go, and find out it's their favourite Christmas film ever. I think there's a spoiler group about it online, but I don't know how reliable it is.'

She glanced down the corridor and smiled. 'You know who likes to go, don't you?'

He shook his head. 'No, who?'

Indira looked at him carefully. 'Skye. She loves it. I'm surprised she hasn't mentioned it already.'

He wasn't quite sure what to say. From Indira's gaze, it was like being under a microscope—he was sure she was watching for any sign of a facial twitch.

'I heard my name, what's going on?' asked Skye brightly.

Indira grinned. 'Jay was just saying that he'd like to go to the Christmas drive-in tonight.'

'He was?' Skye clearly couldn't hide the surprise on her face. 'And here was me thinking you didn't even know that many Christmas films,' she said under her breath.

Jay squirmed, but before he got a chance to reply, Indira spoke again. 'And I was just saying how much you love that, and that you'd probably be going.'

Their eyes met. Both of them had the same deer-caught-in-headlights look, neither of them quite sure how to respond.

But Indira had already made her mind up about this. 'It starts at seven thirty, and it's popular. You'd both need to be there before seven.' She glanced at her watch, then turned to Jay. 'There are always food vans there, so you'll be able to grab some dinner. But you better go home and get changed first.' She carried on as if no one else was involved in this conversation. 'So, you'll pick up Skye about six-thirty then? Better get a move on you two.'

Skye's mouth was slightly open, as if she were trying to interrupt, but Indira locked her with a hard stare.

What could he say?

He had genuinely considered doing this tonight to try and lift his festive spirits a bit. Would it be so awkward to take Skye with him?

'I don't know Skye's address,' he murmured, glancing between both women.

Indira picked up a Post-it pad from the desk. 'Here you go,' she said, scribbling as she held Skye's gaze. 'It's easy to find.'

An awkward silence stretched out in front of them. Then Jay gave a brief nod of his head.

'Better get ready then,' he said, moving quickly down the corridor before Indira started dissecting him like a specimen.

By the time he pulled up outside Skye's, he wondered what on earth he was actually doing. He didn't want to have a relationship with a co-worker. It was clear Skye didn't want to have a relationship with him. He'd half expected her to text him with an excuse—he would have gladly taken it.

Skye's place was a semi-detached townhouse in a reasonable part of Edinburgh. The whole row of houses had different coloured front doors. Quirky, but also fun. There was a warm glow from her windows, which made him wonder what the inside was like.

It was good manners to go to the door but, before he had a chance, Skye opened her green front door and came out wearing a practically matching green coat. She had some things in her hand and blinked at his car.

He could have left it in storage back in London. But his father's old, red Alfa Romeo Spider had been his pride and joy, and it was in pristine condition. Most places that Jay took it someone offered to buy it.

Skye's eyes widened at the sight. 'Where did you get this?' she asked as she climbed inside.

'It was my father's. He restored it and loved it. When he moved to Brighton and said he wouldn't use it any more, I had it shipped over from Ireland.'

'You drove it up from London?'

He gave a short laugh. 'Did you think it wouldn't make it?'

She looked around the old-style dashboard, the convertible roof. 'Did it?'

He nodded. 'The engine is probably in better condition than most humans.' He waited a second and then twisted in his seat to face her. 'If this is too awkward, just say. I did mention to Indira that I was thinking about going, it was her who mentioned that you'd gone before.'

She raised her eyebrows. 'Haven't you realised yet that you don't argue with Indira?'

He let out a short laugh. 'I felt as if I was under some kind of microscope.'

'Me too,' she agreed, then looked at him carefully. 'We both know Christmas films aren't really your thing. Why did you want to go?'

He sighed. 'Honestly, I've been giving out diagnoses these last two days at an alarming rate. I just wanted something to distract me. To let me think about something else. It's been hard,' he admitted—not something he would usually do.

'People think we're made of granite or something,' she replied. 'Just because we chose oncology doesn't mean we won't have bad days like everyone else.'

She got it. She really did.

He nodded. 'I just wanted some kind of pick-me-up. Plus, you guilted me into it.'

'I what?' She was shaking her head.

'You shamed me,' he said matter-of-factly. 'You let me know that, if I get caught in some pub quiz, I only know the names of two Christmas films. It could be the difference between winning or losing.'

She gave him a smug smile. 'I'm glad that you take your pub quizzes seriously.'

Jay started the car and pulled out. If Skye didn't want to be here, then she wouldn't have come. He started towards Portobello.

'Did you eat?' she asked.

He shook his head. 'Indira said there are food vans.'

Skye pulled a face. 'I didn't really have a chance to warn you. It will be hotdogs, half-cooked burgers, chips and likely some kind of kebabs.' She pulled out her phone. 'But there is good news.'

'Tell me, please. From the description of the food, we'll both end up being referred to public health with some kind of gastro disaster.'

She turned her phone to face him, a genuine smile on her face. 'The film,' she said. 'It's *The Santa Clause*.'

He glanced sideways. Her eyes were shimmering. 'Is that a good one?'

'You've never heard of *The Santa Clause*?' her tone was incredulous.

He shook his head as he kept his eyes on the road. 'Should I have?'

She threw up her hands. 'Tim Allen. An ordinary guy hears a noise and goes outside to find Santa has fallen off his roof. He has to take over, and starts to turn in Santa. It's brilliant.'

'It is?' Jay wasn't convinced from the brief description.

But Skye settled back into her seat. 'If you're looking for some kind of pick-me-up, I guarantee you, this is it.'

'If you say so.'

They continued along the road, whilst Skye kept telling him parts of the story. The more she talked, the more enthusiastic she got. By the time they reached Portobello, they had to join a long line of cars to pay their entry fee and get in.

She nudged him with her elbow. 'See? This is all because they've seen on the spoiler page what film it is tonight.'

'I'll take your word for it,' said Jay as he flashed his card at the machine. The barrier lifted.

'Park over here,' said Skye, directing him to a certain part of the drive-in, which was really just a large retail car park surrounded by warehouses. The screen was huge and rippling in the wind.

'Did you bring anything?' she asked as he slid his seatbelt off.

Jay felt momentarily panicked. 'No, how—what should I have brought?'

She held up the bag she had with her. 'Drinks, crisps, chocolate or, if you prefer fruit, I have tangerines.' She dangled the big string bag in front of his nose and he started to laugh.

'I've failed,' he said, then lent over her, accidentally brushing against her leg as he made a grab for the glove box. 'I might have some ancient mints in here.'

Even though it was dark in the car, he could still see the green of her eyes. Their gazes clashed and held for a moment.

He knew. He knew she'd felt the same buzz he had.

He leaned back into his own seat, but didn't break their

gaze. Skye licked her lips. He knew it was likely just a nervous reflex, but it sent his senses into overdrive.

'How about some chips?' he asked, hand grasping for the door handle.

She gave the tiniest of nods and he stepped out into the cold night air. Anything to cool his flushing skin.

He joined a snaking queue before realising he hadn't even asked if she wanted anything on hers. A quick executive decision was made to take one bag with salt and vinegar, and the other with salt and tomato sauce. He was happy with either, so would let her choose. He grabbed another couple of diet sodas and headed back to the car.

The screen had been playing adverts whilst the rest of the viewers had moved into their places around the car park. It was literally mobbed. He'd never seen anything like this before.

As he climbed back in, he suddenly realised that the Alfa might not be the best car in the world for this. The roof was in place, but it did let in a few drafts, and with the temperature due to drop to below zero it might be a cold watch.

'Salt and vinegar, or salt and sauce?' he asked as he pulled out his insulin pen and injected in his stomach.

'Tomato or brown sauce?' she queried.

He scoffed. 'Tomato. Who puts brown sauce on chips?'

'Me,' she answered as she took the bag with salt and vinegar.

As soon as they opened their bags the steam started fogging the windscreen. Jay started the engine again to clear the window.

'This car might not have been the best idea,' he admitted.

'Why?'

'Let's just say that, in a car this old, things can be a little draughty.'

She stared up at the roof above them and touched it with her hand. 'What's it made of?'

'Mohair.'

'What?' A deep furrow creased her brow. 'Are you serious?'

'Entirely. I'm just not sure it was expected to last this long.'

'It's rain proof?' She looked mildly panicked.

'I haven't got wet yet.'

Before she had a chance to say anything else the film started, sound booming from speakers at the front and sides of the car park.

It was odd. He'd never been to a drive-in before. The screen was big enough to see easily, and he could see cars filled with multiple people around them.

'How long is it going to take to get out of here?' he asked.

Skye took a quick glance around the large car park. 'Probably about an hour. But don't worry. I'll teach you about other films whilst we're waiting.'

The film was surprisingly good, but the temperature in the car was plummeting fast. After half an hour, Skye gave a sniff and pulled her coat further around himself. She'd already told him to put his engine off, in case it drained the car battery, and the truth was he couldn't remember the last time he'd renewed the battery.

'There's an age-old way to keep warm,' he said quietly.

'What's that?'

'Body heat.'

She stared at him. 'I can't believe you just said that.'

'Are you cold, or are you cold?'

'I'm cold,' she admitted.

'And if we were stuck in the Antarctic somewhere, would you worry about getting body heat from someone you don't really like?'

'We're in Portobello,' she bit back. 'And I didn't say I don't like you.'

He gave her a smile and held out his arm. 'Then keep warm.'

Her jaw was slightly clenched, and he wondered if she wanted to get into a fight about it. But, after a few seconds, he could see her relent, before she shifted slightly in her seat and let her body press against his.

Okay, so it wasn't ideal. The car made things a little awkward. And it wasn't the optimum way to keep warm, but it was better than nothing.

'You should have a blanket,' she scolded. 'What if you got caught at the side of the road in a snowstorm?'

'I don't take her out in the snow,' he said quickly.

'Her?' She turned to face him.

He shrugged. 'Miriam.'

'You called your car Miriam?'

He was conscious how close they were. How he could intermittently see tiny freckles on her nose, depending on the way the light reflected from the film screen.

'My dad called his car Miriam,' he replied, 'and I have absolutely no idea why.'

She seemed to pause, just staring at him for a bit,

and he wondered if he'd managed to get tomato sauce on his face.

'What?' he asked.

After last time around, no matter how much he was tempted to lean in and kiss her, he wouldn't. Not after she'd left so quickly. And not after their conversation where she'd made it clear she wasn't interested.

His curiosity was piqued. 'So, you don't—*not* like me then?'

She gave him a hard stare, but didn't make any attempt to put any distance between them. Heat was starting to spread.

She blinked. 'I think you're okay.'

'Okay?' He couldn't help but smile again. 'As in, okay to work with, okay to talk to if there's no one else around, or okay to consider if he were the last man standing?'

The edges of her lips crept upwards. 'All of the above.'

He let his head flop back. 'I'm going to die of happiness from the compliments tonight.'

Her gaze narrowed slightly and he sensed her stiffen. 'I'm not anyone's rebound girl.'

Now it was his turn to stiffen. 'Why on earth would you think that?'

'From what you said the other day in the canteen. You know that you're prickly and push people away. You also told me that you wanted to get away from watching your ex celebrate her new engagement. You're clearly on the rebound.'

He shook his head in bewilderment. 'If I was on the rebound, I'd still have feelings towards my ex. I don't.

I'm just not entirely sure that workplace romances are the best thing.'

'You think that because you're still hurting,' she insisted.

Jay could feel his hackles rising. 'I think that because—like I explained to you—I don't like being the subject of gossip at work.'

She just stared at him, as though she didn't really believe what he was saying.

'Let me give you an example. I've been here—what, three weeks? I barely know anyone at the Great Northern. But, in the last few days, I've heard gossip about the potential father of Poppy Evans' baby, I've heard others talking about a guy called Max, and taking bets on when he might lighten up, and if some other female doctor might be the person that's affecting him. Do you know her? Tamsin O'Neill? And I've heard rumours about a maybe affair between one of the radiographers and his secretary.'

He shook his head. 'It's intrusive, and potentially harmful. But hospitals are notorious for gossip. I just don't want to be part of it.' He waited a second as she continued to stare. 'And none of that—*none* of that—means I'm still in love with my ex. I actually wonder if I was ever in love with her in the first place.'

She shifted, her body, which had been aligned with his, moving back to her own seat.

All of a sudden, the space seemed immense.

'Let's just watch the film,' she said.

There was really no arguing with that. He settled back

in his own seat, frustrated, and wondering where on earth those thoughts had come from.

After a few long minutes Skye reached into her bag and brought out a cardboard box of chocolates. She opened the box, took the first one, then handed it wordlessly to him.

The box passed back and forward between them for the next half hour until the film ended.

He gathered up their rubbish and took it to the nearest bin, relieved when he got back in the car and it started with no issues.

As he got back in, he caught the aroma of her perfume again—his heart rate quickened. She was still having a crazy effect on him.

How could he blame her for getting the wrong end of the stick when his brain told him one thing, and his body another?

His heart sank as he looked at the queue ahead. Skye had been entirely right. This would take an hour at least to get out of the venue.

They exchanged glances and she gave a conciliatory smile. 'Truce?' she asked.

'Truce,' he agreed, feeling a wave of relief. They really didn't need for things to be awkward between them.

'Great,' she said as she sagged back in the seat. 'Now, which Christmas film do you want to see next?'

CHAPTER SIX

SKYE LOOKED AT the piles of notes on the table on her desk. In days gone by, it hadn't been unusual for patients to have three or four volumes of ancient paper files with their medical history enclosed. In a lot of cases, these had been scanned and converted to a digital system. But sometimes the scanning process hadn't been accurate. And if a patient had previously lived in a different area, chances were their notes were still on paper. Which is why her desk was currently deluged.

Jay hadn't been joking about the sharp rise in diagnoses recently. All of these people who'd had tumours biopsied were potential candidates for her research project.

But, like any research project, there were a strict range of parameters for any patient being allowed to have their data examined by the AI programme. And those parameters meant an extensive deep dive into their past history to ensure they didn't have anything to exclude them from the project. It wasn't just time consuming, it was exhausting. And Skye didn't want to ask anyone to assist in this process, because one mistake, one tiny detail missed, could affect the impact and reliability of the whole study.

It was making her antsy. Just like working alongside Jay on a daily basis.

Since their Christmas drive-in—which Indira had asked them both about—it had almost felt as if she was walking on tiptoes around him.

He'd clearly been unhappy with her suggestion he was on the rebound. And she'd fixed that idea in her head so much she hadn't really considered other possibilities.

Maybe this was partly her fault. Her previous relationships hadn't really been a success, with any partner—whether or not they worked in her hospital. All of the guys she'd dated had eventually got fed up with placing second to her work. So maybe she was actually trying to scupper this one before it could even start?

It was easier to blame him, and feel offended, than look at herself.

And the more she thought about it, the more a little flame flickered inside her. Jay Bannerman was *not* on the rebound. If she'd hadn't run off that night at the market, could their relationship have started to blossom further?

In the car the other night she'd still felt that sizzle, that heat. Neither of them had acted on it. But deep down, apart from Indira's organising, she'd wanted to go with him. If she hadn't, she could have made an excuse at any point. But the fact was, she did want to spend time in Jay's company. What could that even mean now?

She pushed the files aside, knowing she needed maximum concentration when she was looking at them. She didn't want to risk missing anything.

Leah was still on the ward, as was their new patient, Kelly Robertson, the forty-year-old with metastatic cancer. Skye decided to review them both.

'How you doing, Leah?' she asked as she entered her room.

Leah's colour was looking rosier, and she'd been eating better the last few days. She looked up from the book she was reading. 'Sorry, what?'

Skye laughed as she sat down. 'Am I disturbing you? What are you reading?'

Leah held up the hardback book. '*Thursday Murder Club.* Dr Bannerman brought it in for me. He says he has all four if I like them.'

Skye was a little shocked. 'Jay gave you that?'

Leah smiled and nodded. 'Apparently he reads like a fiend.'

She started to get curious. 'And what do you think of it?'

Leah held it to her chest. 'I love it. It's great. Just what I need.' It was actually the happiest Skye had seen her since she'd been admitted. And it was lovely to see—Leah had had a tricky start to her treatment, and it was nice to see things settling down.

Skye could see she was almost three-quarters of the way through the book.

'I had no idea Dr Bannerman was a reader.' Skye smiled. 'Maybe you should give it to me when you've finished, and I'll give it a try.'

Leah gave a calculated look at the book. 'I'll be finished in another hour.'

Skye asked her another few questions about her treatment, her symptoms and her pain relief, making a few minor tweaks to her plan, before carrying on down the corridor.

Kelly took a bit longer to assess. Hers was a slow-growing cancer, which had spread, but was actually still at a manageable stage. Once they had her pain completely under control, she would be able to go home.

When she was finished she headed into Jay's office. He was behind his desk eating some chocolate.

'You okay?' she asked straight away, the alarm sounding on his phone.

'I will be in five minutes,' he said, silencing the alarm. She noted he was eating the chocolate from the advent calendar, which was actually really small.

'How about I go and get you a coffee and a chocolate digestive from the secret stash in my desk?'

He stared for a moment, and she wondered if he was going to argue. But he pulled out his own pack of digestives from his drawer. 'Actually, I'd love a coffee.'

She brought it back five minutes later and sat down with her notes. 'Okay to talk about some patients?'

He nodded.

She ran over the minor changes she'd made for Leah, and the plan she had for Kelly. Jay, in turn, talked about two of the older patients in the ward, both with breast cancer, but both managing well. Neither of them were steady on their feet, and with their cancer treatment there was always a risk of osteoporosis, which could lead to broken bones. The physiotherapist and occupational therapist were assessing them both.

'I didn't know you were a reader,' said Skye with a tinge of amusement.

He arched one brow. 'Who gave away my secret?'

'Leah. She's a teenager, what do you expect? Plus, she's loving that book you gave her.'

His face brightened. 'Great,' he slid his arm under the desk and came out holding a blue-trimmed book, 'I brought her the second. I knew she would love it.'

'I might have to read these,' said Skye, her fingers brushing against his as she took the book, flipping it over to read the back. 'What else do you read?'

'Mainly crime, a little sci-fi at times and any non-fiction that involves shipwrecks or Antarctica.' He watched her eyes skimming the blurb at the back of the book. 'Do you read?'

Skye sat back in her chair and crossed her legs. She noticed him watching her legs as she did it, and it gave her an illicit thrill. The ward was quiet now—most people had gone home. Could they engage in some harmless flirting again?

'Do I read? I'm never happier than spending a day in one of Edinburgh's many brilliant bookshops. I especially like shops with those moveable ladders. You know the ones? It's on the ambition list with the dogs.'

He sat back and gave her an amused glance. 'Well, I didn't see inside your house, but you must have one of those large front rooms. Surely you could put one of those bookcases there?'

She pulled a face. 'Old house. The floors are a bit uneven, and the wall is not exactly square. I would need to get someone to custom build for me, and in Edinburgh that's very expensive.'

He blew out a long, slow breath. 'I can only imagine.'

Then he leaned forward with a glint in his eye. 'The place I've got has built-in book shelves.'

She scowled at him. 'You'd better be joking.'

He leaned back and stretched out his legs. 'Nope.'

'I'm beginning to regret making you a coffee now.'

He stretched out his arms. 'It's getting late, why haven't you gone home?'

'Why haven't you?'

He shot her a glance. 'What is this, tit for tat?'

She leaned forward, speaking in a low voice. 'And why would you think that?'

She was watching his eyes again, and this time they went straight to her cleavage. Skye never really wore anything revealing at work. Her red wraparound dress covered all the parts of her it should, but when she'd leaned forward, he might have had the opportunity to catch a glimpse of the now deep V at her neckline.

As his gaze lifted, their eyes met. She held that gaze. Not looking away. Jay didn't seem embarrassed to have been caught looking, instead the edges of his lips turned upwards. His voice was low, almost a whisper. 'Seems when you work later, you can get distracted.'

She toyed with the gold necklace around her throat, knowing that those actions would taunt him. He shifted slightly in his chair, and that made her smile.

'So, today's lesson is that you're a book lover,' she said. 'As well as the old news that you're a Christmas film virgin.'

'I'll have you know that I take my lessons seriously. I've watched *Die Hard*, *Home Alone* and *Bad Santa*.'

'The list is much bigger than that.'

He shrugged. 'I know, but I've got to start somewhere.'

She straightened up, letting her back arch. 'Why don't you come and help me with the research? I've got a dozen files to read, and two sets of eyes are better than one.'

He paused for a moment before standing up, a little closer than normal. She could practically feel the heat from his body.

'Is there a reward?' he asked, his voice huskier than she expected. It sent a shot up her spine. Those brown eyes of his were enveloping, like some kind of treacle, just trying to pull her in. She could easily get lost.

She licked her lips. 'There could be.' She spun around and walked out of his office, swinging her hips a little more than necessary.

He was right on her heels. As he walked into her office he closed the door behind them.

She let her finger drag on the desk as she pulled up a chair next to hers. 'Be my guest.'

'Is this the part where we sing?' he joked.

'I don't think I can quite manage Angela Lansbury,' she replied as she sat down, letting her wrap dress naturally position itself. She didn't adjust it to hide the way it revealed part of her thighs.

He sat down next to her, his leg brushing against hers, then frowned when he saw the packed files on the desk. 'You weren't joking. What are all these?'

She sighed. 'The patient files that aren't digital. I need to go through them to make sure all patient histories are declared before they join the study.'

He put his elbow on the desk, leaning closer to her. 'You're doing this yourself?'

She leaned towards him. 'Well, who else would do it?'

His muscles tensed around his neck. 'Why wouldn't you get a research assistant or some admin help you?'

He was so close—she inhaled his woody aftershave. The top button of his shirt was unfastened and she could see some tiny dark hairs at the base of his throat. Her fingers wanted to reach out and touch them.

But he'd asked a question he expected her to answer. She tugged down the clip that had been holding up her hair. Her dark curls fell around her shoulders. 'I won't have this study compromised. If I miss something, then it's my fault. But I won't miss anything, so that's why I do it myself.'

He looked a touch annoyed. 'But why would you want to spend hours doing this, when your time could be better spent on other parts of the study?'

She twisted a bit of her hair around one finger. 'These are the things that compromise a study. Something missed, which is then discovered way down the line. That Patient One Forty-Four had a strong family history of cancer, which could have meant a genetic component was involved. That Patient Seventy-Six was given an experimental vaccine as part of another study thirty years ago, which they'd subsequently forgotten about.'

She took a deep breath and looked him in the eye. 'Attention to detail is important.' She gave a hint of a smile. 'You should know that.'

She let those words hang in the air between them. Jay reached up and took a tress of her hair, winding it around his own finger in slow motion. He gave it the lightest tug and she moved her face closer to his.

'But not all the details have to be yours,' he said, his warm breath close to her cheek.

'I'm a control freak,' she said hoarsely. 'I think you should know that.'

His lips were only inches from hers. She could almost taste them.

He gave a smile. 'I think I can live with that.' His voice was a whisper, pulling her in further.

This time when their lips met there were no spectators. They were behind a closed door in a ward with minimal staff. Her hands wrapped around his shoulders and back, and his mouth moved quickly, from her lips down to her throat.

That connection took her breath away. That feel of his slight stubble against her soft skin made her want to grab him and not let go.

She let out a soft moan as his jawline scraped the base of her throat. He moved closer, then kissed up the other side of her neck to her ear, moving back to her lips.

Even though his mouth was on hers, he was too far away. She shifted, moving from her chair onto his lap. Heat emanated through his shirt to her hands. She toyed with the top buttons.

Her head really wasn't on work right now, although in the background a voice was whispering words of warning. She started to undo those buttons so she could place her hands directly on his warm chest.

It was Jay's turn to shift now and let out a little groan. But he didn't stop kissing her. He kept going. The guy should get awards for this. She didn't want to know where he had practised, she just wanted him to keep focused on her.

Her hands ran through his hair. It was already tousled, but she liked the fact it was little longer than normal—it gave her something to grab hold of.

Her wrap dress was moving. The soft jersey gave way easily to Jay's hands as they slid around her breast.

She was losing focus and concentration and she pushed herself harder against him.

There was a soft knock at the door. 'Skye? Are you still here?'

They froze. Like cartoon characters, eyes wide, mouths open. It must only have been a millisecond, but it felt too long.

Skye jumped up and pushed her dress back into place. Thankfully the soft jersey obliged. She had no idea what she'd done with her hair clasp, or what she actually looked like. She took a few strides towards the door in the hope of intercepting anyone who might want to get in, giving Jay a few more seconds to fix his shirt.

She pulled the door open. Soo Yun was a Korean medical student who worked part time in medical records to supplement her studies. She had a pile of notes in her hands and was struggling with them.

'I've got the rest of the files you requested for your study.' She smiled.

'Fantastic,' said Skye, standing back with the door wide open, making room for Soo Yun. They'd talked about the study on a number of occasions and Soo Yun was genuinely interested.

As she spun around, Jay was sitting behind the desk, his head leaning on his hand in the most casual way.

'More files?' He smiled. His shirt was intact, and his hair actually looked less rumpled than normal.

Skye had a ten-second panic. Was her make-up halfway across her face? Did she look dishevelled? But Soo Yun hadn't reacted in any way when she'd opened the door. And by now Jay was on his feet, taking half the notes and making space on the desk for them.

'Next time bring a trolley.' He smiled at Soo Yun. 'Don't want to hurt your back with all those files.'

'I weight-lift,' she said matter-of-factly as she slid the rest of the pile on the desk. 'They're not heavy, just...' she stared at the wonky pile '...uneven.'

'Thanks so much,' said Skye. 'This should be the last for a while.'

Soo Yun gave a nod and waved her hand as she headed to the door. 'Let me know if you need any help.'

She disappeared back into the corridor as Skye tried to catch her breath.

As she looked up at Jay, he started laughing. It was infectious. She started laughing too.

She leaned back against the wall, hand on her heart. 'Oh my, can you imagine if we'd been caught?'

He walked over, just inches away. 'Maybe not ideal,' he agreed. He licked his lips and paused a few moments. 'Shall we call it a night?'

'Yes.' The word was out quicker than she really wanted it to be, and he gave the merest flinch.

'See you tomorrow.' His voice sounded casual, but she wondered if she'd just offended him for the second time.

Two strikes and you're out, a little voice said in her head.

Hers was the last office in the row. There was no hospital room opposite and no one in the corridor outside.

She leaned forward and brushed the briefest kiss on his cheek. 'See you tomorrow.'

She sat back behind her desk. By the time she looked up, Jay was already gone.

CHAPTER SEVEN

HIS EYES FLICKERED OPEN. He hadn't shut his blinds completely and he could see the sun struggling to rise in the deep purple sky outside, giving the horizon a strange glow.

It was Saturday. He had no on-call. And he knew that Skye was off too.

He reached over and grabbed his phone, scrolling social media for a whole ten seconds before he pulled up his contacts.

Skye Campbell was in there. Was it too early to text? She struck him as an early riser, but he could be wrong.

He still hadn't had a chance to buy a Christmas tree for his place. He still had some stuff down in London, and was merely renting out his place right now. But he wasn't such a Grinch that he didn't at least put something up for Christmas.

He wouldn't buy a real one. Mainly because he wouldn't know where to go. But there were a few other things he wanted to pick up today. Before he gave himself time to reconsider, he sent a text.

Do you have plans?

His reply came within a few seconds.

What did you have in mind?

Then a few moments later:

Don't tell me someone's phoned in sick at work?

He laughed.

No. No work issues. But wanting to get a few things for Christmas and see a few sights. Want to join me?

After another few moments, he realised he was holding his breath waiting for a reply. He could see the little dots on the screen. How much was she typing?

Since you're awake, I know a place that does a great breakfast. As long as your Christmas shopping will allow me to introduce you to Edinburgh's best bookshops, I'm in. There's also a Christmas brass band concert in Princes Street Gardens. Bring your walking shoes and some warm clothes!

She sent him a pin on a map—obviously the place she wanted to go for breakfast.

Thirty minutes?

He couldn't reply quickly enough. Thirty minutes later he was in a quirky café on Leith Walk. He found a table and Skye appeared, wearing a bright pink coat and a grey hat with flaps over her ears. She had sturdy boots on, and took off her jacket to reveal jeans and a jumper.

'Did you know I love Christmas shopping?' She smiled as she sat down.

'I guessed you might. Plus, I need some help,' he conceded.

She gave a wave to the guy behind the counter. 'Do you know what you want?'

'Haven't even looked.'

'Do you trust me?' Her green eyes were dancing with mischief. It was a good start.

'I may live to regret this, but go on.'

She beamed. 'Aldo, can I just have my usual, times two?'

Ten minutes later, two plates of toast with scrambled egg and bacon, and two skinny lattes appeared.

She lifted her knife and fork and then paused. 'Okay for your diabetes?'

'Absolutely,' he said, checking his phone, then taking out his insulin pen and injecting.

She wrinkled her nose. 'Aren't you supposed to do that a bit before you eat? Sorry, I should have told you what I'd ordered.'

He shook his head. 'Everyone is different. For me, the fast-acting insulin works *fast*. It was a bit of nightmare when I was a junior doctor and carrying a page. I learned to always order something I could eat on the move, because if I'd already jagged, then sat down to eat and page went off…' He was still smiling as he let his voice drift off.

'Ooh,' she said as she pulled a face.

'Right.'

They ate leisurely as she queried his shopping list.

'I need a tree, but we'll probably have to buy that last.'

'Not really, we can buy from somewhere that will deliver. They probably won't do it till the end of the day.'

'Okay,' he said as he sipped his coffee. 'Then, I'm absolutely up for the bookshops. I always buy my sister and my mum and dad books. And I'll buy them some other things to go alongside.'

'Anything in particular?'

He turned over his phone and showed Skye a picture of his sister. 'She has quite similar taste to you in clothes. Probably a jumper or a shirt? My mum likes jewellery, so if there are any places with quirky jewellery I'm sure I'll find her something.'

'And your dad?'

There was the tiniest difference in tone when she asked the question. He reached and put his hand over hers.

'Sorry, you don't need to help me pick something for my dad.'

She shook her head, and her expression was genuine. 'No, it's fine. Honestly. It's actually kind of nice. I can't pick something for my dad, but I'm happy to help you find something for yours.'

Jay watched her carefully. 'Okay,' he agreed. 'Well, my dad likes art. Not fancy art. But genuine hand-painted stuff. So, if there are any arts and crafts shops around, probably something from there?'

She smiled. 'Some of the bookshops we'll visit also sell

art. One has kind of Scottish landscapes, and the other has more cats and dogs kind of stuff.'

He looked at her coat. 'How many coats do you actually have? I don't think I've seen you wear the same one twice.'

She sat back proudly. 'I have coats in many colours, and lots of leopard, zebra and snake prints too. I've bought them over the years, and just take care of them. I love a good coat.'

He pointed. 'Hats and scarves too?'

'And gloves. There are never enough gloves in the world.'

'Well then, let's get started.' Jay paid the bill and they left the café together.

'Know what I like best about this café?'

He frowned. 'Apart from the good breakfast?'

She nudged him. 'It's literally fifty feet away from a bookshop—' she paused for effect '—with ladders.'

The expression on her face made a surge of warmth spread through him. He really enjoyed being in her company. She could easily have said no today. And whilst he was sure he could have searched the city to find what he needed, it was so much better doing it with a friend.

They spent the next hour in the bookshop. It was on multiple levels, with shelves up to the ceilings, so the ladders were essential. Skye spent quite a bit of time in the fantasy section, and Jay found a new release from his favourite crime author. He also found a cosy crime for his mum, and a dark historical that was right up his sister's alley.

Skye came over and looked at what he'd picked.

'Interesting,' she said, putting the latest TikTok sensation on the counter at the till. 'What about your dad?'

Jay gave another glance over his shoulder. 'Truth is my dad loves Irish fiction, but he's read most of it. He's started to read some Australian crime authors and is really enjoying them. So, I'll see if I can find him something along those lines.'

'Is it the authors he likes or the setting?'

'Oh, definitely the setting. Anything set in the outback, far away from civilisation, that's his thing.'

'I'm sure we'll find something.'

After they'd paid for their books, Skye took him to a department store, where he ordered a medium-sized pre-lit tree and some decorations that could be delivered later that day. Then she took him down some side streets, and they found a few craft shops with jewellery, before he picked a necklace in a waterfall design with abalone shell, and a matching pair of earrings.

There were also a few boutiques and they browsed through them. Skye disappeared to try a green jumper dress, which matched her eyes—and hugged all her curves—and Jay found a similar one in violet that he was sure his sister would love. He paid for them both as she was getting changed again. When she went to the till, the assistant smiled, folded the dress, wrapped it in tissue and put it in a paper bag, before refusing payment and nodding at Jay.

She came over with her eyes shining, holding up her bag. 'You bought me this?'

'Of course, you looked fabulous.'

She tilted her head to the side a little. 'But what if I hadn't liked it?'

He gave her a nonchalant look. 'Then my sister would have got two.'

He could tell from the moment she'd caught sight of her reflection in the dress that she'd loved it. And she'd looked fantastic. He hadn't been able to resist buying it for her.

She gave him a shy kind of smile. 'Thank you,' she said, accepting the bag he offered.

'Lunch?' she asked. 'There's an Italian pizza place around the corner?'

He nodded.

They had a relaxed lunch with some wine, before heading out into the cold Edinburgh air again.

The city had got much busier. The streets were full of people who were obviously on tours, and those who were on day trips to the theatre.

'You wanted to sightsee?' she said, a crafty tone in her voice.

'Oh, no, but what do you have in mind?' he asked.

'Is your blood sugar okay?'

'Why?'

She'd slipped her arm into his as they'd threaded through the streets, but now she stopped and looked upwards. 'Because the best view in Edinburgh is up there.'

Jay looked up. 'We're going to climb the Scott Monument?'

The tall gothic monument was close to the train station, and towered over the main street in Edinburgh.

Jay knew it was a tribute to the Scottish author Sir Walter Scott.

'Just as long your blood sugar can take it,' she smiled.

He looked up again. 'Of course I can.'

Two hundred and eighty-seven steps later—spotting different statues all the way up—they were on the highest viewing platform with a panoramic view of the city. The breeze was more than a little brisk, and he pulled his hat from his pocket, tugging it down over his hair.

'Wow,' he said as Skye started to point out different parts of the city to him. The view was truly amazing, but even on a cold and windy day like this, the monument was busy. It wasn't long before they had to climb back down the spiral stairs to reach the bottom.

'We're in the perfect place now,' Skye declared.

'Why?'

'Because we're right next to Princes Street Gardens, and the brass band is playing next to the fountain.'

They made their way down to the gardens, which were full of people and multiple refreshment stalls. They bought some coffee and a muffin for Skye, then made their way to where the brass band was set up. The band members ranged in age from young kids and teenagers to adults and pensioners, all wearing gold-buttoned black jackets with matching hats. Another part of the gardens was set up as a Winter Wonderland, with an ice rink and a Ferris wheel, but they settled in with the rest of the crowd to listen to the brass band.

Even though it was cold, the atmosphere in the gardens was warm. People were there to enjoy themselves.

Families, couples and groups of friends, all with smiles on their faces, surrounded them.

The band started with some Christmas carols, which most of the crowd sang along to, before moving to some more modern Christmas tunes. That had people raising their voices even louder as they all sang along to 'Last Christmas' and 'Fairytale of New York', albeit very out of tune.

As Jay watched those around him, he was struck by how happy he actually was to be there. And part of that was down to who he was with. He'd spent so much time in his head, vowing he would never have another relationship with a colleague, but here he was, with a colleague, and all could think about was what had happened in her office, and what might have happened next.

Skye Campbell wasn't Jessica, his ex-fiancée. Now that he could look back with clearer vision, he could see the faults in their relationship. But that also made him wary. Both he and Jessica had been completely devoted to their work. Much like he still was now, and much like the traits he also admired in Skye. But how much time could two doctors—devoted to their work—actually give to each other? Maybe he was a fool for actually considering things in his head again.

But somehow, he just couldn't stop thinking about her. He could see people around them giving occasional glances. Making assumptions. And he wasn't sorry. If he met anyone from the hospital now, he wouldn't try and hide the fact they were there together. He was happy to be there with her. No, he was proud to be there with her.

Skye threw her head back to try and reach the last

note of 'Merry Xmas Everybody' and he winced, then laughed. Okay, maybe not proud of the singing. It was entirely in its own key.

She slapped his arm, her face lighting up. 'Are you laughing at my singing?'

He slid an arm around her waist. 'I think the whole of the gardens is laughing at your singing,' he joked.

She leaned towards him. 'Feeling festive yet, Dr Grumpy?'

He looked down at the bags at their feet, and at the people around them. It had started to get a bit darker and the lights in the gardens had come on.

'I'm definitely feeling something,' he admitted.

She glanced down at the paper programme someone had passed them. 'Only two songs to go.'

'How about some dinner before we finish?'

She gave a small smile, her hands resting on his other arm. 'Sure.'

Skye was having the best day. From the moment she'd received his text this morning, her heart had been jumping.

She couldn't quite put her finger on what was so perfect about all of this. Was it the fact she knew she'd brought a genuine smile to the face of the guy who'd been nicknamed Dr Grumpy? Or was it just the fact she was getting to know him more and more, and liked everything she found out?

From breakfast, to shopping, to sightseeing and lunch, her day had been just perfect. Jay Bannerman was good company, whether he meant to be or not.

She could easily have bought her own dress—and

would have—but it had been a nice gesture on his part that he'd paid for it.

If she'd been on her own today, what would she have done? Much the same as this, but she wouldn't have had someone to share it with. She was an independent woman and liked her own space, but sometimes it was nice to have someone at your side. Whether it was merely friendship, or something else, she wasn't entirely sure.

The other night at work they could easily have ended up as friends with benefits if they hadn't been interrupted. But in a way she was glad they had been. First, she would hate to be caught in a compromising position at work. Second, she really wasn't a friends-with-benefits kind of girl. She might not be particularly good at relationships, but she wasn't really casual either. It struck her that maybe she just hadn't met the right person yet. Or maybe she had and had been too focused on work, letting them slip through her fingers.

But no one had really given her the buzz that Jay did. As soon as he started talking, she practically swayed to the tune of his voice. It was magical. Not that she'd let him know that.

No one had lit a fire in her belly when she'd been kissed the way Jay had. When his hands had slid inside her dress…

She shivered, and felt him pull her against him. The gardens were cold, but the brass band were great and as they played their final song, she was almost sad they were finished—even if she couldn't feel her toes any more.

'Anything in particular you'd like for dinner?' she asked him.

He held out his hands. 'I'm easy. You've done good at picking so far. So just pick some place that you like.'

Skye put her hands on her hips and thought for a moment. 'What I really want is a cocktail,' she admitted, then something came to mind and she clicked her fingers, pointing at Jay.

'You've still to get something for your dad, and there's a Scottish restaurant down one of the side streets, near some small shops that have some paintings in them.' She glanced at her watch. 'It's only five o'clock—the shops stay open to eight on a Christmas Saturday night in Edinburgh, and the restaurants won't be busy yet, so we should be fine.'

Jay gathered up the bags at their feet. 'Lead the way.'

It took around ten minutes for the crowds to file out of the gardens. Lots of them were heading in the direction of the ice rink and Ferris wheel, but thankfully Skye and Jay were going in the opposite direction.

As they bustled through the people, Skye reached out and grabbed his hand, keeping them together when people unexpectedly stopped in front of them, gathered in crowds or slowed to admire some lights or a view.

They ducked down the smaller street, which instantly felt as if it were in a different century. Shop windows weren't wide panes, but more small squares that were slightly bevelled as if they had been there for ever.

Skye pointed to a wooden sign hanging far in front. 'There's the restaurant, but there're a few shops here that might suit.' She directed him to a craft shop, the stone shopfront painted in cream and brown, several items on display in the window. Jay looked for a second, then gestured he wanted to go inside.

It was one of those kinds of shops that, when two people were in it, felt easily crowded. They kept their elbows tucked in as they admired the glass cabinets and pictures on the walls. Some were paintings, some were sketches. There were golf courses, a few of Edinburgh Castle at different points in history, a few street scenes, and some darker ones that matched some of the history of Edinburgh.

The man behind the counter gave them a smile as he continued reading his paper. 'If you need any help, just ask.'

Jay was glad. There was nothing worse that someone hanging over your shoulder, remarking on everything that fell into your line of sight.

'I've found my favourite,' whispered Skye.

'Where?' Jay scanned the walls, trying to think what one she might pick.

She nudged him and pointed down near the floor. He bent down and picked up the small, framed sketch. He turned it one way, then the other.

'Is that a blue dinosaur?' He was totally confused.

She was still grinning. 'Looks like it.'

He glanced at her. 'But dinosaurs weren't blue.'

'Prove it.' She kept smiling. 'It's not like any of us have seen them.'

'What even is it?' he whispered back.

'When I was at school, we called them a diplodocus, but I think the proper name is something else.' She gave a shrug. 'Or I might be mixed up.'

Jay held it closer. He could see the fine lines of varying depth. The drawing was meticulous, and he wondered where on earth the artist had been inspired.

'This is your favourite?' he asked again.

She nodded without shame. 'Absolutely. The hint of blue just gives it an edge. Makes it that bit different.'

'A blue dinosaur?' he asked again, shaking his head. He really wanted to start laughing.

'Maybe not for your dad,' she said as she continued around the small space. 'What about this one?'

He moved next to her. This was a painting of Edinburgh Castle. It was set a few hundred years ago. The castle looked damp, dirty and tired. It was nightfall and little pockets of light—clearly where fires had been lit—gave the painting an unusual glow. There was something quite mesmerising about it.

'Has he ever been to Edinburgh?' she asked.

He nodded. 'A few times. He had a placement in Edinburgh during his training.'

'His training?'

He gave an ironic smile. 'My dad's a doctor. At least he was—he retired a few years ago.'

'What kind of doctor was he?'

'A GP. He loved it, but I remember him getting called out at all times of the day or night. He worked incredible hours—and didn't think anything of it.'

'So, you're glad he retired?'

'Absolutely. He and my mum bought a camper and have been halfway around Europe, getting into all sorts of trouble.'

'Really?'

'Oh really. My dad thinks his accent will literally let him get away with anything.'

'And does it?'

Jay pulled a face. 'Mainly. I think it's safe to say my dad's blessed with the Irish charm.' And before she got a chance to say anything, he added, 'You know, the thing I forgot to pick up on my way out the door?'

She laughed and put her hand on his arm. 'Don't worry, you're starting to heat up. Maybe someone sent it in the post for you to pick up.'

'What? I'm not Dr Grumpy anymore?'

He held the painting under one of lights in the shop to get a better view. Skye looked at him carefully, a small smile on her lips.

'You're getting better,' she said in a voice that sent a lightning bolt down his spine.

Their eyes connected. 'And what does that mean?'

She smiled, as if she were thinking of something all to herself, before looking up again. 'It means, we'll see.'

The owner was staring at them now, so Jay paid for the painting, with delivery promised for tomorrow, before they headed back out into the street, towards the restaurant.

As she threaded her arm through his, his brain was asking the obvious question. What did he really have against a relationship with a colleague? One bad experience was just that—one bad experience. Did it mean he had to shut himself away from other opportunities when they came?

The restaurant was downstairs, and the steps slightly uneven as they made their way down. The tables in the cellar were cramped. Not close enough to be touching the people at the next table, but close enough to hear their conversation. Skye darted her way through, holding some of their bags high above their heads in an attempt not to bump any elbows. They ended up at a table in the back corner, away from the main traffic.

As soon as they sat down, the waiter filled their glasses with red wine and left a single piece of paper on the table. The menu only had two choices for each course.

'What kind of place is this?' whispered Jay as he shrugged off his coat.

'A drink-what-they-give-you and eat-what-they-bring-you kind of place.' She smiled. 'It's all Scottish produce, so I've always just told them to bring what they think. I've never been disappointed.'

Jay almost held his breath at those last few words. *Never been disappointed.*

It was like there had been a low-lying hum in the air all day between them. He liked it. He liked it more than he wanted to, and more than he should.

He looked around the cellar restaurant. The ambience was good, the lighting not quite dim, but low enough to be intimate.

Most people were talking in low voices, leaning in to each other. The waiters moved seamlessly, and their wine glasses were always topped up. Jay went with the flow, and told the waiter to being whatever he recommended.

They had a lamb starter, followed by sea bass, then an intricate dessert—neither of them could work out what it was. But the array of sweet and tangy kept their taste-buds interested.

As the night continued, Jay held up his glass to admire it.

'What?' she asked.

'I've never been a red-wine fan,' he admitted.

'And now?' she asked.

'Now...' he nodded slowly '...I'm contemplating a change.'

As he sat the glass down, they looked at each other. There was so much he could say—so much they had already revealed to each other.

'I'm contemplating a change too,' she said in a hushed voice.

They both breathed quietly.

'The one thing I was sure about when I came here,' he said, 'was that I wouldn't be dating any colleague. I wanted to focus on my work.'

Skye gave a nod. 'Men have always got bored with me. I spend too much time at work, and then talk about it as soon as I get home. I always have the next day to look forward to. And, whilst I like the idea of another human in my life, I just can't prioritise it.'

'Can people really change?' he asked her, his voice husky.

'I think we can change if we want to find something else in life,' she said slowly. 'But...'

'But?' His heart was clenching in his chest. Was this where it all went wrong?

'You've barely been here a month. I don't like to jump into things.'

'You want to take things slow?'

She bit her lip. 'I think that twice we've just jumped ahead of where we should have been.'

He smiled. He couldn't help it. 'Those memories are the ones that keep me awake at night,' he admitted.

She sipped at her wine. 'They might have kept me awake too,' she conceded.

'Then what are we going to do about it?'

Skye looked thoughtful for a minute.

'We date.' She gave him a careful stare. 'And we decide if we want anyone to know about it.'

Jay shifted in his chair. He knew what she was doing. She was giving him a get-out-of-jail-free card. She knew about his past experience, and knew he didn't want their every move watched. And if they announced they were dating? The hospital grapevine would sing, and every glance, every smile and every scowl would be recorded. Every conversation with a member of the opposite sex could potentially start rumours. It was ridiculous. They both knew that.

But the reality was…had people already noticed the way he looked at her? The interactions between them? The gentle flirting? Did he really want to stop any of that?

He wasn't sure. He held up his glass. The truth was he just wanted to spend more time with her. He'd loved every moment of today, and wanted more days just like this.

'To what comes next,' he said with a smile.

'To what comes next,' agreed Skye, clinking her glass against his.

CHAPTER EIGHT

SKYE WATCHED THE man in his early fifties, who had a mild look of panic on his face.

'Can you say that again, please?' he asked.

She did. 'Mr Lucas, your cancer is at an early stage. The bowel screening test is an early indicator. The colonoscopy and biopsies have confirmed a few Stage Two areas in your bowel. A further scan shows that it doesn't look like there are any further spots. So, we'll start your treatment tomorrow if you like.'

He took his wife's hand. 'But we have a holiday planned.'

Skye gave a nod. This frequently came up with patients newly diagnosed. 'When is your holiday booked?'

'Over Christmas,' his wife said, 'but we can cancel.'

Skye took a breath. 'It's entirely up to you what you want to do. We can delay your treatment until you come back if that's what you want. But I would have to advise that you let your travel insurance company know about your diagnosis.'

'What would you do?' his wife asked.

It was the million-dollar question. Chemotherapy could make patients very ill. Should they go and have a nice holiday first? Maybe. But if they did, was there a chance the cancer could continue to develop and spread? Maybe.

Skye was always honest with her patients. She put her hand on her heart. 'I would start treatment,' she said, her mind always going to back to her father. If his cancer had been diagnosed sooner, he might have responded better to treatment. She didn't know that for sure, nobody knew that. But the little spark was still there.

'But this is your decision,' she continued. 'Why don't you go home and speak to your family and friends? I have another doctor on duty—Dr Bannerman. Do you want to speak to him as a second opinion?'

They exchanged nervous glances. 'You don't mind?'

She stood up and gave them a smile. 'Not at all. I'll go and get him.'

It only took a few moments to find Jay. The last few days with him had felt strangely like floating on some kind of cloud. The world was tinged with pink.

They'd gone to the cinema—indoors this time—and to see a pantomime in the nearby theatre. They'd also spent a few late nights working at the hospital, concentrating on the research project.

There had been no big announcement. But Skye was pretty sure that several of their colleagues were on to them. Luckily, in the run up to Christmas, people were distracted. Everyone had shopping to do, things to organise, Christmas outfits to buy and food to plan. It was a good time of year to be dating almost under the radar, and she was enjoying it.

She walked into Jay's room.

'Hey,' she said, in a tone that seemed to have been made just for him.

'Hey.' He looked up, smiling, speaking in a similar tone.

She gave a sigh and carried the tablet over. 'The fifty-two-year-old man I mentioned this morning. He's here with his wife, and they're wondering if they should go on holiday before he starts his treatment. I offered them a second opinion.'

Jay nodded, and looked over the history, the biopsy results and plan for treatment.

'No problem,' he said as he stood up.

'You're not going to ask me what I advised?' she said, a little curious.

'No,' he said, brushing the briefest kiss on her cheek. 'Because your decision will have been sound. And I don't want it to influence mine.'

He disappeared down the corridor and into her office, whilst she went to check on some other patients.

He came back a while later, his arm clearly against hers. 'He's going to start treatment tomorrow. His wife will rebook their holiday in six months when his treatment is finished, and it will coincide with their silver wedding anniversary.'

She gave him a grateful smile. He'd agreed with her opinion, and a warm feeling spread through her. She hadn't been entirely sure what he might say, because she, too, could have easily gone the other way. There could be valid arguments for both decisions. But somehow knowing he agreed with her gave her reassurance.

'Time for coffee?' he asked, and she nodded and leaned over the desk towards Indira and Ronnie.

'Can I get you guys anything from the canteen? How about the Christmas cinnamon scones?'

Ronnie patted his stomach. 'Oh, go on then, they're great.'

She gave a smile and they headed down, buying coffees for themselves and scones for the staff upstairs.

They sat down at a nearby table, and Skye couldn't help but let out a big sigh.

A furrow creased Jay's brow. 'What's up?'

She shook her head. 'Nothing really. I've just got something coming up soon that makes me nervous.'

She could tell he was surprised. 'You? But you're never nervous.'

'Of course I am,' she said quickly.

'When?' he challenged. 'On the meetings with the other research experts you are calm, confident and able to answer any question they throw at you. You give good alternatives when issues arise, and always manage to keep things on track. When hurdles come up, you problem-solve. I've never seen you nervous at all.'

She waved her hand. 'But that's entirely different. A meeting is just a few people in a room, or on the other end of a computer.'

'But you're the same with patients, their families and if you're teaching students.'

'But that's always personal too. We have a maximum of six students to teach. And they are always keen and willing to learn. This…is different.'

He leaned his head on one hand, looking a bit bemused by all this. 'Okay then, tell me what it is that's got super-researcher and doctor Skye Campbell shaking in her boots.'

'You're mocking me,' she said as she stirred her coffee. Her stomach was actually fluttering.

He slid his hand across the table and touched his fingers to hers. 'Tell me.' This time his voice was reassuring.

'So, you haven't been here at Christmas before.'

He shook his head. 'No.'

'Well, what you haven't found out yet, is that every year at Christmas there is a huge Christmas gala in aid of cancer research at the poshest hotel in Edinburgh. It's on the twenty-third of December, and…' she licked her lips, because her throat had actually just dried up '…I've been asked to speak at it.'

'But that's fantastic. You're the perfect person to speak at it. I can't think of anyone more qualified.'

She put her hand to her throat, now feeling a bit sick. She swallowed. 'But that's just the thing. I hate public speaking. I get nervous in crowds. I just look out and see a sea of faces.' She intertwined her fingers with his and squeezed. Maybe a little bit too hard.

He crooked his head. 'But haven't you had to do it for things before?'

She took a breath and closed her eyes. 'Well, I had to do some presentations at university during medical training. But they broke us into groups. So, it wasn't the whole class of a hundred and twenty.' She shuddered. 'It was a maximum of fifteen people in the class. That I could just about manage.'

'Have you ever spoken in front of a crowd? Maybe it's just because you haven't done it before.'

She pulled a face. 'Well, I've not. But I've won a few awards, and any time my name was called, I swear, my heart was racing, my hands were sweating and I felt as if I couldn't breathe. I couldn't even say thank you in a normal voice, let alone do a thank you speech.' She tugged at her shirt. 'I'm feeling nervous just thinking about it.'

Jay looked thoughtful. 'Why? What is it that just makes you so nervous?'

She pulled her fingers back from his, and started drumming them on the table. It was hard to put things into words. She'd never really talked to anyone about this before.

She looked up—his brown eyes were fixed on hers. 'It's personal,' she said. 'I would be okay if it was about the research, or cancer signs and symptoms, and treatments. I could talk about all that until the cows come home.' She stopped for a breath. 'But they asked me to talk about my experience. About how my dad getting cancer and dying changed my course in life, and how I'm now devoted to this.'

'And that's great.' She could see him thinking. 'You managed to tell me about it.'

She held up her hands. 'But that was different. It was just you and me. It wasn't a room filled with four hundred people expecting me to talk from the heart about something that still impacts me.'

Jay stayed silent for so long that she wondered if he was just going to give up on her.

When he spoke, he kept his voice low. 'Grief has no

timespan. It's one of the biggest lessons I've learned when treating patients with cancer. People always assume that in a few years they'll feel better after losing a relative. And for some people, in a couple of years, they can start to get their life back. But, one of the first doctors I worked with had lost a child. And it didn't get better. Every birthday was a memory lost. Milestones that his child would never reach. He was haunted by it. And who had the right to tell him he shouldn't feel grief?' He reached over and took her hand again. 'It's the same for your father.' He kept his voice low again. 'You would have wanted him to see you graduate as a doctor?'

Her skin prickled and she sniffed, feeling tears well up in her eyes. She just gave a nod.

'You would have wanted your dad to walk you down the aisle at some point, and hopefully one day hold your first baby?' The tears started to fall. He wasn't saying any of this to be mean, and she knew that. He was telling her that he understood. She nodded again.

Jay reached over and caught one of her tears with his thumb. 'I don't want you to be unhappy. If this is making you feel like this, should you be doing it?'

She hated herself right now. Hated herself for crying in the hospital canteen—she could see glances being cast their way. The very thing that Jay had not wanted. But to be fair, he didn't look as if he was noticing.

'Do you think I should back out?' Her voice was breaking.

'I think you should do what you feel is right,' he said in a smooth tone. 'They asked you to do this because they want to hear your story. But it's entirely up to you if you want to share. No one can force you to do it.'

'What good would it do?'

Jay looked at her carefully and licked his lips, clearly considering what to say. His gaze was sincere. 'I think you could do a lot of good. I think you might give hope to some people, fire to others and comfort to some. Remember that most people who support cancer research or cancer charities have been affected in some way. It could be that some are struggling with grief. Maybe they too could channel how they feel another way? Maybe they just need to hear that, even though it's been a few years, you still have full, vibrant memories of your dad. Some people are scared they might forget things. You're going to prove to them that you don't.'

The tears were still falling, but his words were a big comfort. He was making sense. She hadn't really considered this point of view before.

Jay kept going. 'You might inspire other people to be doctors, nurses or researchers. To volunteer. To raise money for the research.'

Skye nodded—she was feeling calmer. He was helping. He was giving her a bit of confidence to know that her talking might be important and might inspire others.

'Do you have a date?' he asked.

The question caught her unawares and she let out a laugh. 'What?'

'A date. Is someone going with you?'

She shook her head. 'No. I hadn't even planned ahead. I still wasn't sure I could actually do it.'

'How about I come with you—only if you want, of course.'

She smiled at him. This guy, who'd started here prickly and pushing everyone away. The same guy who didn't really want people in the hospital talking about him, but hadn't been afraid to reach out and take her hand in the middle of the canteen.

'I'll give you a pep talk on the way there. I'll distract you, keep your mind off things. Anything you want really.'

She said the only thing her heart would let her. 'You don't need to sell yourself. I'd love it if you came with me.'

CHAPTER NINE

IF HE WAS HONEST, Jay was feeling a tiny bit nervous himself. He'd checked his bowtie at least five times before he'd climbed in the car to pick up Skye.

He'd asked her about her dress but she'd been very coy, just saying it was something special.

As he rang the door, he wondered if the flowers he'd brought was going overboard. But the expression on her face as she opened the door told him everything he needed to know.

'Oh, they're beautiful,' she said, taking the large bouquet of Christmas flowers from his hands. Red, greens, whites and golds along with a huge red bow in an already filled clear glass vase, meaning Skye could carry them straight to her table in the hall.

As she turned, he caught a glimpse of green sequin. Once she sat the flowers down and spun around, he got the full effect.

'Wow,' was all he could say.

She grinned. 'You like?' She gestured with her hands to the full-length green sequined dress that hugged her body perfectly. The top had a low V and thick straps. Her dark curls were styled around her shoulders, her green eyes looking darker than normal alongside her pale skin and red lips.

'You look stunning,' he breathed, wondering how on earth he got so lucky. 'How are you feeling?' he asked, remembering his role here today.

He stepped inside and put his hand on her hips. She gestured back to the table where she'd sat the flowers. Now he noticed the shredded paper. 'What's going on?'

She picked up a silver sequin bag and held it up.

'It's tiny,' he said, stating the obvious.

She nodded. 'Room for my house key, my phone and lipstick. That's it.'

Jay glanced at the paper. He could swear that at some point there had been writing on it. 'So, what is that—your speech?'

She nodded. But she didn't look worried. Her spine was straight, her shoulders back. 'I decided I didn't need it. I'd written it five times, scored parts out, and it was actually making me worse.'

He noticed the tiny tremor in her hands and took them both, pressing them up to his chest. 'Speak from the heart, that's all that matters and all that counts.'

She nodded her head and took a deep breath. 'You're right. Now let's go.'

He put her black coat around her shoulders and they headed outside.

By the time they reached the hotel, there was a queue of cars. He squeezed her hand. 'Well, at least you don't need to worry about the biggest disaster for a fundraiser event.'

'What do you mean?'

He smiled. 'No one turning up. Look at the queue, that's fantastic.'

She gave a tiny groan. 'Think of the all the people in the room.'

'No. Don't. Only think of the people in the room when there's a fundraising moment and they do one of those charity auctions.'

She nodded her head, as if she were trying to convince herself. The car edged forward again until they were finally in front of the hotel. Because it was one of the main roads in Edinburgh, valet parking was a must. So when the suited valet appeared with a ticket in his hand, Jay jumped out to take it, before coming around to take Skye's hand as she emerged from the car.

There was a tiny second—as the ripples of her dress fell into place around her body—when he caught his breath. Did she have any idea how beautiful she was?

They walked up the steps to the hotel and through the main doors, instantly hit with a wave of heat.

It only took a few seconds to see how seriously this hotel took Christmas. The tree in the main entrance was huge, and it looked real, decorated in silver. The pink and purple logo of the cancer charity was matched by subtle decorations throughout the room.

It was only a few moments before they were offered a drink from a silver tray and ushered through to the ballroom.

Skye stopped mid-step, and he instantly understood why. The ballroom was spectacular, with a stage at one end, the silver, pink and purple theme carried on throughout, with around one hundred and fifty tables set, filling out the room. The bar at one side was the whole length of the ballroom and already had wait staff dashing back and forward from it, carrying trays.

Whilst he thought the place was spectacular, he could see it entirely from Skye's point of view. Volume.

He heard her shaky breath as he slipped his arm around her waist. 'Just be you. They will love you.' He kissed her cheek and she gave a nod of her head.

She slid her hand into his and they made their way across the ballroom, greeting the hosts and sitting at one of the tables near the front. It wasn't just Skye who was talking tonight. There was a whole host of entertainment for the gala, as well as a charity raffle, followed by a full-on disco.

The room filled quickly as people in spectacular outfits found their tables. The hotel kept things running smoothly, ensuring hors d'oeuvres and drinks flowed. It would have been easy to take another glass of the bubbles, but Jay had seen that Skye was sticking to her original glass and had only taken a few small sips. So, he decided to do the same.

There was a room reserved at the hotel in their name, so Jay didn't need to worry about driving later.

He could see her taking deep breaths and forcing herself to relax. He gently sat his hand on her leg underneath the table, and she dropped her own hand on top of his, squeezing it in appreciation.

'Ready?' he asked quietly. As he leaned in, he could smell her perfume again, and for a moment he wondered how he'd ended up here.

Here. With Skye. Feeling like this.

The compere for the gala started, and a few entertainers came on, getting the spirits in the room high. Both he and Skye laughed at the comedian, and watched in awe at the magician, trying to work out how he did his tricks. Then, one of the charity choirs came on to sing a host of Christmas tunes. Food appeared before them as if by magic, with the plates swept away as soon as they were finished. The hotel staff had this all down to a fine art.

Then, the chairperson of the cancer research committee appeared to remind everyone why they were here, and why their work was so vitally important in the fight against cancer.

This was it. This was Skye's moment. As her name was called, he saw her momentarily freeze. Her whole body went rigid, her face like stone.

He moved his arm back around her waist and whispered in her ear. 'You are a wonderful doctor, and a great daughter. Go and tell the people how much you love your dad, and how your work honours his memory.'

She gave the briefest shiver, as if something had just danced along the length of her spine, then she turned to him, her face relaxed but with a determined air. 'You bet I will.'

As she climbed the stairs to the stage, and stood behind the podium, Jay had only one thought. He'd never loved this woman more.

Skye had been momentarily stunned with nerves, but having Jay by her side, being her cheerleader, was exactly what she'd needed. Before she'd spoken to him, she'd started to build this thing up in her head to something unachievable.

But now she was here. All five versions of the speech she'd tried to write had shot from her mind like a cannon ball, leaving no trace behind. But as she looked around the sea of faces, a few started to stand out. A patient she'd treated. Another who'd recently had a baby. Colleagues who worked in other areas. All pieces of a jigsaw puzzle that made up parts of her life.

Then there was Jay. The guy who'd appeared out of nowhere like the baddie in a Christmas movie, who finds the joy of Christmas, and turns his life around.

But it was her life that was turning around from the impact they were having on each other. She was finding it hard to admit to herself how much she was falling for him.

She didn't want to. She didn't want to end up disappointed. Wouldn't he eventually go back to London? She knew her old supervisor's knee replacement had gone well and he was currently in rehab. But once he was back to full health, he would be expected to return on a permanent basis. So where would that leave Jay?

They hadn't even talked about that. But then again, they hadn't really talked about *them* either. Was there even a them?

As she stood on the podium under the spotlight, a wave of emotions flooded through her. As she blinked under the bright lights, her eyes went to one place. Jay.

As handsome as any film star, sitting in his tuxedo and bowtie, as if he were waiting for the Oscar ceremony to start. His slightly tousled hair, the shadow along his strong jaw line, and—if she had been close enough to see them—those brown eyes that would be cheering her on. She knew that.

She'd never felt like this about anyone before. She'd never been so drawn to someone, or at times so annoyed by them. His accent made her want to float. His touch made her want to cry. His kisses took her to a whole other place.

In general, he made her want to sing, like one of those cartoon princesses with an array of animals forming a choir. If only they would do her housework too.

'Skye?'

A voice made her jolt, and she realised the chairperson was looking at her with concern.

She breathed, smiled, pushed her shoulders back and adjusted the microphone.

'Thank you for joining us tonight at this Christmas gala in aid of cancer research. My name is Dr Skye Campbell, and I have both professional and personal reasons for being here. Let me tell you why.'

Her stomach was doing its own version of a ceilidh. But she wanted to do justice to the invite she'd been given. So, she started by telling stories about her dad. The fun relationship they'd had. The time she'd slipped over in the waves at the beach, and her father had practically stampeded over everyone to get to her. The time she'd refused to attend ballet because she wanted to do karate, and he'd marched her across the road in her tutu, immediately putting her in the other class.

How proud he'd been when she'd been accepted into

medicine. How sad they'd both been when she'd moved from home to the university halls to begin her new life.

How excited she'd been at first, then how she'd noticed a change in her dad when she'd visited for holidays. The small and seemingly unimportant symptoms, which had never been alarming but merely annoying. The way that neither she, nor her parents, had put things together until it reached a crisis point.

How she'd been devastated by his diagnosis, and the progression of the disease. How it had made her channel all her focus at university into studying cancer. How she, and her mother, had nursed her father at the end. How unfair everything felt. How unfair it still felt. How, the what-if game still played in her mind. What if she'd stayed at home and made her father take his mild symptoms more seriously? What if he'd visited the doctor sooner, and started treatment much earlier? What if doing those things would've meant he'd still be here today?

How even now, years on, those thoughts still haunted her. Skye knew that her voice was cracking. She knew she was shedding tears on the stage. But the only thing she was aware of was the fact that she could practically hear a pin drop.

She told them how she'd focused on becoming a doctor of research, as well as a doctor of medicine. She talked about the importance of research to give a better understanding of the disease, and how to stop it. She talked about AI, and embracing technology that might give them the answers they needed. She joked about *Star Trek*, and the fact she was sure that one day they would indeed have a medical tricorder, which could tell them what's happening in the human body in an instant.

She talked about some forms of cancer—like high-risk neuroblastoma in children, where five-year survival rates were still not great.

She put her hand on her heart, and told them that she honestly believed that someday, in the future, they would find a cure for cancer, and that she dearly believed it would be in her lifetime. And that every time they supported a cancer research charity, they were helping to do that.

By the time she was finished, Skye felt exhausted. At first there was silence, then applause erupted around the room, and the whole room stood on their feet.

The chairperson came to her side sniffing, and thanking her, saying there wasn't a dry eye in the house, and she managed to grab her dress and get down those steps to her table again.

Jay wrapped his arms around her, and she let herself just fall into them. It was so nice to have someone here. Someone who believed in her and supported her. Who knew her history, and why she did this. Someone who'd told her she could do this.

'I'm so proud,' he whispered in her ear. 'You were magnificent.' He released from their cuddle and held her by the shoulders, looking into her eyes. 'And I just know that your dad would be so proud of you, too.'

He wiped her tears and handed her a drink. She looked at it blankly for a moment. 'You told me your favourite cocktail the other day. I ordered it in advance.'

As she took a sip, she was surrounded by well-wishers,

all thanking her for her speech and telling her how it affected them. It was as if her speech had caused a buzz across the room, and as the next part of the evening was the charity auction, it seemed it couldn't have been better timed.

For the next hour, she relaxed into Jay, sipping her cocktail and watching the auction. A whole host of weird and wonderful items were bid on in the room, as well as online. Some of the amounts were staggering, and word was that some celebrities had decided to bid online in support.

By the time the auction was finished, the total amount raised was flashed up on a screen over the stage, and it made her cry again.

An array of canapes were set up in the adjoining room, and guests were encouraged to move through whilst the dance floor and the band were set up.

As they moved through the crowds, hand in hand, people were still stopping to speak to her, to tell their stories and offer their support.

After a while, Jay gave her a nudge and whispered in a low voice. 'Fancy some air?'

She nodded gratefully and the two of them stepped outside into the cold Edinburgh night. He slipped his jacket around her shoulders. 'Okay?'

She nodded and smiled. Her heart was happy—it felt as if she'd done a good thing tonight. 'I just feel exhausted,' she admitted. 'I'm not sure how long I can last on the dancefloor.'

'Then why don't we have a party of our own?'

She gave him a secret smile. 'What do you mean?'

'I mean, I booked us a room here. Just in case it all got too much for you. I wanted you to have somewhere you could go if you needed some time out.'

'You did?' She was surprised and more than a little flattered by his consideration. Then she frowned. 'I heard the rooms were booked out months ago.'

He smiled. 'They probably were, and we just got lucky when I phoned.' He pulled a key from his pocket. 'Want to go and see?'

She leaned forward, putting her hands on his chest, noticing instantly how cold his shirt was already. 'Some women might be suspicious of this planning,' she teased. 'They might think you were trying to send them a message.'

His breath was warm on her face. 'We've been sending each other messages for weeks. Honestly, I didn't tell you about the room because I didn't want you to think that. If I was a better planner, I would have warned you in advance to bring some overnight clothes—likely some fleecy pyjamas.' He gave a wicked smile as he held up his hands. 'But it seems I forgot.'

He licked his lips and looked down at her through his thick lashes. 'I still only had a few sips. If you want to go home I can collect my car, I can take you home right now.'

She looked thoughtful for a moment, though she'd made up her mind instantly. 'I have a better idea. How about we slope off to the bar for an hour and get a bit tipsy? Then we can head up the stairs.'

'Your wish is my command,' he said as he put his arm back around her, leading her up the steps and into the dark wood-panelled bar. They sat in deep comfortable leather armchairs whilst their waiter brought them a bottle of champagne.

'If you'd told me five weeks ago this is where I'd be, and this is who I'd be with, I might not have believed you.' She smiled as they clinked their glasses.

'What's that supposed to mean?' he said, but he had a big grin on his face. He put one hand on his chest. 'You say that as if my reputation had preceded me.'

She leaned forward, giving him a clear, intentional view of her cleavage. 'I have no idea what you mean,' she replied, letting his eyes linger before she sat back up.

Her mind was swirling. Maybe it was the champagne. Maybe it was just how overwhelming the night had been. But all of a sudden, she was considering what it might be like to have it all.

To be able to come home to someone at night. To have a loving relationship and successful career, in a way she'd never thought possible before.

Little voices played in the back of her head. Jay wasn't here permanently. She knew that. He would have to leave, and likely soon. But, for five minutes, couldn't she pretend to have it all? Her heart was bursting tonight. She'd spent so long living in fear.

Once you'd lost someone you loved to cancer, a permanent guard formed around you. Going through the pain once was bad enough—the thought of loving someone again, and risking losing them, was just too much.

But right now, it was just her and Jay, and the most wonderful time of year. 'Would it be terrible if I told you I wanted one dance before we go upstairs?'

He gave her a guarded look. 'And what might that dance be to?'

'Just my favourite Christmas song of all time.'

He groaned and leaned forward. 'I'm going to have to do a request, aren't I?'

She smiled broadly. 'I'm sure it's on their playlist. Will you ask for "Last Christmas"?'

He sat down his champagne glass as he narrowed his gaze a little. 'Isn't that a sad song?'

'Not when you're dancing with your perfect person,' she replied.

Jay disappeared out of his chair, and within a few moments he was back. He held out his hand to her. 'You're in luck, or you just have perfect timing. We're up.'

She slid her hand into his and they made their way back into the ballroom. The Christmas lights were twinkling, the main lights dimmed and she let Jay lead her to the middle of the floor as the first notes started.

They'd never danced together before, but Jay had rhythm and Jay had moves. Even though she was pressed up close to him, and could feel the heat from his body next to hers, he spun her around the dance floor as if they'd been dancing partners for years. It was a slow song, but by the time they were finished she was giddy, laughing as she kept her arms wrapped around his neck and his mouth firmly on hers.

'Take me upstairs,' she murmured as she ran her fingers down the length of his spine.

His dark eyes fixed on hers. 'Are you sure?'

'I've never been surer,' she replied, meaning it from the top of her forehead to the tips of her toes. Nothing had ever been as magical as tonight.

CHAPTER TEN

JAY WOKE UP in the pristine linen sheets—the feel of Skye's body next to his—and couldn't be happier.

Things had changed rapidly between them. It had been inevitable—they both knew that. And from the moment they'd entered the room last night, they hadn't wasted any time. He smiled at the clothes lying littered around the room and wondered if they might find them all this morning.

He couldn't remember ever feeling like this. Not even with Jessica. It was only hindsight that meant he could see it.

Should he order breakfast? Neither of them were officially scheduled to work today. It might be nice to have some room service before they decided what they would do with the rest of the day.

He stroked one finger down the side of Skye's face. She was lying with her back to him and breathing slowly.

'Hey,' he murmured, 'happy Christmas Eve.'

There was a moan, and then a murmur, before she turned around to face him.

He didn't wait for her to open her eyes. 'I've been thinking,' he said. 'That this connection between us,' his fingers were still touching her skin, this time her shoulder, 'is so strong, we shouldn't ignore it. We should listen. We should see where this takes us. Embrace it.'

Her eyes opened. She still looked sleepy. And she hadn't spoken, so he just continued.

'I know I'm heading back to London soon, and I've never had a long-distance relationship before. But I think we should try—if you want to. I don't want to walk away from this. This… This isn't casual.' His fingers moved from her shoulder, and he very gently traced one down her cheek. 'Not for me, anyhow.'

She blinked, and he wasn't sure what it was he could see behind her eyes. But she surprised him with her sudden movement—she sat up suddenly and leaned back against the pillows.

'I think we should keep seeing each other,' he pressed. 'I think we should see where this goes.'

Skye was terrified. Terrified by everything.

By the strength of her feelings last night, the connection between them and, most of all, by the way her heart was telling her to hold on tight.

And that onslaught of emotions was sending her into panic mode. Jay was right here. Right beside her. On one hand telling her that he was leaving, but on the other that he wanted to make this work.

She felt as if she couldn't breathe. Everything had been so perfect. Like the final scene in a film. And everyone knew that all the characters got their happily ever after following the final scene. So what was wrong with her?

She blinked her eyes and knew in an instant. When you loved someone this hard, what happened if you lost them?

A car crash, a bad flight, an electric storm, a disease. A rogue cell growing into something it shouldn't.

A look or a glance from someone else once Jay got back down to London. A beautiful, intelligent woman, who wasn't emotionally stunted like she was, who would feel free to love and embrace him. He might feel this connection again, and it wouldn't be with her. What then? A broken heart that she might never recover from?

It was truly amazing what could flash through the human brain in the blink of an eye.

She'd been through the heartbreak of losing someone before. And whilst she knew that a family member was different to a romantic partner, at the end of the day, it came down to a similar premise. Love.

She'd learned how to be resilient. She'd had to. And maybe that was part of why no relationship had really worked for her—she hadn't put herself out there. She'd been too scared. Too cautious. Letting herself love someone else would instantly put her heart at risk. Could she actually cope with that?

And what about Jay? The guy with the deep brown eyes that sent her spiralling, the gorgeous accent, the gentle touch that was like an electricity bolt to all her senses.

She wanted it. She wanted it all. She wanted him. But the truth was—she was just too scared.

His eyes were fixed on hers. Her chest was tight. But she needed to talk. She needed to give him an answer—even if she knew it wasn't what he wanted to hear.

'I'm not sure,' she finally said.

Jay flinched, almost as if she'd slapped him with the palm of her hand. His face had had a dreamy quality about it only seconds before, and it was clear that he'd thought she would agree with what he said.

'We've never talked about long-term,' she said quickly, wishing for all the world that she wasn't actually naked under these sheets with an equally naked Jay next to her. 'Long-term has never been in the picture. You came up here for six weeks to supervise the research project. A project that I still need to work on.'

Her voice became a little more impassioned. 'You've seen me. You've seen how many hours a day it takes up, over and above the day job. How on earth do you think it's even feasible to carry on a long-term relationship when I have those kind of work hours? It's not realistic, no matter what way you try to stretch it.'

Her heart was clenched in her chest right now, because Jay's face told her everything she needed to know. He was devastated, and it was her who'd done this to him.

She honestly didn't deserve him.

She swallowed and tugged at the sheet on the bed, keeping it against her chest as she stood up and looked frantically around the room for her clothes. What had happened to her bra?

She caught a flash of sequin and made a grab for her dress, hauling it up her body in a way it probably wasn't designed to go.

Jay sat upright. His face was pure confusion. 'This is honestly how you want things to go?'

She took a shaky breath as her dress finally adjusted into place and she located her shoes. She dropped the sheet.

'It has to.' She struggled to navigate her feet into their strappy shoes. 'This could never work for us. Not really. I have to focus on the project. I can't get distracted. I have to put all my time and energy into the thing that could make a difference to people. You heard me talk last night. You know where my heart lies.'

She couldn't look at him. Not now. She couldn't look into those brown eyes knowing what she'd just done.

It was true. What she'd said was entirely true. She should focus everything on the research project. It was the best thing to do for herself, and to pay tribute to her dad.

She picked up her black coat and swallowed, her throat horribly dry. She couldn't look at him as she left.

'You're a wonderful person, Jay. I'm sure you'll find the right person soon.'

And with those final words, she walked out the door before she started to cry.

Jay was numb. He couldn't believe what had just happened.

More than that, he couldn't believe he'd been such a fool.

He'd been burned once, he should have learned his lesson then. But no, he had to be a fool and misread a situation totally.

He put his head in his hands. It didn't seem real. He'd

finally found someone he'd felt a real connection with. Someone he thought he could trust.

He'd thought Skye Campbell was worth the risk. Worth the risk of opening up his heart again and taking a chance on love.

But he'd been wrong. So wrong that he kept rethinking things in his head.

The dates, the flirting, the buzz between them. Their first kiss, and then their second. All of last night and just how magical it had been for him—for them—or so he'd thought. Had he been living in fairy land? Had all this just been a game to Skye?

He'd been sorry. Sorry at the thought of having to leave Edinburgh and go back to London. He'd already been half thinking about trying to find another job in Scotland. Thank goodness he hadn't taken any steps.

He pulled out his phone, searching for the first flight down to London. He didn't even care which airport. He would worry about his father's car later. The lease on the house had been twelve weeks minimum, so he could still leave the car there until he got things sorted.

But in the meantime, all he wanted to do was get away. He didn't even care about his clothes and other items he'd left at the house. He looked at his jacket hanging over the back of the chair. He could hardly fly home in a tux—he supposed he could collect the minimum of his personal belongings. What did he even actually need?

As he walked about the room searching for his clothes, he was cursing himself the whole way.

He'd fallen hard. He should never have let himself.

From the moment she'd sparked his attention he should have just shut down and kept himself and his heart safe.

This wasn't worth it. And even worse, it was Christmas. He didn't have any plans. His sister was already off to his parents' house and he would never turn up unexpectedly. That would only result in a whole host of questions he just didn't want to answer.

But even he knew it was the worst time of year to be alone. Christmas seemed to echo louder amongst those who were alone, and he wasn't prepared for that. His penthouse flat back in London would be pristine. That is to say, bland and undecorated. He didn't have a single piece of food in the fridge and likely only a few random things in the freezer. He wasn't even sure he'd have enough time to food shop after he landed. His Christmas food might end up being whatever was on sale at the airport and his packet of emergency digestive biscuits. Fantastic. Happy Christmas.

As he fastened his shirt and picked up his wallet he groaned. People would have seen them last night. Lots of people, and likely word would have spread quickly.

It almost felt as if the Great Southern and Great Northern had some kind of grapevine all of its own. If he had thought things were bad before at the Southern, he would be lucky if he was only known as a laughing stock now.

But something struck him.

Did he really care? Did he really care what other people thought of him and his disaster of a love life?

He grabbed his jacket and keys. *No.* No, he didn't. And what did it matter anyway? Because there was no love life to speak of. And that's exactly the way it would continue.

CHAPTER ELEVEN

SKYE WAS MOVING on autopilot. She stumbled out the hotel—ignoring the stares of other guests in reception, as it looked as though she was doing the walk of shame from the night before—grabbed a taxi and sobbed all the way home.

It was Christmas Eve, and she wasn't scheduled to work. But work was always Skye's solace. So, she scrubbed her face, tugged on some thick woolly tights and the first piece of clothing she came across, and headed straight back to the Great Northern.

If people were surprised to see her, they didn't say so. She'd grabbed a coffee and muffin on the way in, and after a quick check to make sure all the patients were fine, she headed into her office, closing the door behind her with a sigh—and then another sob.

As she looked at the piles and piles of medical records in front of her, a new sensation swamped her. Was this it? Was this it for her life?

And was this it because she'd chosen it?

Her phone beeped and she looked down at the text.

Catching a flight to London. Will continue to support the project.

Her heart stopped. That was it. Nothing else. But what did she expect?

She'd seen Jay only a few hours ago, but she was missing him already. The realisation hit her like a snowball to the head.

She picked up the coat she'd just taken off and brought it to her nose. There it was. An indistinguishable scent to others, but distinctive to her. She could smell the faint aroma of his aftershave. She'd been with him the last time she'd worn this coat.

As she breathed in, she had a startling realisation. She loved him. She loved Jay Bannerman. She loved his tousled brown hair, his deep dark eyes, the little lines around his eyes, and that fantastic voice. She loved the way he frowned, and how he had just as much of a work ethic as she did. She loved the way he'd embraced his sense of fun, when he'd started at the Northern so buttoned up. She loved the way he'd admitted to his own apparent weak points—that he hated being talked about—and that made her stomach plummet. He'd trusted her with that information, and what had she done?

She started to feel sick now. The aroma of sweetness from the muffin and coffee weren't helping. She'd done everything wrong.

A man she adored had proposed a way forward for them both. And instead of grabbing it with both hands, and shouting her glee from the rooftops, she'd disappeared quicker than a rat down a drainpipe.

A rat. It felt like an apt description right now.

She took a deep breath and tried to be rational. She could remember all those fleeting thoughts in the hotel room that had filled her heart with fear. The risk of loving someone else. The risk of losing someone else, and wondering if she could ever survive it.

Her stomach clenched. Those feelings were still there.

There was a knock at the door and Indira stuck her head in. 'If you wouldn't mind, could you have a quick check over Mr Lucas's medications? He's feeling really queasy and needs something to settle his stomach.' Her brow creased. 'You look terrible, by the way. Anything I should know?'

Indira. Always a defender of the truth. Just what she didn't need. 'No, everything's fine. I'll be there in a minute.' Indira nodded and left.

She sighed and put her head on the desk for a moment, taking a few breaths. Mr Lucas, the man who should currently be on holiday, but who'd agreed to stay and start treatment. Most of the patients should be getting day passes for Christmas Day to go home and spend time with their families. She would need to make sure he was fit enough to do that.

She left the office and picked up her tablet to check his meds before she got to him. He'd been moved into one of the side rooms and, as she approached, she could hear people talking.

It was Mr Lucas and his wife. Both sounded upset, and she stopped, not wanting to intrude on a personal moment.

Normally she would move away, not listening to what was being said, but for some reason the few words she did hear made her feet almost stick to the floor.

'But what if I don't get better? What if this treatment makes me sicker than ever?'

'Don't say that, honey. They always say you'll feel worse before you feel better. It's just a bad day.'

His voice cracked. 'The Bahamas was always your dream. I'm sorry it took us twenty-five years to book it. We should have gone sooner. We should have started our bucket list whilst we were still young and fit.'

'Don't say that. We'll still get to the Bahamas. We'll still get to all the places on our list.'

'But what if we don't?'

Skye could hear the anguish in his voice.

But his wife's voice was calm and assured. She spoke with complete and utter conviction. 'Then I have no regrets. John, I married you because I loved you, and because I wanted to spend all my time with you. It doesn't matter where in the world we are, what's important to me is that I'm with you.'

'But all those extra hours at work. All those missed weekends. All the business trips that I should have sent someone else on, but insisted I had to go myself.' He sounded tearful. 'I'm sorry. I should never have let work prioritise my life for me. I should have never thought it was more important than us, more important than you. I should have spent all that time with you. And here I am now, lying in bed, ruining your Christmas for you. You love Christmas Eve. It's your favourite time of the year. We used to make a day of it, taking the kids out for lunch and then going to see whatever blockbuster was on at the cinema. I can't even keep water down right now.' His voice dropped low. 'You probably regret dancing with me all those years ago.' He gave a choked laugh. 'You should have picked the other guy.'

The wife's voice came back, strong and solid. 'Stop it,' she said firmly. 'There's no room for regrets here. Everyone could live a better life with hindsight if they knew what was ahead, but we've not been granted that gift. I wouldn't change a thing about our life, and I don't have regrets. We met when we were supposed to meet. I wasn't supposed to dance with the other guy, I was supposed to dance with you. The time we've had is precious and it will continue to be. I fully intend to make wonderful memories for our twenty-fifth wedding anniversary in the Bahamas. We've had plenty of great Christmases. And we'll make this one our own too—even if it has to be different. What's important, and what's always important, is that we are together.'

His voice was croaky. 'I know they said they caught it early. I know they said there is a good chance of success. But what if that isn't me? What if this is terminal? I don't want you to have a miserable few years because I'm sick.'

'John Lucas. That's enough. In sickness and in health. That's the vow we made. It could just as easily be me in that bed instead of you. I know you. I know you would do exactly what I'm going to do—stay by your side. We're a team. I don't regret a single minute with you, and I'm going to celebrate every single minute I can get.'

There was a reason her feet were frozen to the floor—it flooded over her like a tidal wave. It didn't matter that she shouldn't have eavesdropped. It had struck every nerve she had. Because, despite the crushing weight of grief from losing her dad, she did not regret a single minute she'd spent with him. That had always been blindingly clear to her.

All moments were precious.

Skye almost choked. The fear that had been sitting all around her, like a hidden barrier, just needed to be stepped through. She had no guarantee of what lay ahead for her, or for Jay, but what she did know was that she didn't want to waste a single minute. She wanted to grab the chance of a relationship with him—a chance of her own happily ever after—with both hands.

For a moment, she thought she might be sick as she remembered the look on his face when she'd made excuses not to be together—not to give them both a chance.

She glanced at the ward clock, then back at the tablet in her hand. She had a duty to try and make John Lucas feel better, to try and make Christmas pleasant for him. Once she'd finished with her patients, she would do a mad dash to the airport.

A single tear fell down her cheek. She could only hope that Jay would forgive her.

CHAPTER TWELVE

JAY HAD ALWAYS loved his London home. But right now it just felt empty.

The heating was on, he still had his gorgeous view of Canary Wharf and he'd managed to grab a few things from the posh supermarket at the station on his way back. It was hardly Christmas food, but it was better than an empty fridge.

As he padded across the floor of the living room and stared out at the view, all he could notice was the echo around him, the emptiness.

Jay Bannerman had always liked his own space. He'd loved buying his own place after house-sharing with others. He'd taken pride in decorating and the upkeep of it. He'd never noticed before that there seemed to be a few things missing.

He shook his head. He was feeling melancholy, it was just the time of year. It did this to lots of people. Maybe he should have thought about joining his parents and sister, but since he'd left his car in Scotland that would be tough. And it had just started to snow—the road to Brighton wouldn't be clear.

He sighed, wishing he had some Christmas decorations. He did have some in a box some place, but they were right at the back of a cupboard that he had no energy to rummage through.

He was trying so hard not to let his mind go back to this morning. He'd spent the whole flight going over things in his head, wondering how he'd got it all so massively wrong.

Was he just a really poor judge of women? Or was he just not capable of the type of commitment a relationship needed? Maybe that's what she'd been trying to tell him?

He contemplated a beer. He'd bought a whole four and they were in the fridge. He'd just started walking to the kitchen when there was a buzz at his door.

He frowned. He certainly wasn't expecting anyone. And to be honest, he wasn't in the mood for company.

It must be a neighbour. Anyone else would have buzzed from the main entrance. He'd never had an unexpected neighbour visit, and he hoped they didn't want to borrow the traditional sugar or milk—because he didn't have any.

He sighed as he opened the door, and his breath caught somewhere in his throat.

Skye. Looking more than a little dishevelled. Her cheeks were pink, her hair sticking out everywhere. But what surprised him most was the fact she looked just as shellshocked as he felt.

'I'm sorry,' she said rapidly. 'I'm so, so sorry. I just freaked out this morning. I panicked. Can I come in?'

He stepped back automatically, not really finding words.

She stepped inside and paused. 'Whoa.'

He closed the door. She was staring straight at the

view, caught unawares by the sight of London stretched out before her.

He moved beside her, but didn't speak.

After a few seconds she turned back to face him. But then she kind of crumpled and put her face in both hands.

He could hear her breathing heavily.

'Do you want to sit down?' he asked, not entirely sure if that was wise or not.

She didn't answer for a second, then pulled her hands back. Her eyes had filled with tears. She nodded, shrugging off her black coat as she sat on his cream sofa.

Her voice was shaky. 'I behaved really badly this morning, and I hurt you. I should never have done that.'

He just looked at her, trying to take in the fact that he'd been thinking about her five minutes before, and now she was in front of him.

'You came from Edinburgh? On Christmas Eve?'

She was starting to shake. 'I didn't know what else to do. I couldn't phone you. I couldn't text. No one who has screwed up as much as I did should apologise like that. I had to do it in person.'

Now he was starting to get annoyed. 'But this morning you were sure about things. You said what was on your mind and left.'

She shook her head. 'I said what a panicked idiot says, when the man she's fallen in love with offers her a chance of a real relationship that she doesn't think she's worthy of.'

'What?'

There was a long silence between them. She put a hand to her chest and gave him a sad smile.

'Jay Bannerman, I wonder if you've actually realised I'm a complete mess? My life is all about work. I tell myself it's because I'm devoted to it, but the truth is, and I only just got this myself, it's because I'm too scared to let myself love someone. I'm too scared to take the risk that I might lose that person.' She shook her head. 'I've suffered loss. I came out other side, and I just don't know if I can do that again.' The tears were flowing down her cheeks. 'Or I thought I couldn't. But then I heard Mr and Mrs Lucas talking today. Talking about every minute counting, no matter what.'

She shook her head again and looked at him with pleading eyes. 'I've just done all of this wrong. I didn't want to like you—I really didn't. But I couldn't help it, I just did.' She held up both hands. 'I couldn't ignore the buzz between us, I've never felt anything like that before, then that first time you kissed me…' Her voice tailed off.

It was like someone put their fist around his heart and squeezed. He felt this, he really did. But he just didn't know how to deal with it.

He couldn't live like this, catapulting from one emotion to the other. This morning he'd started the day happy, then been devastated at her words and actions. Now, hours later, she was here, taking it all back?

He held up his hand. 'I can't do this. I can't rollercoaster from one minute to the next. *I* wanted things to work this morning, and you didn't. You didn't want any kind of relationship with me, and certainly didn't want to work at it. You can't just change your mind and turn up at my door as if that didn't happen.'

'I'm sorry,' she said. 'I didn't mean for things to go like this.'

Anger surged inside him. He wanted to yell and shout and just tell her to leave, but part of his heart was still responding to her every word. Hoping and praying that pieces of what she'd said might be true.

He sighed and ran his fingers through his hair. He met her gaze. 'You can't do this to me, Skye. It's not fair.'

She reached over and took his hand, threading her fingers through his. 'I watched two people earlier, telling themselves that they had no regrets. That they wanted to spend every moment together, in sickness and health.' She put her other hand to her heart again. 'And what I knew right away was that if I didn't get on a plane, to tell you, face to face, exactly how I felt, I would regret it for the rest of my life.'

She squeezed the fingers that were threaded with hers. 'I love you, Jay Bannerman. Probably from that first time you kissed me. It didn't matter that you'd been grumpy, it didn't matter you'd pushed people away. I got that. I understood. I just didn't understand myself.' She took a deep breath. 'But I hope that I do now. Tell me to go away. Tell me I ruined things and that it's all my fault. But just know that I made a mistake. And I'll always regret it, no matter what the future holds.'

Jay had been listening. Really listening. It was so easy to let his defences fall automatically back into place. It would be even easier to shut himself off the way he'd done for the last year.

But the last six weeks of his life had been different. For the first time in a long time he'd glimpsed happiness. He hadn't wanted to acknowledge it, but he wasn't a fool. Would he really let her walk back out of his life?

He took a shaky breath. 'I don't want to have a life with regrets either.' He straightened his shoulders. 'But I can't go back and forth. I love you, Skye. And you broke my heart this morning, you made me feel as if I'd read things all wrong between us. Because I've felt the heat between us too. You know I didn't want to date another colleague, you know I didn't want to do anything that would make me the talk of the hospital. But then I met you, and all those good intentions went out the window. I've spent the last few hours feeling like an absolute fool.'

She winced as he kept talking in a low voice. 'Neither of us knows what the future holds. I live in London, you live in Edinburgh. I don't even know how we'll make that work. But I'm willing to give it a try. I'm willing to see where this goes.'

A frown crept across her face.

He was surprised. He'd thought she'd be happy, but she turned to face him, pulling him a bit closer.

'No,' she said firmly. 'I don't want to see where this goes. I want more than that. I want the whole shebang. I want a happily ever after. If I have to move to make that happen, then I will. I want to be with you.'

'You do?' His dark eyes were wide, a smile finally hinting at the edge of his mouth. Was he willing to take this jump? Yes, without a shadow of a doubt.

She gave a smile as she wound her hands up around his neck, brushing her lips against his. 'We might be taking it a little too fast, but I do.'

EPILOGUE

Christmas Eve, one year later

'Where are we going?'

'It's a surprise.' Jay winked. He pulled into a rural estate with a large grand house tucked behind Arthur's Seat in Edinburgh.

She shot him a glance. 'Did you invite your parents here for Christmas? My mum? Is that what you're up to?'

Skye had no idea what was going on. Things between them had just got better and better. As his last act in Edinburgh, he'd given approval for the next stage of the project. It had only taken two months for him to transfer up to Edinburgh on a permanent basis, and they'd been working together ever since.

Did people talk about them in the hospital? Probably. But only to say how sickeningly happy they both seemed.

As they pulled up in front of the grand white house, Skye could see the main hallway festooned with red decorations. As she stepped out the car, Jay couldn't hide the big smile on his face.

'What have you done?' she asked again, feeling very suspicious.

They walked inside and Jay's parents, his sister and

her partner, and Skye's mum and her charming boyfriend were waiting for them. Skye let out a squeal and hugged them all. 'You're all here for Christmas!' she exclaimed.

She adored Jay's parents and his sister, and her mum was now settled with the fellow widower she'd met in Spain. She narrowed her gaze as she saw them all exchange glances.

Jay's voice at the back of her neck startled her. 'Not exactly,' he said.

She turned around and he was down on one knee, box already opened towards her. 'You told me you wanted a happily ever after, that you didn't want to wait to see where this goes.' He was beaming. 'Will you marry me?'

Skye let out a squeal. 'Of course I will.' She hugged him around the neck, then jumped up and down as he slid the elegant diamond on her finger.

He was still down on one knee as he surprised her once again. 'You know I don't want a long engagement?'

'What?' she asked, a little confused. 'Well, yes, I know that.'

He stood up. 'Good. So how do you feel about getting married today?'

For a moment her legs were like jelly. 'What?'

She looked at the faces around her. All of them beaming, just like Jay's. 'You're all in on it, aren't you?' she asked, pretending to frown even though she couldn't stop smiling.

Jay pulled a face for a second. 'You can shout at me later, but I might have posted the notice about our wedding in the hope you would actually say yes.'

Her mum gave a shrug. 'I might even have picked you a dress,' she said, her voice a bit shaky.

Skye enveloped her in a big hug. 'Oh, thank you.' Everything was falling into place for her. The one thing she'd always known she'd miss at her wedding was her father's presence. But here, now? Doing it this way meant she didn't have time to think about it, or to wallow. The fact that Jay had obviously enlisted her mother's help for her dress was just perfect. And she absolutely trusted her mother's taste.

'You've organised all this?' She tilted her head as she looked at Jay.

'Well,' he admitted, nodding to a woman in the corner with a clipboard. 'Maddie has actually played a big part.'

Maddie stepped up. 'If you're ready, Ms Campbell, I'll take you up to your room to get ready.'

Her stomach gave an excited flip. They were really doing this. Right now, in this gorgeous venue, at her favourite time of year.

He couldn't have planned this more perfectly.

Half an hour later, Skye stood blinking at the mirror in her Audrey Hepburn styled, smooth boat-necked dress. It had a nipped in waistline and a three-quarter-length skirt in pale satin.

'I couldn't have picked better,' she murmured to her mother, who handed her the bridal bouquet of off-season orange gardenias, paired with dark green leaves. She felt something against her palm and lifted the bouquet to inspect it.

A silver chain was wound around the stems, with the

words *With you always*, coupled with a small photo of her dad in a silver locket.

She let out a sob.

Her mother wrapped her arms around her. 'This is meant to be a happy day.'

'It is,' she said, tears flowing down her face. 'I would have always wanted Dad to be part of this, and this is just perfect.'

'Are we ready then?' asked her mum. She'd changed into an elegant dark green dress and jacket—she even had a fascinator in her hair.

Skye gave a nod and checked her make-up, covering the tear tracks and putting on a lipstick that matched her flowers. Her heart was singing.

Everything was perfect. A beautiful venue. The man that she loved. The people that were important to them both. And the best time of year. Jay Bannerman knew her. Every part of her.

She would have hated the fuss and worry of a big wedding. She would have fretted about who to invite. How to arrange time off. Now, it was all done for her.

She wasn't even going to tell them that she might have glimpsed the wedding notification a month ago, when they'd been selling their houses, buying a new one together and sorting out insurances. Skye was a doctor—she'd never sign anything without paying attention and reading every piece of paper on her desk. But everything about this was perfect.

She took a last glance in the mirror, then opened the door, her mum beside her, and made her way along the corridor to the main stairs.

Their wedding venue was a beautiful room at the back of the house that looked over the snow-covered gardens.

As she walked in, she let out a gasp as she saw their celebrant. It was Connie, their receptionist from the ward.

Both Jay and Connie shot her conspiratorial glances. Connie was wearing a beautiful navy dress.

'I've been training,' Connie admitted. 'Only Jay knew. This is my first wedding.'

Jay was in a traditional Irish kilt in shades of green and a black Argyll jacket. Skye couldn't stop beaming. She leaned over and whispered in his ear. 'You look spectacular. And at some point, I'll kill you for all this, but right now, I'm just so happy.'

'You're stunning,' he whispered back as he kissed her cheek. 'And your mum couldn't have picked you a more perfect dress.'

They clasped hands as Connie started the ceremony. It didn't take long for her to invite them to talk.

'We have the option of traditional wedding vows at a ceremony, and, if things are planned in advance, sometimes brides and grooms like to write their own. But…' she smiled broadly '…we know that one bride didn't get a chance to do that. However, I'd still like to give them an opportunity to tell each other why marriage is right for them.'

They faced each other and Jay held both of her hands whilst looking her in the eye. 'A year ago today, I got together with the person who was made for me. That's the way I like to think of it. When Skye and I first met, there were sparks, but not all good ones. Anyone would think I annoyed her?'

Their family members laughed as he continued. 'But as we got to know each other, I found it hard to resist Miss Sunshine, as she's known at the hospital. Skye Campbell, I love you. You have the biggest heart, the best attitude and are one of the best and most caring doctors I've ever worked with. Your research is your heart, and everyone knows it. But I hope that I have a little of your heart too.'

She gave him the biggest smile.

He continued. 'I can't imagine what my life would be like if I hadn't met you. You're the first thing I think about when I wake up in the morning, and the last thing I think about at night. And most of those times—work willing—I get to be beside you. You make me see the better side of life. Everything I do with you is fun—no matter what it is. Because we both know how precious minutes are. So, I stand here today, saying the words in sickness and in health, because we both know how important they are.'

Skye's lips started trembling. Her heart was so full it could explode. She pulled Jay's hands up to her heart.

'Dr Grumpy,' she started. 'Jay Bannerman. The man who walked into my life with only work on his mind. I'm so glad you came to Scotland, I'm so glad we got to work together. But most of all, I'm so glad we got to know each other, because those first weeks were the best thing that ever happened to me. You gave me confidence and supported me to talk in front of hundreds of people. You believed in me when I didn't believe in myself. And when I panicked, and ran,' she gave him a smile, 'you forgave me, and told me you loved me.' She reached over and touched his face. 'You are my happily ever after, Jay. And I can't wait for "for ever" to start.'

And, with that, he embraced her, leaned her back and kissed her as their families cheered them on.

* * * * *

Neurosurgeon's IVF Mix-Up Miracle

Annie Claydon

MILLS & BOON

Cursed with a poor sense of direction and a propensity to read, **Annie Claydon** spent much of her childhood lost in books. A degree in English Literature followed by a career in computing didn't lead directly to her perfect job—writing romance for Mills & Boon—but she has no regrets in taking the scenic route. She lives in London: a city where getting lost can be a joy.

Also by Annie Claydon

One Summer in Sydney
Healed by Her Rival Doc
Country Fling with the City Surgeon
Winning Over the Off-Limits Doctor

Discover more at
millsandboon.com.au.

CHAPTER ONE

MONDAY LUNCHTIME. Eight months pregnant and summoned to the fertility clinic by a telephone call from her doctor that morning. Just for a *little chat* to tie up some loose ends. If she could come at lunchtime, that would be perfect. Would half past twelve suit her?

Poppy Evans wasn't entirely buying it. Dr Patel had sounded positive and upbeat, but had also insisted firmly that their meeting couldn't wait until later in the week. In her experience, that kind of invitation wasn't usually issued for loose ends of no consequence, and Poppy had spent the short taxi ride from the Great Southern Hospital to the fertility clinic trying not to list out possibilities in her head.

She was keeping it all under control. After all, she was a neurosurgeon—the kind of person who always had a steady hand and a cool head, whatever the situation. But as she approached the young woman behind the reception desk she felt her heart lurch with anxiety.

'Poppy Evans for Dr Patel.'

The receptionist smiled, turning to a computer screen. 'Thank you, I'll let her know you're here. Would you like to take a seat in the waiting room?'

Poppy remembered to return the smile, before walking through to the large, sensitively organised space. Groups of seats were organised around small occasional tables, with green plants and low-level partitions giving some semblance of privacy. No one needed to meet anyone else's gaze if they didn't want to, and Poppy had appreciated that when she'd first visited the clinic. She'd been able to pretend that the pregnant women, waiting with their partners, didn't have everything that she'd once wanted.

If only Nate were here now…

Nate would understand how she felt. He'd listen to every one of her fears and wouldn't try to dismiss them or tell her not to worry. He'd simply take her hand between his and tell her that he'd always be there for her, and that whatever came next they'd get through it together.

But Nate wasn't here. When they'd made their vows and promised to love each other for the rest of their lives, neither of them could possibly have foreseen that Nate's heart was a ticking time bomb. They'd been together for seven years and married for barely three on that fateful winter's morning when Poppy had stood on the touchline, cheering the Great Southern team on in an inter-hospital football match. Nate had been the goalie for the team and just before half-time he'd made a dive for the ball. His heart had stopped before he hit the ground, and despite heroic efforts by his teammates he'd been beyond saving.

Poppy had spent every waking moment aching with grief. Every sleeping moment dreaming of the love she'd lost. The children that she and Nate had wanted together, deciding to wait for a few years after their wedding because they had all the time in the world…

Then Nate had come to her rescue. He would never have expected her to live her life alone, and although Poppy couldn't bear to love anyone else the way she'd loved him she had plenty of room in her heart for a child. She'd taken her time to grieve, then gone through counselling and made new promises for the future, which had brought her here.

'Hey there, baby...' Poppy shifted uncomfortably in her seat, trying to find that elusive position of perfect relaxation, her mouth forming the shape of the words. *'It's going to be all right. You and I, we're in this together.'*

Somehow, that gave her the answer she needed. Poppy took a breath and then another, as instinct and unquestioning love began to steady her nerves.

'Dylan Harper. I'm a little early.' A voice that she knew floated over from the reception desk and Poppy looked up. The man was facing the receptionist, but one glance at the shock of blond hair and the perfectly fitting grey suit was enough to tell Poppy that she hadn't misheard. However unlikely, this was the Dylan Harper she knew.

Not well—although she and Dylan were both neurosurgeons at the Great Southern Hospital, he had a busy schedule. It wasn't easy to combine his role of hotshot surgeon, a man who could take on the most difficult cases and achieve the best possible result, with all of that gorgeous charm and sex appeal, which he shared liberally with a string of different partners. Their paths had inevitably crossed, and she'd been impressed with his skill and professionalism, but she'd left it at that. His deep blue eyes didn't have the same power over Poppy as they seemed to wield over practically every other female member of the department.

Forget it. She had her own concerns and now wasn't the time to wonder what business Dylan might have at a fertility clinic. Poppy rolled her eyes, annoyed with herself for wondering what Dylan was up to when it really wasn't any of her business, and with him for... She wasn't quite sure what Dylan had done to annoy her. A multitude of small niggles that boiled down to the fact that he didn't appear to value the things that she did.

The receptionist was waving him straight through to the corridor behind her, where the consulting rooms were located. Apparently, he wasn't going to be asked to wait, even though he was early. Poppy shifted again in her seat and saw Dr Patel hurrying towards her.

'Hi, Poppy.' Something about her smile lacked its usual warmth. Perhaps she was just having a bad day. 'How are you?'

'I was thinking that you might tell *me*.' Poppy was getting a little frustrated, and wished that someone would get to the point and tell her why she was here.

'Yes...yes, of course. This isn't a medical matter...we just need to have a chat.'

Enough with the code words and vague reassurances. 'My baby's all right?' This wasn't really the place to ask, but the waiting room was empty and it was the only question that Poppy needed to know the answer to.

Dr Patel suddenly looked her straight in the eye. That was better. 'I've reviewed all your notes and your baby's fine. Come with me, and we'll talk.'

Okay. Dylan had disappeared now and Poppy followed Dr Patel to her consulting room. She refused the offer of a cup of herbal tea, and was waved over to an informal seating area to one side of the desk.

Dr Patel sat down opposite her. 'As you know, Poppy, we have very strict procedures to ensure that the rights and confidentiality of both our donors and recipients are protected.'

Poppy nodded. That was exactly what she'd wanted. This baby was the one that she'd longed for, and which she and

Nate couldn't have. The list of traits which had helped her to choose a father for her child had been all the better for being impersonal.

'I can only apologise for this—'

'Get to the point!' Poppy regretted the words immediately and shot Dr Patel an apologetic look. 'Please. I've always appreciated your straightforwardness, and that's what I need from you now.'

Dr Patel nodded, concern flashing in her eyes. 'I have to tell you that the biological father of the child you're carrying is not the donor that you chose.'

What? Poppy pressed her lips together, aware that she should probably keep her first thoughts to herself, and give the information a chance to sink in. Dr Patel was watching her, a concerned look on her face, and thankfully giving her time to process it all.

'You mean…?' Poppy still couldn't think of a coherent question. 'Say that again…'

Dr Patel nodded, swallowing hard. 'A mistake was made at the facility we use to store donations, and your eggs were fertilised with sperm from the wrong donor.'

Okay. That didn't leave any room for doubt. Poppy took a breath. 'How on earth did this happen?'

'As you know, we use an independent storage facility.' Dr Patel repeated the information a second time, in case Poppy had missed it the first. 'They informed us as soon as they were aware, and have cooperated with our request to give us access to their records. All of my enquiries over the weekend have convinced me that this is a genuine mistake.'

Poppy waved her hand abruptly and Dr Patel fell silent. 'When did you know about this? My baby hasn't been DNA tested—what makes you so sure that there even *has* been a mistake?'

'The facility called and spoke to me late on Friday afternoon. I spent most of Saturday there, going through their procedures, so that I would have a clear report to give to you today. There's a complete audit trail, backed up by hard copy records, which confirms exactly who the biological father of your baby is.'

'And it's not the person I chose.'

'No, it isn't.'

So there was no doubt. Poppy was about to have a child and had no idea who the father might be. The baby inside her seemed to pick up on her agitation and started to kick. She absentmindedly rubbed her stomach to soothe it, and realised that she wasn't thinking straight. This was *her* baby. She'd carried it for eight months, looking after it for every step of the way. Nothing could make her love it any less, and it wasn't humanly possible to love it any more.

'So… If the records are so unequivocal, how did this happen?'

'The storage facility and this clinic have agreed on a joint enquiry, and I've been nominated to lead it. We're committed to maintaining transparency and keeping you informed.'

Right. Poppy wasn't used to being on this side of the conversation. She'd feel a lot happier if she was in control—making enquiries and drawing conclusions herself. She might have to fight those battles later, though, because she had a more pressing question.

'And the biological father of my baby…?'

'He was contacted yesterday and Dr Neave, the director of this clinic, spoke with him. He agreed immediately that you should have sight of his medical records, and also suggested that if you would like to meet with him he would be prepared to waive his own confidentiality rights.'

Another person who'd been told before she had. But it put Poppy in charge of at least part of the process, so she'd let that slide for the moment. The biological father probably wouldn't have the same medical understanding she had, but his gesture meant that she could ask him all the right questions, and hear his answers first-hand.

'Okay. I don't *want* to meet with him, but I think I need to. I'd be grateful if you would arrange that as soon as possible.'

'We can arrange it for you now. He's agreed to make himself available and is in this building, with Dr Neave. Or you can think about it—maybe sleep on it?' Dr Patel hesitated. 'Whatever you decide, I want you to know that I'll be with you all the way.'

There was nothing *to* decide. Poppy shook her head. 'You understand that I'm well equipped to make the best medical decisions for my child.'

Dr Patel smiled suddenly. 'Yes, I do.' She got to her feet, walking over to her desk to pick up a folder, which she handed to Poppy. 'For our own records, we need you to sign a waiver first, with regard to your own confidentiality rights.'

'You have a pen?' Poppy scanned the three copies of the document inside.

'Yes, I do. But you're going to take your time and read everything through first. And I'm going to fetch you a cup of herbal tea, whether you want it or not.' Dr Patel's practical, dry humour surfaced and Poppy smiled.

'Yes, okay. Thanks. On second thoughts, I think I could do with a drink.'

* * *

Dylan Harper had thought about little else since yesterday afternoon. It had come as a shock to find that his sperm donation, which had been frozen some years previously, had been given to someone by mistake. A process that was shrouded in confidentiality suddenly seemed intensely personal.

He couldn't allow himself to have feelings, though. When the director of the fertility clinic had called him, Dylan had insisted on meeting with him straight away. Dr Neave had explained all his options and Dylan had made a decision. The anonymous woman who was carrying his baby was clearly the most vulnerable person in all of this and, as such, her needs and decisions should take priority over his. He'd waived his own confidentiality rights, and made himself available today.

The needs of the expectant mother—who Dylan was struggling not to think of as the mother of his baby—clearly didn't involve him at the moment. He'd been sitting in Dr Neave's office, waiting, for more than half an hour. Dr Neave had tried to engage him in conversation for a while and when that hadn't worked for either of them he'd left Dylan alone to read a magazine.

Maybe this had been a wasted journey. Dylan stared at the clock, wondering if he should leave, and then decided that he shouldn't because, however this turned out, the journey hadn't been wasted at all. It was all about options—and if the expectant mother rejected the option of meeting with him today, that was fine.

He sighed, leaning back in his seat and staring at the ceiling. Then jumped as Dr Neave came back into the office.

'The mother would like to meet you. Are you ready?' Dr

Neave had already expressed his reservations about Dylan's insistence that she should take priority in everything, and told him that he was here to advocate for him.

'Far from it.' Dylan ignored Dr Neave's suggestion that he was perfectly within his rights to wait a while. 'Let's go, shall we?' He wasn't in the habit of going back on his decisions once they were made.

It took a slightly irritable hurry-up glare before Dr Neave joined him in the corridor, heading for one of the consulting rooms at the far end of the corridor. Dr Neave tapped on the door, waiting for a moment until a woman's voice sounded, inviting them in, and Dylan was ushered into the room.

Then the thunderbolt hit.

Two women were sitting on the sofa. The one who clearly *wasn't* pregnant would be Dr Patel, the deputy director of the clinic. And the one who very obviously was…

'Ms Evans.' The sudden, enforced intimacy of the situation felt as if it were strangling him and Dylan instinctively tried to draw back from the sensation. But even though they didn't know each other well, he and Poppy had never gone quite as far as referring to each other as Ms Evans and Mr Harper. 'Poppy…'

That might have been a wrong move. Poppy's eyes filled with tears and Drs Neave and Patel were looking at each other, seemingly at a loss. No surgeon liked to be wrong-footed, least of all Dylan Harper, but he knew exactly what he needed to do. Poppy's care was the one and only priority.

That wasn't going to be as easy as he'd imagined it might be. Dylan had always liked Poppy and moreover he respected her. She was the best surgeon in the whole department, with the possible exception of himself, and her intelligent, no-nonsense approach would beguile any man.

And she was beautiful, too. When she'd first come to work at the Great Southern Hospital he'd regarded Poppy as gorgeous but strictly off-limits, because she was married. Then, when she'd lost her husband so tragically, Dylan had kept his distance even more assiduously, a little ashamed that Poppy's slim figure, red hair and expressive hazel eyes should still provoke a reaction in him.

And now she was in the full bloom of pregnancy, which seemed to push all of his buttons as well. Poppy had always been professional in their dealings, but if Dylan had to take a guess at her opinion of him he'd probably settle for mild dislike. Which didn't make him much of a candidate as biological father of her unborn child.

Of course, she'd never wanted a father for her child. She'd wanted an anonymous donor, who had passed all of the genetic screening and health tests. Even this much contact was more than she'd ever envisaged, and the fact that they knew each other made everything even worse.

One tear rolled down her cheek in the silence. Maybe he should say something, but for the life of him he couldn't think of anything that might be either helpful or appropriate. Telling her that surely it wasn't so bad to find that he was the biological father of her child felt more like a salve for his own ego than a reassurance.

'You're not operating today?' Poppy's voice quivered a little.

Fair enough. If she wanted to ignore the elephant in the room and discuss his operating schedule, then that might give them both a chance to get their breath back.

'No. I had two early morning procedures, and I may need to see a patient late this afternoon. Dr Shah will fill in for me if necessary.'

Poppy nodded. 'I was in post-op this morning. Both your patients are doing well.'

'That's good to hear. Thank you.' Dylan resisted the temptation to ask for a more detailed update. Right now, he could hardly remember what he'd been doing in the operating room this morning, which was unusual as he could usually give a blow-by-blow account of every procedure he'd performed at the end of each day.

He reminded himself that he'd decided to take on the role of protector, even if that had never been an option for either of them before. He walked forward, sitting down in the armchair opposite Poppy.

'This is a shock for both of us.' He took a breath, letting go of everything that his suddenly vulnerable heart wanted. 'I just want to say…'

Dylan fell silent as Poppy held up her hand, clearly not ready to hear what he had to say just yet. He was vaguely aware that Dr Neave had come to sit down in the seat alongside his, and that he was giving Poppy the same kind of professional smile that he'd given Dylan.

'Poppy, you clearly know Dylan, which is something that couldn't have been anticipated when we started on this journey. I think we need to take a moment to reframe the conversation.' Dr Neave spoke and Dylan resisted the temptation to tell him that calling this a journey wasn't going to make it into a walk in the park.

'This *journey*?' Poppy flashed back, and Dylan suppressed a smile. This, more than anything, convinced him that Poppy was going to be all right.

Dr Neave nodded. 'I'm sorry. You have every right to be angry and that was a bad choice of words. Shall we break for a cup of tea and see where we are in half an hour?'

'No more tea.' Poppy was beginning to sound much more sure of her ground now, and that was exactly what Dylan wanted. He turned to her, catching her gaze, and saw a warmth in her hazel eyes that he'd never stopped to notice before.

'What do you want, Poppy?'

CHAPTER TWO

WHAT POPPY ACTUALLY wanted was to be back at work. Or at home, looking forward to the time when she'd be able to hold her child in her arms, in the sure knowledge that the biological father had given her this immense gift without wanting anything in return.

But she needed to pull herself together. Despite her own horror, she'd seen the wounded look in Dylan's eyes at her dismay when she'd realised that he was the biological father of her child. Somehow, that had made him seem so much more human. Someone who could be hurt, despite all his self-assurance.

And even if what she wanted was now beyond anyone's grasp, Dylan had made a good first step in asking her. Cutting across Drs Neave and Patel's smooth assumption that they were at the centre of this decision-making process made it a *very* good first step.

'I'd like a few minutes with Dylan. To discuss this alone, please.' Poppy glanced at him, receiving a small nod. Somehow, the look in his clear blue eyes seemed to reassure her. If the eyes really were the windows to the soul, then Dylan's soul might be enough to see her through this situation.

'Poppy. Are you quite sure?' Dr Neave leaned forward in his seat, his thoughts difficult to read behind his smile. 'In a situation such as this, you should consider working with an advocate, who can act as an intermediary.' He gestured towards Dr Patel, in a signal that she might be such an advocate for Poppy.

What was Dr Patel going to do? Follow her back to the hospital and mediate in any discussions that might involve Dylan? Tell her things that she already knew about the medical and emotional implications of her situation?

Dylan leaned back in his seat, crossing his legs. Poppy glanced at him and he extended his fingers in a gesture which implied she knew all of the facts and that the decision was hers alone. Then she knew.

He might be autocratic. Irritating. Dylan's charm might follow him like a scented aura, infecting far too many of the women they both worked with. But he was honest. He made life-or-death decisions every day in the operating theatre and was aware that she had too, before her pregnancy had meant she was temporarily assigned to the less physically demanding role of post-operative care. However annoying he might be, he was the one person in the room who trusted that she could speak for herself, and appeared ready to listen.

'As I said, Dr Neave, I'd like a few moments with Dylan, please.' She heard a certainty in her voice that she didn't feel, and Dr Patel nodded, gesturing to Dr Neave that they should leave the room.

She'd made her decision now, made the first cut, and now she had to follow it through, quickly and cleanly, with every bit of the expertise she had at her disposal. Poppy waited until the door closed behind Drs Neave and Patel, then focused on Dylan.

'You knew about this yesterday?'

He nodded. 'Not that it was you. I found that out at exactly the same moment you did.'

Poppy nodded. 'I guess that a *the sooner the better* invitation to a fertility clinic is a little lower down your list of priorities if you're not eight months pregnant.' Somehow, now that they were alone, it was easier to speak her mind.

'Yeah. But when they told me *when* the mistake had taken place the situation very rapidly shot to the top of my to-do list.' He reached inside his jacket, pulling out an envelope and putting it on the coffee table. 'These are the results of my medical screening. I asked them to do a few extra tests, and to supply me with the raw data of the results, but that would have spoiled the line of my jacket.'

Surely no one was *that* vain. Poppy looked up at him and saw a self-deprecating smile. She hadn't guessed that Dylan was capable of not taking himself completely seriously. 'You don't need to do that.'

He ignored the words, and Poppy picked up the envelope. He must realise that this was the first thing she'd wanted to know. 'Now that I know you're qualified to read it, I'll make the longer report available to you.'

'Thank you. I'd like to see it.'

He nodded. 'You'll have it tomorrow.'

'I'll treat it in complete confidence, of course.' Poppy should have remembered to say that before now.

'Thanks. How do you feel about keeping all of this quiet? I understand that you may need to talk about it, but in general…' Dylan frowned.

Poppy nodded. 'I'd be grateful if you didn't say anything to anyone at work. You know how it is, tell the wrong person something and in twenty minutes everyone in the department knows. By the next morning it'll be up in

Scotland.' The open lines of communication between the Great Southern in London and the Great Northern in Edinburgh worked to good effect in many ways. One of the unintended side-effects was the unimpeded transmission of gossip.

Poppy saw Dylan turn the corners of his mouth down. She might not be guilty of spreading gossip about him, but she'd listened. Dylan never had much to say about his personal life, so how else would Poppy have known about his conquests?

'You're right. Let's keep this to ourselves, shall we? Unless, of course, there are medical issues which require disclosure, it's no one's business but our own.'

Was there a trace of vulnerability in his eyes? Or maybe Poppy was just finding that she too was susceptible to Dylan Harper's charm. Was he really trying to make a difficult situation better, or did he feel that was the best way to get what he wanted?

Now wasn't the time to think through whether she trusted him or not. That would have to come with time, and was the result of actions and not words. Suddenly Poppy felt she'd heard too many words today already.

'What do you say…? We've covered some of the basics.' Poppy pursed her lips.

'You want to get out of here?'

'Yes. I do. Unless Dr Neave has something more to say.'

Dylan's smooth composure had returned now. It was like watching water being poured into a glass, effortlessly finding its own level. 'I imagine that Dr Neave has a great deal more to say. But if you've had enough for today, then he can wait. Whatever happens next happens when you're ready, and not one moment before.'

* * *

Dylan was as good as his word. He'd ended the meeting tactfully and firmly, leaving Drs Patel and Neave as reassured as they could be in a situation like this. He wasted no time in shrugging his overcoat on and ushering Poppy through the main doors of the clinic and into the lift. As the doors closed, leaving them alone, Poppy let out a sigh of relief.

'Coffee?' He corrected his mistake quickly. 'I meant… decaf? Or herbal tea?'

Poppy smiled up at him. In the confined space, Dylan seemed very big. Very reassuring. 'Herbal tea doesn't have quite the same ring to it, does it?'

'I'll join you. I'm sure there's something to be said for it.'

'No need. If you stick with coffee, then I can at least smell it.'

He thought for a moment, clearly trying to gauge the medical ramifications of smelling coffee. 'Fair enough. Whatever gets you through the day.'

He was close, suddenly. Protective. As he ushered her out of the lift, through the lobby and into the street he seemed to move with her, always there but never actually touching her. Poppy looked to the left and then the right, wondering if she should make the decision to head for one of the half-dozen coffee shops that lined the street ahead of them, but it seemed that Dylan had other ideas. He held out his arm, in a quiet invitation for her to take it.

She was pregnant, not ill. But Poppy's legs were beginning to shake now, the third option of shock starting to take hold. She took his arm, feeling the soft material of his overcoat—cashmere, probably—and Dylan started to walk, taking the first side-street that they came to.

The coffee shop was just slightly off the beaten track, and smaller than the others. A little less shiny, but it was warm and clean. Dylan led her past the crowded counter and down three steps, into a larger, quieter room with framed posters on the walls and comfortable seating.

One of the nice little places that he just happened to know? Poppy dismissed the thought. If he *did* happen to know a few nice places where you could ask someone for a getting-to-know-you coffee, then so what? This wasn't a situation that might lead to an evening meal and then something more. They both had a different mission, and this was somewhere in the heart of the city which provided a moment of much-needed calm.

He left her to choose a seat, and Poppy made for the far corner of the room, taking off her coat and hanging it on the back of an armchair that stood next to a small table. She looked around, wondering if a waiter might appear, and he gestured towards a large blackboard on the wall which listed out the various offerings. Poppy perused the list.

'Blackcurrant and apple sounds nice...' She dragged her gaze away from the list of different coffees.

'Yeah.' Dylan didn't sound any more convinced of that than she was. 'Take a seat, I'll go and get the drinks. Anything to eat?'

Poppy still felt a little sick and shaky. Maybe...maybe not. He seemed to see her indecision. 'The croissants here are good.'

Maybe she'd feel a little steadier if she had a bite to eat. Poppy nodded, sitting down.

Dylan was gone for a while, and she could breathe now. Maybe she should make a list of things that she wanted to ask. She took a napkin from the holder on the table and a pen from her bag, and then couldn't think of anything to write.

HELP ME!

She'd doodled the words in capitals on the napkin, and then scrunched it up quickly, reaching to put it into her coat pocket when she saw Dylan reappear with a tray. This was *her* pregnancy. *Her* baby. She didn't need Dylan's help, even if every instinct was sending the unlikely message that she wanted it.

The croissants were warm and smelled great. His coffee smelled wonderful. Poppy concentrated on her mug of herbal tea, taking a sip. 'That's nice.'

He nodded, taking a sip of his coffee. 'There's something I want to tell you.'

Clearly, he'd been using his thinking time to better effect than she had. Poppy wondered whether Dylan had brought her here to deliver yet another shock, and decided that it was better to get it over with. At least she was sitting down and in the company of a medical practitioner. She took one of the croissants from the plate, putting it into her saucer and breaking a corner off it.

'I'm listening.'

'When I...' He looked around and even though there was no one within hearing distance he lowered his voice. 'When I donated my sperm, it was for one purpose. My brother and sister-in-law couldn't conceive and...'

Poppy hadn't thought of that possibility. It seemed incongruous that a man who made no long-term commitments should have done something like that, but she was coming to the conclusion that Dylan was a nicer guy than she'd thought.

'You helped them?'

'Yes. My sister-in-law had no issues in that area, but my twin brother...'

'You're a *twin*?' Suddenly Poppy was thinking like a doctor again, and there were several very obvious questions she wanted to ask.

He took his phone from his pocket, stabbing at the small screen with his finger and then turning it towards her. Two men standing together, laughing.

'You're the one on the left?'

He raised his eyebrows in surprise. 'Yeah. Was that a guess?'

No, not really. Dylan was the one with the raw sex appeal, but Poppy wasn't inclined to give him the satisfaction of hearing that.

'I suppose I had a fifty percent chance of being right.'

He nodded. 'Sam and I are very alike, but we're fraternal twins, not identical. Since we don't share all our DNA, then it's perfectly possible for just one of us to have fertility issues.'

That was the question that was bothering Poppy. She nodded, blushing.

'Since there's already been one mix-up, it's not too much of a leap to think there could have been two. I questioned Dr Neave very closely on that when I first found out and, although they're in damage limitation mode at the moment, I believe him. And here's the proof that I *can* father a child...'

Dylan picked up his phone, scrolling through photographs. His face warmed suddenly as he found the one he was looking for and he turned the screen towards her. A little blond boy, about four years old, with a toy train.

'Oh! Look at that smile! He's very cute.' Instinct spoke

before caution had a chance to modify the thought. Poppy swallowed hard. 'What's his name?'

'Thomas.' Dylan flipped the photo to one side, showing her another. 'That's him with Sam, and his wife Sophie.'

Dylan's brother had one arm around his wife and the other around his son, who was sitting on his lap. They were all smiling for the camera, but there was more than that. Every syllable of their body language showed close bonds of love.

'What a lovely picture. You and your brother *are* very alike.' Only Dylan's brother seemed happier in his skin somehow, with laughing blue eyes and less precisely coiffed hair. Maybe Poppy was over-thinking this.

Suddenly she saw the same warmth in Dylan's eyes. 'Yeah. My brother Sam is his dad, he's been with him every step of the way and I'm not sure it would be possible for him to love Thomas any more than he does. I'm his uncle, so I insist on spoiling him a bit...' He fell silent, scanning Poppy's face. Maybe he could see all of the questions forming in her head. 'Ask. Please.'

'You don't think of him as your child?'

Dylan chuckled, leaning back in his seat. 'He's my nephew and my godson. That makes him a part of me, but not in the same way that he's a part of my brother. I haven't been there when he wakes up crying in the night, or when he's sick. I can't be and it wasn't what I signed up for. I have a demanding job and my own life.'

He put everyone in their right place. Maybe Poppy was finding a place in his definition of what a family meant, but he would never think of her child as his own. She reminded herself that when she'd first realised that the biological father of her baby wasn't the donor she'd chosen she'd feared this unknown man might want to claim her child as his, and that this was exactly what she'd wanted.

'Does the rest of your family know?'

Dylan nodded. 'Yes, family and close friends. Sam and Sophie will talk to Thomas about it when the time's right, but it's not something they consider a secret. He knows who his mum and dad are.'

'And he'll know that you gave his mum and dad a precious gift?'

'Yeah. Medical science did too. And Sam and Sophie wanted a child so much—it was their determination which made it all a reality.' Dylan shrugged. 'This was one of the best things I ever did, and I don't regret anything about it.'

There was no trace of any regret in his face either. As far as his nephew was concerned, Dylan had exactly what he wanted, no more and no less. And he was in shock too. He'd never counted on his donation being used for anyone other than his own brother and sister-in-law.

And now he was a father again. *Biological* father. That one word meant a very great deal in terms of distance.

'Do you regret this?' Her fingers strayed to her stomach.

Dylan thought for a moment. 'I regret that this wasn't the way you had things planned. I don't think I have it in me to regret being part of the making of a life, though. However awkward it is, that's something that's bigger than both of us.'

Good answer. Very good answer. Poppy nodded. 'I have to admit that I didn't think I'd be sitting here drinking tea with you. We've not had a great deal to do with each other at work and…if I'd had time to think about this, I would have reckoned on you running for the hills. But you haven't.'

'And how do you feel about that?' Dylan's gaze was focused entirely on her now.

'I'm not sure. I almost wish you *had* run for the hills.' Poppy heard a touch of defensiveness in her tone.

She could see the hurt on Dylan's face and pressed her lips together. That wasn't going to take the words back. He'd given her all of the right answers and she'd thrown the wrong one back at him.

One small part of her wished that he *had* just walked away, and that they could pretend that this had never happened. That Dylan would be the anonymous donor that she'd wanted. But the door on that option had closed behind them now, and to Poppy's surprise she'd found a kind and committed man, someone who might love her child. However complicated that was, she couldn't deny her baby that possibility.

'I'm sorry. I didn't mean it that way.' He hadn't openly reproached her, but his reaction hadn't been difficult to miss.

'It's okay. I'd rather hear what you think than what you reckon I want to hear.'

CHAPTER THREE

RUNNING FOR THE HILLS. Was that really what Poppy thought of him? She could be forgiven for that. Dylan was aware that he was capable of charming women but he never stayed around for too long.

His father had been a man who'd run for the hills, and Dylan had always felt that if he never made those promises he couldn't break them. His brother, Sam, was the product of the same broken home, and although his actions seemed very different the motives behind them were the same. Sam and Sophie's relationship was based on promises that Sam knew he could wholeheartedly keep. The brothers who were so alike in some ways and so different in others were just a demonstration of the fact that human beings weren't simply a set of predictable flow charts.

Donating his sperm had been easy with Sam and Sophie, they'd sat down together and worked out answers to every possible question in advance. He and Poppy had found themselves with a fait accompli, and if his own feelings of shock were anything to go by, she must be really struggling. A lot more than he was, and she was also eight months pregnant. Dylan only had to look at her to realise that he needed to be the one to support her, not the other way around.

'May I ask you something?' He took a sip of his coffee

and then another, disappointed to find that caffeine was overrated and didn't make the question any easier.

'Yes, of course.' Poppy was still a little pink from what she clearly saw as a faux pas and Dylan wished he could get inside that beautiful head of hers. He was just going to have to be as honest as his heart would allow.

'I know you never wanted this. That you decided to bring this baby up on your own. But I can't undo what's happened or how I feel. I'd like to be there for you, as much or as little as you want. And if you'll accept me as a friend, I'd very much like to be an uncle to your child, too. Not just for birthdays and Christmas, but for whenever I'm wanted or needed.'

That didn't sound too pushy, did it? Too needy or too demanding. Poppy had lost her husband and asking whether he could be a stand-in father sounded as if Dylan was trying to take his place. He couldn't be a father, but he knew that he could be a loving and committed uncle and, if she would let him, he knew that he could promise her that.

Poppy didn't answer immediately. That was okay, she was giving it serious consideration. Dylan focused his attention on his coffee, trying not to put her under any pressure by staring.

'I guess… Since I have two sisters, there's a vacancy for an uncle that I'm looking to fill. I'm going to need someone with experience.'

Dylan felt a smile rise from his heart. 'May I send you my CV? I could provide references…'

She laughed. 'That won't be necessary. There's no salary involved and I hear that the hours can be terrible. Don't you want to think about it and come back to me later?'

'No. I'm taking the job.'

Dylan leaned back in his seat and she gave him a smiling nod. He really ought to feel more. This had been a shock and it had opened up a whole new world of commitment that he'd never asked for. But they were just echoes now, and the only thing that really gripped him was a sense of relief that Poppy wasn't going to shut him out.

It felt as if they'd settled something. Not everything, but it was more than enough for today. Poppy was sipping her tea in silence, tearing bite-sized portions from the croissant, and he reminded himself that he'd promised to let her dictate the pace.

'We're not done yet, are we.' She shot him a knowing glance. 'But I should probably be getting back to work.'

'Me too.' Dylan considered the practicalities of this next step. 'I think I'll walk, but I'll go and hail you a taxi.'

'You'd *prefer* to walk…?' She gave him an enquiring smile.

Dylan gave up. 'Maybe I'll join you and ask the driver to stop around the corner. That way, we won't be getting out of the taxi together in full view of the whole hospital.'

'Sounds like a plan.' Poppy got to her feet, putting on her coat. Apparently, sitting here while he went outside to hail the taxi wasn't on her agenda either.

She allowed him to open the door of the coffee shop for her, and as soon as she stepped out onto the pavement and raised her hand a taxi came to a stop next to them. Giving him a broad grin, she climbed in, waiting for Dylan to follow.

So this was what impending fatherhood was like. His sister-in-law had joked about his brother's over-protective attitude, and his brother had just laughed and shrugged.

Sam hadn't been able to change the way he felt, and Dylan couldn't now.

As they neared the hospital he leaned forward, telling the taxi driver where to stop. When he got out, handing over a note to cover the fare and the tip, he saw Poppy wrinkle her nose and, just to annoy her even further, he asked the cabbie to take her right to the dropping-off area outside the main entrance.

They'd come a long way in just a few hours, from stunned silence, where just one word might be disastrously wrong, to cautiously teasing each other. But they were both surgeons, they knew exactly when concentration was needed, and when it was possible to step back a bit and lighten the mood. Dylan was under no illusions, there would be plenty of difficult decisions, wordless moments ahead of them.

But somehow… Somehow, he was looking forward to it. Not just the challenge of learning how to be a father, but getting to know Poppy a little better. Before now, he'd studiously ignored all of the things about her that sent tingles up his spine, but now he was noticing the light in her eyes, which changed subtly according to her mood. The way she tilted her head slightly when she smiled. The precise, graceful movement of her hands, and the burning feeling that accompanied the thought of what her touch against his skin might provoke. Dylan was trying very hard not to think about that…

'Hi, Mr Harper.' A cheery voice brought Dylan back into the here and now. One of the receptionists who manned the main desk in Neurology had clearly decided to take a late lunch hour and was walking straight towards him.

'Oh. Hey, Paul. I was miles away…' It was a little late to try and draw Paul's attention away from the taxi, which had stopped at the lights a little further down the road, but Dylan reckoned it couldn't do any harm to try. 'I don't suppose you saw any urgent messages for me this morning, did you?'

'No, just the usual stuff. I'll be back in ten minutes, but they're all in your inbox.'

'Great. Thanks.' Dylan shot Paul a smile and kept walking.

Paul was a nice guy, and everyone appreciated his cheery efficiency. Maybe he hadn't seen Poppy's red coat in the back of the taxi. Maybe he wouldn't put two and two together and come up with the right answer. Dylan just had to hope.

Poppy walked through the reception area of the hospital, deep in thought. What if the baby looked like Dylan? Had his blue eyes and blond hair? That wouldn't be so bad…

His quiet sense of humour. The way he seemed to understand what she was feeling. That smouldering look, which seemed to ignite in the face of a challenge. All good qualities, but they might make for some unexpected challenges during her child's teenage years. But they were a long way away, when just getting through today was proving a major challenge.

She'd be okay if she took this one day at a time. One decision, one thrill at the way he smiled at her. Maybe those thrills would wear off after a while and leave her alone with Nate, the one love of her life.

When she stepped out of the lift, Maisie was alone at the reception desk of the neurology department and Poppy stopped to talk. She'd seen that on TV mystery movies, people stopping to talk to someone so that they had an alibi for the time of the crime. She dismissed the thought. Neither she nor Dylan had committed any crime.

'How did it all go?' Maisie asked.

'Fine.' Poppy hadn't thought to make any secret of her visit, and her nerves at the sudden summons to the clinic must have been obvious. 'Just tying up some paperwork.'

'They haven't heard of email?'

Poppy shrugged. 'They pride themselves on their personal touch.'

She walked to her office and took off her coat. Sat down and nudged her computer into life. Funnily enough, the world still appeared to be turning, in just the same way as it had before she'd left the hospital this morning.

It was finally possible to take a breath. Close her eyes and let her mind wander, instead of feeling that every word might provoke a catastrophe. Dylan was still there, ever present in her thoughts, but somehow his blue eyes seemed less challenging now.

What would it have been like if they'd made this baby together the traditional way? If his tenderness had turned to heat… Since Dylan wasn't here to notice the small shudder of excitement that the thought provoked, it was a risk-free fantasy. A 'what if' that had never been a part of Poppy's plan, and was seriously *never* going to happen.

She relaxed back into her chair, shifting slightly as the baby began to kick.

'Simmer down. We can do this, together.' Poppy wasn't sure whether she was speaking to herself or to her baby, but the words seemed to reassure them both.

It had occurred to Poppy, for the first time, that she didn't need to do this alone. A friend, an uncle for her baby… It all sounded a little bit too good to be true. She'd wait to find out, but while she was waiting she needed to be a bit nicer to Dylan. That comment about whether she would rather he ran for the hills had hurt him.

Nate had liked her outspokenness. He would have shrugged and told her that it wasn't the most practical option and not taken it too personally. But then she'd chosen Nate and he'd chosen her. The way they just got each other had been a big part of the appeal.

Neither she nor Dylan had had any choice in this. They were both vulnerable, both forced into a situation that hadn't been of their making. Which brought her full circle, back to the thought that she really *did* need to be a little nicer.

Poppy leaned forward, checking her messages. This late in her pregnancy, she was confined to consultations and post-op care and she was due on the ward in fifteen minutes.

She'd spent almost two hours carefully assessing and reassuring her patients. The intense concentration that surgery took always cleared her mind of everything else, and although her temporary role was a little different it still required her full attention. When she saw Dylan making a beeline for the ward manager at four o'clock her heart almost missed a beat.

Almost. Somehow his blond hair seemed lighter, as if he'd found some sunshine hiding in a corner somewhere and brought it with him. He was clearly fresh out of the operating theatre. There must have been an emergency this afternoon which had claimed his attention. His presence here meant only one thing, that there would be a new patient coming up to the ward soon, and he had concerns about them.

Poppy looked at her watch. If she left at four-thirty then she'd miss the worst of the rush hour and get home without standing, squashed and uncomfortable, and feeling that she was about to faint in a crowded underground train. If she was going to have to work late, maybe it would be better to wait until after the rush hour had subsided a bit…

'Hey.' He was relaxed and smiling as he approached Poppy, but she could see the remains of a steely concentration in his eyes. Dylan's habit of stretching and taking a few breaths before he left the operating theatre, to shake off the stress, hadn't entirely worked this time.

'You've been operating this afternoon. Was there an emergency case?'

He nodded. 'A young mum. She was walking her older child home from school, with the younger one in a pram. They were hit by a car.'

That was bad enough news at the best of times. These days it was enough to bring a tear to Poppy's eye, and she blinked it away quickly. 'Injuries…?'

She'd tried to make that one word sound brisk and professional, but the softness in Dylan's voice told her that he saw through it. 'The baby and her big brother were fine, their mum pushed them both out of the way. She had two broken legs, and a tear in her jugular vein.'

The broken legs were the most obvious injury, but the tear to the vein in the back of the neck was the most dangerous.

'You've repaired it?'

'I was lucky to have the chance to do so. Apparently, one of the grandparents waiting at the school gate was a retired nurse, and she kept the bleeding under control until the ambulance arrived.'

'Any damage to the vagus nerve or carotid artery?' Every step of the delicate emergency surgery that Dylan had just performed was clear in Poppy's head.

He leaned forward a little, a smile playing around his lips. 'Not telling you. I'll be here and will be keeping an eye on her for a while.'

'That's *my* job, Dylan. I'm going to hazard a guess that everything went well, and there were no complications. You're not the kind of monster that jokes around if that's not the case.' Poppy pressed her lips together. Hadn't she resolved to be nicer to Dylan?

But he grinned. 'Am I the kind of monster who can persuade someone to go home on time, without too many arguments?'

'To tell you the truth, I'm rather banking on you not being any kind of monster.' Poppy realised that her hand had strayed to her baby bump and she snatched it away before anyone saw and concluded that she and Dylan were talking about her pregnancy.

'Good point. I'll do my best to convince you of it. Will you *please* go home? You could accept my promise that I'll be here for our patient, and humour me.'

Our patient. Poppy had never heard Dylan say that before. He went to extraordinary lengths for the patients that he operated on, and often seemed reluctant to give them up to someone else's care. Maybe he was getting used to the concept of shared responsibility, since he knew he couldn't just walk in and take charge of her baby.

'I could do with going home and putting my feet up for the evening. It's been an unexpected kind of a day.' This time Poppy managed to curb her tongue. *Unexpected* didn't carry quite so many value judgements as *monster*.

He nodded silently, his blue-eyed gaze catching hers. The feeling of warmth that this new connection with Dylan had started to provoke was even more inappropriate here than it had been in the coffee bar. But it just wouldn't give up, and Poppy couldn't entirely push it away.

'Unexpected for me, too. I'm hoping that we might be able to turn that into a positive.'

Poppy nodded. *Unexpected* hadn't been her favourite thing, ever since Nate had died. But she was working on that, and now might be a chance to break some new ground.

'Me too. I'll see you tomorrow.'

The emergency operation that Dylan had carried out this afternoon hadn't been quite as straightforward as he'd allowed Poppy to believe. Repairing the broken vein had been difficult, and there had been several other issues arising from the blow to the back of the woman's neck as she was thrown against the kerb. Dylan had used all of his skill, and given her the best chance he could, but she would need to be carefully monitored tonight.

Then there were the factors that had nothing to do with cold calculation, and everything to do with emotion. Faith Carpenter had two children, both far too young to do without her. Dylan had met her husband, Peter, when he'd returned to the hospital after collecting the children and taking them to their grandparents, and something about his quiet determination to do everything he could for his wife and children had touched Dylan.

Both parents wanted to be there for their kids, and that was something that Dylan hadn't had. He couldn't change that, bring his father back and make them all a happy family. But he could change this. He'd had to struggle to push that thought away more than once as he'd operated, because concentration was everything.

One of the high-care rooms on the ward had been readied, and Faith was carefully transferred into the bed. Dylan checked all her vitals, then went out to the waiting room to meet her husband, who sprang to his feet as soon as he saw him.

'I've just examined Faith, Mr Carpenter. She's sedated, but she's come through the surgery very well. We'll be keeping her under close observation tonight to make sure she continues to improve.'

'Thank you.' Peter Carpenter leaned forward, taking his hand and shaking it. 'Thank you for everything you've done. May I see her, please?'

'I'll speak to the ward manager and ask if you can go in for just five minutes. Faith will be very drowsy. She might not know you're there.'

'That's okay. I'll know it, won't I. If there's anything you could do, I'd be so grateful…'

Dylan nodded. 'Wait here. Let me go and see.'

He obtained the ward manager's blessing, and shepherded Peter Carpenter into his wife's room, after warning him that the bruises on her face looked worse than they actually were. The tears in Peter's eyes when he first saw his wife were quickly brushed away and Dylan motioned him to the chair placed next to Faith's bed.

'Hey there, darling. The doctors all say you're doing really well. The kids are both fine, they're with your mother…'

Faith's eyelids fluttered, but she didn't respond. Dylan

told Peter that it would be all right to take his wife's hand, and he reached forward, gently winding his fingers around hers.

It didn't matter that Faith might not know Peter was there, because maybe she did. Suddenly Dylan could detach himself from hard facts, and hope for miracles. Maybe because a miracle was exactly what he needed. Something that might allow him to be a real father. He might have rejected the thought for all his adult life, but suddenly that was all he wanted to be. Everything he wanted to find out *how* to be.

He stepped back, picking up the notes that he'd already read and studying them, in an effort to give Peter and Faith some semblance of privacy. After ten minutes, he stepped forward again, catching Peter's attention.

'Time to go and let her get some rest. If you leave your number with Reception, we'll call you later this evening to let you know how Faith is. If she needs me, I'll be here. I'm on call tonight.' That wasn't entirely true, but since Dylan reckoned he would grab a few hours' sleep in one of the on-call rooms, it was close enough.

Peter nodded. 'I've got to go now, Faith. The doctors will look after you tonight, and I'll be here to see you in the morning. I'm going to give Andrew and Chloe both a big hug from you when I get home. We all love you...'

Dylan swallowed the lump from his throat as Peter leaned forward, kissing his wife's hand. He could usually keep this feeling under control a little better. But going home now was impossible. That was about the only solid fact that he was sure of at the moment.

CHAPTER FOUR

GET SOME REST. That was a slightly more complex procedure than it had been when Poppy had been able to fall into bed, sleep in whatever position she happened to hit the pillows, and then wake up refreshed after eight hours. But between getting home at five o'clock and leaving again at nine the following morning, Poppy had alternated between snoozing on the sofa and sleeping in her bed for a total that approximated eight hours. In between times, she'd eaten, tried not to worry and almost convinced herself that this was just a matter of her making it very clear to Dylan what was going to happen next.

That last part was the thing she was most uncertain of. Dylan was a law unto himself, talented, excellent at his job and completely unpredictable when it came to his personal life. That had never bothered her before, because she'd had nothing to do with his personal life and Dylan's approach to his job was quite different. But it mattered now. The baby that moved inside her was a part of him, too.

It wasn't unusual not to see Dylan at work, she could go for a week without catching sight of him. It *was* unusual to want to know where he was. A casual enquiry had established that he wouldn't be operating until eleven, and when she'd visited the ward she'd found that he'd been here all night. Maybe his patient hadn't been quite as well as he'd suggested, but when she'd asked about Faith Carpenter she'd found that she was doing better than expected.

Since Dylan wasn't in the cafeteria, there was really only one place he could be hiding out. Poppy tapped gently on the door of his office and then entered, wondering whether his smile might have the same effect on her that it had yesterday.

Oh! His office chair was empty, but there was an inflatable mattress on the floor which looked comfortable enough. Or maybe Dylan was just very tired, because he was fast asleep under a couple of hospital blankets. He was wearing a white T-shirt which did little to disguise a very fine pair of shoulders, and the idea of tracing her finger along the muscles of the arm that was flung across his face seemed suddenly very tempting.

'Dylan!' Her voice might be a little harsher and louder than it really needed to be, and he woke with a start. 'Sorry...'

'Uh...' He rubbed his hand across his brow and then focused on his watch, tapping his finger on its face. 'That's okay. You beat my alarm by about ten seconds.'

'You've been here all night?' Poppy wasn't sure how she felt about the idea that he might have been covering for her.

Dylan propped himself up on one elbow, rubbing his hand across the top of his head. Blond spikes made him look more boyish.

'It's not the first time.' He looked a little apologetic. 'At least I have my own office now, which is a lot quieter and much more comfortable.'

But why? If she and Dylan stayed overnight for every patient whose future was uncertain they'd never leave the hospital. Poppy decided not to ask, because how he managed his life really was up to him.

'I'll go and fetch you some coffee, shall I?' Poppy smiled at him. That was the obvious thing to say in the circumstances.

'No, that's fine, thanks. I'll pop into the canteen and get something on my way down to the pre-op meeting, and then shower and scrub up. How did you sleep?'

'Fine. You?'

'Like a baby.'

'Good.' Poppy didn't want to discuss babies right now. Not when Dylan was looking like the guy that everyone would want to say good morning to. 'I'll get on then. Sorry to…um…'

She turned, making for the door before either of them had a chance to say anything else. It appeared that Dylan was going to get the last word, though.

'I'm not sorry. About anything,' she heard him murmur quietly as she closed his office door behind her.

Dylan was reaching new heights in working cooperatively. He'd asked whether he might pick up some lunch so that they could go through some of her notes on pre-op patient consultations together, and turned up in her office with a bright smile and a carrier bag from the local health food restaurant, which was much more tasty than anything the canteen had to offer.

He walked through into the recovery suite more often, too. Or maybe he'd always done that and Poppy just noticed when he was in the room now. He seemed to spend more time on the ward, as well, and always stopped to exchange a few words with Faith Carpenter and her husband.

He never once alluded to what bound them together. Although Poppy couldn't help feeling that the odd slip—some reference to their situation—might be reassuring. Ever since Tuesday morning, they'd both carefully avoided the subject.

And then, on Thursday, she'd walked past the open door of his office, carrying two muffins in a bag. One of them had been intended for Kate, one of the doctors in A&E who Poppy was particularly friendly with, but when Poppy found herself stopping in Dylan's doorway it became obvious that Kate was going to have to fend for herself calorie-wise this afternoon.

'Hi. Blueberry muffin?' That was the only excuse she had to interrupt him, and Poppy held up the bag.

'Yes. Thanks…' Dylan leaned back in his seat, smiling. She couldn't go back now. Poppy walked into the office, pushing the door to behind her, half-closed to allow a little privacy, and half-open to suggest that there was nothing to see here.

He wasn't slow in picking up the signals. 'You want to talk?' Dylan asked as she sat down on the other side of his desk.

'Um… Not right now. Do you?'

He shook his head. 'No.'

Okay, then. Perhaps they'd just eat in silence, and Poppy would leave. She supposed that would be fine. She'd made her move, given him the chance to say what was on his mind, and that was going to have to be enough. She reached into the bag, aware that Dylan was watching her.

'This is one of those Sam and Sophie situations…'

Clearly, she wasn't supposed to know what that meant, and a reaction was required. Poppy raised an eyebrow, wrapping one of the muffins in a napkin and passing it to him. 'Sam and Sophie?'

'Yeah. I email Sam, telling him something, and he replies. Every time. Sophie replies when she has something to say, and the rest of the time she just assumes that I'll know that she's read it and has nothing to add.'

Poppy thought for a moment. 'They've both got points in their favour.'

He nodded. 'Yeah.'

Time to give a little something. They were relative strangers, and maybe they did need to set the ground rules that came naturally in a situation that felt this intimate.

'I think I'd probably fall into the same category as your brother Sam.'

He nodded. 'I've got a bit more in common with Sophie's style.'

Right then. Things really were as they seemed. Dylan had told her that nothing happened until she was ready, and he was keeping his promise. He was still there, waiting for her to collect her thoughts.

'That's...good to know. Thank you.'

He grinned. Dylan's smile was still capable of reducing her to a quivering wreck, if she allowed it to. More so because she'd been noticing him a lot more recently. The way he moved. How his scrubs were always better fitting at the shoulders than at the waist, because Dylan had a great pair of shoulders. Reassuringly broad. Actually... gorgeously broad...

'Suppose I get the muffins tomorrow?'

Dylan knew exactly what was going on here. Poppy wasn't ready for another conversation right now, but she still needed some ongoing reassurance. Along with the rest of the department, she was well aware that he was a problem-solver, and that the solutions he applied in the operating theatre were both elegant and effective. She was learning that his approach to life in general added delight to the recipe.

'Sounds good. Surprise me.'

Red rag to a bull. The curl of Dylan's lip told Poppy that if it was possible to make a muffin surprising he'd do so. Before she was tempted to start flirting with him, Poppy grabbed the bag containing her own muffin and got to her feet, hearing Dylan's soft goodbye as she fled the room.

The following morning, when she opened the door of her office, the smell of warm baked goods greeted her. There was nothing on her desk but, after looking around, Poppy found a wholewheat strawberry muffin from a local bakery, behind a stack of patient leaflets on the bookshelf.

Friday sped by and then the weekend, a little easier because Poppy knew that nothing had changed and Dylan was still there. She almost couldn't wait to get to work on Monday morning, and he didn't disappoint. Poppy opened the top drawer of her desk, and the scent of a banana muffin from the health food restaurant assailed her.

She'd spent the weekend alone, and that degree of separation had helped her to think. Poppy sat down, breaking a bite-sized chunk from the muffin and savouring it for a moment. Then she picked up her phone and texted Dylan.

Dylan had waited, and Poppy had come through for him. It hadn't been as easy as he'd made out, and it wasn't all about differing email styles. He'd known she needed time to process this, and it had been hard to back away. But now Poppy had responded.

He baulked at her choice of lunch venue, though. The hospital garden was a nice place to take a walk, cool in the summer and sheltered in the winter, but it was overlooked by practically every window at the back of the building.

He texted back, hoping that didn't sound as if he was chickening out.

My office?

He received Poppy's okay to the change in plan, along with a smile emoji, and breathed a sigh of relief.

When she appeared in the doorway, at one o'clock on the dot, all the feelings he'd been trying to suppress hit him straight in the chest. He'd missed her. And now it felt that all he'd ever wanted had just burst back into his life, accompanied by a shimmer of sunshine.

Poppy was wearing a green flowery maternity top with a chunky green cardigan, leggings and comfortable flat-heeled boots. Her bright hair and eyes, accentuated by her pale skin, made a practical work outfit into something gorgeous.

'Coffee?' She was holding two cardboard beakers and placed one of them down on his desk. 'I smelled it on the way over here.'

Dylan laughed, feeling suddenly perfectly happy. Smelling his coffee without asking first seemed like an act of perfect intimacy. He stood, motioning her towards the group of comfortable chairs in the corner of the room, and Poppy sat down, depositing the drinks on the low table in front of her. He followed, closing the door as he went.

'Do you smell everyone's coffee?'

'No. Just yours.' The teasing look in her hazel eyes was

there for only a moment before she turned the corners of her mouth down. 'Do you mind?'

'Not in the slightest. May I ask you something?'

'Of course. Anything.'

Dylan saw a flash of alarm in her lovely eyes. Even now, Poppy was trying to pretend that nothing had happened, and that they were just in his office chatting casually. That didn't work for him.

'Would you mind being a little less nice to me? Maybe telling me what's on your mind?'

Poppy paused for a moment, taking a sip of her tea. 'That's a big ask.'

'Yeah, I know. We're on unfamiliar ground though, and I can't imagine how you must feel about it. I'm not even sure that I can tell you how I feel, not straight away. I think we need to be honest with each other if we're going to come to an arrangement. Something that's best for the baby, and that we can both live with.'

Poppy smiled suddenly. 'Those are your priorities? Best for the baby comes first?'

'We did this. The one person that can't suffer as a result of our actions is the baby we made.'

Poppy reached forward, brushing her fingers against the back of his hand. Her touch made the hairs on his arm stand suddenly to attention. 'I like those priorities very much. It's exactly how I feel. I'm afraid I can't be any less nice about the idea.'

'That's okay.' Dylan thought for a moment. 'Why did you suggest the garden, Poppy?'

She blushed suddenly. 'You don't like the garden? It's so pretty with all the white Christmas lights in the trees. One of those secret places in the heart of London.'

Dylan nodded. 'Only it's not so secret, is it? Anyone could see us there together.'

'And sitting in your office with the door closed is more discreet?'

Dylan had to admit it felt that way. 'I close the door all the time. When I'm with a patient or a colleague that I want to discuss something with. When there's a noise outside and I want to concentrate.'

'Yes. Of course.'

'But…?' He'd say it himself if he had to but he'd rather Poppy did.

She shrugged. 'We're colleagues. Being seen together isn't really the problem, is it?'

That was as far as she seemed to want to go, but Dylan caught her meaning.

'Look, Poppy, I'm aware of my reputation…'

'Are you saying that you just have to stand next to a pregnant woman and everyone automatically thinks you're the father of her child?'

He'd asked for her honesty and he couldn't complain if it made him uncomfortable. Sometimes his own actions made him feel uncomfortable, as if he was deliberately shutting off a part of his life that he knew he couldn't handle.

He shrugged. 'I'm single and I like the companionship of women.' Her raised eyebrow told him that she knew exactly what he meant by companionship. 'I've been known to flirt, and people talk.'

He'd never flirted with Poppy. He'd felt an attraction, but that had only made him draw back. She'd been grieving, vulnerable, and he really *wasn't* a monster.

She puffed out a breath. 'This was what I wanted to talk

to you about, Dylan. I'm afraid it's a little too late to stop people from gossiping.'

'Are they? About us?' This was exactly what he hadn't wanted. 'I have to admit that…last Monday…'

'Paul happened to see you getting out of the taxi. I heard.'

Dylan winced. 'I should have mentioned it. I didn't want to worry you unnecessarily. Who told you?'

'My friend Kate from A&E. Three people have asked her already if it's true that we were at the fertility clinic together last week. She said that was nonsense and that I'd gone alone, but I didn't really help matters by telling everyone that I'd just been called in to tie up some paperwork, when I got back.'

'But who does paperwork at this stage?' That sounded a little as if Dylan was finding fault, but Poppy just nodded.

'Yes, exactly. I didn't want anyone thinking that there was anything wrong with the baby, though. That would be worse.'

There *was* something worse than his being the father of her child. It was obvious, but now that Poppy had said it, an obscure feeling of happiness washed over Dylan. Not being the worst thing that had ever happened to her allowed him a little flexibility to rise to the moment.

'I'm sorry, Poppy. I really thought that we could keep this quiet.'

'Then you had your head in the sand.' Her smile told him that she was trying out the not-being-so-nice idea, and he smiled back. 'We work together. We're looking at caring for a child together…?'

She shot him a questioning look, and Dylan nodded. Yeah. If she'd let him, that was exactly what he wanted.

'I agreed with you that we should keep this a secret, because it was such a shock and I needed time to think it all through.' Poppy turned the corners of her mouth down. 'But, practically speaking, it's not going to float. What happens when you ask the pretty new nurse in Orthopaedics out on a date and then say you can't make Wednesdays because that's your babysitting night?'

'I can have a babysitting night?' That gleaming prospect was all that Dylan took from Poppy's words.

She rolled her eyes. 'I thought you wanted to be involved. That doesn't mean you just get to hold a nice clean baby.'

'I know how to change a nappy. Do you?'

Poppy laughed. 'I practised on the doll, during my antenatal classes. How hard can it be, I'm a surgeon?'

'That's what I reckoned with Thomas. My brother almost cried with laughter the first time I tried it.'

Poppy waved her hand dismissively. 'Forget nappies. I was scared that people would find out too, but I did a lot of thinking about it over the weekend and we've done nothing wrong. I wanted a baby to love and care for. You donated sperm to give your brother and his wife a very special gift. We don't have to tell everyone about it, it's not their business, but we don't need to sneak around like a pair of criminals.'

'You're happy with that?'

'Um… Well, no, not really. I might need you to remind me of what I've just said, at some point.' Poppy was fighting back now. Dylan had rejected her veil of niceness and a strong, principled and loving woman had emerged. 'But if you feel that you can own this, then so do I.'

The thought made him shiver. It wouldn't be easy because owning it gave him the opportunity to let Poppy down, the way his father had let his mother down. But although Poppy had support from friends and family, it seemed that there was no one else who would take on the role that he so badly wanted for himself.

'How do you feel about taking a quick stroll around the garden, then? Inspect the Christmas tree. Let everyone see us, and they can think whatever they like, because we really do have nothing to be ashamed of.'

She gave him a dazzling smile. 'That sounds great. I'll go and get my coat and we can get soup from the canteen and take it with us.'

It was difficult to miss Poppy's bright red coat, and the green knitted beret that was pulled down over her ears at a slightly jaunty angle. And Dylan couldn't have been more proud.

They'd taken a walk around the hospital garden, stopping to sit down and drink their soup, in full view of half the hospital. Dylan hadn't touched her once, although he'd been tempted to offer Poppy his arm. All the same, if anyone wanted to accuse them of walking slowly, or of smiling at each other under the white Christmas lights in the trees, then they were guilty as charged.

When Dylan opened the door for Poppy to enter the building, she brushed past him—or rather her coat brushed past his—without the need for either of them to flinch back.

'I had a few Braxton Hicks contractions at the weekend. I called down to Maternity and they've booked me in for a scan tomorrow, after I finish work.'

'Yes?' Dylan tried not to sound too overly excited about it. It was a routine part of Poppy's care, and she probably didn't want to turn up with him in tow. 'You're going to get pictures?'

She laughed. 'I always get as many pictures as I can, so I can spend time staring at them later. If you're not busy, you could come along if you wanted.'

Busy? Dylan remembered that he was a surgeon and that he had a job to do. He'd temporarily forgotten what his schedule was for tomorrow…

He pulled his phone from his pocket and tried to focus on his diary entries. Poppy seemed to sense his confusion and leaned against his arm to see for herself. 'Nothing there. Unless of course you're on the ward?'

'Uh… No, I don't think so. I can always swap with someone if I am. Would it be okay with you if I… I could stay in the waiting room if you want. Perhaps you'll share some of the pictures…?'

Poppy raised her eyebrows. 'Dylan! I never would have put you down as a squeamish type. How does that work for you in Theatre?'

Maybe he should get used to asking for what he wanted, since Poppy was more than capable of answering back.

'I'd really like to come in with you and see the baby…'

She smiled up at him. 'Good. I'm really looking forward to it as well.'

CHAPTER FIVE

POPPY HAD TOLD him that there was no point in his sitting with her in the waiting room and, since he was already in the hospital, she'd phone him when she was called in for her scan. Dylan had sailed through his morning surgeries, optimism lending an edge to his concentration, and then afternoon consultations with patients who were scheduled for surgery next week. Then he'd spent thirty minutes in his office, pacing up and down, as the nerves hit him.

What if Poppy had changed her mind, when faced with the realities of having to explain his presence? That was okay, he'd be disappointed but he could handle that. He'd already told her that everything went at *her* pace and not his, and that she should do whatever seemed right for her.

But what if there was something wrong, and she was rushed down to Theatre and no one knew to inform him…? Sudden panic gripped his heart, and he was reminded of his brother's wry comment that he hadn't known what worry really was until Sophie had become pregnant. Dylan shelved the idea of emergency procedures, since that option was very unlikely, and then jumped when his phone rang.

'Busy?' Poppy's voice sounded on the line.

'No.' Dylan choked the word out.

'Hurry up, then. I've just been called in…'

Something else to panic about occurred to Dylan and he

swallowed hard, telling himself that he could face a receptionist and ask which room Poppy was in, without having to explain his presence in detail. He could leave his own interest vague—no one needed to know whether he was there as a colleague, a friend or a father.

'Dylan...?'

Poppy's voice again. If he wasn't equal to this situation then what real use could he be to her?

'On my way. I'll see you in a couple of minutes.' He thrust his phone back into his pocket, stopping at the basin in the corner of the room to wash his hands. There was no real need for that, he wasn't attending this consultation in a medical capacity, but it made him feel a little better. Then he hurried down to the hospital's maternity unit.

Poppy had clearly told the receptionist that he would be coming, because she waved him straight through. He knocked on the door of the consulting room and heard a soft woman's voice calling for him to come in.

She was lying on the couch and the sonographer had switched on the scanner, ready to go. Poppy gave him a slightly nervous grin and the sonographer smiled at him, nodding towards his rolled-up sleeves.

'I don't think we'll be delivering this baby just yet. You can sit there, Dylan.'

He wasn't Mr Harper here. Dylan wasn't even a doctor, he was here with Poppy and he did as he was told. Poppy flashed him an amused look as he obediently sat down.

'Right then. Let's say hello, shall we?' The sonographer omitted the explanations about how an ultrasound scan worked, but she still provided some well-practised reassurance, noting aloud that everything looked good. That was a relief, because right now Dylan couldn't recall a single thing from his rotation to Maternity during his training and could only see the wonder. From the look on her face, Poppy felt the same.

He counted fingers and then toes. Imagined that he saw something of Poppy in the baby's features. When it moved and then settled again, he felt Poppy take his hand and realised that it had strayed to the side of the gurney she was lying on.

And... A girl. A baby daughter. The information rushed in on him and Dylan felt the last vestiges of his self-control slip away as he started to grin helplessly.

'She's beautiful. Perfect.' His voice sounded a little shaky, and Poppy turned her head towards him.

'Isn't she just.'

'And she's fine as well.' The sonographer had been concentrating on the screen and her smooth tones told Dylan everything he needed to know. 'It won't be long now, Poppy. Everything's as it should be for a delivery early in the New Year...'

Dylan didn't need to hear anything more. His gaze was fixed on the screen in front of them, taking in every second. When the sonographer pronounced herself satisfied and lifted the sensor from Poppy's stomach, all he wanted to do was to tell her to switch the screen back on and let him take a second look. Instructions to fellow medics worked in the operating theatre, but almost certainly not here.

'We're done.' Poppy nudged him. 'I'll bring the photos up to show you.'

'Right. Thanks...' Dylan gathered his wits and got to his feet. He turned to the sonographer, thanking her too, and she smiled.

'You're welcome.'

There was no hint of a question in her face. No surprise and no judgement. Dylan supposed that, like most people here, she'd seen pretty much everything and knew how to act professionally. If there were any rumours surrounding his accompanying Poppy, then they wouldn't be coming from her.

'I appreciate…everything.' He got to his feet, turning quickly to walk from the room.

Poppy had followed Dylan up to his office, handing over the images from the scan for him to look at. His face was one picture that Poppy could scarcely drag her gaze from. All the wonder that she'd felt as she'd watched her baby grow in a succession of scans. The feeling when she'd first felt her daughter move. All the ways she'd bonded with her child, rolled up into one. Maybe she should have brought a stethoscope with her, just to check that he was all right, but she hadn't expected this.

'It's a girl, then,' he murmured. 'I didn't think to ask.'

Maybe he had, and maybe not. Poppy had thought about telling him, and decided to find out where he stood before she did so. Right now, there was absolutely no question about that.

He smiled at her silence, seeming to understand. Then the pictures from the scan claimed his attention again.

'Do you need to get back to work?' Hours weren't really an issue, Dylan worked the same hours she had before she became pregnant, and it was always more than they were contracted for. She was just a little worried that he might have forgotten something that he needed to do.

'No, that's fine.' Dylan shook his head. 'I was in at six this morning, and picked up a procedure that the night staff couldn't handle. I've been working through since then, there's nothing more.'

'Okay.' He'd already stared at each of the photographs three times, and that probably counted as giving him enough time to take all this in. 'I don't want to burst your bubble...'

He looked up at her. 'I hope you realise that it would take a pneumatic drill to burst this particular bubble. What is it?'

'Just a letter from the fertility clinic. You've probably got one too, but I'd like to compare notes some time.'

'I haven't heard anything from them. What does it say?'

Poppy shrugged. She'd been worried when she'd received the letter in this morning's post, but resolved to wait until after the scan to show it to Dylan. Maybe this wasn't quite the right time to discuss it, either.

'It's really nothing urgent. When you've got a minute tomorrow...'

He looked up at her questioningly. Then Dylan chuckled. 'I can't pretend I'm not putty in your hands at the moment, and you could probably get me to agree to anything. We may have to put a coping strategy in place for that, so it'll be good practice if you show me the letter now.'

It was difficult to tell whether he was joking or not and Poppy decided not to enquire, since Dylan might not know the answer either. She took the letter from her handbag and slid it across the desk towards him.

'I want your opinion. Not just a *whatever you want*, please.'

He nodded, his face hardening as he read the letter through.

'My opinion? You're sure?'

'Yes, Dylan.' Poppy felt a quiver of uncertainty. Dylan

hadn't put a foot wrong so far, which was more than she could say for herself. It suddenly occurred to her that this might be the exception to that.

'Well, for starters, I think that writing to you just weeks before you're due to give birth shows more concern for themselves than for you. Putting that aside, my preference would be that neither of us signs anything. Do you need the money?'

'Of course not.' A surgeon's salary was a lot more than enough for Poppy's lifestyle and she'd thought very carefully about all of the costs involved in bringing up a child.

'Okay. Then a confidentiality agreement is going to give you nothing. The fertility clinic—or, more likely, their lawyers—are probably worried about the newspapers and so on, but what if you wanted to tell someone? A friend, or maybe someone you have a relationship with at some point in the future? Someone who's advising you about your own needs or those of your child?'

'I'm not intending on starting another relationship…' Dylan was right in every other respect.

'And I wasn't intending this. It's happened, and now I wouldn't undo it for the world.' His expression softened suddenly and he glanced again at the photographs on his desk, before resuming the brisk pace of the discussion.

'We decided that we aren't going to sneak around, or feel that this is some kind of guilty secret. If that's what you want, then don't sign the confidentiality agreement, however much they offer you as a *"gesture of good faith"*. I'm your child's biological father and that means I can make those kinds of gestures, too.'

For a moment Poppy wasn't quite sure what he meant

and then it hit her. She recoiled from the thought. 'I said that I don't need money. Not theirs or yours…'

'Okay.' He held his hands up in surrender. 'I know. I'm just saying.'

'And the other contract?' Poppy hardly dared ask now.

'I'm all for that. You entered into this on the basis that the biological father would have no parental responsibilities or rights over your child, which is a standard arrangement. As such, your rights over your child are probably protected, but I'd be keen to sign a document which confirms this and shows that I understand the legal situation. This is not me running for the hills, by the way, I just want you to retain control.'

'I get that.' Poppy felt a wave of relief that she hadn't realised she'd been waiting for. 'So you think we should ask them to draw up those documents and sign them?'

'I'd like to suggest something a little different. When I donated sperm for Sam and Sophie we had an independent solicitor, who specialises in family law, draw up a contract. We'd already agreed everything between us but…' Dylan shrugged. 'It was really important for us to know exactly how the family relationships were going to work and for us to all feel secure about our roles. Knowing that Sophie and Sam are Thomas's real parents allows me to get the most out of being an uncle.'

'No. It's sensible…' Poppy could never have anticipated sitting here, having this conversation. Having a baby with anyone other than Nate… A paralysing wave of guilt hit her. She'd wished Nate might be there for all of her other scans, but when she'd seen the look on Dylan's face she'd thought of no one but him.

'We can instruct anyone you choose, but the solicitor that

we used is very good and made sure that the document we signed exactly reflected everyone's wishes. And in case you're wondering, she isn't cheap but she's the best. I'll be covering her fees.' Poppy opened her mouth to protest and Dylan shook his head. 'I want everything to be as you intended it, Poppy. This is a cost that you hadn't anticipated, and I'm going to insist.'

'You're being very reasonable about all of this.'

He laughed, leaning back in his chair. 'This is what I want, Poppy. Now you have to take a few days to think about it, and tell me what you want.'

'I don't need a few days. You're right about everything, apart from paying the solicitor's fees.'

'Okay, I'll reserve the right to disagree with you on both of those points. Sleep on it, and tell me again in a couple of days, because this is something that affects the rest of our lives and it's important. We can resort to pistols at dawn over the solicitor's fees later.' He planted his elbows on the desk, leaning forward. 'How did we do?'

'I think we handled it pretty well. Why don't you come over to my place at the weekend for lunch, and we can make a final decision then? Unless you have anything else planned?'

'Nothing planned. Thanks, we'll do that. My car's in the staff car park, so I'll give you a lift home this evening. You don't want to be on the Tube during rush hour.'

No, she really didn't. Poppy had been reckoning on a taxi home. 'Don't you want to scan those photos first?'

He grinned, nodding. 'Do you have a scanner?'

Poppy pointed to the printer on his desk. 'You have a scanner, Dylan. That doesn't just print things, it scans them as well.'

'Does it? You want to show me how to do that?'

'Dylan! You don't know how to use your own scanner?'

He grinned at her. 'My nephew tells me that a four-year-old is better with this kind of thing than I am. He should know, since he *is* a four-year-old.'

Poppy had saved the scans onto Dylan's phone, wondering whether he'd look at them again tonight. She couldn't help hoping that he might.

She had *someone*. The person whose number you gave when anyone asked if there was someone they could call. Someone who came into work at six in the morning, bringing his car, so that she didn't have to make her way home with the regular crowds that flooded into busy London stations every evening. That person who she'd show a problematic letter to, and who could come up with an answer that she was comfortable with. Someone who might love her child in the same way she did—maybe not quite as much, but who might just feel from time to time that their baby daughter was his first priority…

No. She'd gone too far. Nate had been her *someone*, the person who'd always put her first. She might feel that Dylan would do that, but perhaps every woman he'd been associated with—and there were a lot of them—had felt the same way. That was his charm, his appeal. Poppy was getting carried away, forgetting that this baby was the one that she and Nate had never been able to have. She didn't really belong with Dylan and neither did her child, it had all been an accident that was never meant to happen.

All the same, when he'd suggested they go and get something to eat, because the roads would be crowded at this time in the evening as well, she'd agreed. That was just a practicality. And when she'd wondered aloud whether they might stroll up to one of the stores in either Oxford Street or Regent Street, to pick up some Christmas gifts for her nieces, his reaction was clearly one that moved beyond the bounds of putting time on their hands to good use.

'You want to take me to a toy store?' He was grinning like a four-year-old.

'Can't you go in on your own? Or are you worried about getting lost?'

Dylan chuckled. 'A second opinion's always good. I'm still deciding what to get Thomas for Christmas. How many nieces do you have?'

'I'm only buying for my middle sister's two girls. Our oldest sister lives in Germany so her son and daughter's presents are all sorted.'

He nodded. 'So you won't be seeing them at Christmas?'

'No, they're going to her husband's family. My mum and dad, along with my middle sister and her family, are going over to stay with her in Cologne for a couple of weeks before Christmas. I dare say they'll be doing a tour of the Christmas markets for some presents. They'll be back the day before Christmas Eve and we'll have Christmas together.'

'You're buying for two girls, then? Any ideas yet?'

'The eldest is quite sporty and my sister says she needs a new kit bag, so I'm going to get her that. The younger one likes taking things apart and putting them back together again, so I thought I'd get her one of those sets of bricks that you can put together to make something that works.'

Dylan's brow creased. 'Okay then, a store with a sports department *and* a toy department...'

'What about Thomas—what are you thinking of getting for him?'

'Uh…no idea. I usually just go and play with everything and see what catches my eye. I'm slightly behind on that this year.' Dylan thought for a moment. 'I'll just come and play with the bricks, shall I?'

She was seeing a whole new side of Dylan, one that he kept carefully hidden at work. And it was a really nice side, carefree and buoyant. Christmas shopping suddenly seemed like a new adventure.

'Okay, then. I'll buy and you play.'

He sprang to his feet. 'Sounds good. Hurry up and get your coat, then…'

CHAPTER SIX

DYLAN HAD OFFERED his arm for the short walk to Oxford Street, and Poppy had taken it. When the relatively quiet backstreets opened up onto bright Christmas lights and crowds in the main thoroughfare he became protectively close, and Poppy didn't draw back. It was nice to have someone with her, even if Dylan could never be *the* someone.

It appeared that he was intent on inspecting all the children's sports bags thoroughly, sliding his hands into the pockets, turning them inside out and fiddling with the straps. But a smiling, 'Decision, Mr Harper!' snapped him back into work mode for a moment, and he pointed to the style that Poppy had thought might be best.

'That one.'

'I agree. What do you think of the dark purple one?'

He nodded. 'Yeah. That's nice.'

Job done. Poppy took a reusable carrier bag from her pocket and unrolled it, giving it to the cashier who was dealing with her purchase, and Dylan retrieved it from the smiling woman. Just a man carrying his pregnant partner's bags. They must see that all the time over Christmas, but it sent a shiver down Poppy's spine.

When they got to the toy department, he slid the bag over his shoulder to leave both his hands free. His eyes had lit up like warning signs and he was looking around with an expression of dazed wonder on his face. Poppy took his arm, propelling him over to a large display of toy bricks, before he got caught up with anything else.

'This is wonderful…' He leaned forward, turning one of the moving circular arches of a space station with his finger.

'It is, isn't it. But it's a bit too complicated for Anna, I think. It'll drive my brother-in-law crazy trying to help her put it together.' Poppy moved on, pulling Dylan with her.

She decided on a smaller model of a water mill, which had moving parts that transferred water from one container to another. Since Dylan had played for a while with the display model, it would probably suit little Anna too. She nudged him in the ribs and he jumped, grinning.

'Hey. You want to look at some more of these? For your nephew?'

'You think he'd like one? I could mention it to Sophie.'

The answer to his question was obvious. If the boy was anything like his biological father, then yes, he'd love one.

'Can you give her a call and ask her?'

'Right. Yes, good idea, I can show them to her.' He manoeuvred Poppy into a seat beside the display, which someone had just vacated, and fiddled with his phone, speaking loudly over the hubbub around them.

'These are the ones…'

Poppy rolled her eyes. This might take a while, but she was sitting down and she didn't have to worry about bags or trains home. Dylan turned the phone around and she caught a glimpse of a laughing woman with dark hair.

Maybe she should have looked the other way, pretended that she wasn't with Dylan. But his sister-in-law probably wouldn't think twice about seeing Dylan with an unknown woman, and the screen was moving too fast and probably not big enough to reveal her pregnancy bump. Poppy reminded herself that she was *accompanying* Dylan and not *with* him.

He pointed the phone towards the display, carefully panning around to take in as much as possible. Then a few spoken words and he nodded, ending the call.

'Sophie says she thinks he'll love something like this. His birthday's in March and they were thinking of getting him one then, but Christmas is fine. She said I could help him put it together.'

Poppy nodded. Dylan hadn't just chosen something, he'd asked first. If this was a blueprint for the way he intended to go with their daughter, the arrangement would be fine with her.

'Did she say which one?'

'No.' Dylan frowned. 'She couldn't see them all that well, so she's left me to decide.'

'Well, you can start with the ones that have his age range printed on the box. Then pick the one you think he'll like the best. I'll stay here for another minute or two.' Or maybe three. The shop was crowded, but the seats were placed in such a way that she could see the display without being jostled.

'You don't mind?'

'No, take your time.' Poppy was starting to enjoy this. Dylan's excitement and the boyish look on his face. Even his indecision, which was never part of his persona at work, made her smile.

'Thanks...' His gaze turned towards the space station,

lingering on it for a moment, and Poppy shook her head. That would be for ten to twelve-year-olds, at least.

Forget champagne. He was with an intoxicatingly beautiful woman and this was one of the best evenings that Dylan had spent in a long while. He'd done something practical, and got Thomas a present that both he and Poppy agreed that he'd love. Sam would understand how much that meant to Dylan. Their father had always considered that any effort on his part should produce tangible results, and when he'd gone to live with his divorced lover and her daughter, all of his time and money had been spent on them. Dylan and Sam's mother had struggled, and everyone had to understand that Christmas wouldn't be the same.

Things were different now. Their mother's car was beginning to show its age, and he and Sam had bought her a surprise gift of a shiny new runaround. Christmas at Sophie and Sam's place would be everything that a family Christmas should be—full of warmth and tradition, with presents for everyone under a huge tree. That was the way that Sam dealt with it all, but Dylan hadn't been able to forget so easily.

But somehow, he'd forgotten when he was with Poppy. Her smile, the baby inside her. That was what Christmas was all about. But there was the glitter too, and the excitement of buying presents. He'd picked up a catalogue so that he could study the full range of construction kits in detail at home, and they'd stopped to get some wrapping paper on the way to the rooftop café.

It was a little chilly for Dylan's taste, but it seemed to suit Poppy's current temperature gauge perfectly. And the view was spectacular, with Christmas lights spread out below them as far as they could see.

'What's that?' She meandered towards some activity that was going on in a darkened corner of the space, and Dylan followed with the tray. Suddenly the white painted walls glowed with light as someone started to fiddle with some equipment on a small table.

'Ah—I see, it's a star projector. Do you want to sit here?' He indicated a nearby table.

'Yes, please.' Poppy plumped herself down, mesmerised by the display. Dylan couldn't drag his gaze from the look on her face, and almost spilled her herbal tea as he unloaded the tray.

'Would you like a leaflet?' A young man approached them. 'The stars are all absolutely correct and you can get different filters that give you the view from different parts of the world.'

Poppy laughed. 'Any spaceships?'

'Um… I don't think so. I can check…'

'No, that's okay. We've got a spaceship construction kit already.' She glanced at Dylan and he nodded. One spaceship at a time, and the projector seemed a little too advanced for Thomas.

'It'll do a few other things. There's a filter that does snowflakes, which looks great on a wall. Maybe for the baby?' The young man was clearly covering every sales point that occurred to him, and Dylan smiled, leaving Poppy to correct him.

'Newborns can't see as far as a wall, they're very shortsighted. But I'll take a leaflet if you don't mind. To think about for next year, maybe.'

'Have a great Christmas.' The lad brightened at the idea

of a willing recipient for his leaflets and gave one to Poppy and an extra one to Dylan before moving on to the next table.

'It's not really for kids, is it.' He glanced at the leaflet. The price and the assertions about the scientific accuracy of the projection made the gizmo an adult toy.

'No. It's gorgeous though, isn't it. Imagine going to sleep under the stars.'

Dylan chuckled. 'Maybe it *does* work on babies. If you're calm and happy then that rubs off on them, doesn't it?'

'That's an excuse, Dylan.' She looked up from her copy of the leaflet. 'However much I like the idea, I'm not going to fall for it. I've got far too many things to get for the baby as it is.'

Right now, Dylan wasn't thinking of the baby, he was thinking about Poppy and he so wanted her to have something nice for herself. But it was far too soon to offer. Maybe next year, when they'd agreed what he could and couldn't do and he'd shown that he could stick to that. That was killing him right now, but he had to show Poppy that he was going to do this the right way. The way *she* wanted it to be.

'Why don't you get one for yourself?' Poppy grinned at him.

'Nah. I'd never get to see it. I fall asleep the moment my head hits the pillow.'

She gave him a fleeting look of disbelief, quickly hidden by a smile. She was right. If Dylan had company for the night, he never allowed himself to be the first to fall asleep. But stargazing was different. Part of a relationship that was entirely different to the ones he usually had with women, and which had to be made to last.

'Are you warm enough?' Poppy was undoing the buttons of her coat and loosening her scarf.

'Yeah, I'm fine.' Dylan decided that he could at least take his gloves off, because his coffee was hot. And sitting here, amongst stars and Christmas lights, was one of those special moments that he wouldn't miss.

Neurology was busy. The approach of Christmas didn't allow any let up in emergency patients, and the pressure to treat those who were scheduled for operations wasn't any less either. But people wanted to take leave, to sort out their own Christmases, and that left all of the remaining staff working to capacity.

'No!' She heard Dylan's voice as she passed the open door of the surgical office. 'One of my usual team is away today and another two have been co-opted onto other teams. I know we're busy, but I'm really not confident that I can give this patient the best care without a full team. I'm going to need another surgeon present.'

'I understand all that, Dylan, really, I do. But I can't magic a surgeon up out of nowhere.' The surgical coordinator's voice sounded stressed. Paula had a difficult job at the best of times, everyone wanted the best for their patients and human resources were always the most valuable commodity.

Guilt, at being one of the surgeons who *wasn't* available, stopped Poppy in her tracks. Then she thought again. She walked into the office, scanning the board. The department *was* unusually busy today, and Paula was quite right.

'I'm a surgeon.' The obvious answer sprang to her lips and she tried to qualify it with a joke. 'Not a bad one, actually.'

Dylan turned. 'No, Poppy. You're one of the best, but

we have a patient coming in by ambulance with extensive head trauma. From what I'm told, it'll be a complex operation and you can't be expected to stand for that long.'

'So get me a stool.' She turned to Paula. 'Not one of the little ones, something a bit more supportive… You know what I need.' Paula had three kids of her own.

'Yeah, okay. If you're sure?'

Dylan opened his mouth to answer, but Poppy beat him to it. 'Yes. Thanks, Paula.'

Paula hurried away, leaving her to face Dylan's wrath. That felt like a challenge Poppy could rise to suddenly.

'I'm not happy with this, Poppy. I'm not prepared to put one person at risk to help save another. I'll find someone else.'

'Who?' Poppy gestured towards the board. 'There are plenty of surgeons up there who are doing something else. And one standing in front of you who isn't.'

Doubt showed in his eyes. Dylan was clearly agonising over this decision, and it wasn't one that Poppy would have liked to make for someone else either. But he didn't have to make her choices for her. He didn't have the right…

'Mr Harper. You need a surgeon?'

'Yes, but…'

Poppy shot him her best *Don't you dare* look, and he fell silent.

'Then I'm perfectly capable of making this decision. Go downstairs and wait for the patient to arrive and do an initial assessment. I'm going to go and get ready, which might take a little longer than usual because I can't reach my feet. My hands are, however, at your disposal.'

Dylan tried one more imploring look and Poppy ignored it. 'Yes, Ms Evans.'

'Paula's put it down for Theatre Three?' Poppy glanced at the board. 'I'll see you there.'

'Poppy…' Dylan caught her arm. 'If you feel under stress you have to stop. Please.'

'Dylan, you don't have to worry about me. I know what all the risk factors are, and this is well within my capabilities. If I do find myself in difficulties, I'll tell you. But, in the meantime, I know I can help. Is that all right with you?'

His gaze searched her face and he gave a brisk nod, before turning to hurry away.

Poppy could have handled that better. She was confident that she could assist Dylan, and she could have taken him to one side and acknowledged his fears. Maybe pointed out that in the best of all worlds she shouldn't be in the operating theatre, but not every situation had to be ideal to make it workable. But pride, and the rigid determination she'd had from the start, that this was *her* pregnancy and she could do it alone, had got in the way.

By the time she'd finished scrubbing up, the team was already assembled. Paula had done a good job, and found a surgeon's stool with a backrest from one of the other theatres. Poppy nodded to the rest of the team and took her place, sitting quietly amidst the focused activity. She needed to save her strength, and then everyone would get through this just fine.

Dylan arrived, and gave her a guarded nod. And then the patient was brought in and lifted onto the table.

He was right. No one person could do this alone. A crushed skull, major bleeding—this kind of injury was going to leave its mark and it was their expertise that would dictate how much of a mark.

'Right then. I'm going to start with the major injury, here.' He indicated the mass of blood and shattered bone on one side of the patient's skull. At least his head was already shaved, and Poppy thanked their lucky stars for that sartorial choice.

'I need you to assist and also keep an eye on the other injuries. There will be times when I can manage on my own, and when I ask you to take a break, that's exactly what you do.' She saw his eyes lighten in a smile. 'Got it, Ms Evans?'

'I've got it. If I feel I need to take a rest, I'll give you as much warning as I can. Got that, Mr Harper?' Poppy grinned back at him. They'd disagreed but that was forgotten now.

'Yep.' He looked up, his gaze moving around the assembled team. 'Okay, everyone. We'll take half an hour to see what's what, and then we'll have some music, shall we?'

Poppy would never have put Dylan down as a lover of classical music, his body was made for wilder rhythms. But somehow the soft strains of Bach seemed to suit his precision. The music wasn't loud enough to intrude on the constant to and fro between them, but just enough to help focus their concentration.

'Can you see how far that sliver of bone is embedded?' Once the mess of impact had been cleared, the patient's brain was relatively free of injury, but there was still a long way to go.

'No. It may be deep…' Poppy pointed to the chart that was being updated as each piece of bone was extracted.

With shards this small, it was difficult to tell whether they'd got everything or not.

'That's what I'm thinking. See that gap, right there...' Dylan stopped to study the chart. 'I'm going to take another scan and do some exploratory work. Comfort break, Ms Evans.'

'I could do with one, Mr Harper. I'll be back in half an hour?'

'Make it forty-five minutes.' The use of their surnames was becoming a private joke between them, somehow more intimate than the use of first names. And there *was* intimacy between them now. The understanding of two people who'd found they could work well together, each anticipating the other's every move. There was no manufacturing it. Sometimes it happened in Theatre, and sometimes it didn't. Everyone knew that you accepted it for what it was, and made the most of it when it did happen.

How did he do it? Poppy needed more rest than usual, and Dylan had made sure she took it, but he'd worked without a break. Concentrating for hours on end, performing the most delicate work under both mental and physical stress. Even the strongest and fittest of surgeons needed to take time out during a long procedure, but Dylan seemed tireless.

'Nice one.' He'd carefully extracted the last piece of bone from their patient's brain, and Dylan stood back, flexing his shoulders. 'Don't you need a break, Mr Harper? I'll stay and keep my eye out for any bleeding.'

He thought for a moment. Dylan might push himself, but he wasn't rash, and his patient always came first. 'Ten minutes, Ms Evans.'

'Make it fifteen,' she called after him. 'I'm not going to need you back before then.'

Dylan reckoned that every woman he'd known had taught him something. That was broadly true, although recently there hadn't seemed quite as much to learn. Or maybe he just wasn't so interested in learning it. But this was ridiculous.

Poppy made him feel like a raw recruit in the theatre of life. She was vulnerable and in a bad situation, and she seemed at a loss sometimes. But she still knew how to be strong and she definitely had no difficulty in making her voice heard.

She'd been right when she'd snatched the right to decide whether she could go into Theatre back from him. But she had the grace to know that Dylan had only been trying to protect her and acknowledge that too.

'Okay. I think that's everything now. We'll close?' Having Poppy to refer to at every stage had made him strong. Someone who could see what he saw in a situation and pull him up if she saw something he didn't.

'Yes, I agree. You're going to use a temporary implant?'

Dylan nodded. It would take time to make a new prosthetic covering for the brain and it was necessary to protect it in the meantime. Poppy watched while he carefully finished their work and dressed the wounds. Then he stood back.

'Go well, Craig.' Poppy murmured the words as the patient was wheeled out of the operating theatre. Dylan probably had seen his name written on the board, but he'd taken no notice. He turned to her with a smile and Poppy shrugged.

'They can't hear me, obviously. I just say it.'

Nice. Dylan stretched his aching limbs, wondering if he might come up with a version of it. Something like Poppy's, although he wouldn't steal her exact words.

'Oh.' He heard her catch her breath and looked round. Poppy was leaning forward slightly, clearly trying not to make a fuss.

'Braxton Hicks?' He tried to make the enquiry sound casual.

'Yes. They go pretty quickly and it's not like a proper contraction. More like menstrual cramps.' She looked up at him, grinning. 'You don't have much of a reference point there, do you.'

'No. But I get the general gist of it. Come on. Time to get back to your office and put your feet up. I'll finish up here, and then take you home.'

'I've been sitting down all afternoon…' Poppy slid to the edge of the stool and seemed to stumble slightly as she put her weight onto her legs. Dylan caught her, holding her tight.

'Okay. I've got you.' There were still a few people left in the operating theatre, checking equipment and cleaning up. That made no difference. Dylan wasn't letting go of Poppy.

'So you have. I'm okay, my leg went to sleep.'

'All right, then. Just start walking and I'll stick around until it wakes up.'

Poppy didn't put up a fight. She seemed wobbly and suddenly tired, beyond just pins and needles in her leg, and she clung to him as he supported her to the doors, which swished open as he punched the control. It was the sudden fatigue that hit almost everyone after a long operation was concluded, and Poppy was experiencing it more acutely than usual.

He took her into the de-gowning area and sat her down. She looked up at him, pressing her lips together. 'I suppose you can say it now.'

'What? I told you so? You're the one who proved me wrong. I couldn't have done that procedure without you and you were right, we made it work.'

She grinned. 'Okay. I don't mind if you're nice to me.'

That was a relief, because Dylan didn't have much time. He had to check that Intensive Care had all the information they needed, and then go and see the patient's relatives. Craig's relatives.

'I have to go…' He didn't need to explain all that to Poppy and she nodded. He looked around, seeing the medical student who had been present during the operation.

'Candace, would you help me out, please, and sit with Ms Evans until I get back? Whatever you do, don't let her persuade you that she's okay and you don't need to stay.'

'No, Mr Harper. You can count on me.' Candace sat down next to Poppy.

Poppy raised her eyebrows. 'Don't worry about me, I'm not going to move a muscle. I'll take Candace through some of the points she may have missed during the operation.'

Dylan chuckled. Poppy was unstoppable, and he certainly wasn't up to being the immovable object that could change that. Candace was grinning from ear to ear at the prospect of a senior surgeon's undivided attention for half an hour.

'Great. Good idea.'

CHAPTER SEVEN

POPPY HAD TIDIED up a bit, and even gone to the lengths of giving her flat a more thorough vacuuming than it had received in the last few weeks. Two weeks till Christmas, and with another three weeks to go of her pregnancy, she was suddenly feeling heavier. Maybe she was going to have to take her mum up on the offer to come round for a couple of days when she got back from Germany and help with a spring clean.

All the same, the place looked okay in the low winter sunshine, which slanted through the south-facing windows. It was the first thing she and Nate had seen about this flat—the space that was large enough for a seating area at one end and a dining area at the other, and the way that it flooded with sunlight in the late mornings and early afternoons.

She'd put her laptop, along with a pad and her list of talking points, on the dining table as a nod to the strictly business tone of the morning. Dylan would be here soon, and when he'd said that he could book a conference call with the solicitor who had handled his own agreement with his brother and sister-in-law, Poppy had agreed. It was a nice touch that a family lawyer arranged meetings with people out of work hours and in their own homes, and Poppy hoped that she'd like Vera Chamberlain. Or...she didn't really need to *like* her, just to feel comfortable with her advice.

The doorbell sounded and Poppy picked up the remote, buzzing Dylan in and telling him to come to the sixth floor and turn left. When her own doorbell sounded, she released the lock to let him into the flat.

'Through here,' she called to him and when he appeared in the sitting room Poppy gave him a welcome smile from her armchair. Dylan shed his padded winter jacket and draped it over the back of the sofa, clearly more than happy to shift for himself.

'Glad to see you're putting your feet up today.' He grinned at her. Blue eyes, broad shoulders and the subtle scent of something gorgeous. Poppy tried not to think about any of that.

'Would you like something to drink?' She slid to the front of her seat, ready to stand, and he shook his head.

'Why don't you stay there? If you point me towards the kitchen, I can make the drinks.'

'On the other side of the hallway, back towards the front door. Thanks, mine's a blackberry and apple, please.' Dylan turned and she called after him. 'There are biscuits and some cake in the second cupboard on the left…'

'I'll manage.' He disappeared, leaving the door open, and she heard the sound of kitchen doors opening and closing. Poppy couldn't resist picking up her phone…

'Whoa…'

She heard his exclamation of surprise as the coffee machine started up. Then he appeared in the doorway.

'Is that a robot coffee machine, or just a freak lightning strike?' He pretended to frown at her laughter.

'There's an app.' She held up her phone. 'I filled the machine before you got here.'

'In the interests of scaring the guy who only uses his

phone for telephone calls and the odd photograph?' Dylan was taking it pretty well, grinning broadly now.

'It wasn't premeditated. It only just occurred to me.'

'That makes it okay, then. Crime of passion. Is the kettle going to attack me if I reach for it?'

'You don't need to reach for it, it'll be boiling in...' Poppy picked up her phone, fiddling with it '...one minute. My sister gave me some automatic plugs that you can control with an app for Christmas last year. It's surprising how handy they've become all of a sudden.'

'So if I were to ask whether you want biscuits or cake, do I need to duck while a knife flies across the room?'

'Sadly not. A couple of the lemon cookies would be nice. There's ginger cake in the cupboard as well...'

'Cookies are fine.' He turned back towards the kitchen. 'I'll stick with the no-knives option, just in case...'

Dylan returned with the drinks and sat down. The stupid practical joke, played on a whim, had worked to break the ice. It had been nagging at the back of Poppy's mind that this was the flat that she and Nate had bought together, and now Dylan was here to talk about the baby that she'd wanted with her husband. But she had to face things as they were today, not as they had been.

'Your flat's great. Really roomy for one person...' He pressed his lips together suddenly, as if he'd just realised that he'd said the wrong thing.

'It's okay. You can ask.'

He considered the option for a moment. 'Not my place. Maybe the answer will come up in conversation at some future date.'

Dylan wasn't pushing, although he must want to know.

It occurred to Poppy that it was probably just as difficult for him to come here as it was for her to play host.

'This was the flat that my husband and I bought when we got married. When he died I felt that I couldn't leave, but I didn't really want to stay either. So I decided to wait a while to see how I felt when I got over the shock.'

Dylan nodded.

'I had counselling before I started with the fertility clinic, and that was one of the things I discussed. I don't want a shrine to my husband, I want a home. I had the place redecorated and replaced some of the furniture—the mortgage was paid off by the insurance policy we'd taken out. Nate's still in my heart, but I've made sure that there are no ghosts here any more.'

'That's… It sounds like a good place to be.' He shot her a look which implied several gentle questions.

'It does, doesn't it. I still have my moments but… I just don't want you to think that your being here is making things difficult for me.' That was a little aspirational as well, but it was where Poppy wanted to be. Where she *was* for most of the time.

'To tell you the truth, I was wondering. It's really not my intention to try and take anyone's place, because I know I can't.'

'We'll find our own places, Dylan.'

He nodded. 'Is it my place to notice that you don't appear to have a great deal in your fridge?'

'I sent you into the kitchen, so I can hardly say *no*, can I?' All the same, Poppy wished he hadn't. This sudden slowing down had caught her unawares and she was a little embarrassed. 'I'm buying little and often at the moment.'

'Make a list. I'll go out and get some shopping, after we've spoken with Vera.'

No *Would you mind* or *If you want*. Dylan had taken everything she'd said on board, and Poppy was in no position to argue if he was exploring a little, to find out what his place might be. She didn't much want to argue, because a line of shopping bags on the kitchen counter sounded like pure heaven at the moment. Independence could wait until after the baby was born.

Vera had explained everything to them, and Dylan was pleased to see that her common sense and down-to-earth approach obviously impressed Poppy. Then came Vera's questions, which in Dylan's experience were generally very much to the point.

'Dylan, I'm seeing an inconsistency here. On one hand you're keen to sign an agreement that gives you no rights or responsibilities. But you also say that you wish to be a part of this child's life.'

'I need to earn that.' Dylan realised that this was the first time he'd said it so bluntly. In the window that displayed their images on the screen, he saw Poppy turn suddenly, and look at him.

'You don't think you already have?' Poppy's murmured words felt like a dagger of sunlight, plunged straight into his heart.

'It takes longer than a few weeks.'

This was what he needed. If he could prove himself then he wouldn't feel so guilty about hoping that Poppy would want to give a little more.

Vera pursed her lips, clearly setting the matter aside for the moment. The opinion on the confidentiality agreement was more straightforward, and Poppy spoke for them both. Once Vera had reassured herself that Dylan felt the same way, she told them that she would write to the clinic on their behalf and deal with the matter. End of story. She added her own warm wishes for the baby, told a joke about the birth of her first child, who was now a father of two himself, and they were left with the image of her smile as she briskly ended the video call.

Poppy leaned back in her seat, rubbing her back. 'Nice lady.'

Dylan nodded. 'Yeah. She can be ferocious when she wants.'

Poppy laughed. 'Oh, I got that. Are we sure that we want to set her on the clinic? They've been really good to me…'

'She'll handle it. Vera knows how to apply a velvet glove approach—the iron fist only appears if she sees her clients being bamboozled into something.' Dylan valued Poppy's instinct to be kind, but she needed to stop worrying. 'We're not on our own with this any more, Vera will come back to us and propose a way forward.'

'Yes. Good.' Poppy got to her feet, walking over to the sofa and sitting down, a look of pure bliss on her face. Dylan caught up her writing pad and a pencil from the table.

'Now we can worry about the list, eh? Or shall I just visit the kitchen again and look in all your cupboards?' The smiling threat was enough to make Poppy comply, and she started to reel off a list of everything she needed.

Poppy ordered the list in food groups—fruit, vegetables, dairy… That was probably the order that Dylan would find them in the local supermarket she'd suggested as well. But she'd missed out one thing…

'Anything for Christmas? Before the shelves empty out?'

She shook her head. 'No, that's all sorted. Mum's already got everything organised, and her next-door neighbour will take in the last-minute shopping while they're away in Germany. Dad's going to come and pick me up on Christmas Eve.'

'Any other bits and pieces? Decorations?' It was impossible for Dylan to look pointedly at Poppy's Christmas decorations because there weren't any, so he'd just have to say it.

'I meant to get a tree last weekend, but things caught up on me a bit. I'll give it a miss this year, I think, and have a really great one for next year.' She turned her mouth down in an expression of regret, which was quickly replaced with a smile. 'Baby's first Christmas tree, eh?'

The baby was going to be well provided for, if his nephew's first Christmas was anything to go by. Right now, Dylan was more concerned with *this* Christmas and with Poppy. But he sensed he was approaching Poppy's hard limits in terms of daily offers of help, and that he should leave her in peace and go to the supermarket. Tomorrow might be another matter, but he'd meet that challenge when it came…

From the antiseptic scent that had pervaded the kitchen when he'd left yesterday afternoon, Dylan had done some surreptitious cleaning. Poppy resisted the temptation to text him to remind him that they hadn't yet negotiated any rights concerning household chores, because she appreciated the gesture. And there was something about sparkling clean appliances, a full fridge, and the thought that Vera was on their side, which allowed her to relax for the evening.

And then, late on Sunday morning, her phone had rung.

Dylan had said he was in the area, and asked whether he might pop in. Poppy had gulped down the quiver of excitement at the thought of seeing him again, replied in the affirmative, and then Dylan had ended the call. Clearly his approach to the telephone was much the same as his attitude to email, and he had nothing more to say.

'Any ideas what he might be up to now?' Poppy wasn't really expecting an answer. If she didn't know, she doubted her baby girl would. Maybe she should tidy up a bit, but standing up just to put the TV remote away seemed too much effort for too little reward. She was at least up and dressed, and had finished breakfast, and that was going to have to do.

The doorbell rang. His definition of *in the area* was clearly parked outside in the street. Poppy heard Dylan's voice on the intercom and buzzed him in.

He was a long time making his way upstairs. Poppy opened her front door, looking out, and saw the lift doors open.

'Dylan!' He was wearing a bright grin and holding a Christmas tree, tied up in netting. Poppy felt her heart lurch. The effort of manoeuvring a large tree out of a small lift without scratching the wooden panelling emphasised his strong body and although his intention was clearly that the tree would promote delight, she only had eyes for him.

'Stand back,' he instructed unnecessarily. 'Don't try lifting it.'

Poppy rolled her eyes. Independence was one thing, but carrying Christmas trees quite another. Dylan strode back to the lift, where he'd left a large bag, and just as he picked it up the doors closed on him. Poppy watched as the indicator lights showed the lift travelling steadily down to the ground floor and then pausing before it made its way back up to the fifth.

'Did someone call it?' she asked as he emerged.

'There was no one there…' He put the bag inside her front door and then came back to where Poppy was standing by the tree.

'That lift looks really good, but it has a mind of its own.' Poppy shrugged.

'Suits you down to the ground, then.' Dylan picked up the tree and Poppy stood back as he manoeuvred it along the hallway.

'I'll take that as a compliment,' she called after him. A very nice compliment, because right now she felt heavy and awkward and the idea of looking good was the last thing that occurred to her.

'That's just as it was intended.' He got the tree through her front door and laid it down in the hall. Poppy followed him, shutting her front door behind them, the feeling of excitement that was rising in her chest not entirely focused on Christmas decorations.

Now that he wasn't fighting to get a large bag and a Christmas tree under control, Dylan was suddenly still and uncertain. Maybe he had his doubts about this.

'Do you mind? I can take it away if you don't want it…'

'Don't you dare, Dylan!' Poppy put herself between him and the tree. 'You'll have to go through me first before you lay one finger on this tree.'

He laughed, his face brightening. 'You like it?'

'No, I don't like it. I love it, and it was a really kind thought.'

'Good.' He turned away quickly, as if to disguise his reaction. 'Where do you want it to go?'

Poppy chose a spot in between the living and dining area, by the window. Dylan opened the bag, drawing out a tree stand, and fixed it securely in place, and then removed the netting. It was a great tree, a little bigger than the ones she'd had before, and she wondered whether her lights would stretch far enough to reach the top, but Dylan had thought of that as well. He had a box of lights in the bag along with some extra baubles, glass and gold, which would match anything. He fetched her box of decorations from the walk-in cupboard in the hall, and Poppy laid them all out on the dining table in order.

'Your decorations are lovely. Each one has a memory?'

It didn't sound like a casual enquiry, and Poppy chose her words carefully. 'These were the ones I bought for my first tree.' She pointed to a set of glass icicles. 'I seem to break one of them every year, but it doesn't matter since I started off with quite a lot of them. The wooden ones are from the Christmas market close to where my sister lives in Cologne, I got them the first year she moved out there. My mum made the fairy for me.'

'She's great.' Dylan picked up the porcelain-faced fairy, dressed in white satin with sequinned netting. 'A very special lady.'

There was no point in pretending there was nothing of Nate here. 'I bought these for the first Christmas after I was married. I was trying for a more sophisticated feel to the tree.' She laid her fingers on the sparkling white snowballs.

'They should have pride of place,' Dylan murmured.

'There's room for everything, these will be beautiful with the lights.' Poppy reached for one of the glass baubles that Dylan had brought. 'They're the ones that I'll have on my pregnancy Christmas tree.'

He smiled, clearly happy with the idea. 'I'll put the lights on, shall I? Then you can hang some of the decorations, if you want.'

'Without mince pies and hot chocolate? Dylan, whatever are you thinking?' He'd added a box of mince pies to her shopping list yesterday.

He chuckled. 'Okay. You can heat the mince pies while I make a start on the lights...'

It took two hours to decorate the tree. Poppy spent a good deal of that time on the sofa while Dylan dealt with the top and bottom branches, but she insisted on helping with the middle ones that she could reach easily. Finally, Dylan carefully secured the fairy, moving her arms so that her wand was pointing in the direction of the sofa, which Poppy took as a hint. He cleared the boxes away, then re-appeared from the storeroom with the vacuum cleaner to get rid of the fallen needles and sparkle on the carpet.

'Can you stay for something to eat? It'll be dark soon and we can have a grand switching on of the lights.' Poppy hoped that Dylan could stay a little longer, she didn't want this to end. But he'd spent a good proportion of his week-end here and surely he had somewhere else to go. Some-*one* else to spend his evening with.

'That would be great, thank you. Unless you want to take a nap?'

'If I fall asleep you can wake me. I'm too excited to miss anything.'

The afternoon had been everything that Dylan could have wished for. He couldn't bear the idea of Poppy going with-out a proper tree, after all the Christmases when his mother had gone out to find fallen branches in the park and meticulously painted and arranged them before hanging baubles on them. He and Sam had always told her that it was better than a boring old Christmas tree, but they all knew that it wasn't. The bare twigs were a symbol of everything they'd lost.

But Poppy had liked her tree. She'd accepted the baubles that he'd brought, making them something special in his eyes. And she'd hung the ones that reminded her of her husband, rather than hiding them away. It was all good.

She was tired now, though, and after they'd eaten she'd gone to sit down, while Dylan stacked the dishwasher. When he came back into the lounge, she'd rolled over onto her side and was snoring gently.

Maybe he should go. Or maybe wake her up, so that she could switch the lights of her Christmas tree on. Dylan sat in the darkening room, trying to make his mind up, and then Poppy shifted sleepily on the sofa.

'Uh… Sorry. I wasn't snoring, was I?'

'Only a little. I mistook it for the sound of angels singing.' Dylan chuckled as Poppy sat up straight, shooting him an indignant look.

'Come over here. I want to wash your mouth out with soap.'

She could do whatever she liked to him, as long as she was happy.

'Later. Don't you want to switch the lights on first?'

'Oh! Yes!' She was suddenly as excited as Thomas always was at the prospect. Poppy got to her feet, walking over to the tree, and Dylan caught up the remote for the lights and followed her.

'Right, then. Three…two…one… It's *Christmas*!'

Poppy flipped the button on the remote and the tree lit

up. She waved her arms and began to cheer, and he followed suit. This really was Christmas. The way it should be, with the prospect of a new life and tenuous new hope tugging at him.

'It's beautiful, Dylan. Thank you so much.' Poppy turned suddenly, her hand on his shoulder pulling him down so that she could plant a kiss on his cheek.

He was powerless to resist her. Shaking suddenly from the feel of her lips brushing his skin. Her gaze met his and an action that might easily pass between friends became something that could only be shared between lovers.

'Happy Christmas, Poppy. Who knows what next year's going to bring, eh…?' It could be anything. A thousand different sensations that he'd never allowed himself to feel before.

It was both terrifying and compelling. Because one touch of Poppy's fingers, a brief kiss, had made him feel all of the things he knew he ought to feel for a woman. So much more than he'd ever felt before. If they wanted to call it friendship then he would, for Poppy's sake. But Dylan knew exactly what friendship looked and felt like, it was something he'd always treasured. This wasn't the same.

She smiled. 'I guess we'll just have to find out, won't we. Happy Christmas, Dylan.'

He longed for her lips, but they were very dangerous territory right now. And the thought this this would be the first of many Christmases—another departure from his usual modus operandi—brought him to his senses. He reached for her hand, pressing a kiss lightly on the back of her fingers. These old-fashioned marks of regard were underrated, because it felt like everything.

And he could see that *everything* in her eyes. Her face,

streaked with light from the tree, tilted up towards him. Her hand lingered in his for a few moments more than it had to, and he felt the warm pressure of her fingers sending shivers up his spine. Somehow, he knew that she was feeling that same delicious pleasure.

He drew back at almost exactly the same moment she did. This wasn't in their agreement, and Dylan knew that feeling was no excuse for doing. His head was scrambling back over the line he'd crossed, even if his heart begged for more.

'Do you have to go home and do your own decorations now?' Her smile still had the hint of that special moment, which was now beyond their grasp. And Poppy always seemed so keen not to take too much of his time for herself.

'No, mine are already done. There's a company who sneak in while you're at work and put your tree and your decorations up for you.'

Her hand flew to her mouth. 'No! That's awful!' She turned the corners of her mouth down. 'I mean…very useful for a busy person. You could have just given me their number, though.'

No, he couldn't. Being here had meant far too much to him.

'They get booked up very quickly. And just in case you were wondering… No, I don't have a date tonight either.'

He could see from the look on her face that she *had* been wondering. She turned away from him suddenly, walking back to the sofa.

'I've been thinking about…what Vera said.'

Vera had said a lot of things. Dylan knew exactly which thing Poppy meant, because he'd been thinking about it too. He'd been all in favour of the idea that Poppy should have full custody of her daughter, not just for their sakes but for his as well, and at the same time pleaded for her to allow him to be part of their lives. Vera had seen the inconsistency and now Poppy did too.

And she'd been so upfront about the way she felt, going out of her way to reassure him that their relationship could take its own course and was quite separate from the one with her husband.

'Should we talk?' Dylan couldn't help framing that as a question, even if there was no doubt in his mind. 'About… where I'm coming from in all of this?'

She nodded firmly. 'Yes. I'd like to know, Dylan.'

CHAPTER EIGHT

DYLAN HAD BEEN putting this off. He made tea for Poppy, and she went through the smiling joke of sniffing his coffee. Perhaps she knew that it was difficult to find somewhere to start.

'You have a Christmas grinch somewhere in your past?' She'd clearly decided that he needed a bit of a nudge, and Dylan smiled.

'Yeah, I guess. My father left my mother when Sam and I were eleven. He'd been having an affair with someone at his office, a divorcee with a child.'

'I guess that messed up Christmas,' Poppy prompted him gently.

'It messed up everything. My mum hadn't seen it coming and she was devastated. So sad… I didn't help her much. I started to cut school and generally act up. My father had always been a bit of a role model for me.'

'Isn't that how it should be? For an eleven-year-old boy?'

Dylan shrugged. 'Maybe. I chose the wrong person. My father seemed like someone you could rely on, but that was only because it suited him. After he left, it was very much a matter of *out of sight, out of mind.* All his attention went to his new partner and her child.'

A tear rolled down Poppy's cheek. 'I'm so sorry, Dylan. That must have been devastating for you.'

'Much more so for my mum. She was determined to be there for me and Sam when we got home from school, but she had to get a part-time job just to make ends meet. My father had obviously been planning this for some time, he had his own business and his new partner was an employee, so there was room for some creative accounting. He paid very little child maintenance.'

Poppy shook her head. 'So you and your brother probably didn't have all that much at Christmas.'

'Not much that you need money for. Mum made the best of everything and went without herself. Things got better, Mum got a full-time job when Sam and I were older, and when we both went to university we agreed to pool what money we had and give Mum the Christmas she deserved. We got a tree and some nice presents for her, and cooked lunch. Imagine two eighteen-year-old lads in a kitchen…'

'I'm sure she loved it. However you did.'

'Actually, we didn't do too badly. We got together and planned it down to the last moment. Mum had to intervene a couple of times, but mostly we did it ourselves. Sam nearly singed his eyebrows, he was a bit too generous with the brandy on the Christmas pudding, but apart from that we had no casualties.'

Poppy chuckled, leaning forward to reach her mug and take a sip of her tea. Still waiting. She was sometimes a bit too perceptive, and she knew that this wasn't just a guided tour of his Christmases past.

'I can't commit, Poppy. I think of all the promises my father broke, all of the pain he caused, and it just terrifies me.'

She regarded him steadily. 'But from what I hear you say about your brother… What makes you think that you're like your father and not him?'

Good question.

'Sam and I are alike, we're both pretty certain about not making promises we can't keep. He knows for sure that he can keep his promises to Sophie and Thomas.'

'He's had the time to think that all through, though, hasn't he. I've had time to think through exactly what I want with this pregnancy. You really haven't.'

Dylan nodded. Maybe he'd found something in Poppy that he'd been looking for all his life, but he couldn't be sure. And his fears were bearing down on him, too heavy a weight to resist.

'You don't often find that thing that Sam and Sophie have.'

'I think I see it now. You don't want to sign up for something you think you may not be able to fulfil…' Poppy thought for a moment. 'But Thomas…?'

She'd done him the favour of listening, and responding without judgement.

Dylan smiled. 'I'm his uncle. I make a really good job of that.'

'Okay. I get it. This is somewhere for us to start from, and we can work out how we want things to be as we go. I just wanted to know that you weren't doing all of this because you felt you had to.'

'I don't. It's what I want, Poppy.'

She nodded, smiling at him. 'Well, the baby loves your Christmas tree.'

Dylan threw her a sceptical look. 'And you know that how?'

'She makes her presence felt. Sometimes she kicks and moves around and sometimes she's calm. When we switched the lights on I felt her almost dancing with excitement.'

Just the way Poppy had been. He wanted so much to ask—to lay his hand on her stomach and feel the baby kick. But that seemed a step too far.

Then Poppy reached out, taking his hand. 'You want to feel her?'

'Do you really have to ask?'

She shook her head, laughing. Poppy put his hand onto her stomach and he felt nothing. No movement. He wondered whether he should take his hand away, lifting it slightly.

'No, stay there. But more pressure.' Poppy clasped her hands over his, pushing a little. Then he felt it.

'Whoa! Does she do that all the time?'

'No, that was a big one. I think she's settling down again. Maybe she knows it's you.'

The idea hovered in the air, shining and magical. And then Dylan tore it down, unable to contemplate it. 'She feels someone.'

'She can hear voices—she's been able to hear mine for ages now. And yours is lower, she responds differently.' Poppy gave him a searching look. 'Before I was pregnant, I knew all about babies because I'm a doctor. I've learned a great deal more since.'

Dylan nodded. As long as Poppy allowed him to keep his hand right there and feel his daughter kick, he didn't much care whether the baby knew it was him or not. Just that she knew it was someone who loved her.

'Do you have a name for her yet?'

'I did think of a few when I first knew it was a girl. I couldn't work out which might suit her best, and thought I'd make up my mind when I got the chance to meet her face to face.'

'Good idea.' Maybe he'd get the chance to be there when Poppy did that. Be one of the first to call the baby by name. That was unlikely. By the time the baby was born, Poppy's family would be back in England and they'd be the ones to witness those first momentous decisions.

There was something more he could do, though. If Poppy took pleasure in it, then maybe their baby girl would feel that. He took his hand from her stomach, bidding a silent *See you later* to his daughter.

'I saw a box of other decorations in your hall cupboard. Tinsel and greenery. Were you thinking of using them this year?'

Poppy laughed. 'I'd come to the conclusion I wouldn't be using any of it. I usually put those around the fireplace.'

'I could… You could tell me where you want everything…' Dylan shrugged, leaving the offer as open as he could so that Poppy could say no if she wanted to.

'Yes, Dylan, thank you! That would be wonderful…'

Sleeping well wasn't really an option these days, but Poppy had gone to bed early and, apart from the now regular trips to the bathroom, she'd stayed there for some time. All the same, just getting to work was an increasing effort, even if her first glimpse of the decorations in the sitting room buoyed her.

There was an oat and banana muffin hidden away behind her printer. It got her through three pre-op consultations, carefully explaining to each patient what to expect, and checking on their condition. Then the fourth…

Mrs Wise had wobbled into the hospital with the aid of her walking stick, and someone had taken the precaution of putting her into a wheelchair. She had a relatively small meningioma, and its position didn't account for her unsteady gait. Poppy could see in the notes that Dylan had referred her to Orthopaedics but, as far as she knew, ancient Tyrolean walking sticks weren't standard issue.

'I see that Mr Harper referred you down to Orthopaedics.' Poppy peered at the screen in front of her. 'For your knee?'

'Yes, that's right. When you get to my age you always seem to have more than one thing at a time. They're going to keep an eye on it.'

'Okay. It says here they've given you some exercises to do.' Poppy was mentally measuring the distance between the desk and the couch, and wondering how she was going to carry out an examination without one of them falling on the floor.

'Yes, dear. I do them every day. Are you looking forward to the baby?'

'Yes.' Poppy decided not to elaborate. It was Mrs Wise's condition that they were supposed to be discussing.

'Is it your first? My Keith was a difficult birth, you know...'

Poppy didn't much want to hear it. Childbirth stories from forty years ago weren't her favourite subject at the moment. 'I'm fine, Mrs Wise, thank you. This appointment is for us to discuss how *you* are...'

Mrs Wise leaned forward. 'Boy or girl?'

Enough! Reaching for her phone might be an unwelcome sign that she couldn't cope. Right now, Poppy didn't care because examining Mrs Wise was going to involve an obvious breach of Health and Safety guidelines.

'Just a moment, Mrs Wise.' She couldn't help a sigh of

relief as Dylan answered his phone. 'Mr Harper, do you have ten minutes, please?'

There was a short pause as Dylan assessed the situation. Then, 'Yep. What's up?'

'Mrs Wise is here. Since you're the surgeon who'll be carrying out her meningioma procedure next week, I wondered if you might like to pop up and see her.' Poppy added as much information as she could.

'On my way...'

Poppy managed to steer Mrs Wise away from any potential medical issues surrounding the birth, and stuck with telling her that she didn't have a name for her baby girl just yet. Then a knock sounded on the door, and Dylan appeared. His eyes travelled from the wheelchair to the examination couch, and he gave a small nod.

'Mrs Wise.' He sat down in the chair next to her. 'Remember me? I'm Dylan Harper and I saw you last time you were here. I'll be carrying out your procedure next week.'

'I remember. Hello, Doctor.' Mrs Wise smiled politely. At least she wasn't calling Dylan *dear*. Poppy turned her computer screen towards him so that he could see it.

'I referred you down to Orthopaedics, didn't I? Have you seen anyone there yet?'

'Yes, they were very good. Very nice. I have exercises.' Mrs Wise beamed at Dylan.

'And they gave you a walking frame?' That wasn't a particularly inspired guess, it would have been an obvious move.

'Yes, but I left it at home. I prefer my stick.'

Dylan regarded the stick with interest. 'It's a nice one. Where did you get it?'

'My late husband brought it home from a walking holiday when he was eighteen. We used to walk everywhere together, you know, and he always took his stick.'

Poppy could identify with that. She'd used Nate's things, worn his sweaters at first, just for the comfort they'd brought. Then she'd made a resolution and gone through everything, saving some things as mementos and giving the rest to the charity shop.

'I understand.' Dylan looked up at her when she spoke, his blue eyes suddenly thoughtful. 'It's a very precious thing, isn't it.'

'Yes, Doctor.'

'Then I think you should keep it at home, where it won't be lost or broken, and you'll always have it to remember him by. The walking frame is just something to help you, it doesn't matter if it gets damaged.'

Mrs Wise thought for a moment. 'Yes, I think you're right. I'll do that.'

'That's great.' Dylan shot a smile in Poppy's direction and then turned his attention to Mrs Wise. 'Now, I'll just help you over to the examination couch and check you over to make sure everything's as it should be before your operation. Then you can go home, and I'll see you next week.'

'Yes, Doctor. Thank you.'

Dylan was perfect. Smiling and authoritative, with a trace of mischief in his blue eyes that seemed to indicate he was on his patient's side as he checked her reflexes and reviewed her scans. Anyone would fall for him. He helped her down from the couch, installing her safely back in the wheelchair.

'Right, then. Everything's as it should be, Mrs Wise. I think we'll organise some hospital transport to get you home, shall we? Unless that's already sorted out.'

Mrs Wise shook her head. 'I came on the bus. I didn't want to be any trouble.'

Somehow, Dylan managed not to roll his eyes. 'It's no trouble. Making sure you get home safely is one of the things we're here for. I'll just wheel you out and speak to the receptionist, and she'll look after you.'

Mrs Wise gave Poppy a cheery wave, wishing her all the luck in the world with the baby, and Poppy grinned at her, telling she didn't need any luck for her operation next week because Mr Harper was the best surgeon in the department. She caught a flash of Dylan's blue-eyed smile before he turned, manoeuvring the wheelchair through the door.

'Thanks, Dylan. Was that your lunch break, or can I buy you lunch?' Poppy was feeling a little annoyed with herself that she'd had to call him for help, even if it had been the obvious right thing to do.

'I've only got fifteen minutes. You can buy me lunch tomorrow if you like.' He sat down in the chair on the other side of her desk, clearly willing to spend that valuable time with her.

'I'm seeing a new side of you. Charming all your patients…' Poppy shifted in her seat, trying to get comfortable again.

'Really?' He flashed her an amused look. 'Are you suggesting that I switch on the charm to get what I want?'

'Face it, Dylan. You can be charming and you wanted to get through to her for her own good. I'm just seeing a different side of you now, one that doesn't get much of an airing at meetings and in the operating theatre.'

'Ah. That's all right then. I'd hate to think that it was my principal contribution to the department.' He was teasing, but there was a wry edge to his humour. Poppy had heard the way the nurses talked about him, and she'd be annoyed if any of the male members of staff said those things about her.

'I've always respected you as a fine surgeon. Now that I've got to know you out of work, I appreciate your charm. Getting through to people is a thing as well.'

His lips twitched as if he was trying not to make too much of the compliment. 'Thank you.'

'You're welcome.' Poppy decided to change the subject. 'I'm going to have to slow down a bit, aren't I? Not being able to operate until after the baby's born is one thing, but if I need to call someone in to help with consultations then I'm becoming a liability.'

'Liability's a bit harsh. But you're less than three weeks from your due date, and maybe it's time to think about spending some time at home.' He smiled suddenly. 'Ideally, of course, you'd go into labour around lunchtime, have the baby and then be back at work the following morning.'

Poppy chuckled. 'You know that's not going to happen, don't you? I'm really looking forward to my maternity leave, and spending some time with our little girl.'

Slip of the tongue. Poppy had caught herself thinking of her baby as Dylan's child too, and the idea had escaped into the open air now.

If he heard it, he said nothing. That was good, because Poppy didn't entirely know how she felt about it.

'I'm looking forward to seeing her.' His gaze was scanning her face, looking for a reaction.

'You can come and see her any time you like.' Poppy had told him that often enough, but Dylan always seemed to want to hear it one more time. 'You can bring whatever you like as well. Supplies from the supermarket. You could bring coffee, even. For me, that is, not her…'

He chuckled. 'Aren't you supposed to stay off the coffee after she's born?'

'For the most part. I can have a cup a day, as long as it's not right before I feed her.'

'Ah. Well, you can call and demand emergency coffee any time you like. Day or night. As long as I'm not working, of course.'

'Careful what you wish for, Dylan,' Poppy teased him.

'I am.' Dylan murmured the words but there was no doubt in her mind that he meant them. It was hard thinking of him as the man she might rely on, but when she looked into his clear blue eyes it became frighteningly easy.

He looked at his watch. 'I've got to go. I've got a surgery scheduled. If I leave my charm behind on your desk, would you look after it?'

Poppy chuckled. 'Of course. I'll give it a saucer of milk and lock the door in case it escapes.'

He laughed, making his way to the door. 'Get something to eat. Sounds as if your blood sugar's beginning to drop.'

Dylan closed the door behind him, and suddenly the room felt darker. Poppy wriggled in her seat, trying to get comfortable, and then decided to get up and walk a little. Pacing seemed like a good idea right now.

Spending more time at home would be hard. She'd miss her morning muffins—she could hardly expect Dylan to deliver them to her flat. And she'd miss the reassurance of seeing him every day, even if it was just a fleeting glimpse of his smile, or catching sight of him at the far end of a corridor. Letting herself flirt with him from time to time.

But then, when she got back home she'd see the photograph of her and Nate's wedding, sitting next to the plant he'd come home with the day before he'd died, which Poppy had nurtured so carefully in the weeks and months after she'd lost him. And she'd feel guilty about wanting to be with Dylan because she and Nate had been so happy, made so many promises, only a few of which they'd had time to keep.

Poppy knew what Nate would say about that. They'd talked about it once, feeling safe in the knowledge that all their what-ifs were never going to happen. Nate would want her to move on and live her life. But she'd disagreed with him then, and it seemed wrong not to afford him the respect of disagreeing with him now.

Moving on and living your life was a lot easier to say than it was to do… But the baby was moving on and so was her body. Dylan's suggestion that she slowed down was a good one, and it was time she listened to it.

CHAPTER NINE

DYLAN HAD TEXTED HER, saying he couldn't make lunch on Tuesday, and so Poppy had conceded to the inevitable and gone to see the head of Neurology instead. He'd suggested that she confine herself to seeing patients in the morning and go home in the early afternoon for the rest of the week, and since she'd be taking time off over Christmas anyway it made sense for her to start her maternity leave officially next week. The department would miss her but they'd cope and he already had a replacement lined up, who would be able to cover Christmas and the New Year.

It was sooner than she'd expected, but Poppy could see the sense in it. Someone who was able to take on her usual workload would make staffing over the holidays much easier, and she'd started to feel the strain of needing to be at work every day. Poppy had reluctantly agreed to the plan.

She'd texted Dylan to tell him, and he'd sent back a smile. Clearly, he was busy, and she shouldn't be needy when he had patients to attend to. And, for this week at least, she still had morning muffins, a different flavour every time. On Friday there had been a note attached to the bag, saying that he could leave work a little early to take her home, if she would wait for him, and Poppy had texted back to thank him. Several heavy hints from Maisie at Reception had told her that there would be goodbyes to say at lunchtime, and she could spend the rest of the afternoon packing up her personal belongings.

There had been cake, and a whip-round had afforded presents for both Poppy and the baby. Poppy had cried when she'd read the messages in the large card, and spent the next two hours thanking everyone, as people dropped in and then left again to go back to work.

At three o'clock, Maisie had taken care of the paper plates and cups and the empty soft drinks bottles and her office was spick and span again, apart from some chocolate cake which had been trodden into the carpet. Poppy was sitting with her feet up on the empty box that she was supposed to be taking her personal belongings home in when a knock sounded on the door and Kate burst in.

'Sorreee…! Sorry I missed your party, honey.'

Poppy smiled. 'I know you would have made it if you could. Busy down in A&E?'

'Frantic. But I've got fifteen minutes to myself now, and I came up to see if you were still here.'

'You haven't got rid of me quite yet. Dylan's operating today, but he's going to take me home afterwards in the car.' Poppy tapped the box with her foot. 'I've still got to pack my things up. Do you want some cake? I saved you some.'

'You star. Yes, please. I haven't had anything since breakfast.'

'Have some of my tea, I don't really want it.' Poppy pushed the freshly made cup of herbal tea across her desk and took a large foil-wrapped slice of cake from her desk drawer.

'Mmm. Thanks.' Kate unwrapped the cake, beaming at it. 'You've been seeing a bit of Dylan lately.'

'Yes. I should tell you…'

Kate held up her hand. 'You don't need to explain. I don't listen to gossip and it's your business.'

Poppy wanted to tell someone, and Kate was her closest friend. 'It's okay. I want you to know. There was a mix-up at the fertility clinic. Dylan's the father of my baby.'

Kate lost interest in the cake, staring at her open-mouthed. 'It's true, then. What's Dylan doing donating sperm? He's already seduced half the hospital.'

'Not *half*...' Poppy turned the corners of her mouth down, regretting that this had been one of her first thoughts, too.

'Okay. A good proportion of the single women under thirty-five. And it's a big place.'

'He had his reasons, Kate.' Poppy didn't feel comfortable talking about Dylan's nephew. 'And this wasn't his fault any more than it's mine—he's been really good about it. I have full custody and responsibility for my baby, just as I wanted, and he's...he says he'd like to help out. As a friend. He'll be her uncle, just as you're going to be her Auntie Kate.'

'Hmm. Sounds cosy.' Kate took a sip of tea, looking at Poppy thoughtfully.

'Give him a chance.' Poppy frowned at her friend. It wasn't like Kate to be so negative about people. 'He's been there for me. He leaves breakfast muffins in my office every morning.'

Kate nodded. Poppy knew that would impress her. 'Where from?'

'Don't worry, they're not all fats and sugar—he gets most of them from the health food restaurant.'

'Hmm. Better than a *Thinking of you* text, I suppose. You do know he's seeing someone?'

Of course Dylan was seeing someone. By all accounts, he was rarely without a partner, however uncommitted those relationships were. It didn't mean anything. Dylan had told her how he felt about commitment. That didn't mean he couldn't love their baby when she was born.

'Yes, I know. I told you, Kate, we're friends. I don't want anyone else, not after Nate.'

Kate turned the corners of her mouth down. 'You and Nate were special. Just as long as Dylan respects that, and he's being straight with you. Not stringing you along with muffins and promises. The ones from the health food place are enough to turn anyone's head.'

'It's okay, really. We've sorted everything out between us, and Dylan's done a lot to make sure that everything's the way I wanted it. Who's he seeing?' The question slipped out.

'So you *didn't* know...?'

'I knew. I don't know who.'

'Jeannie from Orthopaedics. I saw them in the canteen together, very wrapped up in whatever they were saying. I happened to walk out behind them...' Kate shrugged as Poppy raised her eyebrows. 'I did really just happen to finish at the same time they did. Dylan had his arm around her as they got into the lift and, just as the doors closed, I saw them hug each other. It wasn't a friendly hug either.'

'You were taking notes?'

'No, of course not. Don't be obtuse, Poppy. We all know the difference between a *See you later* hug and a *See you later between the sheets* one.'

'When was this?'

'Tuesday. I thought you said you knew?'

'I did. In general terms.' Although Tuesday... That felt

a bit like a slap in the face because Dylan had cancelled lunch with Poppy to meet Jeannie.

And Poppy *knew* Jeannie, she wasn't just an anonymous name. Tall and willowy, with long dark hair… Poppy didn't want to think about her blue eyes, or that Dylan might find them just as mesmerising as his own were. Or her easy-going nature, which had to be a relief after all that she and Dylan had been through recently.

Time for a change of subject. Poppy had been quite clear that she didn't want to get in the way of Dylan's love life, and she needed to swallow down whatever she felt now and stick to the plan. She didn't want Kate to think badly of him either, they might be bumping into each other at her place after the baby was born.

'It's not a problem, Kate. I'm more interested in you and Jon. How are things going?'

'Good. Really good, actually. You were right—the problems we've been having aren't because there's anything basically wrong, it's just that we never get to see each other with Jon working nights. He's on days again now for the next five weeks and he's going to ask about making that permanent.'

Poppy nodded. 'They're sure to agree. Jon's a really valuable member of staff and they won't risk losing him. He just needs to be a bit less accommodating about what everyone else wants.'

'Yeah.' Kate's fingers strayed to her engagement ring. 'When I got home last night there was a trail of rose petals leading upstairs and he was running me a hot bath. And we're spending the weekend at a hotel in Hampshire, it's a really nice place.'

'Fantastic. Where did Jon get rose petals from at this time of year?'

Kate rolled her eyes. 'Trust me, honey, that was the last thing on my mind at the time…'

It had been a long week. Dylan had been busy and he'd missed Poppy's goodbye party, but he made it up to her office at four o'clock, after spending six hours in the operating theatre.

'How did it go?' Poppy was reclining in her office chair and gave him a smile.

'Well.' The surgery had taken longer than he'd anticipated, but he was pleased with the results. 'I've spoken with the relatives—are you okay to stay another half hour while I check on the patient in Recovery?'

'As long as you like. I've boxed up all my stuff now, and it'll take me a good half hour to make a quick tour of the department and say goodbye to everyone.' She produced a bottle of water from her empty desk drawer, smiling up at him. 'Sit down for a moment, you look tired.'

He didn't feel tired, but that would hit him later on, probably after he got Poppy back to her flat and settled in. But she knew that he'd be thirsty and he sat down, taking the bottle gratefully.

'I saved you some cake as well. I had such a beautiful card, and such thoughtful gifts.'

Water first. Dylan took a long swig from the bottle, nodding to indicate that was just what he needed. Then he looked inside one of the gift bags on Poppy's desk. There were things for the baby, some sleepsuits in various sizes and a warm quilted snowsuit.

'This is very cute.' He pulled the snowsuit out of the bag, examining the three penguins embroidered on the front.

'Isn't it. And look, they got something for me, too. It's my favourite scent.' Poppy's tone was a little flat, her smile not as glowing as usual. Maybe she was just tired, and needed to get home after what must have been an emotional day for her.

But she pushed the second gift bag across the desk towards him and Dylan looked at the bottles inside. Body lotion, hand cream and scent, an expensive brand. Poppy was gorgeous just as she was, but this gift was a little luxury, designed to make her feel that way. He wished he'd thought of it.

'It's lovely.' Dylan thought he saw tears in her eyes when he looked up but she dabbed them away quickly. Today had been more taxing for Poppy than he'd thought. 'I'm sorry I couldn't be there for your party.'

'It's okay. We're not joined at the hip. We have our own lives.'

Maybe Poppy had been having doubts. They'd seemed so close last weekend, and Dylan couldn't deny that it had given him pause for thought. He would never abandon his child, he was sure of that, but he needed also to think about a sustainable relationship with Poppy. He'd been so careful with words, never promising anything he wasn't sure he could deliver, but maybe he needed to be a little more careful with his actions.

'I can take your box down to the car and we can meet outside. Whatever you're more comfortable with.'

'You're giving me a lift home, Dylan. People can think whatever they like.' Poppy thought for a moment. 'It's up to you, though. You're going to be the one staying here and facing the music.'

A swell of warmth suddenly burst in his chest. There would be plenty of time to work out their boundaries later. If Poppy needed, or even just wanted, his support today then he'd be proud to give it. 'There's nothing to face. Let's waltz out of here together.'

Finally, she smiled. A *real* smile, not just the pale glimmer that had been playing around her lips. 'Very smooth. Am I going to have to deal with your charming side all the time, now that we're not officially working together?'

'Yep.' He grinned back at her. They were both tired, that was all. 'I'll be back in half an hour. Don't eat my cake.'

Three-quarters of an hour later, he pulled out of the hospital's underground car park, into the dark streets. Just for the hell of it he took a detour along Regent Street so that Poppy could enjoy the Christmas lights, and then headed north to her flat.

She walked ahead of him up the steps to her building, as if she couldn't wait to get home. Her life was entering a new phase, and somehow her eagerness to meet it allayed his own fears about the changes ahead. He hurried to open the main door for her, and she walked towards the lift.

'Oh!' Poppy stopped suddenly. Yellow and black striped tape was secured across the lift doors, and there was a laminated notice taped to them.

'Five days!' He glanced at the notice, reading it quickly. 'Since when does it take five days to mend a lift?'

'It's an old lift. They have to use a specialist company.' Poppy shot him a dismayed look. As well she might, because there were six floors of steps between her and her home.

'Come back to mine. We'll go from there.'

Poppy stiffened with disapproval. 'No, I can make it up there. If you help me.'

'And then you'll have to make it all the way down again to get back out. It's fifteen minutes to my place, and we can sit down and decide what to do.'

'But… No, Dylan. I need my things.'

'We can come back tomorrow for anything you need.' Dylan was happy to give way to Poppy on most things, but not this. 'If you won't come to my flat, then I'll take you somewhere else.'

'But I have a perfectly comfortable flat, which has everything I need. It's just a few stairs. You could help me up them, couldn't you?' Poppy shot him an imploring look which almost broke his resolve.

'Yes, I could, but I'm not going to. I wouldn't be doing you any favours.'

'Dylan…!' Poppy pressed her lips together, nodding at a couple who were just entering the lobby. 'The lift's out.'

'Not again.' The woman grimaced. 'Are you going to be all right…?'

'Thanks, but we'll be fine. We're going to my place.' Dylan spoke before Poppy had a chance to, and was aware of her frowning at him. The woman nodded, and made for the stairs with her companion.

'So you're turning down offers of help on my behalf, now?' Poppy practically hissed the words at him.

'Do you know her?' Dylan asked, ignoring her glare.

'Only to say hello to. But they live on the third floor and I expect they wouldn't mind my sitting down for a while to get my breath back, before I tackle the rest of the stairs.'

'I'm not worried about you getting out of breath, I'm

worried that you'll fall. And you're just making things unnecessarily difficult. If there's a friend you'd prefer to stay with then I'll take you there. What about Kate?' If Poppy refused to stay with him, Dylan would just have to accept it, but he wouldn't leave her to depend on the help of virtual strangers.

Poppy puffed out a breath. 'Kate and Jon, her fiancé, have been going through a rocky patch. They've been making time for one date night a week and they're going away this weekend. My turning up at short notice is hardly going to put them in the mood for scattering rose petals.'

Probably not, although that was what friends were for. But at least Poppy was beginning to realise that she couldn't stay here.

'Family?'

'I'd usually go to Mum and Dad's or to my sister's, but they're in Germany at the moment.'

'Right then. Since I'm still in the country, and not having any relationship problems, it sounds as if you're stuck with me. Is that really so bad?'

Suddenly her defences dropped. 'No, it's really nice of you. I'm sorry I just...panicked for a moment. Home's always the place you feel safest.'

And it was where Poppy had lived with her husband. Dylan understood that, and didn't underestimate her need to feel its comfort right now.

'There's nothing to be sorry for. It's just for tonight and we can weigh up the options in the morning. If you give me your keys then I'll go and fetch whatever you need.'

She opened her bag and handed her keys over. 'I've got my hospital bag already packed, that has everything I'll need for a night, and it's in the hall. Would you bring my

V-shaped pillow, please, it's on my bed. And there's another memory foam pillow as well.'

'Okay. You go and sit in the car while I take on the stairs. Give me a call if anything else comes to mind…'

CHAPTER TEN

POPPY WAS FEELING a little ashamed of herself. She'd hoped that Dylan might take her home and then find an excuse to leave, because jealousy was one of those emotions that was better handled alone. But she knew that staying here was a really bad idea, and she was just going to have to make the best of things. She obediently went to sit in his car, and when she saw the lights in her flat come on she called Dylan with a few more things to add to the list.

She heard the tension in his voice lighten, and several minutes after the windows on the top floor of the block darkened he walked back towards the car. Leaning in, he put the fairy from the tree into her hand.

'I thought she might like to come too.'

Poppy smiled at him, trying not to cry. Dylan seemed to take her weepiness in his stride, but she was starting to become impatient with it. She really wanted her mum at the moment, and the fairy was just perfect.

'I brought some of your tea as well.' He grinned and Poppy laughed, wrinkling her nose.

'I just can't get away from the tea, can I? I was hoping that we might call this an emergency and have to drink coffee.'

Dylan chuckled. 'I'm afraid it's not that much of an emergency...'

His flat was in a large, solidly built block. There were two lifts, and when he pressed the call button the doors of one slid open. They rode smoothly up to the penthouse, and Dylan ushered her through a small lobby to his front door.

It looked as if his was the only apartment on the top floor of the building, set back a little from the façade of the lower floors. The double-height windows at the front gave a marvellous view of the lights of London, and at the back steps led up from the huge living area to a deep gallery, which appeared to be Dylan's private space. Poppy looked around, wondering where she was going to sleep, and he smiled, walking to a door that led to a covered space under the gallery.

'This is the spare bedroom.' He leaned into the room, depositing her case by the door, as if she'd already taken up residence there and it was out of bounds for him. When Poppy looked inside she saw a cosy room which boasted a large double bed.

'The bathroom's next door—' he indicated another, closed, door '—and the kitchen's just around the corner from there.'

The three rooms, bedroom, bathroom and the open-plan kitchen, were all tucked neatly under the gallery. Dylan's bedroom space must be almost as large as the seating area downstairs, and when Poppy looked upwards she saw the top of bookshelves at one side. He must have an office up there, too.

The Christmas decorators had done a good job. There was a large tree, standing by the full height glazing in the living space, garlands threaded along the top of the steel and glass barriers that bordered the gallery, and shimmering clusters of tinsel and baubles by the windows. Poppy clutched her mother's fairy protectively to her chest.

'Not quite as Christmassy as yours…' He smiled, nodding towards the fairy. He was right, the fairy might not have so much shine but she was one of a kind. These decorations were beautiful but they were the sort of thing you might find adorning any public space at this time of the year.

'It's lovely, Dylan.'

He nodded, turning away. Dylan was nothing if not perceptive, and he must know the difference between a gorgeous piece of architecture and a home. 'Make yourself comfortable. Would you like some tea?'

'Thank you. That would be great.' Poppy walked across to the seating area, where a large sofa and several chairs were placed around a glass-topped coffee table. Almost defiantly, she draped her coat untidily across the back of an armchair, although she was sure there must be a concealed cupboard for it somewhere, and sat down, putting the fairy down on the coffee table in front of her. At least the two of them were in this together.

He reappeared, carrying two cups of tea, and sat down in a chair opposite her. They sat for a moment in silence as Poppy tried to think of something to say. Preferably something that didn't have anything to do with Jeannie.

'You have a lovely view here. There must always be something different.'

He nodded. 'Yeah, I like it.'

'I'll be okay on my own, if you have plans…' Maybe the plans involved staying in rather than going out. Poppy would just have to hope that Dylan would go to Jeannie's place, since the open-plan gallery would make it difficult to ignore a second guest for the night.

'No plans.' He shifted in his seat suddenly, leaning forward to reach for his tea. 'You must be hungry. I'll make some dinner.'

'Don't go to any trouble. Have you got any bread? Maybe peanut butter?'

He chuckled. 'You call peanut butter sandwiches dinner? I was going to do shepherd's pie with lentils and plenty of vegetables. I've got some ice cream in the freezer.'

Dylan's menu choice sounded surprisingly homely. And delicious. Her stomach began to growl appreciatively before she had a chance to tell him that he shouldn't go to any trouble. Dylan grinned and got to his feet.

'I'll take that as a yes. Sit tight, it'll be thirty-five minutes.'

Dylan sat alone, staring out at the lights of London. They were usually calming, the world going by beneath him something that he could lose himself in. Tonight, his thoughts were in overdrive and difficult to ignore.

Poppy had been quiet all evening. Probably tired—today had been a busy day for her, and one that marked a big change in her life. It was her defensiveness that bothered him, because Dylan had thought they'd set that aside and reached an understanding.

It was still fragile, though. He'd stepped back a little this week, telling himself that Poppy needed to find her own space. But maybe he was the one who needed to find some space.

They ate in the kitchen, because that seemed rather more homely than the large table out in the main living space.

Poppy helped him stack the dishwasher and then curled up on the sofa, obviously exhausted, and she'd agreed readily when Dylan suggested she might like to watch some TV in bed. He unlocked the door between the bathroom and the spare room, telling her he'd use the shower room upstairs, and then drew the curtains and found the remote for the TV. Poppy picked up her Christmas tree fairy, bidding him a smiling goodnight.

Now that the fairy was gone, the remaining Christmas decorations seemed somehow cold and lifeless. Dylan climbed the steps to the gallery, kicking off his shoes and flinging himself down onto the bed. This evening had handed him just the opportunity he'd wanted, hadn't it? An emergency, which hadn't hurt anyone, but had given him the chance to come to the rescue and show Poppy that she could rely on him. But it tasted bitter. Poppy really hadn't wanted to come here, and Dylan was having his doubts about how they'd manage, living together for five days. They'd both had their reasons for deciding to live alone, and this was a sea-change that had maybe come a little too soon.

Poppy's warmth, her sharp but forgiving tongue and her creative approach to life might be challenging, but Dylan had a feeling that it might just save him. Tomorrow might turn into a mess of conflicting emotions and uncertainties, his and hers. But he could deal with that far better than he could deal with the distance which seemed to have opened up between them this evening.

Poppy had watched a little TV and slept for a while. But keeping herself confined to the spare room and the adjoining bathroom had provided the rest that she so badly needed. She knew what she had to do now. It was okay for Dylan to be involved with the baby, but they both had their own lives.

She almost faltered when she found that he'd been up before her. He'd clearly been at some pains to let her sleep in, and came hurrying down the steps that led to the gallery when he heard her moving around in the kitchen. Breakfast was a process of emptying one of the kitchen cupboards to provide her with a choice of cereals, and Dylan's smile as he spun different boxes of tea in the air to encourage her to choose.

He seemed so alive. Casual clothes, jeans and a sweater suited him so well and his blond hair and blue eyes seemed brighter when they weren't combined with the greys and dark blues of the suits he wore to work. He made coffee for himself and kept her company at the kitchen table while she ate.

'I've decided…' Poppy had finished her granola mixed with yoghurt and raspberries and her spoon clattered into the empty bowl. 'It's really good of you to put me up here, but I'd like to go to a hotel until my lift's back in action.'

His gaze darkened suddenly. 'A hotel?'

She'd missed this too. Someone to call her out on her decisions. People had gingerly offered advice after Nate had died, but the common thread had always been that she should do whatever felt right and that there were no rules. Dylan was different, and he had no hesitation in telling her what he really thought.

'Yes.'

'Why?'

Poppy took a breath. 'I'll have all my meals prepared

for me, I can do just as I please, and I won't be in anyone's way.'

Dylan looked around, as if searching for a point that he'd missed. 'You can do all that here, can't you? We're not exactly falling over each other.'

'Yes, but… It's really nice of you, Dylan, but you have your own life.' Poppy decided that she shouldn't make it all about him, even if his life was probably a bit more eventful than hers at the moment. 'I do, too.'

His questioning gaze seemed to bore into her. 'What's going on, Poppy? You didn't find a plague of insects under the bed, or an odd smell in the bathroom, did you?'

'No! Your guest room's lovely and so is the bathroom. I was very comfortable last night.'

'But you won't be comfortable tonight?'

'No. I'd prefer to go to a hotel.'

It was one thing to know that Dylan and Jeannie were probably spending their nights together, but actually being here and having to watch him go… That was far too much information. Poppy was trying very hard *not* to be jealous right now, and finding it much more difficult than she'd anticipated.

His brow darkened. Dylan got to his feet, grabbing her empty bowl and putting it into the sink, his movements betraying a strand of anger. Then he walked through to the main living area, clearly looking for something that needed to be tidied away and finding nothing. Poppy took her phone from her pocket, scrolling through the list of hotels she'd found at two o'clock this morning, before falling asleep again. If Dylan was going to sulk… Fair enough, he'd get over it and she'd just get on and do what she'd decided already.

Then he marched back into the kitchen, leaning against the counter, as if coming any closer might bring her within the radius of an angry emotion that he didn't want to share.

'What?' Poppy glared at him. She might be pregnant but she was quite capable of arguing with him if she wanted to.

Dylan folded his arms, thinking for a moment. She wished he wouldn't do that—he could say what he thought without censoring anything that might be too blunt.

'You obviously have something on your mind, Poppy, and I'd be grateful if you'd just say it. If you just don't want to be around me, then say so. I might not like it very much, but it strikes me that being honest with each other is the only way that we can make our arrangement work.'

Honest. That worked two ways.

'I know you're seeing someone, Dylan. Clearly, my presence here is cramping your style...' Maybe that was a bit *too* honest.

'What?' He looked genuinely puzzled. 'You think I have the time to see anyone right now? Or the inclination?'

'I have no idea what your inclinations are, Dylan. I just think that respecting each other's space and that we have different lives is a good way to move forward.' That sounded a bit more constructive.

He spread his hands in a gesture of frustration. 'I agree, Poppy. If either of us is seeing anyone, then it's probably a good idea to mention it. It's okay to mention it, because we're friends and we both want to do the best thing for the baby. But I'm not. Are you?'

Poppy rolled her eyes. 'Of course not.'

'So what makes you think I am?'

She didn't want to bring Kate into this, but light was already dawning on Dylan's face. 'Kate told you, didn't she.

That she'd seen me and Jeannie in the canteen together. I noticed her staring at me and then looking away.'

'She saw you on the way to the lift as well.' Poppy defended her friend. Seeing two people together in a canteen was jumping to conclusions, and Kate had acted on a little more than that.

'Uh... I didn't notice that.' Dylan walked across the room, sitting down opposite her. 'Here's the full story. Jeannie and I *were* seeing each other a couple of years ago. She's moved on now, but we're still friends. Her sister has epilepsy and she has frequent fits. She's just found out that she's a candidate for fibre optic laser therapy.'

Poppy swallowed down the unwelcome wave of relief that washed over her. 'I've heard a lot about that.'

'I saw it done up in Edinburgh, at the Great Northern Hospital. Far less invasive than conventional surgery and patients have a much faster and better recovery. But neither Jeannie or her sister know much about it, and they don't really understand her surgeon's recommendations. I told Jeannie I'd be happy to get the notes and test results and give a second opinion.'

Stupid. Poppy could feel herself reddening now. She'd not only been wrong, but she'd betrayed her own dismay at the thought of Dylan being involved with someone else.

'Sorry.' She ventured onto safer ground. 'Is Jeannie's sister all right?'

'Since Jeannie knows how everything works, she was able to push through the request for her sister's test results and I saw her on Thursday evening. I reviewed everything, and I agree entirely with her surgeon—he just hadn't explained the options all that well. When I talked it through with them, they both understood why he'd made his recommendations. Jeannie texted me this morning to say that her sister's feeling much better about everything and has decided to go ahead with the surgery.'

At least he didn't produce his phone and show her the text. That would be too humiliating for words.

'Got it. I'm the bad guy, Dylan. I can only apologise.'

He reached forward suddenly, the tips of his fingers almost touching hers. Not quite, but the effect was still electric. 'No, you're not the bad guy. I should have explained when I said I couldn't make lunch on Tuesday, but it was the only time that Jeannie and I were both free and she and her sister were both stressing out about things.'

'You don't need to tell me anything, Dylan. This is Jeannie's business, and her sister's. Not mine.' The words tasted bitter because Dylan had done exactly the right thing, and she'd jumped to the wrong conclusion so easily.

'You need to be able to trust me. I hadn't realised that Kate had seen me give Jeannie a hug, and I guess that if two people have already been in a relationship then there's a slightly different level of reserve. I wish Kate had asked me, but she's your friend. That means taking your side and talking to you first.'

'I may just kill her the next time I see her…' Poppy joked, shrugging awkwardly. If he wasn't careful, Dylan was going to end up far too good to be true.

'Don't. Please.' His blue eyes were suddenly clear and thoughtful. How could she have doubted him? 'Whatever Kate thinks about me, she's probably right.'

'You care about what anyone thinks, all of a sudden?' Another question that seemed to have slipped past the usual filters. Poppy couldn't help liking the way they always made Dylan smile.

'I care about what you think. And that *you* care about what I do.'

Poppy stared at him wordlessly. She couldn't think of a reply which didn't betray everything she'd been thinking and feeling. Dylan seemed to see her confusion, and thankfully didn't push for an answer.

'It's only till your lift gets mended, Poppy. Let's take it one day at a time, eh? Perhaps I could interest you in another cup of tea, in a brazen attempt to get you to stick around for a bit longer...?'

Poppy had been jealous. Dylan had seen it in her face, and he'd had to stop himself from smiling at the thought.

It was a new perspective. He'd always felt that jealousy was one step away from possessiveness, and two from commitment, and as such he reckoned it was a major red flag. But he'd welcomed Poppy's jealousy. In his head he regretted the hurt it had caused her, but his heart took an irrational pleasure in it.

And...instead of wordlessly skirting around the issue, making up their minds that this was one area of incompatibility that would push them further apart, it had brought them a step closer. This relationship was demanding more from him than he'd ever offered to anyone, and it came as a surprise that suddenly he knew how to give it.

It came as a surprise that he *wanted* to give it as well. Dylan was beginning to wonder whether Poppy might be the woman who peeled the spots from this leopard's back and applied a few new ones.

His hand shook as he made the tea, even the familiar process of boiling a kettle seeming somehow new and different. They sat together in the kitchen, making a list of all the things she needed from her flat, and then Dylan encouraged Poppy to add a few things to make her feel more at home here.

He stopped off to do a weekly shop on the way back and when he returned to the flat he heard Poppy's voice in the kitchen. His hands full, he kicked the door closed behind him and found her staring at her phone.

'You know that Oliver Shaw's daughter Kayley was in a car accident during the week?' Poppy looked up at him, and Dylan left the carrier bags where he'd dumped them on the counter.

'Yeah, I went down to Intensive Care to see them when I heard.' Dylan had worked with both Oliver and his ex-wife Lauren, who both specialised in reconstructive surgery. 'This must be tearing them to pieces, Kayley's twelve weeks pregnant.'

Poppy nodded. 'Yes, Lauren told me. I left a message for her, saying there was no need to call back, but so she'd know I was thinking of them. But she's just called me.' She looked up at Dylan. 'And all I could think of to say to you was to ask about your current sleeping arrangements.'

'That's different. We're all thinking of Oliver and Lauren, even if we don't talk about it. Is there any news?'

'Kayley's stable but she's still in a coma. The baby…only time will tell but right now Kayley's still pregnant. I said that I was staying with you for a while, and that we were both thinking of them. I knew you'd want me to send your best wishes as well.'

Dylan nodded. 'Thanks. I was going to suggest we called together, later on, just to keep their phone time down a bit. But it's better that Lauren called when she wanted to talk.'

Poppy got to her feet, walking towards him. 'It's made me realise what's really important, Dylan.' She caught his hand between hers, laying it carefully on one side of her stomach. Dylan felt their daughter kicking almost immediately and everything else in the world melted away.

'She's lively this morning.'

'I think she's saying hello to her dad.' Poppy laid her head on his shoulder and the feeling took his breath away. The scent of her hair, feeling their baby kick. He put his arm around her shoulders and she snuggled against him.

This. Just this. There was nothing more that he wanted. And then Poppy grinned up at him, and he realised that her smile had been missing from his list of life's necessities.

'Just be there for her when she needs you, Dylan. I'm tendering my resignation as your intimacy co-ordinator.'

Poppy was joking about it, and that was a very good sign.

'What if I'm not planning on any intimacies for the foreseeable future?' That wasn't quite true. The one person he wanted to be intimate with, in so many different ways, was Poppy. But she'd already pointed out to him that wasn't on her agenda, and it would be wrong of him to mention it.

'I hear that board games are a good distraction.'

Dylan chuckled, feeling the baby move beneath his fingers. Maybe their baby girl was giving this new understanding her seal of approval. 'I have board games. You want some distraction?'

He saw Poppy's usual response to a challenge firing

up in her eyes. 'I have to warn you about my competitive streak.'

'You have a competitive streak?' Humour twinkled in his eyes. 'That's good, because you're just about to face your nemesis...'

CHAPTER ELEVEN

THE LAST FEW days had been exactly what Poppy needed. When Dylan had gone into work the following week it provided a framework for her. She could rest as much as she wanted during the day, and Dylan was there to share the evenings with her. Preparing dinner and eating then staying awake to talk might be simple pleasures, but they were spiced with a heady attraction that made time spent with Dylan something to look forward to.

It had been a mixed blessing, though. She'd lain awake at night, thinking that this was so like the life she'd had with Nate. The one she'd promised she wouldn't have with anyone else.

Promised Nate? Or promised herself? Maybe it was a little of both. All of the promises in the world hadn't allowed Nate to stay, and as her relationship with Dylan had become more precious to her Poppy had begun to realise how much she feared losing him.

But getting up in the morning, seeing Dylan's smile as he rushed out of the door to work, made her brave. Cooking for him, enjoying his appreciation of their evening meal, turned her into a warrior queen who could face any kind of peril. And then the nights alone, broken by discomfort and regular visits to the bathroom, let in all of her fears again.

'Craniotomy.' On the day before Christmas Eve that

wasn't a commonly heard greeting, but it made Poppy sit up straight. Dylan had been sharing his days at work with her, taking her through some of the complex procedures he'd performed. It wasn't quite as compelling as doing them herself, but it was good to talk about something that took her mind off her ever-changing body and made her feel like someone with a brain.

'Really? It was an emergency?'

Dylan nodded, slinging his overcoat across the back of the sofa, leaning down to deposit his briefcase on the cushion next to Poppy's feet. 'Yes. Very successful. You want to hear about it?'

She nodded. 'Yes, please. I have a large pot of goulash in the oven, and it'll be another forty-five minutes until it's ready.'

'Okay. I'm just going to make some tea and I'll be right with you.'

He walked over to the kitchen, reappearing carrying two cups of tea. He'd taken off his jacket and rolled up the sleeves of his white shirt, and when he sat down on the other end of the long sofa he slipped off his shoes. One of his plain navy-blue socks had a green toe and heel, and the toe and heel of the other was red. Poppy couldn't help smiling.

'You've got another pair just like that?'

Dylan grinned. 'Yep. Green and red are good Christmas colours, aren't they?'

'Make sure you don't get the two pairs mixed up. I never had you down as someone who wears odd socks.'

'Seems you didn't have me down as a lot of things.' He made that sound as if it wasn't quite a rebuke, but he was right. Poppy had always looked at his immaculate surface, never allowing herself to wonder what lay beneath it.

He reached for his briefcase, opening it and drawing out the spiral-bound notepad that he used to jot down the salient points of his day. Poppy felt her toes begin to curl with anticipation. Dylan smelled so nice and he looked gorgeous too. Lean in all the right places, but his shoulders and arms were bulked with muscle. Her own body confidence felt a bit like a swinging barometer right now, some days partially sunny and others freezing rain. But it was nice to have him around and dream…

'Ow!' Pain suddenly shot through the arch of one foot and along her calf. She could feel her toes continuing to curl into a solid, painful ball and when Poppy tried to reach them she couldn't. 'Ow! Cramp… My foot!'

Dylan's briefcase fell from his lap, scattering papers onto the floor. He took hold of her foot, stripping off her sock, and straightening her toes. That felt better and when he slipped his hand under her knee, expertly straightening her leg and pushing her foot upwards, the pain in her calf muscle suddenly abated.

'That's…good. Thank you.' Poppy went to pull away from him and felt another twinge running along the side of her foot.

'Don't move. If it feels better just stay there.'

Poppy decided to take his advice. 'I'm glad that one of us can reach my feet…' She gave in to the feeling of his fingers probing her leg. Not actually touching her skin, but even through the fabric of her leggings it felt almost like a caress.

'You've been getting cramps a lot?'

'A bit more than usual. No more than expected—you don't need to go and fetch your doctor's hat.'

Something ignited in his eyes. A tenderness that seemed to come from the man and not the doctor. He increasingly had the ability to slip out from behind all of the labels she'd given him—doctor, friend, uncle—and she was in the presence of a man. The father of her child.

One thumb was under her toes, stopping them from beginning to curl again. The other hand was on her calf muscle, probing gently.

'That's it. Right there.'

He nodded. 'I can feel it.' His touch became firmer, a little more searching. More pleasurable…

Poppy amended the thought quickly. More therapeutic. She could feel him working the muscle, which responded to his gentle fingers and began to relax.

'Your toes are cold.' He'd turned his attention to her foot now. When he let go of her toes they started to curl again, and he pulled them back straight. 'Hold on. I'll just get something to warm them up a bit.'

He laid her foot back down onto the sofa and got to his feet. Dylan spent only two minutes in the bathroom before he emerged with a bowl of steaming water, a flannel and a towel, but Poppy's muscles were already beginning to cramp again. He spread the towel over a cushion, propping her foot up, and then dipped the flannel into the water, wringing it out. Then he wrapped the warm fabric around her foot, massaging her toes.

Heaven. Pure heaven. There was none of the reassuring technology of the hospital but the traditional techniques had a thing or two going for them as well. Watching Dylan as he concentrated on the task in hand, the whisper of a smile on his lips as he felt her begin to respond and relax. Suddenly her feet were no longer a distant country, they were centres of warmth and feeling.

What couldn't they do with this moment? The thought of the forbidden was sending warm tingles down her spine.

'Your ankles aren't too swollen,' he murmured and Poppy nodded.

'It feels much better, thank you.'

He tapped her other foot lightly with his finger in an unspoken invitation. Poppy cordially ignored the fact that she felt no trace of cramp in it and shifted round, propping it onto the soft towel.

He knew. Poppy saw a sudden flash in his blue eyes and the trace of a smile. The way he stripped her other sock off seemed slightly more sensual, more sure of himself. She'd almost forgotten how it felt when her body responded to someone entirely of its own accord. When just a look or a smile was enough to start the slow, delicious journey into arousal.

Maybe he felt that too. He warmed and massaged her other foot with the same gentle fingers, but somehow it was less relaxing and more pleasurable. Then she felt his thumb pressing on the soft hollow beneath her ankle...

'Too much?' His fingers stilled suddenly.

It wasn't enough. Poppy pulled herself back from the warm tide of sensation that was making her toes tingle. Dylan's gaze found hers and she saw everything that was unspoken between them in his eyes.

'It's fine. It feels much better.'

She wanted so badly to reach for him. There was something about the way he was looking at her which made her feel beautiful. As if he wanted her touch just as much as she wanted his. That suddenly seemed so much more important than her doubts and fears.

Then his smiling look of regret brought Poppy back down to earth. This couldn't happen. They mustn't even say it, because that would acknowledge something that neither of them could handle. But Dylan handled *not* saying it really well.

'We'll leave it there then?'

Poppy gave him a smiling nod. He dried her toes with the towel, then put her socks back on and covered her legs with a throw from the back of one of the armchairs.

'Thanks, Dylan. I don't think I ever fully appreciated the value of foot care before I was pregnant.'

'And that's just the time you can't reach them.' He chuckled. 'One of the more annoying tricks that life plays on a person. Did you call to find out whether your lift has stopped playing annoying tricks?'

'Yes, I did. It's been mended and working fine now. Hence my special goulash, as a thank you.' Hence maybe allowing herself to forget that she and Dylan were bound by the baby inside her, but still very different people.

'We'll need to get up early so you'll be home in time for your father to pick you up for Christmas.'

Poppy shook her head. 'Actually, there's been a slight change of plan. I video-conferenced with them today, and they're snowed in. It happens—the smaller villages near to Cologne get quite a bit of snow in the winter.'

'So they won't be back? Come over to Sam and Sophie's with me on Christmas Day.'

'Thanks, but...' That might be a step too far, and she'd been taking too many of those lately. 'They're trying again tomorrow. Mum says the roads should be clearer then, and they should make it home by the evening. Dad'll come and pick me up on Christmas morning.'

Dylan nodded. 'Okay. But give me a ring if they don't make it.'

Poppy nodded, leaning forward to catch his hand. A brief squeeze and then he was on his feet, picking up the bowl and flannel to take back to the bathroom.

Dylan was going to miss Poppy. Those early nights when he went up to the gallery and lay on his bed, reading or watching TV with the sound turned down and subtitles switched on. Listening for her. Keeping watch over her and the baby as if he were a real dad and not just a biological father.

He was already head-over-heels in love with the baby girl that Poppy was carrying, and things were moving fast in that direction with Poppy as well. He'd shared his flat before, partners had come and then gone again, but they'd always left the place much as they'd found it. Poppy had made it into a home, turned his kitchen into a comforting refuge, filled with warmth and the scent of cooking and the Christmas tree into a twinkling source of light that seemed to radiate all of the magic of the season.

There was a price to be paid for that, though. Those delicious moments when they stepped over the line they'd drawn for themselves had given him a glimpse of what he and Poppy could be together. But however right that had felt, it had also felt right to draw back again. If he couldn't protect her from the possibility that he might fail her, then how could he expect to protect her from the thousand other things that could hurt Poppy or their child?

Time was ticking slowly forward. Through the night and into the dawn, when Dylan rose from his bed and took a shower. Steadily marking a beat as they ate breakfast, and checked that Poppy had packed everything. When she put on her red coat, adding a red hat with a white pom-pom, and picked up the fairy from her post by the bed in the spare room his flat seemed to darken.

Snow tumbled against the windscreen as they drove, and Poppy's phone rang in her pocket. 'Unknown number. I bet it's a scammer or a sales call.'

'On Christmas Eve? When it's snowing? Far more likely to be a lost reindeer wanting directions.' Dylan grinned and she laughed, answering the call.

Someone spoke at the other end of the line, and suddenly she was all smiles. 'Thank you so much. Give Lauren and Oliver my love, won't you. And from Dylan Harper too… No, it's okay, you can tick him off your list. I'll let him know right now.'

'Whose list have you just ticked me off? And is that what I think it is?'

'Yes! That was a friend of Lauren's calling round to let us all know that Kayley's woken up. She's weak, of course, and she'll need care but she's going to be all right. The baby's fine too.'

'Wonderful news.' Suddenly it really *was* Christmas, and there was hope in the air.

'I sent my love, and yours too. We'll be able to pop in and see Kayley when she gets out of the ICU.'

'Who said that there's no Christmas magic, eh?'

'Dylan! I distinctly remember hearing you tell a student that there was no magic in medicine. Just hard work and precision.'

He laughed. 'It's never too late to learn…'

Poppy was bubbling with excitement by the time they

reached her front door. Dylan had made sure that her plants and the Christmas tree were watered and left everything tidy when he'd come to pick up her things. He'd brought a bag of food from his own fridge and as soon as the place warmed up a bit everything would be back the way it should be. Apart from just one thing…

'You want me to put the fairy back onto the tree?' Poppy was still holding the fairy between her gloved hands.

'Yes. Thank you so much, Dylan.'

He could just reach… Dylan stretched up and fixed the fairy back at the top of the tree. Poppy was clapping and laughing the same way that she had last time, her face glowing with joy. Everything was the same, and he wasn't really losing her after all. He turned, putting his arm loosely around her shoulders, and Poppy looked up at him, her eyes moist with tears.

Good tears. The tears which overflowed from a heart that was full of joy. One of them escaped her eye and Dylan wiped it away with his finger. Tenderness overwhelmed him, and he brushed his lips against her cheek.

She was still looking up into his gaze, melting him from the inside out. Passion began to stir, something new and all-encompassing that made everything else seem like a mere murmur of feeling. He felt her fingers pressing softly on the back of his neck and couldn't resist. Gently, he gathered her in his arms, leaning down, and Poppy kissed his mouth.

A real kiss, not the kind that was gone before it had ever really been there. Sweet, a little hesitant, but full of Poppy's firm resolve. He kissed her again, and this time Poppy responded with all the hunger that he felt. Slowly they deepened the kiss, in a complex dance of questions and answers that felt natural and right.

'You're so beautiful.' He brushed a strand of hair from her cheek, kissing the skin beneath it. Dylan knew she needed to hear that. He'd seen the way she turned the corners of her mouth down when she awkwardly sat down, reaching helplessly for her swollen ankles. Poppy loved being pregnant, and it was everything she wanted, but sometimes his compliments fell on deaf ears.

But this time she believed him. She was looking up at him with that clear warmth in her eyes which held nothing back. She must feel his desire. He couldn't have feigned the way his body was reacting to hers if he'd tried.

'She feels us...' Dylan had been dimly aware that the baby was moving but when Poppy twined her fingers in his, placing his hand on the side of her stomach, it felt as if the little girl had decided it was time for a workout.

He kissed her cheek, feeling almost embarrassed, and Poppy laughed at his sudden hesitancy. 'She feels the warmth, Dylan. She doesn't know what's on your mind.'

Poppy knew, though. And when she kissed him again it was quite clear that she had the exact same thought as he did. Her body was a little busy at the moment, making a miracle, but the look in her eyes told him that one day, maybe soon, she'd have time just for him.

And their daughter was a part of that. Cocooned safely between them, maybe feeling the heat that had been absent when she'd been conceived. Now that Dylan was getting used to the idea, his thoughts were running away with him, leapfrogging over the years to find that Poppy was there with him, a constant and loving presence. Someone who could give him everything that his heart and his body craved.

It was too soon for an *I love you.* That would surely come

later. But when Dylan kissed her he felt love in his heart, and saw it in Poppy's gaze. He fell to his knees, resting his cheek against her swollen stomach. If Poppy's love was more than he'd ever need in his life, this was something different but more. A next step, taken before their first, which made everything suddenly come together.

Dylan rose, seeking the warmth in her eyes, the tender feel of her lips again. But Poppy had looked up and seen something beyond the cocoon that had formed around them.

He didn't need to turn—he could see it in her face. Poppy's wedding photograph stood in the alcove next to the fireplace behind him. A reminder of all the things that might tear them apart if they took the risk of loving each other. He tried to reach for her, forget the feelings that engendered, but he couldn't.

Dylan's kiss had been everything. Everything that Poppy had thought she'd never feel again…

No. It had been more than that. For those sweet moments it had been Dylan alone. Just him, like a first love that hadn't yet learned how to fear loss. It had seemed impossible that she might start something new when she was so heavily pregnant, but he'd made it seem so right. As if suddenly all the pieces in her life had clicked together.

And then there was the desire. The feeling that he found her immeasurably beautiful. Her aching legs and complaining back were suddenly lost in the wash of wanting him. Wanting to explore that hard, perfect body of his, and knowing what her touch might do.

But she'd looked up. Hesitated and then baulked. Maybe if he'd turned her head away, gone back to the beginning again and talked her through it, the way he'd done with some of the other issues they'd faced, it would have been different. But Dylan simply didn't do that with his relationships, and there was no way that Poppy could do it on her own.

'That was nice...' His smile had lost its ardour, and seemed like part of a plan for what he needed to do next. And *nice* really didn't cover it. It was practically an insult to what had gone between them.

But Poppy couldn't go back now. Guilt was sweeping over her like a great wave, and Dylan had been thrown clear and was too far away now for her to reach. She'd lost Nate, the man she'd promised to always love. And if she could lose Nate then she could lose Dylan as well.

'Yes.' She stepped away from him, looking helplessly around the room for something that urgently needed to be done. When the earth had moved between them, surely it had left some trace... But there was nothing. Even the fairy on the tree looked serene and unruffled.

'You must have things to do. I should let you get on.'

Dylan didn't look convinced. 'I don't have much to do. Some present wrapping...'

Present wrapping on Christmas Eve sounded nice, but right now even the thought of that festive warmth was an impossible agony. 'I'll be okay. Go and wrap your presents.'

He nodded, picking up his jacket and walking into the hallway. Poppy stopped in the doorway that led into the sitting room. No fond goodbyes at the front door.

'Happy Christmas,' she remembered to call after him and he turned. She could see the quickly hidden scepticism at the idea in his face.

'You too. Call me if there's anything you need. I'll see you after Christmas.'

They both knew that neither of them would call over

Christmas. And right now *after Christmas* seemed far too far away to even think about. But Poppy nodded and Dylan opened the front door, letting himself out.

Maybe she should have run to him. Poppy adjusted the thought to her current best effort of a brisk walk. Dylan was obviously hurt, and she should have explained. Given him one loving touch to reassure him. But she couldn't. Any relationship she had with Dylan would be based on the pretence that she was able to love again without dreading its consequences, and that wasn't something that Poppy wanted for either of them.

She walked back into the sitting room, picking up her wedding photograph. Nate's face was shining, so proud and happy. And she'd been so in love with him. He was gone now, but that moment would last for ever…

Suddenly she felt it. A wave that started at the top of her uterus and moved downwards. Poppy put her hand on her stomach, feeling it harden as the pain increased. Any second now…

It didn't stop. She let out a whimper, trying to breathe, and the picture frame fell from her hand, clattering against the plant pot and then slipping down behind the sideboard. Somewhere in the distance she heard breaking glass, but instinct had taken over and all she could feel was the pain.

'Not yet, sweetheart…' She gasped out the words, knowing that they'd make no difference.

This baby was coming, and Dylan wasn't here. Poppy looked for her phone, remembering that it was still packed in her handbag in the hallway.

Then she saw the remote for the door, right in front of her, where she'd left it six days ago on the sideboard. She picked it up, thumbing the intercom. Dylan would be going through the main doors on his way out, and surely he'd hear the buzz.

Unless he'd already gone. The pain had subsided now, and Poppy gingerly took two steps towards the window. His car was still parked outside in the street. She thumbed the intercom again.

'Dylan! Dylan, I need you…' She kept her thumb on the buzzer, gasping as the second contraction began to build. This one was stronger, and she yelped, holding onto the intercom for dear life.

Breathe. Just breathe. She could get to her phone and call the midwife. Poppy got as far as the sofa and decided to rest for a moment, bending forward and planting her hands on the armrest. That felt a little better…

Then she heard Dylan's voice, followed by a loud rapping on the front door. 'Poppy…? Poppy, press the door release. Let me in…'

She fumbled for the intercom, almost dropping it, before she managed to disengage the lock on the front door. She heard it slam behind him and his hurried footsteps in the hall, and then he was there, gently supporting her.

'Just breathe—everything's okay.'

'No, it's not!' Poppy immediately regretted snapping at him. 'I feel a bit better, though. Maybe if I sit down for a few minutes.'

He took her arm and she leaned on him gratefully as he walked her a couple more steps and helped her sit down. Poppy flopped to one side, stretching out, and he lifted her feet up onto the cushions.

'I'll take you to the hospital.' He was smiling now. Reassuring.

'Maybe it's…' Maybe it wasn't a false alarm. Poppy wasn't sure. 'The leaflet says to call first.'

'I don't care what the leaflet says. I'm a doctor.'

He must have seen her grimace, and laid his hand lightly on her stomach as the pain began to build again. Dylan gripped her hand, and she hung on to him.

'You're a neurologist.' Finally, it subsided and she could trust herself to speak without screaming the words at him.

'Yeah, and I did my rotations at medical school, the same as you did. *And* I've been brushing up over the last few weeks.'

He had? 'You didn't tell *me*.'

'No, I didn't. Just breathe, will you. And when you get the next contraction I'll be needing you to make as much noise as you can. Let it all out.' He looked at his watch. Dylan was clearly taking note of how long it was between each contraction, and it must be less than five minutes…

She didn't need to ask. He had that all under control, and her body was beckoning her towards a greater, more all-encompassing task.

'Whatever you think, Mr Harper.'

Did he just roll his eyes? She'd have a word with him about his bedside manner when this was all over.

'Thank you, Ms Evans. You concentrate on what you're doing, and leave the rest to me.'

CHAPTER TWELVE

'*THE REST*' WAS accomplished with startling ease. Before Poppy knew it, she was downstairs and in the car. Dylan took the backstreet route to avoid the Christmas Eve traffic, and fifteen minutes later they were parked outside the maternity unit at the hospital.

'My notes…' Poppy suddenly remembered that she'd been supposed to bring them with her.

'I've got them.'

'My phone…' At some point she was going to have to call her parents to let them know where she was.

'That's in your handbag. Which you're holding. Breathe…' He'd seen her grimace and he got into the back seat of the car with her, waiting for the contraction to subside. Then he hurried to the entrance of the unit, returning almost immediately with a wheelchair.

Everything was happening much faster than she'd expected. The onset of contractions and the way the midwife took them straight through to one of the birth suites, as Dylan quickly updated her on the interval between contractions.

'Your birth partner, Poppy. Can we make a call for you?'

Poppy was still struggling to keep up. 'My sister… But she's on her way back from Germany.' This baby wasn't going to wait for that. She turned to Dylan.

'Dylan. Please…' Maybe this was too much to ask of him, but he smiled, taking her hand.

'With you all the way.'

Dylan had been many things today. A spurned lover. A doctor. A birth partner. And now… Now he was a bemused and besotted father. His daughter had been in a hurry to make her way into the world, and little more than three hours after he'd heard Poppy's voice on the intercom, and run up six flights of stairs, the baby girl was born.

There was quiet activity around them, but for once he didn't care. He was dimly aware that all the correct medical procedures were being followed, and he wasn't a part of that. He and Poppy were in their own small bubble, both focused on the tiny baby that lay on her chest.

'You did so well. Both of you,' he murmured. Dylan couldn't imagine ever tearing himself away from this moment. It would follow him always, somewhere to go whenever the going got tough. And he imagined that it would, although even that had lost its sting right now.

'Do you want to hold her?' Poppy's gaze met his suddenly.

More than anything. He didn't want to break the skin-against-skin connection between Poppy and the baby, which was keeping the little one warm and contented under the thin blanket that covered them both. Nor did he want to ask for more than Poppy wanted to give—he'd only even been here by chance. But acting considerately and well was being drowned out by an instinct to hold his daughter in his arms that just wouldn't let go of him.

'Do you know her name yet?' Dylan avoided the question.

'Listen. What do you hear?'

Quiet voices around them. The subdued noise of the machine which was still monitoring Poppy's vital signs. He shot her a puzzled look, not wanting to direct her thoughts in any particular way other than where they wanted to go.

She smiled. 'What do you think of Belle?'

Now he heard it. The faint peal of Christmas bells, coming from one of the city churches that surrounded them. Ringing out hope for the future.

'I think it's perfect. It really suits her.'

Poppy chuckled. 'Along with Impatience. She really didn't want to wait any longer, did she. We can't really call her that, can we.'

Dylan shook his head. 'Not unless you like unusual middle names. Even then, it carries a few expectations.'

'She's perfect as she is. I have no expectations other than that she be loved for whoever she wants to be.'

She'd be loved. If Poppy wasn't planning on taking up residence in his heart, then it would be all for Belle. Dylan nodded his agreement, a conflict of emotions raging in his chest.

And then, suddenly, they fell quiet. Poppy had murmured a few words to the midwife, and she helped her to lift Belle and wrap her in a soft baby blanket. Then his daughter was placed carefully into his arms. Belle scrunched up her face and he felt her shifting against him, then she settled again as he stroked her head with his trembling fingers.

Cold air and the scrunch of a layer of snow beneath his feet wasn't quite enough to bring Dylan to his senses. But he could drive back to Poppy's flat, sorting out the things she'd need and packing them to take to her in hospital. Glancing across towards the photograph that had changed everything yesterday, he saw only a cracked plant pot and scattered broken leaves. When he went to investigate further, a trail of glass fragments led him to the broken picture frame, which had slid down behind the sideboard.

There were a few hours to kill before he was expected back. Poppy needed to rest and she'd wanted to call her family, to see what was happening with them and introduce them to Belle. Dylan moved the sideboard, clearing up the mess of broken glass and taking the plant to the kitchen to trim its bent stalks. He wound a few rounds of tape around the pot, the emergency surgery would have to do for the time being, and returned it to its place on the sideboard. Maybe a little water would help with the plant's recovery…

Anything. Think about anything, so you don't have to face the one thing that has to be faced. But the shattered frame was still waiting for him. When he picked it up he found that the mounting board had saved the photograph from any harm, and he could carefully extract it from the wreckage.

Poppy looked joyful. Her husband—Dylan still couldn't bear to think of him by name—had all the signs of a happiness that Dylan had presumed to feel. If it had been anyone else then he could have fought for Poppy, but not this man. Not the one who'd captured her whole heart, leaving Dylan out in the cold.

Dylan frowned. Now, he was just feeling sorry for himself, digging down to find all the feelings of rejection—that childish certainty that if he'd been better and more worthy of his father's love then he never would have left. He was the one who'd broken their agreement, not Poppy. She'd compromised with him when she hadn't needed to, let him share the first moments of Belle's life and promised that he would be able to share more. She could no more give him her heart than fly in the air, because it belonged to someone else.

Now he had something to do. If he couldn't be entirely happy then at least he could be busy, and that thought always made him feel strong again. He could live up to his promises, and that would make him the man his father never had been. Belle would have every last piece of him that he could give, and Poppy and Nate would have his respect.

Dylan had come back to the hospital with her things, and Poppy had made it clear that he was welcome to stay as long as he liked. He'd been kind and caring towards her, understanding that she was still floating on a sea of drugs and emotion. And he'd watched Belle hungrily, waiting for any chance he might have to hold her. Poppy had gently tried to wake her, and the little girl's eyes had remained firmly shut. Then somehow her dreams had wakened her, and Dylan had taken her, walking her up and down until she fell asleep again in his arms.

'She's had a big day.' Poppy couldn't get enough of seeing him with Belle at the moment. 'Did you see her eyes?'

'They may well change.' A note of uncertainty sounded in Dylan's voice. He was clearly hoping that Belle might have inherited something of his.

'I hope not. They're such a gorgeous blue.' Poppy had deliberately chosen a donor with the same eye and hair colouring as her, so that she wouldn't be wondering whether the baby was like her or its father. But now that Belle was here, had a name and a personality all of her own, none of that mattered. She could do a lot worse than inherit her father's blond hair and blue eyes.

Dylan bent to plant the tenderest of kisses on Belle's forehead. 'With any luck she'll have your determination to do things her own way. If she doesn't, you'll just have to teach her.'

'I'm planning on doing things one day at a time at the moment.' Right now, the next twenty years were going to have to take care of themselves. 'They may well be discharging us tomorrow, so Belle will be having her first Christmas at home.'

'I'll be here in the morning to collect you both. What time?' Dylan looked up at her.

'No! You've got someone else waiting for you on Christmas Day. Thomas is going to need his bricks, along with his uncle to help him put them together.'

'There's plenty of time to do both. Sam and Sophie usually spread the present opening out a bit and I can be there for the afternoon. Did you call your mum and dad?'

Poppy turned the corners of her mouth down. 'They started out this morning, but it began to snow really heavily and they had to turn back. Dad was ready to set off again when he heard Belle had been born but I insisted they wait until after Christmas. I don't want them taking any risks.'

Dylan nodded. 'Sensible. In that case I'll definitely be here tomorrow. I put the carrycot into my car, just in case you were going to need it.'

'And…' Poppy frowned at him. The carrycot hadn't been among the things he'd brought up to the unit. 'You're not going to make me stay here until you arrive by holding my carrycot ransom, are you?'

He grinned. 'Well, you're definitely not going to need it tonight. And I'll be here first thing in the morning…'

True to his word, Dylan was at the hospital early on Christmas Day. There were a few unfamiliar faces among the staff on duty, and they were clearly busy, but everything went like clockwork. She'd be going home for Christmas.

That wouldn't be quite as joyful an occasion as it sounded. But at least Belle would be introduced to the smiling porcelain figure on top of the tree, and maybe she would sprinkle a little fairy dust their way. She dressed Belle in one of the sleepsuits that Dylan had brought from Poppy's ever-growing collection, adding the festive red and white hat that the hospital had given her, over her soft fuzz of pale blonde hair.

They were ready. There were smiling goodbyes and 'Happy Christmas's.

'You could drive just a little faster, Dylan.' He'd made sure that everything was done in Poppy's own time, even though he must be keen to get to his brother's house.

'Nah…' He turned into Regent Street and suddenly there was another first for Belle. The usually busy road was almost empty but for a few cars, and the Christmas lights twinkled above their heads. Angels appeared to be hovering over them. And…Christmas bells at the top of each lamppost. In the unexpected quiet, Poppy could almost hear them chime.

Even if she'd been awake, Belle wouldn't have been able to see them yet. But Poppy could and she'd remember this piece of Christmas magic. Dylan drove the whole length of the street and then turned back, heading for Poppy's flat.

As they rode up to the sixth floor, Poppy felt a quiver

of excitement grow. Dylan stopped at the front door, carefully taking Belle from the baby carrier and putting her into Poppy's arms. Then he opened the door, standing back so that she could carry her daughter into her new home.

Dylan must have been here already this morning, and the place was warm, the lights of the Christmas tree twinkling out into an overcast and gloomy day. He left Belle and Poppy alone in the sitting room and Poppy leaned back in her seat, glad that her body felt a little lighter now, and testing out the new aches and pains from the birth. Home. She was home, and all the hope and joy of a new little life was stirring beside her now.

Dylan was warming some mince pies and brought them through with two cups of tea, gulping his down as quickly as he could. Poppy knew what that was all about and beckoned him over, putting Belle into his arms. She couldn't get enough of the goofy smile that spread over his face when he held her.

'I bought a turkey crown and that won't need too long in the oven. There are vegetables and all the trimmings in the fridge…' He seemed determined to make today as festive as possible. 'I can put it all into the freezer if you don't feel like it.'

'I have all I need for Christmas, Dylan.' Suddenly she wasn't sure *what* she needed. After all of the emotion of the last few days, the vulnerability and the memory of his kiss…

Some time alone. Time to let her crowded head make sense of it all and settle into the life she'd planned for her and Belle. And she couldn't keep Dylan from his family at Christmastime. That was the life *he* wanted, the one that she'd selfishly snatched him away from over the last few weeks.

'You should go. You can make Christmas lunch with your family if you go now.'

Dylan shook his head. 'And leave you on your own?'

'I'm not on my own, Dylan. Belle and I are just starting to get to know each other. Your nephew's going to be so disappointed if he doesn't see you, and there's that special present for your mum that you were telling me about. She's going to want to hug both of her sons when she sees her new car...'

Why did that make her feel so empty? Christmas spent together had never been a part of the plan and right now, when they were still feeling their way, wasn't the time to start playing things by ear.

'But...what if something happens? I should be here, with you.'

Should. If Dylan had said that he *wanted* to be here then maybe—only maybe—Poppy would have changed her mind.

'Nothing's going to happen. I have a number to call if I have any worries, and I promise I'll let you know too. I want you to go, Dylan.'

Maybe she could have said that a little more tactfully, because Poppy could see the hurt in his face. But suddenly she really *did* want him to go. They both had their own lives, and becoming dependent on each other really wasn't the right thing for Dylan, or for her.

He didn't argue. Dylan had never expected anything, it had always been Poppy who had offered. He got to his feet, kissing Belle's forehead and putting her back into the baby carrier.

'That's the deal, isn't it?' His face was impassive, suddenly. Unreadable.

'Yes, Dylan. That's what we decided was best for both of us. Give me a call after Christmas and let me know when you'd like to come and see Belle. Maybe we'll take her out for her first walk to the park, eh?'

He nodded, picking up his jacket and feeling in the pocket for her spare keys, which he laid on the coffee table. 'Goodbye, Poppy.'

Dylan hadn't said another word as she'd walked through the hallway with him, letting him out of the flat. Poppy had returned to the sitting room, which suddenly seemed a lot darker and dimmer, and reminded herself that she'd never reckoned on this being easy. But she'd done the right thing. When he arrived at his brother's and found that the people he loved had been waiting for him he'd see that.

But there was something about the finality of his words that had cut like a knife. She leaned over, and Belle's eyes fluttered open for a moment. 'Don't you worry, sweetheart. He said goodbye to me. He's never going to say that to you. Do you want to come and see our Christmas tree?'

Belle's eyes closed again. That would be a no, then. The fairy was going to have to wait before she was introduced to the newest member of the family. Poppy stared at the tree, trying to muster up a little Christmas spirit. The presents beneath it were still waiting for her family's return…

And there was another one, added to the pile. Poppy wondered whether that had been one that she'd forgotten having wrapped, and then decided not, since the blue and gold paper was unfamiliar. She walked over to the tree, bending slowly to pick it up, and looked at the tag.

Just one word.

Poppy

And it was in Dylan's handwriting. What had he gone and done?

The shape, the feel of it were familiar. Poppy returned to the sofa, hardly daring to open it. Not daring to look at the empty space on the dresser. A stab of guilt dug at her heart when she realised that she'd forgotten all about that.

She carefully loosened the sticky tape on the present. Stalling for time, hoping this wasn't what she thought it was. Ripping the paper, as she usually did, seemed wrong but she couldn't put the moment off for ever and the paper drifted in one piece to the floor, revealing her wedding photograph. As good as new, in a gorgeous silver frame.

Nate's gaze seemed to bore into her. Her mouthed apology didn't do any good, and she still felt terrible for forgetting him, excluding him from the moment when she brought the baby that they should have had together back home.

This was Dylan's final word. He knew that she belonged with Nate and he'd accepted that. That hurt too, a lot more than it should.

'Belle…' Poppy laid the frame carefully down on the coffee table and turned to her daughter. The one person she'd never exclude from any part of her life. The little girl seemed to sense her mother's presence and maybe her mood too, and started to cry. Poppy picked her up, holding her against her chest and rocking her gently.

'No need for that, sweetheart. Everything's okay, I promise.' Tears were running down Poppy's cheeks too, but the instinct to comfort Belle was more powerful than anything else. 'Hush now, Belle. I love you...'

CHAPTER THIRTEEN

THAT WAS THAT, THEN. Dylan had dared to love Poppy, but he should have known that nothing ever came of a broken agreement. He had to move on. Or rather, move back. Somehow, he found it in himself to arrive at Sam's house with a smile on his face. Hug his mother and then catch Thomas up in his arms, swinging him round before he held him tightly to his chest.

But even his beloved nephew couldn't fill the empty space that Poppy had left. She and Belle had turned him into an adventurer, showing him that he could feel more than he'd ever thought he would. Now that he was back in a familiar place he couldn't settle.

'We've got some news.' Sam had poured them both a splash of brandy and taken Dylan out into the garage to inspect his latest project, a treehouse for Thomas that would be assembled in the spring.

'Yeah?' From the look on Sam's face it was good news, and Dylan could certainly do with a little of that at the moment.

'Sophie's pregnant.'

'Yeah? That *is* good news.' Dylan clapped his brother on the back, hugging him. 'I didn't realise you were going back to the fertility clinic so soon.'

'You think we'd have done that without making you a

part of it, like last time? After all this time spent trying, we finally managed to do it all on our own. Who'd have thought it?'

Dylan chuckled. 'You and Sophie always were the first team. I was just the second reserve.'

'Hey. You *know* you were always the first reserve, Dylan. We were going to tell you and Mum together, but I told Sophie that I wanted to tell you first. You'll have to act a bit surprised when we do tell her.'

Dylan chuckled, throwing his arms around his brother in another hug. 'Tell her soon, eh? I can't keep this to myself for too long. Now's good, isn't it…?'

'Not yet.'

Something prickled at the back of Dylan's neck. 'Why—is anything wrong?'

'No, everyone's fine. It's you I'm worried about. What's eating at you?'

'It's nothing. Hospital stuff…' Dylan's excuse for being late today had been to refer vaguely to having been at the hospital. No one had questioned that—they were used to him being called in from time to time.

'Must have been bad. You don't usually bring that home with you.'

Dylan shrugged. 'You know…'

'Funnily enough, I do. You can convince everyone else that you've just had a bad day at work, but I'm your brother. Twins' intuition.'

'Ah. So we really can read each other's minds, can we?'

When Dylan and Sam were teenagers they'd devised a code that allowed them to fool their friends. Maybe some of the appeal had been that reading each other's minds might make them inseparable. Two lost boys who would always have each other.

'Nah. I can read the look on your face when you think no one's looking your way.'

'Covert surveillance, then.'

It was no use. Sam wasn't going to give up, and Dylan didn't want him to. Sooner or later, he'd know about Poppy and Belle and he and Poppy had agreed weeks ago that it was okay to tell close friends and family. Sam fell into both those categories.

As soon as he started it all began to spill out, like a gush of frustrated emotion. The mix-up at the fertility clinic. How he and Poppy had carefully worked their way towards finding out what they wanted. Their agreement.

'And now you have feelings for her?' Sam was leaning back against the workbench, listening carefully.

Dylan drained the last drop of brandy from his glass, wishing for a moment that they'd brought the bottle out with them. 'I think so…'

'I'll take that as a *yes*. If you didn't then you'd know.'

That made sense.

'I love her, Sam. It's not just Belle, although she's…' Dylan shrugged. 'You know.'

'Yeah, I do. I love Sophie, and I love Thomas. It's not a popularity contest.'

Dylan nodded. 'So what's the answer, then?'

'Search me. If someone doesn't love you, then they don't love you. You can't cure that, Doc. You just have to accept it and do the best you can for everyone else concerned.'

'You always did handle Dad leaving better than I did…' Dylan turned the corners of his mouth down.

'Yeah? Tell that to Sophie—it would give her a laugh.

We've had our moments, as you know, and it was generally over my habit of just letting things happen. You raged over it, Dylan, and that might well have been a more healthy reaction.'

Dylan chuckled. 'Just as well there were two of us, then. Mum could take her pick over which one she felt like agreeing with at the time.'

Every instinct told him to fight right now, but if it couldn't work between him and Poppy then fighting would only make things worse. He had to get this right, there was no more room for mistakes.

'Sophie would say that *you* can take your pick. Sometimes you do have to accept things, but sometimes it's okay to fight—she's told me that enough times. Not that I'm admitting she's right or anything…' Sam grinned.

'No. Of course not.' Sophie had always been good for Sam, and the two of them had found their way together through everything that life had thrown at them. It occurred to Dylan that maybe acceptance would be a more loving thing to do in this situation. Give Poppy some space to work out what she really wanted. It was a new form of challenge that Dylan was unfamiliar with.

'Do you know what you're going to do next?' Sam asked.

'Not really. It's all too new to be able to put it together right now. But it was good to talk.'

'Well, I'm not wishing to break the moment… But you do know that if Thomas thinks we're idling around he'll be out here with a job for you to do. He's got a few construction projects of his own, now that he's opened all of his Christmas presents.'

Dylan nodded. He needed some time to think and the illusion of a happy Christmas had been difficult to maintain this year. But he'd do it, because there was really nothing else that he *could* do.

'Although Mum's dying to help him with the kit she got him.' Sam was watching him steadily. 'Did you see her face when he opened it?'

'Yeah.' Dylan summoned up a smile. 'She'll have another grandchild soon as well. She can do all the Christmassy things with them that she never got to do with us.'

'She's got another grandchild already, Dylan. We might not get to meet her, but Belle will always have a place with us if she wants it. And so will her mother. You know that, don't you.'

'Yeah, I know. I'm going to have to see how things pan out. Poppy did mention babysitting.'

'Okay, well, hold that thought, Dylan. Sophie and I aren't going to push our way in, but we're there for you and we're there for them as well. Always.'

The light in Sam's eyes was something new. Something different. His brother had learned to fight for their family, and maybe Dylan should follow his example and acknowledge that he had a choice about what to do next.

'Thanks. I don't know what else to say, but…thanks. Do we need to get back now?'

Sam shrugged. 'Like I said, Mum'll keep Thomas amused, and if he sees we're busy… Fancy helping me check the measurements for the treehouse?' He nodded towards the large oak tree in the back garden.

Maybe Sam really could read his mind. Climbing a tree with his brother sounded like a fine thing to do on Christmas Day.

Dylan grinned. 'Got an old jacket I can borrow…?'

* * *

'You are *so* busted, Poppy.'

Poppy let out a sigh. She'd cried for a while, and then slept for a while on the sofa. The phone had woken her, and Belle was shifting fitfully in her crib. Not quite awake enough to cry, but getting there.

'Kate…?'

'Yep. Valued friend and confidante, remember? Who didn't even get a picture of the baby… Your mum texted me. You sound sleepy—did I wake you?'

'Yes.' There was no point in being bad-tempered with Kate—she couldn't help it if she wasn't Dylan. 'I mean… That's okay, Belle's due a feed shortly. What did Mum say?'

'She said that she'd seen you and Belle via video call, and wanted to know whether you were as well as you were making out. I texted back and told her yes, and that Jon and I were looking after you.'

'Oh. I'm so sorry Kate, you're a star…'

'No problem. Are you alone?'

Poppy forced herself to smile, hoping it might sound in her voice. 'No. I've got Belle with me.'

'Not what I meant, Poppy. I'm coming round.'

'No… Look, I'm really sorry. Dylan was here when I went into labour and things all happened so quickly that I didn't get a chance to call anyone. And then I didn't phone you because I knew you'd come and…' Poppy felt a tear run down her face, and thanked goodness this wasn't a video call. 'I just wanted you and Jon to have a romantic Christmas together. Hanging around in the hospital isn't much of a break when you work there.'

'Poppy! One of the things that Jon and I like about each other is that we're both part of a caring profession. What's he going to think if I leave my good friend and her day-old baby on her own on Christmas Day?'

Dylan had left her alone, but then Poppy had made it very clear that she didn't want him here. And he'd always listened to what she wanted.

'You don't have to tell Jon. Just get the rose petals out…'

'Too late. He's got his coat on, so it looks as if he's coming too. Hang on…' Kate called to Jon, 'Don't forget the food, sweetheart.'

'You're bringing food?' It sounded as if Kate was serious about this.

'Were you cooking this morning?'

'Kate, it's really kind of you. But I really just want to sleep…'

'You can sleep. Jon can stare lovingly at me holding the baby and make some turkey and cranberry sandwiches.'

Poppy sighed. Actually, turkey and cranberry sandwiches sounded really nice. She was hungry and maybe food and a little company would take her mind off wanting to cry all the time. 'If you're sure… Hold on.' Belle had started to cry and Poppy switched her phone to loudspeaker and picked her daughter up.

'Ooh. I heard her—she sounds so cute. I've *got* to come now…'

Poppy gave in to the inevitable. 'Okay. I'd love to see you both.'

'We'll be there in an hour. Send a photograph, so I can look at it in the car…'

Tidying away the wrapping paper that still lay on the coffee table and returning her wedding photo to its place on the sideboard had made Poppy feel a little better. When she looked at the plant next to it, she saw that the cracked pot had been repaired and there was no evidence of broken glass anywhere. *She* should have been the one to do all this, but Dylan's gesture had shown respect, for her and for Nate. More than that, it had shown a kindness that had been willing to understand her needs.

The thought only made her cry again. But it wasn't all about Poppy's needs. Dylan had given up a lot to support her and she was grateful, but he had his own life to live. Poppy couldn't give him what he deserved and she had to set him free.

Kate and Jon's arrival did take her mind off things a little. They plied Poppy with food, made a fuss of Belle and sat beside Poppy on the sofa for her video call to Germany, convincing her mum that they were all having a great Christmas.

'You guys, I just can't thank you enough.'

'What? Is that a hint, Poppy?' Kate looked at her watch. 'It's not even six o'clock. We're not going yet, are we, Jon?'

Jon chuckled. 'No, we're not.' He rose from his chair, collecting up the plates and glasses, ignoring Poppy when she told him that she could do it.

'You two are both as stubborn as each other.' She put her arm around Kate.

Kate chuckled. 'Yeah. How's your Christmas been so far?'

'Unlike any Christmas I've ever had before.'

'I can imagine. I assume that the *"friend from the hospital"* that your mum was talking about was Dylan?'

Poppy nodded. 'Yes. I was waiting to talk to Mum and Dad about that when they get home.'

'Yeah, good thought. That kind of thing's better in person.' Kate thought for a moment. 'Did Dylan leave you on your own this morning?'

'I know you don't like him…'

Kate held her hands up. 'That's not true! He's very dedicated and he's a really nice guy as well. And I freely admit that I was mistaken over Jeannie, and I'm really sorry that I ever mentioned it to you. But the thing is that we both believed it, didn't we? He's a player, and everyone knows it.'

'He has his reasons.' That sounded as if Poppy was defending him. Maybe she was.

'I'm sure he does. We all have our reasons. But however nice he is, however good-looking, you're the one who's my friend. That's the way it works.'

'I made him go, Kate. Because of *my* reasons.'

'Nate?'

Poppy nodded.

Still in love with Nate. That had once been so easy, so understandable. But it had all become more complicated in the last few weeks. She'd lost Nate and now she was afraid of losing Dylan. She wasn't sure she could explain it to herself, let alone anyone else.

Kate hugged her tightly. 'You have Belle to think about now, honey.'

Belle shifted in her crib, opening her eyes, as if she knew that someone was talking about her. Poppy picked her up, holding the tiny baby in her arms. Just feeling her close seemed to turn on all the right hormones, and it was difficult not to smile. Belle was wide awake now, those blue eyes of hers tugging at Poppy's heart.

'Hello there, darling. You want to see your Auntie Kate?'

Kate grinned, stretching out her arms. 'Yes, she does! I definitely saw her perk up when you said my name. Come here, sweetie.'

* * *

Poppy's mum and dad had left their car in Germany and flown back home, arriving straight from Heathrow. Poppy had tidied the flat, and her mother had cooed over Belle for a while before plunging into the kitchen.

'She's not going to find all that much to do. Kate and Jon got there first—Jon even cleaned the oven.'

She'd given Belle to her dad to hold and he was taking the job seriously, rocking the tiny baby and talking to her. It was a moment before he replied.

'She'll find something. Any plumbing problems? Your mother's a dab hand with a wrench.'

Poppy laughed. It felt strange, when all she'd been doing lately was trying not to cry.

'Since when?'

'Since October. She and her friend have been going to evening classes on home management, and I got home one day to find that she'd mended a leak under the kitchen sink.'

'Good for her. I'll bear that in mind.'

'And what about you?' Her father's attention was suddenly all on Poppy.

'The midwife says that Belle's doing beautifully, she's feeding well and she only really cries when she's hungry.'

Her dad nodded. 'I was asking about *you*.'

Poppy had been trying to avoid that question. 'I'd be lying if I said I wasn't a bit tired, but it was an uncomplicated birth, and I'm getting along fine. The midwife says I'm doing beautifully, too.'

'Not singing the blues, then?'

That was what her dad had said to her when she was little, whenever she was upset about something. He always seemed to know, better than anyone, and he knew now.

'It's hormones, Dad. You remember when Mum had us?'

Her dad chuckled. 'Vividly. Belle's a lot more serene than you were—you were so alert, and it was difficult to get you to sleep at times. She's more like your sisters.'

Or maybe more like Dylan. He was determined and forward-looking at work, but he had a quietness about him at times, the ability to just switch off and relax, that few people at the hospital ever saw. A rock-steady solidity that she'd allowed herself to depend on, even before she'd noticed it.

Don't cry. Dad'll notice, even if no one else does...

'Nate?' Her dad said the name quietly.

'Nate's gone, Dad. It was hard, but this is me moving on now.'

She *was* moving on. She'd always love Nate, but Poppy could say his name without wanting to break down and sob. She could see in his face that her dad didn't quite believe her, but he wasn't going to be satisfied with *It's complicated...*

'I hear you've had plenty of help from your friends while we've been away. Your mother's furious...'

Had they heard something?

'What about?'

'She wanted to be here for you. I've never seen anyone vent so much anger at snow before.'

'Bloody snow!' Mum's voice drifted in unexpectedly from the kitchen, and Poppy laughed with her dad.

'It's good to have you here now,' Poppy called through to her mother.

It was *really* good, better than either of them knew. Belle had seen her tears, even if Poppy had instinctively tried to hide them, and she must be glad her grandparents were here too.

'It's all been fine.' Poppy turned to her dad, smiling and lowering her voice, just in case her mum felt undervalued. 'A friend had popped round to see me on Christmas Eve, and took me straight to the hospital when I went into labour. Then stayed with me during the birth.'

Poppy carefully avoided the use of pronouns, in case her dad picked up on the idea that there was a male friend involved. That would have to come later, when she could tell them about Dylan without betraying her feelings.

'And it was *snowing*...' Poppy grinned at her dad conspiratorially. 'I could hear the Christmas bells in the distance...'

'I was wondering where you got the name from.' Her dad grinned down at Belle, mouthing her name. 'She's a real Christmas Belle, with those blue eyes.'

'They may darken...' Poppy was becoming more and more sure that they wouldn't. Maybe that was just wishful thinking. Something of Dylan's that she could keep for ever. He'd texted every day to ask how she and Belle were, and Poppy had replied, sending new pictures of Belle. Just Belle. There was a void between her and Dylan now that seemed impossible to cross.

'Hey, now...' Her dad had had more practice at baby-juggling than Poppy, and managed to reach over and put his arm around her while keeping Belle cradled safe and secure in his other arm. Poppy realised that a tear had escaped custody and was making a run for it, down her cheek.

'It's nothing, Dad. Hormones will be hormones.'

'I know. That's the trouble with you doctors.'

'What? We have more hormones than everyone else? I'm not aware of *that* condition.'

Her dad chuckled. 'No. You think everything's a chemical reaction. Hasn't this little girl taught you one thing, darling? Some things are all about the heart.'

CHAPTER FOURTEEN

IT WAS ALMOST New Year. Poppy had two New Year's resolutions, the first of which was to get through the day. The second was a little more challenging, because it was to get through the night.

She'd thought the tears might pass, but as she and Belle had started to get into a routine, and Poppy began to feel stronger and more confident, they'd only become more frequent. More focused on Dylan and the agreement they'd made.

He'd asked her if there was anything she needed, pretty much every time he texted. And there *was* something that Poppy needed. He was off work on New Year's Eve and Poppy suggested that he might like to video call, so he could see Belle. His reply had been an enthusiastic *yes* and he'd said he'd be ready any time they were.

Poppy was ready.

She fed Belle and bundled her up in as many layers of clothing as she could. Then took a few layers off again, in case she overheated. A pair of trousers and a zipped sweater that she hadn't been able to fit into for months, but which were now both satisfyingly loose-fitting, would have to do for her, and running a comb through her hair. Because the taxi she'd booked would be here soon. Poppy fixed the baby carrier into the pram attachment, whispering to Belle that now was the time to be on her very best behaviour, and made her way downstairs to wait for the taxi in the lobby.

Dylan almost didn't answer when his intercom sounded. He'd been sitting in front of his tablet, waiting. Poppy had said ten o'clock, and he'd already cleaned and tidied his whole flat, more as a matter of calming his nerves than anything. Practically speaking, just the background of where he was sitting would have done, but then he'd already changed his mind about that several times, and was thinking about doing so again.

The intercom, again. If it was a parcel then they could leave it at the door, and anyone who'd just decided to pop in unannounced would find him unavailable for visitors. But it sounded a third time, and Dylan strode impatiently over to the console.

'What?' Maybe that wasn't a particularly genial greeting for a courier who was just doing their job. 'Would you leave it at the door, please?'

'Leave what at the door? Me or Belle?'

Dylan's heart almost jumped out of his chest when he heard Poppy's voice. He automatically pressed the downstairs door release, and then realised he should say something.

'Poppy? Poppy...'

'I'm coming up. See you in a minute.'

He heard the sound of the door slamming behind her and realised he'd forgotten to ask her if she was all right. Dylan hurried out into the lift lobby, staring at the lights on the two floor indicators.

Think.

Calling the lift and going downstairs to meet her might

well leave him in the main lobby and Poppy up here. If something was wrong, then the quickest way of finding out was to stay put. One of the lift cars was travelling steadily upwards, and he positioned himself by the doors.

Poppy was smiling. That was all he saw for a moment, and it told him everything he needed to know. She looked a little nervous, but there was no emergency. All the same, Dylan asked.

'You're okay? And Belle?'

'Yes. I thought you might like to hold her. And I want to talk…'

'Yes.' There was only one word to say in response to all of that. Talking sounded a little ominous, but not talking had been the hardest thing he'd ever done. Dylan stood back, catching the lift door before it started to close. Everything he wanted, everything he'd ever need, was here right now and he wouldn't waste a moment of it. He'd trusted her and he'd waited. And Poppy had come. Now was the time to put up a fight.

When he ushered her through his front door he wished he'd left the Christmas decorations up for a little longer. But they'd seemed to mock his unhappiness, and he'd called the company who'd put them up and asked them to come and take them down again. They'd left the flat spotless, but feeling cold and unloved. Which had been okay, because it had matched his mood exactly.

Perhaps if he switched on a few lights… But there was no time for that because Poppy was pulling down the hood of the baby carrier, and loosening some of the baby blankets that she'd wrapped around her daughter. Dylan caught his breath.

'She's even more beautiful than I remember.'

Poppy nodded. 'I feel that every morning when I get up.'

Dylan was about to ask if he might hold her and then remembered, running his fingers ruefully across his chin. A five o'clock shadow had been fine for video conferencing, but he didn't want Belle's fingers to reach for him and find stubble. 'I...didn't shave.'

Poppy looked up at him solemnly. Something was up and he could feel cold dread clutching at his heart. Maybe she'd come to a decision that would part them for good. He ran through the options. Meeting someone was unlikely in the circumstances... Emigrating...? More likely, but distance wouldn't get in his way. He'd meet whatever happened next and deal with it.

'Seems that she loves the movement of a car, and she's sleeping now. Could we talk first?'

'Yes, of course.'

Poppy hadn't taken her coat off yet and that was a worry. Then he remembered that Belle was her first priority, and that Poppy had removed all but one of the blankets that were wrapped around her. He waved her over to the seating area, and waited for Poppy to choose where she sat.

'Keep an eye on her...' She parked the baby carrier in front of one of the sofas and pointed to the seat right next to it, indicating that he should sit down. Then she moved to the opposite sofa. Face to face, but too far away.

Dylan turned his gaze to Belle. The love was different, but it was difficult to say which was more overwhelming. He couldn't think about that now. He had to listen to whatever it was that Poppy needed to say, and just take each moment as it came.

Dylan seemed tired. Shocked to see her, and then as nervous as Poppy felt. Maybe she should have given him some warning of this, but he'd asked what she needed. And she needed this. Just this one chance to say what was on her mind, and then he could shut her out if he wanted to.

She took a breath. She'd rehearsed this a thousand times, but she was going to have to wing it, because everything was different now. Just seeing him seemed to change everything.

'We didn't choose this, Dylan. I thought that the way I felt about you was all about the baby, and that I couldn't love anyone after Nate died. But I was wrong.'

She saw him catch his breath. Maybe… But Poppy couldn't even think it, that hope hurt too badly.

'Nate will always have a piece of my heart. I thought that Belle would fill the rest of it, and she has. But somehow there's more. That doesn't follow any of the physiological rules…' She shrugged and Dylan smiled.

'Yeah. I understand.'

He was waiting for her to finish. Waiting to hear what she had to say. Right now, she needed his help.

'Poppy. Please just say it, whatever it is. I know you'll always want the best for Belle and so do I.' There was warmth in his eyes now, and Poppy could feel that some of it was for her.

She took a breath. 'Dylan, you'll always be Belle's father, and there are no conditions on you seeing her, we don't come as a package. But I want you to know that the part of my heart that belongs to today is all yours.'

Suddenly everything was for her. The look in his beautiful eyes, the way that he smiled. Poppy felt heat rising to her cheeks, and realised that some of it was because she still had her coat on. She loosened the buttons and Dylan got to his feet, walking around the coffee table. Her legs almost gave way as she got to her feet and as he helped her out of her coat she realised he was shaking too.

'Belle…' She looked across at the baby carrier, not daring to meet Dylan's gaze.

'She's fast asleep. This is between you and me, Poppy.' Dylan took her hand and she wound her fingers around his, holding on to him.

'You know…you're my worst nightmare…'

Poppy knew what that meant, and returned his smile. 'I'm going to take that as a compliment.'

'You should. I used to dread getting involved with anyone, feeling any of the feelings that went with that. But I couldn't help falling in love with you, Poppy. And I couldn't fight any more. I knew I had to wait and let you come back to me.'

She felt tears form in her eyes. 'You did that for me, Dylan? You're the best and nicest man I know…'

'I did it for both of us. You've been through so much in the last month, but I knew you had the strength to follow your heart, and I just had to find it in my heart to trust you.'

'I'm sorry…'

He laid his finger on her lips. 'Don't you dare apologise. The first promise I made to you was that nothing happens before you're ready, and I'm sticking by it.'

'I'm ready, Dylan. I couldn't bear the idea of losing you, the way I lost Nate, and so I sold you both short, by burying myself in my memories. But I've made my decision and I'm here now.'

'We need a new set of promises.'

'Looks like it…' Poppy wasn't afraid any more. Dylan knew her, better than anyone else, and the tenderness in his face told her that he wouldn't hurt her.

'Poppy Evans. Will you be my worst nightmare? For the rest of my life.'

'That's…a very long time.' If she could believe in Dylan, then she could bring herself to trust that it *would* be a very long time.

He smiled. 'Yes, it is. It may be scary because nightmares often are, and there's a lot we both need to come to terms with. But I promise you that I'll always love you.'

'I'll be your nightmare, if you'll be mine.'

He wound his arms around her shoulders, letting out a sigh. She could feel his body against hers, hear his heart pounding and feel the tremble of his limbs, but that was subsiding now. Warmth began to curl around them, in an exquisite reminder that the here and now were everything. Dylan was everything, even if that flouted the laws of mathematics, because Belle was everything too.

'I'm putting you on notice.' He seemed to have abandoned his usual habit of giving Poppy the options and letting her make up her mind. 'We might stumble a bit, and neither of us knows what the future's going to be like. But I won't leave you. We'll wake up together and face the day together. Every day.'

'That's what I want, Dylan. Because I'll always love you.'

Poppy could feel sweet arousal begin to throb in her veins. She wasn't ready for that, and she wasn't entirely sure that she wanted Dylan to see her body right now. But this was stronger. She kissed him, holding him tight, and his response made her knees tremble. Tender and yet full of that sweet passion that seemed to drive him forward in everything he did.

'Dylan…'

'No.' He held her in his arms and she could feel he wanted exactly the same as her. Even if she was a little afraid. 'Absolutely not, Poppy.'

'Maybe we could… I don't know…'

'Exactly. We'll wait until you *do* know. We have time.'

The thought of time, stretching out before them and beckoning them on, made her smile. 'You're probably right.'

He grinned. 'For the avoidance of doubt… I have the most beautiful woman in my arms and I want to make love to you, right now. The one thing I want more is to wait until you know you're ready. We don't have to prove anything to each other, do we?'

'No, we don't.' Poppy smiled up at him. 'I rather like this new you. The one who tells me exactly what *he* wants.'

He chuckled. 'I'm relying on you to tell me exactly what you want back.'

Poppy could do that. When Dylan's demanding side came to the fore, it was all about how they could move forward together. Not about him at all, but about the best for both of them.

She heard Belle shift, and her head turned instinctively. Dylan's had too. Belle's thin cry sounded and he let her go, making the action seem both urgent and still a little reluctant.

'Our daughter has exquisite timing.'

'Tell me that at two in the morning.' Poppy poked him gently in the ribs. 'Aren't you going to do something about her exquisite timing, then? Since you're her dad.'

Dylan chuckled in delight, moving over to the baby carrier and gently lifting Belle into his arms, making sure she couldn't reach the stubble on his chin. There it was. There had been a thousand pictures of Belle but Poppy didn't need a camera for this one. The image would always be burned into her memory. The man she loved, gently quieting their daughter.

Poppy had sat down to feed Belle and, after a moment's hesitation and her smiling nod, Dylan had taken his place next to her on the sofa, his arm around her. Feeding Belle always gave Poppy a feeling of well-being, but right now her endorphin levels must be going through the roof. Belle wasn't ready to go back to sleep yet, sensing maybe that today was special. Poppy was happy, and the two people she loved most in the world were happy too.

'You want to come back to mine?'

He hesitated. Poppy knew it was nothing to do with her or Belle, and had everything to do with bricks and mortar.

'I've made my peace with Nathan. I'll always love him, but he's gone. It's time to make new memories, and you, me and Belle belong together now.' She grinned up at him. 'Along with a small mountain of baby paraphernalia.'

'Sounds good to me.' He kissed her, and Poppy knew that everything was going to be all right.

'I'll get Belle ready to go, then?'

'In a minute. I've got something for you. A present for you when you had the baby.'

'Dylan, that's so sweet. Can I open it now?'

He chuckled at her excitement. 'Of course. Then we'll go over to yours, eh?'

They lay together on the bed, both propped up on pillows. Belle was sleeping in her crib and Poppy and Dylan were stargazing.

'I love this so much, Dylan.' Poppy snuggled against him, feeling his warmth. 'It's such a beautiful present, stars all the way across the ceiling. And they're so bright and clear.'

He'd made her stay in the sitting room with Belle while he fiddled with the star projector, setting it up and getting the focus right. And when he'd finally called her into the bedroom it had seemed like a whole new world, just waiting for her. He'd changed into sweatpants and a T-shirt, and Poppy had put on a cotton nightdress with a warm dressing gown, ready for their first night together. It was already more than she could have dreamed it might be.

Dylan kissed her forehead. Kissing was underrated and they'd been exploring every aspect of kissing under the stars.

Belle woke a little before it was time for her feed and Poppy picked her up, hushing her. 'Take your T-shirt off.'

'You want to look without touching?' he joked, and Poppy chuckled.

'Yeah, I do. That's not why I asked. It's time you two did a little bonding.'

Poppy allowed herself a smile as he pulled his T-shirt over his head, and then she took off Belle's sleepsuit and laid her down on his chest. She quietened immediately and Dylan's goofy smile surfaced as Poppy laid a baby blanket over Belle's tiny body.

'She's so warm. This feels…'

'Like nothing else?'

'Yeah.' He cradled Belle gently, and Poppy moved to get back onto the bed. This was what he must have felt when Belle was born, a craving to be close to both of them.

Dylan let out a sigh of pure contentment. 'What did I do to deserve this?'

'You promised me the stars, Dylan. Seems you've just delivered…'

EPILOGUE

Three years later

SIX O'CLOCK IN the morning. Poppy opened her eyes to the sound of Belle singing in the room next door. She nudged Dylan, watching as his eyes opened. She never tired of that.

'It's worked. She hasn't got all the words yet, but the tune's almost perfect.' Dylan had been singing 'Chapel of Love' to Belle for weeks now. 'Just in time, as well.'

Dylan chuckled. 'Seems we've done a few things just in time lately.'

They'd started off with everything the wrong way round. Had a baby, and then made love. That first, tender night had been so special, but then Dylan had shown her how perfect could be improved upon. He'd understood why Poppy felt anxious about marriage, and that it was all about her fear of losing him rather than any reluctance to commit herself. But as soon as Poppy was happy with the idea they'd started to look for a venue, finding that it was easier than they'd expected to book exactly what they wanted for a mid-December wedding.

It had been a short and very sweet engagement, made even sweeter when they'd found that Poppy was pregnant again, just last week. Dylan had said that telling everyone after they returned from their honeymoon would be soon enough, and Poppy had joked that they were finally doing things in the right order.

And now Belle was singing just the right song, on just the right day. Dylan kissed her, getting out of bed and pulling on a pair of jeans and a sweater. But Belle's love of moving forward rivalled even his, and she burst into their room.

'Dad… Dad!'

'What is it?' Dylan caught Belle in his arms, swinging her around, then set her back onto her feet, squatting on his heels in front of her.

'Are we all getting married today?'

Dylan chuckled. 'Yep. I suppose we are—because we can't do it without you. You know what happens before that, Belle?'

Belle knew. Dylan was so good with her, encouraging her to be a little less impatient without quashing her natural exuberance and her desire to move forward, which reminded Poppy so much of him.

'Stop. And. Think…' Belle snuggled against him. Two pairs of beautiful blue eyes and two blonde heads, Belle's hair a little lighter and finer than Dylan's.

'Yeah, that's right. We're getting married this afternoon, so what will we do this morning?' Dylan started to count on his fingers. 'We could sit quietly and watch Mummy curl her hair…'

'No!' Belle laughed up at him.

'Right, then. Go to the playground in the park?'

Belle looked at him, undecided. She liked the park, but she knew as well as Poppy did that Dylan always saved the best for last.

'Okay, that's a maybe. Or we could go to the hospital where Mummy and Daddy work and see the Christmas lights in the garden.'

'Yes!'

'Right, then. We'll need to get dressed first. One…two… three…'

'Go!' Belle shouted, running from the room, and Dylan walked back to the bed, kissing Poppy.

'You are *such* a nice man, Mr Harper. That's going to take you almost three hours.' They'd moved away from central London, and the cash from both of their flats had allowed them to buy a house with a large garden.

'Say three and a half, if we stop for breakfast. That gives you time for a lie-in, and then you can go over to your parents' place. Kate'll be there to help you with your dress, and Sophie's bringing Thomas over at eleven. I'll drop Belle over on the way back, and Sophie can help wrangle her into her dress, while I come home and get into my suit.'

'And then we're…'

He grinned, climbing back onto the bed to kiss her. 'Nearly forgot. We're getting married.' Dylan's hand found its way under the covers, caressing her stomach. 'What do you reckon. Boy or girl?'

'Now who's racing ahead? We'll get married, and go on our honeymoon…'

'Northern Lights, reindeer and lots of snow. And Father Christmas, of course…' Dylan grinned boyishly. 'Very long nights at this time of year.'

'So that's something for all three of us. Then we'll come home, take a breath, and find out in due course whether it's a boy or a girl.'

'Good thought.' Dylan kissed her again, climbing off the bed. 'See you later, sweetheart.'

The bedroom door closed behind him, and Poppy smiled, wide awake now but luxuriating in the warm pleasure of not having to get up just yet.

The doors ahead of the bridal party swung open. As soon as Poppy and Dylan had seen this place they'd known that it was where they wanted to be married. One of the oldest banqueting halls in London, it had been recently restored into a high arched space for weddings, which satisfied even Dylan's sense of the dramatic.

Poppy had insisted on a child-friendly ceremony, and her older nieces and nephews were all part of the bridal procession. Sam was at the front, juggling his best man duties with his two-year-old daughter, who would have a good view of the ceremony from her father's arms. Kate was in charge of the other bridesmaids and pageboys, and was chivvying them into their places so that at least they'd start off in a straight line, even if they didn't finish that way.

'Ready?' Her father nudged her, and she nodded. Poppy couldn't take her eyes off Dylan, who was waiting with Sam at the head of the aisle. So handsome in his dark blue suit, the flowers in his buttonhole matching the ones she was carrying. He'd loved her so faithfully and truly, and she couldn't wait to marry him.

'I'm ready.'

Kate let go of Belle's hand, stepping back to walk with the other bridesmaids. Belle raced down the aisle, scattering petals in all directions, while Thomas followed at a more sedate pace with the rings. Poppy's dad guided her forward, blind to everything other than the man she was about to marry. She was dimly aware that Sam had caught Belle's hand, showing her and Thomas where to stand, and then her dad ushered her to Dylan's side.

'You look beautiful.' He murmured the words, taking her hand, and Poppy smiled up at him.

Suddenly the world shot back into sharp focus as the celebrant stepped forward, welcoming everyone.

The words they'd helped write seemed even more beautiful in this setting. So much more binding when spoken aloud in front of their families and friends. When Poppy promised to love Dylan always she saw a tear form in his eye, and she paused for a moment to wipe it away. And when the ceremony was concluded, and Dylan kissed her, it felt as if he was doing so for the very first time.

'How did we do?' Poppy looked up at him. Their walk together, back down the aisle, had been delayed for a few minutes as Belle and the other children crowded around them excitedly.

'I think we did just fine.' Dylan's face was shining with happiness. 'Now it's just the rest of our lives…'

'Piece of cake.' Poppy grinned at him and he chuckled.

'Yeah. My thoughts entirely.'

* * * * *

Keep reading for an excerpt of a new title
from the Historical series,
A MISTLETOE KISS FOR THE GOVERNESS
by Christine Merrill

Chapter One

December 1814

Major Frederick Preston stared out of the window of the hired carriage at the bustle of London, still amazed to be home. It had been five years since he'd been in England, but now that Napoleon had been exiled to Elba, he was confident that the war was over. There was no reason he should not return to see how much his daughters had grown.

'How is the leg?' This comment came from his travelling companion, a captain in the Fusiliers who was sharing the ride into the city.

Frederick flexed his knee, trying not to grimace at the injury that was still not healed, though it had been over six months since he'd taken a ball at Toulouse. 'Fine, thank you.'

In truth, it was beastly. When he had been on the ship from Calais there had been space to walk around and keep the joint limber. But on the ride from Dover, it had grown stiffer and more painful by the mile.

'It will be better once you are home with your family,' the Captain said, ignoring his lie. 'The last time I was in London, I enjoyed dinner and a delightful evening of cards with your daughters. It is most kind of you to open your house to junior officers when you are not there. We are all very grateful for your generosity.'

Frederick smiled and nodded. 'I know how lonely it can be when one is between postings and without the proper time to have a decent meal. The least I can offer is dinner now and then. And in her letters my girls' governess assures me they appreciate the company.'

'Mrs Lewis?' the man said with a smile.

'You have met her then?' he asked, trying not to appear too curious.

'She is never far from the girls when we are there,' the Captain assured him.

'Lewis has been a godsend,' Frederick admitted. 'I hired her through an agency while I was in Portugal and she took everything in hand with barely a word of instruction from me.'

'You have never met her?' the man said, surprised.

Frederick shook his head. 'We correspond frequently, but I have been rather busy these last years...'

The Captain laughed at this assessment of a long and brutal war, then said, 'You will be pleasantly surprised, I am sure. Mrs Lewis is a favourite of the regiment.'

'Like a mother to you all,' he said, for didn't all governesses have a maternal air about them?

There was a strange pause, probably caused as the carriage bounced in a rut. Then the Captain gave a weak nod and said, 'You really have not met her.'

'But I am looking forward to it,' Frederick replied. 'I wish I'd had her on the front lines to teach my Lieutenants how to write reports. Her letters were succinct without missing a detail.'

'A useful skill,' the Captain agreed.

'And the old dear follows orders like a seasoned campaigner. When it comes to the care of my children, I have but to ask and she obeys.'

'The old dear,' the Captain said, smiling into the dark.

The carriage was slowing now and Frederick smiled as it proceeded the last few yards to stop in front of his town house. 'Home at last,' he said, slapping his knees with his hands to pound the blood back into his legs. 'We shall see you at dinner soon, I hope.'

'I welcome the invitation,' the other man said, reaching to open the door for him. 'Give my regards to the girls. And Mrs Lewis, of course.'

'Of course,' Frederick said. While he had missed his children and was eager to come home to them, he felt a similar excitement at the prospect of meeting the woman who had cared for them. After years of correspondence, he viewed her more as a friend than an employee. Her letters had been a source of comfort on some of his most difficult days, giving him little slices of the life he missed to raise his spirits. Even when relaying a domestic crisis, she solved the problem with maturity and wisdom and ended the letter with a happy outcome to assure him that all would be well when he returned.

And now, at last, he was coming home to enjoy the fruits of her governance. He took one last, steadying breath before grabbing his stick and heaving himself out of the carriage with a smile, then limped to the front door.

'Father is here!' Eleanor Preston stood in the little window by the door to the town house, bouncing from side to side with excitement. 'The carriage has stopped. The door is opening.'

'Let me see,' her sister Jane said, pushing her out of the way.

'Ladies,' Charlotte Lewis said with gentle admonition, 'remember your manners. You are no longer children and you do not want your father to think he is coming home to a pair of hoydens.'

The sisters immediately calmed themselves and stepped away from the window to stand side by side and straight ahead like a pair of their father's soldiers.

Charlotte smiled in approval. At sixteen and nineteen respectively, the girls were not quite of age. But they had been children when their father had last seen them and she wanted the Major to be impressed by how much they had changed. They were lovely young women now and a credit to his name.

'I was so afraid he would not be here in time for the ceremony,' Jane whispered, raising up on the balls of her feet for one last peek through the glass.

'He promised he would come,' Charlotte reminded her. 'It would take more than Napoleon to keep him away from your wedding.' He had assured her of it in his letter, but his homecoming had been delayed several times already and it was hard to believe that their waiting was finally over.

She resisted the urge to peer through the window for a first glimpse to assure herself that he was well. In truth, she was just as excited by this homecoming as the girls were, though it was not her place to be so. She was only a servant. Her happiness did not signify.

All the same, her heart leapt when the door opened and a man in a dashing red coat limped though, shaking snowflakes from his hat before setting it on a side table and turning to accept the embraces of his daughters.

She recognised him instantly, for she had seen his face often enough in the little miniature portrait that Jane kept on her bedside table. That picture had been painted years ago, when he had been younger and war had not taken a toll on him. He was still tall and broad-shouldered, but there were touches of grey in the temples of his brown hair and a small scar slicing though his right eyebrow.

She could see lines around his mouth as well, signs of the barely contained pain that his injury must be causing him. It was bad, she was sure, and she ached for him. But she offered a silent prayer of thanks that he was here and on two legs. For some time after the Battle of Toulouse, they had feared him dead. Even after he had been found and taken to hospital, two months had passed when he'd been too weak from blood loss and fever to write them. It had been months after that before he'd been strong enough to travel.

The wait for news had seemed interminable. She'd been as distraught as the girls during that long silence and rejoiced with them when it had ended. And celebrated again, when alone in her room, hugging herself and smiling at the thought that the meeting she'd longed for would finally occur.

His letters had been so much more to her than mundane correspondence from an employer to an underling. He'd filled them with stories of the places and people that he saw, hinting at the glories and terrors and boredoms of his days in a way that her late husband never had bothered with. Though he'd been away at sea for much of their marriage, his letters had been brief and irregular.

But the Major was a natural storyteller. Perhaps that was why she felt such a connection to him. And now here he was, an arm wrapped around each daughter, staring at them in amazement as they squealed in delight.

'So tall,' he said in an awed voice. 'My dear Jane, you are taller than your mother was when she passed.' He glanced to the other. 'And my little Eleanor. Not so little any more.'

'You are being silly,' Eleanor said with a laugh. 'Jane is to be married and next Season I will be out.'

'You certainly will not,' he said with a mocking smile. 'You are far too young. And you, Jane, cannot mean to leave me just as I have finally come home.'

'We already have your consent,' she reminded him. 'Jeremy saw to that before offering.'

'He is a fine young man,' her father agreed, giving her a peck on the cheek. 'But I still have you for several days and mean to make the most of them.'

The footman was bringing in the luggage and Eleanor broke free to open the nearest valise.

'Here, now,' her father said. 'What are you doing?'

'Searching for presents,' she said, showing no shame.

Charlotte cleared her throat to remind her not to be greedy and the Major glanced up, noticing her for the first time. Then he smiled and she felt the warmth to the tips of her toes. 'Christmas is not for two days, Eleanor. Your gifts will wait until then. For now, you must show your manners and introduce me to your friend.'

'Our friend?' said Eleanor with a laugh.

'You know Mrs Lewis,' Jane said.

'She has been here for ever,' Eleanor agreed.

His smile faded as he stared at her, confused. 'Lewis?' he said, furrowing his brow.

She had been longing to hear that single word for months, for he never called her Mrs Lewis in his letters. This abbreviation of her name had come to feel familiar, rather than dismissive, as if he was speaking to a comrade. It was never, 'Lewis, do this' or 'Lewis, do that' as if commanding an underling. Instead, he might write 'The most interesting thing happened the other day, Lewis…' The name felt like a touch on the shoulder, drawing her into a private conversation, away from the rest of the world.

But now it was spoken with confusion, as if he could not quite place who she might be. Had he really forgotten her, after all the letters they'd exchanged? She hid her disappointment beneath a professional smile and dropped a curtsy, eyes bowed. 'Sir.'

'Lewis,' he said in the same dazed tone, then gave a small shake of his head and said, 'Of course.'

'It is good to have you home, Sir,' she said, for what harm could there be in saying so? 'Tea has been laid in the sitting room, in anticipation of your arrival.'

'Tea,' he repeated in the same dull tone.

'And sandwiches and cakes,' she assured him. 'If you prefer something stronger, you have but to ring.'

'Of course,' he said, still staring at her as if she was a stranger.

If she were a lady, she might have flounced away at this cold greeting. But she was his servant. It was not her place to come and go as she pleased. He needed to dismiss her and she prayed it would be soon, for she could not stand another moment of this unexpected awkwardness between them. 'If there is nothing else,' she prompted, 'I will leave you alone with your family.'

At last, he seemed to remember himself and said, 'That will be all, Lewis.'

'Thank you, Sir.' She turned before he could see her expression of disappointment and hurried up the stairs to her room. What had she been expecting? He was tired after a long journey and she was only a member of the staff.

She would take this time alone to get hold of herself and banish any nonsense she'd imagined about their first meeting, how he would greet her as an old friend, or perhaps, something more. If she did not learn to hide her feelings, it might mean the end of her position here. Her affection for him would be an unwelcome embarrassment.

For now, she would stay away until summoned. The family did not need her to watch their reunion. They had much to talk of and she had no part in it.

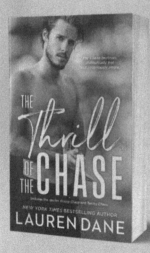

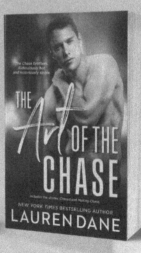